ECHOES OF A SHATTERED AGE

LEGEND OF TAKASHANIEL (BOOK 1)

RAMÓN TERRELL

TAL PUBLISHING

ECHOES OF A SHATTERED AGE

ISBN: 978-0-9937236-8-1

Cover painting by Martin Maceovic
Cover Font by Nick Deligaris
Tal Publishing
Published by Tal Publishing Vancouver BC
e-book: January 2017
First Edition: January 2011
Printed in the USA

RAMÓN TERRELL

ECHOES of a SHATTERED AGE

LEGEND OF TAKASHANIEL #1

To Moms, unconditionally loving and always willing to give her last.
And Pops, who is now among the ancestors.
What do you say when "I love you both" is not enough?

1

I s the octagon complete?" Zreal rasped. "It must be perfect for this to work, or we are doomed."

"Do what you do best and leave the octagon to me," Brit scolded.

"We have never tried something this big before, my lord! The octagon must be perfect or we will beg to perish for our folly."

"Quiet, idiot," Brit hissed. "I created the octagon with my own power. Do you not think I know how to manipulate it and what the cost is for failure? Be silent."

"As you wish," Zreal replied. He looked upon his superior with fear and admiration. Brit was powerful, standing at eight feet tall with long, powerful arms that looked as if they could strangle an elephant. His hands were rough and gnarled, an indication of how he drew the earth's energy and twisted it to his will. His fiery orange hair lay in stark contrast with his burgundy skin. His massive legs were as large around as Zreal's entire body. His face was wide and rock-like, as if he could split a boulder with his forehead.

The most intimidating feature about Brit, Zreal thought, was his eyes. A wicked blend of red and blue, those burning orbs looked as if a simple angry stare could cause an agonizing death. Zreal knew not how old Brit was, but if the tales of the Drek's battle with a Daurak were true, that would make him several thousand years old. It seemed inconceivable.

The prehistoric-looking animal was said to be more vicious than any living predator of modern times, and its appearance resembled the two-legged dinosaur predators from this world's ancient years.

Remembering this, Zreal did not bother his master any longer. He didn't dare to doubt Brit's abilities, but dealing with Quentranzi demons was another affair altogether.

Long after Zreal left the circular room, Brit continued perfecting the octagon. Human practitioners of the darker arts would use a circle or five-point portal to summon a denizen of the lower planes. Brit used methods that did not originate from this world. The octagon was Brit's own creation, and a more effective tool for summoning the more powerful demons of the abyss. In summoning fiends, one must have a powerful circle to produce an effective hold. If the demon happened to be a particularly powerful one, the circle would have to be perfect, which was a rare ability amongst humans.

Zreal smirked when he thought back to the whispers amongst humans, of a sorcerer who summoned a major demon using an imperfect circle. Once summoned, the demon inspected and destroyed the circle within seconds, slaughtering the sorcerer and ravaging everything in sight. It took the combined effort of ten sorcerers to bring the fiend under control and banish it back to the lower planes.

Quentranzi demons were altogether different in nature and motivation than any other in the abyss. The most powerful and arrogant of sorcerers shuddered at the thought of trying to summon a Quentranzi. Some rare sorcerers' tomes and books of the Secret Order described these monsters as super-demons, capable of unspeakable turmoil and devastation. They possessed the power to will their summoner to release the hold on them, even if the seal was perfect. According to these ancient tomes, even major demons feared and avoided Quentranzi. To summon such a creature would require an indomitable mind, an unbreakable will, and an internal strength alien to this world and its weakling inhabitants.

Brit was well aware of the many potential dangers of summoning such a terrible creature, but he needed power in the right places and knowledge beyond his own. He needed other-worldly knowledge that a Quentranzi could provide. "It is finished," Brit said. He stood back from the octagon and inspected it. The octagon was far more effective than the circular seal because of its otherworldly nature. Each corner of the octagon could pierce the summoned fiend if need be, cowing it.

Reassured of the octagon's perfection, Brit summoned Zreal back to the room and began making the customary preparations for a summoning. When Zreal arrived, he was amazed at the level of detail at which everything had been prepared. The octagon was perfect, the light sourcing was just right, and the figure was charged with twisted earth energy to shield against any attempts by a demon to use their innate abilities to extinguish the lights and break the seal.

"You summoned me, my lord?" Zreal asked.

"You would not be here if I had not," came the retort.

"Do you wish my help in summoning the Quentranzi?" Zreal asked, wanting nothing to do with this business.

"I do not necessarily require your help, but I do wish to further justify your presence here by incorporating some of your limited talents into my plans ... of course, if you don't mind."

Zreal knew better than to take that last statement as a request rather than the intended sarcasm. "Of course, my lord. Whatever you wish of me. Quentranzi are well known for their ability to project power outside of the barrier even while physically restrained within as well as their particularly strong and cunning psychic attacks. You wish me to help in fending off these attacks?"

"Quite perceptive, Zreal. I would spend my undivided attention on the Quentranzi without troubling over its games." Brit moved to stand in front of the figure while Zreal stood in the shadows to the right. As the summoning began, Zreal steeled his nerves. He had never actually seen a Quentranzi before, but if the power and horror that the lesser major demons were capable of was any indication, the octagon had better be perfect.

Brit softly chanted in a language Zreal did not understand, and a dull green light began to pulsate in the lines of the octagon. Brit repeatedly chanted the name 'Kabriza' with increased intensity.

* * *

IN THE LOWER PLANES OF the abyss, a large gray demon was devouring a smaller fiend. It raised its massive, horned head at a distant call. The call was coming from one of the higher planes, but the thing had never heard of such power coming from there. The rage caused from hearing its name gave way to curiosity, and thus Kabriza heeded the call.

* * *

THE LINES of the octagon began to glow wildly, pulsating between green and blue. To Zreal's surprise, the octagon expanded to accommodate the large abysmal denizen. Foot-high flames appeared at each corner of the octagon seal that also flickered in hues of green and blue. The center of the seal was distorted with haze, and the wall nearest the seal began to blur. A sickening sense of wrongness crept into the room that was so strong, Zreal thought he might choke. It was as though the air he breathed was becoming tainted.

After a few moments that seemed like hours to Zreal, the seal darkened until it was pitch black, and through that blackness stepped Kabriza. If it were not for the strict instructions by Brit to remain hidden, and the fear of disappointing the Drek, Zreal would have cried out at the sight of the monstrosity. His eyes widened in amazement at the sight of the thing.

It stood fourteen feet tall, and its arms were so long that its clawed hands hung merely two feet from the floor. Its huge gaping maw was littered with sharp zigzagging teeth that resembled a pile of broken daggers. Two horns protruded from the bottom of its forehead, pointing straight out and curling upward like long hooks. The spikes protruding from its back looked as if they could cut through the strongest armor, and its legs were as thick as the branch of a great oak. It narrowed its glowing red eyes at Brit. For a time it stood there, arms hanging in front of its torso, tapping the sixth toe on its left foot. Brit faced the fiend, unmoved and calm.

2

Kenjiro's robe—like *Yoroi* and *Hakama*—ruffled in the morning breeze as he sat, eyes closed, legs crossed, and body erect in his daily morning meditation at the base of his favorite oak atop Mt. Yamanake. A frown creased his forehead, and his eyes snapped open.

He took several steadying breaths while he reoriented himself. Something dark and incredibly evil had thrown him from his meditation, and the effect was jarring. *What was that?*

He looked over his shoulder in the direction of the house he shared with his younger sister. Had she felt it? Kenjiro figured she must have. He doubted whatever that evil was that had snatched him from his serenity could be anything from this world.

He took his time, stretching out his legs and arms, then stood. He took a deep breath of the cool morning air and blew it out in a mist in front of his face. This wouldn't be good.

* * *

WEST of the hill where Kenjiro sat in meditation, a small house was nestled at the base of yet another hill that was covered in grass and towering, moss-covered trees. The exterior of the house was unremarkable, yet the interior was decorated with immaculately polished wood paneled floors and rice paper sliding doors connecting the various rooms throughout the house.

Akemi stood at the window of the living room, admiring the nightingale that lived in a tree outside her room. Although it usually sang to her at night, it sometimes perched outside the living room window, and she would sometimes throw a few bits of food to it in exchange for a morning song.

She stepped outside the house and filled her lungs with the crisp mountain air. Her smile changed to a frown when she felt a darkness creeping on her. She looked to the sky, as though the infinite blue canopy sprinkled with puffy white clouds held the answer.

"Evil energy," she thought aloud. It had been some time since she'd hunted. Had that time come again?

She stepped out of the trees to see the familiar mated pair of swans floating across the surface of the nearby lake. Her smile at the sight of the beautiful birds was tinged with regret. The world was such a beautiful place, but it was colored with such horrible darkness.

She moved on, passing through the trees. The location of her home always left the opportunity to explore something new, for the mountains and hillsides of Yamanake were vast and plentiful. She came upon a large tree that looked to be at least thirty feet tall. *Nice place to have a look around,* she thought. The muscles in her legs tightened, and Akemi crouched then leaped atop the nearest branch. She continued to leap from branch to branch until she was at the very top of the tree where she surveyed the miles of land below, stretching into the distance as far as she could see. There was a village not more than a few more hours away that would be awake by now.

"You can't move quiet enough that I cannot hear you, brother," Akemi said, not bothering to turn and face Kenjiro as she spoke.

Kenjiro grunted. He'd spotted Akemi and pursued her until she had come to the tree. He'd waited for a more undetectable approach, slipping from branch to branch of the neighboring trees making little sound before he'd crept behind her. Just once, he wanted to catch her unaware. It was a game they'd played since they were children, and one he'd always lost.

"Today is strange," he said.

"You feel it, too?"

"There are strange energies everywhere," Kenjiro said. "Evil energy. I have a feeling we will see a bit of excitement soon."

"Perhaps," Akemi replied, and a heartbeat later, Kenjiro was gone as quickly and quietly as he'd come. The ninja smiled to herself. Samurai never traveled through the trees. As much as her brother claimed his disdain for the methods traditional to the ninja, some of Akemi's methods had crept into his own, even if he wasn't as proficient. She reached behind her back and drew out her sword, *Sekimaru*. "Perhaps," she repeated as she analyzed her sword, remembering their past battles together.

She slipped the sword back into its sheath and made her way home.

3

Kenyatta stood on top of the jagged rocks overlooking the ocean. In Jamaica, the ocean water was a beautiful blend of blue with a slight hint of green. Through the clear water one could see the many exotic fish that were commonplace to the island, although lately he was seeing some specimens that were new to the place.

The waves from the ocean collided with the rocks below, spraying Kenyatta's clean-shaven face. He closed his eyes and basked in the wonder of the ocean. The wind seemed to blow in a soothing rhythm, and was just the right temperature between cool and warm. Kenyatta crouched on his rock and eyed a most colorful fish. It was a strange, almost diamond-shaped fish with a black body and white dots and bits of yellow. It snapped at any fish that came too close. It reminded him of his grandfather, and Kenyatta smiled. He, too, was a snappy one.

Kenyatta remembered once when he was a child and had gone into his grandfather's room to look for some money to buy a snow cone with. He found some money, and quickly and quietly took what he needed and left. Just before he was able to turn the knob on the back door, he received a hard smack on the back of his head. He'd turned to see his grandfather staring down at him, arms crossed, a scowl on his face.

"Grampa! I was jyas goin' ta get me a cone." Before the young Kenyatta could utter another word, his grandfather struck him across the back of the head again, gave him a long period of fussing and scolding, and told him not to do it again. Then he'd given Kenyatta extra money and told him to buy a cone for both of them. Kenyatta had wanted to smile but thought better of it and just took the money and did what he was told.

Thoughts of his grandfather always brought a smile to Kenyatta's face. Grandpa was a snappy old badger, but deep down he was as kind as the breeze of the ocean.

His mind snapped back to the present, and he leaped backward in a back flip and landed in a skid behind the man who had just charged him from behind. The stranger spun and charged again, throwing a series of sideways kicks and straight angled punches. Kenyatta parried and dodged, then counterattacked.

The attacker threw a wide left-hook punch, which Kenyatta blocked with his forearm. The attacker anticipated the block and countered with a straight snap kick to the groin. Kenyatta threw his hips back, and the other man punched straight out, connecting with the top of Kenyatta's forehead. Accepting the blow, Kenyatta returned it with a backward leaning sideways kick to the attacker's chest.

Both stumbled back, but recovered. For several heartbeats they studied each other. The attacker straightened and laughed.

"I guess I can give you credit. You never would just take a hit and be done with it."

"How else me sending the message dat me adversary choose wrong in a fight wit me?" Kenyatta replied, his smile just as wide. "Ya know ya cyan't be sneakin' up on me like dat no matter how quiet ya be. Ya not catchin' me off me feet like dat."

Kita snickered and ran a hand through his short black hair. He stood about five feet six inches tall and was of a light brown complexion. His slender build showed muscles not large, but defined nonetheless, and Kenyatta's stinging forehead told that his friend was much stronger than his size insinuated. "You looked so caught up in the scenery that I couldn't resist."

Now Kenyatta laughed. "Ya come a long way to be harassin' me, man. Da Philippines not just a quick swim, ya know."

Kita shrugged. "I had to come. There's something goin' on out there, and I wanted to be here when it happens."

"Watcha mean by dat? Sure ya not sayin' that there's a big commotion on the mainland? And even if it was, why would dat be concernin' us?"

Kita frowned. "This is different. I know you can feel it. When you were sitting here deep in thought, didn't you feel a weird energy?" Before he could finish the question, Kenyatta was already nodding his head.

"I did feel it. It's like the energy in da so tense right now. I didn't tink much of it till ya mention it now."

The two friends looked out at the ocean, wondering what this strange energy was and where was it coming from. Kita looked sidelong at Kenyatta. "Hey, Ken," he said, lightening the mood. "You remember when we first trained together in the hills?"

"Ya mean back in da Philippines before we trained with Sensei Akutagawa? Ya, man. I remember. Long time ago. Us only seven back den."

"Yeah, I know. It was a long time ago. Fifteen years to be exact."

"Old man," Kenyatta said in a trembling voice.

"Are we no longer the same age?" Kita asked. Kenyatta shrugged and Kita rolled his eyes. "I remember the first thing we learned."

"Da first ting ya get to learn in fighting?" Kenyatta replied. "I was tinking we would learn to jump off walls and fight wit swords and all dat."

Kita smiled. He'd had those same assumptions.

"We learn how ta breathe and sit still, for weeks." Kenyatta grimaced. "For weeks just sittin' der, quiet and still. I was not tinking to be sittin' der for so long only ta learn to stretch and learn stances after that!" The two friends laughed as they turned their backs to the ocean.

"Man, dat was a long time ago. Him make us do it for so long, and then when we did train more, we were wishing we could sit and breathe again."

"Yeah," Kita responded. "We never got much of a break, and when we did, it was only for a few minutes for water and then back to work."

"Yeah, man. I remember him used to say that we have great tings in us. Great power and spirit, and it was his job to begin our journey to unlock dat greatness."

"Think he was right?" Kita asked, smirking.

"Ya a funny man. Nope, ya got no skills at all, man, but ya do make a good sidekick."

"Right," Kita replied dryly.

"Hey, ya wanna do some *Capoeira*? Been a long time since we practice togeder, and me know ya gettin' rusty."

"Rusty!" Kita was incredulous. "I've always been better than you!"

Kenyatta's mouth fell open, and Kita laughed as his friend rattled off all sorts of insults and taunts in an accent so thick, he could only understand one word in four.

"Why does your accent come and go like that?" he asked. Seeing the responding confused look, Kita let it go. "Never mind," he laughed, giving his friend a playful punch in the chest. "Let's go."

As they walked across the white sands of the beach, they had many laughs and reflections of the past in the Philippines, where they grew up together. It was during that time when they were both children that Kita's parents were on vacation in Jamaica and had rescued a small boy from a band of foreign rogues who had come in off the eastern coast of the island for no better reason than to cause trouble and steal from the villagers.

* * *

THE GROUP of ruffians had come to a humble home with a garden consisting of jacaranda and sago palm trees, with multicolored river rock resting beneath a tranquil pond of clear water. The garden was decorated with many different types of bright green shrubbery and bushes, as well as a section where Kenyatta's grandfather grew vegetables so plentiful they couldn't eat them all and shared with the neighbors. The walls surrounding the yard were covered in ivory and tomato vines that the young Kenyatta would pick right off the vine to eat.

KENYATTA'S GRANDFATHER had a passion for landscaping, and would spend hours in his garden, perfecting the look and feel of the yard. He would pay attention to the most intricate details, ensuring the health and condition of every plant. The effect was a small rainforest surrounding the humble house. When the foreigners came to the house, no one was in sight and they destroyed every piece of decoration that was found.

It was in the midst of this that Kenyatta's grandfather showed up. At six feet, five inches tall, the seventy-year-old man's eyes had burned with the fire of a man half his age. His dreadlocks ran down to the center of his back, with barely a hint of gray. He was a stocky man, retaining the majority of his muscular build since youth, and he emitted an unshakable aura of confidence and spirit.

"Watcha wan' now!" Grampa yelled. "You and ya bombaclot goons comin' ere trashin' me garden! I been spendin' more time in me garden den you four fools been alive! Get outta 'ere now before I bust me broom across ya bombaclot head!"

Just as Grampa was making the threat, two of the troublemakers were circling around his back. They assumed him an easy target since he was such an old man. They smiled at each other and moved in.

One of them threw a punch at the back of Grandpa's head, but when the old man ducked, he overbalanced and Grandpa grabbed his arm and used the force behind it to launch the attacker sideways into a tree. The poor fool squirmed on the ground, groaning and holding his back.

"Be glad ya back not broken!" Grandpa yelled.

The other three men had seen enough and charged in together in hopes of overwhelming the deceptively strong old man. One of the men came in from the left with a sloppy kick, which Grampa sidestepped. While he was recoiling his leg, Grampa grabbed the attacker's foot and delivered a rather powerful kick to the unfortunate man's groin. As the crying wretch curled in on himself on the ground, the old gardener ducked as a roundhouse punch from the third rogue came in aimed at the side of his head. All in one motion, he used the man's arm as a shield to the fourth man's roundhouse punch.

Before the man could utter so much as a grunt from his pained elbow, Grampa pulled the rogue's arm and forced him to overextend his footing. He plowed the rogue face first in the dirt, where he lay cradling his broken elbow.

The last of the four men stepped back and looked at his three friends, lying broken and squirming on the ground. He knew that he could not win a straight fight with the aged gardener, so instead he reached into his belt and drew a crude pistol. Grampa stared at the man. He despised the leftover weapons of the long-past Age of Technology.

"So dis what it come down to, ya?" the old man growled, face hot with anger. "Since ya cyan' fight me, ya just pull a damn pistol and prove ya cowardice. If ya wan' shoot me then do it, but ya still no more a man, and prove ya no more than a coward hidin' behind a gun. No honor!" Grandpa spat on the ground and stared the rogue in the eye.

The ruffian had thought himself superior for having the gun and thus having the upper hand, but the gardener, that old gardener that had seemed so defenseless, had just taken that away.

The rogue grew angry at the fact that he could not look the old man in the face and that he had been humiliated and beaten before he'd even attempted to fight. His anger swelled and he pulled the trigger.

Just as the shot went off, a young boy no older than two or three years old had lumbered to the door and peeked out of the house to see what all the commotion was about. The thunderous report echoed through the village, and people everywhere turned and looked about or crouched low to the ground, trying to discern the location of the sound.

A family of three was shopping on the street when they'd also heard the sound. Mateo looked to his wife and motioned for her to take their son and find a safe place to await his return. Patting his hand against her protests, he promised he would be careful, then left.

Why am I doing this? He thought, as he raced through the streets. *I have a family that I must look after, and this is not even my home. Whatever is happening, it doesn't concern me.*

He couldn't tell himself why, but it was as though some undeniable force, or presence, had compelled him to act.

When he reached the house, he saw a few people standing around a man waving a gun and holding a small boy in front of him, yelling for everyone to stay away. The little boy was crying and screaming at the top of his lungs for his grandfather. As he scanned the scene, Mateo saw an old man lying on the ground in what appeared to be his own blood. He shook his head, realizing that this unfortunate man must be the boy's guardian, the grandfather he was screaming for. Acting on pure instinct, he ducked behind the people in front of him, circled around to the back of the man holding the gun and crept up behind him.

When the man turned around to see who was there, Mateo kicked the gun from his hand, breaking his wrist in the process. When the rogue grabbed his wrist, the little boy ran to the old man.

"Have you no honor, threatening a boy and shooting his grandfather like this?" Mateo leveled his glare at the other man. "Come and fight me as a man and not a coward."

The ruffian considered the proposition, but thought the better of it. Cursing, he turned and ran, pushing his way through the wary onlookers. After pushing and shoving through the crowd, he came free and was again facing this new person. "Get outta my way before I cut—"

The threat died in the thug's mouth when he suddenly slumped to the ground and lay paralyzed and shaking. "What … did you do to me?" he whimpered.

"You don't deserve death." Mateo looked down at him. "You will live the rest of your life at the mercy of others, and be constantly reminded of the privilege of life and the simple ability to function normally."

Mateo had struck several pressure points in the thug's body and left him permanently paralyzed from the neck down. "Only through aid will you ever function in daily life again." He turned his back and left the invalid crying and yelling curses and pleas for mercy all in the same breath. Mateo's mouth tightened. The truth was, with just a bit more force, the crippled thug would have been dead.

* * *

WHEN MATEO RETURNED to the house, he sifted through the whispering onlookers. One person had taken the initiative to try to help the child and his grandfather.

"Thank you for watching after this child," he told the woman, who was obviously just as upset as the little boy. "I will see what I can do for them." When he approached the boy, the child instinctively crawled between his grandfather and this new person.

"Go away!" the child yelled. "Leave me grampa alone!" As the child spoke, his voice quivered and tears streamed down his face.

"I'm here to help you," Mateo said in a low, gentle voice.

"I don't want your help," the child sobbed. "Just go away."

"And how do you intend to help your grandfather? Do you know how to treat his wounds, or are you strong enough to move him? Let me help you, little one. I know you have no reason to, but you must trust me."

The little boy looked into the stranger's eyes for a moment, then bobbed his head.

Mateo kneeled over the older man and immediately recognized the flickering life in his eyes. "Sir, my name is Mateo Masin, and I have come to help you and your grandson."

The old man just smiled and nodded his head, but when Mateo moved to ask for help, he held up a trembling hand and cast a concerned look at his grandson. Reading the old man's pained expression, Mateo went to the boy. "I need to talk to your grandfather, okay? Would you please give us a minute?" The child looked at his grandfather, who nodded, and then back to Mateo. He offered a reassuring nod, despite the hopeless situation for the boy's grandfather. After a moment the boy hesitantly moved back to the doorway of their little house and watched them.

"Me grandson only five years old, but him understand much." Grampa winced through a spasm of pain. "Him not like the other children 'ere, and dat is part of the reason I was carin' for him."

Mateo noted the old man's use of the word *was*. "Me time as his guardian is done," the elder continued. "I don't know you, but I can see your heart through your eyes, and I feel you a good man. The boy need a new and younger teacher for his next stage of life." He coughed, then grinned, a tiny line of blood trickling from the corner of his mouth. "Maybe why dis happen. I ask ya, take him as your own and train him. I know ya don't know my grandson or me, but a man know a warrior when him see one, and I see it in you."

After a fit of thick coughing, the old man gritted his teeth through the pain and continued. "Him only five, but a lot faster and stronger den anyone his age. Him have a purpose, and it must be fulfilled. I ask you ... please to take ... care of him and ... raise him as your own."

Mateo's brows knitted together. The old man hadn't much time left.

"Dis is much to ask, but I have ... no time left, and I ... am sure ya were 'ere at dis time ... for a reason."

Mateo looked into the old man's eyes, at the flickering life.

"I'm leavin' dis world, but ... I still ... watchin' you ... and me grandson."

Mateo did not doubt that, and with a sigh, he accepted the old man's wish. Grampa smiled and motioned for his grandson. The boy, still crying, made his way to his grandfather's side.

"Kenyatta," Grampa began, then coughed again. "Me time 'ere ... is about to end ... and don't be cryin' 'bout dat now. I have lived ... a full life and ... I prefer to leave dis world ... fighting for a cause worth ... dying for. You are ... dat cause ... and I have fulfilled ... my ... obligation to ya parents."

He coughed again, a gurgling wet cough, and Mateo knew he was choking on his own blood. He hated the helpless feeling of watching this man die and there was nothing he could do about it.

"Dis man ... will take care of ya. I know ya don't know him ... but ... ya do as he says ... and listen to him ... as if he were me ... or ya parents. I know ya been tru a lot ... in ya short life wit your father, mother and now me ... but be ... strong ... and we all will be ... watchin' ya ... from the other side ... of the veil of life. Ya hear me, boy?"

"Yes, Grampa." The little boy sobbed.

The old man then whispered into Kenyatta's ear something that only the boy could hear, then leaned away and closed his eyes. The young Kenyatta sat on his knees and stared at his grandfather as tears streamed down his round cheeks. Mateo Masin moved back and allowed the boy this private moment. It surprised him that the child seemed to be so strong, sitting next to his dead grandfather.

The young Kenyatta looked into Mateo's eyes. Much pain was there, but there was also strength. There was more to this child than just the physical pain, or the regular mundane trials. This boy was different in the same way as his own son. Mateo had never been able to pinpoint what was so different about his son Kita, but this child held that same strangeness. Before he could attempt to train this boy in any way, he would need to first understand him. He thought of Kita, his son of the same age as this boy, and hoped that a ray of fortune might later shine through the tragedy in little Kenyatta's life.

* * *

LATER THAT SAME DAY, Mateo had introduced a nervous and distracted young Kenyatta to his wife and son, who was only a few months older than Kenyatta. After a long lunch—which Kenyatta barely touched—Mateo explained all that had transpired leading up to his taking the little boy with him. Mateo was reminded once again how much he loved his wife when she took Kenyatta by the hand and left to go to a few stores to buy some extra necessities and some clothes for the boy. She had immediately taken him in with the family and given him the emotional support that he needed. They helped Kenyatta arrange and perform a ritual funeral and burial. After a two-week-long trial with local law in regard to the boy's relocation, it was discerned that the child had no living family to take care of him. Then, after acquiring written and verbal testimonies from nearby witnesses, the family with a new member in tow left to return home to the Philippines.

4

W hen Akemi returned home, she found Kenjiro outside the house practicing the sword. "I haven't seen you unsheathe *Kenzo* for some time." Kenjiro said nothing, just continued. "I've never felt anything like what I'm feeling now. But whatever it is, it's powerful."

"That's why we must be ready," Kenjiro replied evenly, never breaking his rhythm. "I am arming *Kenzo* as you have taught me."

"With the power to slay a demon?" Akemi was surprised. "Then we do share the same suspicions. You surprise me, brother. I, too, believe that whatever is trying to break into this world is, in fact, demonic in origin. I don't think it's found a way into our world yet, but I believe the veil is thinning as we speak. Whatever is coming through to this world is powerful, Kenjiro."

The samurai paused and looked at her.

"Very powerful," Akemi said.

"Then we must be ready," Kenjiro repeated.

Akemi drew her sword out of its sheath and examined it. "It has been a while since *Sekimaru* has tasted the blood of a demon. I think it's time to renew that thirst, that it might be quenched once again." She left her brother to his ritual and went back to the hills.

She would ready *Sekimaru* as Kenjiro did with his sword, but the ninja demon huntress had a different way of doing things.

* * *

AFTER KENJIRO COMPLETED his moving meditation, he inspected his sword. He and his sister had seen many battles together, shared many victories. They'd fought together their whole lives, and so their skills complemented one another.

The samurai thought back to ten years ago when he'd been given the task of forging his own sword. At the young age of fifteen, he was already a warrior of notable skill, with strength and endurance well beyond any of his peers. His parents had begun his training at the age of five, not unusual for children born of a warrior family. After only a day, his teacher had requested to move him to learn in the advanced class, which brought his parents pride, and himself confusion. Kenjiro hadn't felt as capable as Sensei had perceived him to be, but it was not his place to question.

What older students were expected to grasp in one month, he was expected to have mastered in that same period of time. Though every person was different, it was considered unthinkable for a practitioner to expect to achieve mastery inside of a decade. Kenjiro had reached mastery within seven years. Sensei was also adamant about Kenjiro learning *Bushido*, an ancient code of ethics that the samurai adhered to since even before the Age of Technology. Kenjiro remembered the day he began his lessons alone. Sensei purposely separated his young pupil from the rest of the students because of his rare abilities.

"Ego is a dangerous trait that is born in all of us, Kenjiro," the master lectured. "Some of your classmates admire and envy your abilities, which can lead to jealousy. This could interfere with their progress as well as yours. Remember this Kenjiro: Although your innate abilities exceed that of anyone in your class, it is your soul, your very being, that is your true strength. There is always someone physically stronger, but it is within yourself that you will find that true, elusive and intangible power that you seek. Power without perception is useless. Do you know what I mean when I say this?"

"I'm not sure, Sensei," the young Kenjiro had replied.

"Come."

They went for a walk in a nearby garden overflowing with diverse types of vegetation, from weeping willows to bonsai trees to small, green shrubs. Purple flowers bloomed and emitted a sweet smell. As they crossed an arc-shaped bridge, Kenjiro looked down at the many smooth multicolored rocks that carpeted the floor of the stream below. He liked picking the rocks up to feel their smooth texture before throwing them back into the water and disturbing the koi fish that browsed the stream bed. The sound of Sensei's voice brought Kenjiro's thoughts back to the present.

"What do you see around you?" Sensei asked.

"I see nature, Sensei," Kenjiro replied.

"And what about nature? Why do we often say we see nature, when we are in fact a part of it? Why is it when we take a retreat to a park, or go to the mountains or the forest, we feel relaxed and refreshed, and once we come back to this place that we call civilization, we are renewed? In fact, why is it that we call going to the mountains, or the forest, a retreat?" The child shook his head, confused.

"This," the master continued, "is because humans have separated themselves from nature. We once lived complex lives that were very different from today. The machines that we once used in our daily existence had no spontaneity, no vigor. We as humans have struggled to regain that spontaneity and vigor that we almost lost, so many years ago.

"People did just as their machines once did. They got up, performed their daily functions and went home to sleep. In some cases, perhaps I should refer to the relationship between people and machines differently. Instead of saying people and their machines, perhaps I should say machines and their people. People created these artificial workers to make their lives easier, but as a result, life grew even more complex than the people of previous ages could have ever dreamt it would be. Life and artificial life had interwoven themselves into each other. Though life is different now than it was, we as a species are still struggling to understand life and live it without the unnecessary complications we are so adept at creating."

Sensei spread a hand out to encompass the garden. "Kenjiro. When you see nature, what do you see?"

"I see something that is beautiful and simple, Sensei."

"Explain," Sensei said in an approving tone.

"When I look at nature, I see things going easy, like everything is doing what it does without having to think about it. It just does what it does. Everything seems to happen as it is supposed to, and there is nothing forcing anything to do anything. Flowers always bloom, fish always swim through the water perfectly, and birds fly just as if the sky picked them up and carried them away."

"Good, Kenjiro," Sensei replied, smiling at the child's simple explanation. "I said earlier that power without perception was useless. *Now* do you understand what I meant by this?"

"I think you were meaning to say that every living thing is able to work in life perfectly without any limits or distractions."

"Close," the teacher nodded encouragingly. "Watch that bird." Sensei pointed to a bird roosting in a tree. "Do you see what it's doing?"

The young boy nodded uncertainly.

"It is waiting patiently," Sensei continued. "Scanning for food. From its perch, it can see everything below with more detail than we can." Just as Sensei finished speaking, the bird crouched, then leaped from the branch and glided downward. Several feet from the ground it spread its wings and evened out its angle, scooping up a cricket while avoiding impact with the ground by mere inches.

"You see, Kenjiro? Without an outside influence it would never miscalculate and collide with the ground, because it need not calculate at all. It simply *does*. Without thought. It is in tune with itself and its surroundings. Unlike most humans who stumble through life, the bird acts according to the flow of life using its innate qualities, intelligence, and instincts."

"For example, a bird is born with the ability to fly, but must be taught by its parents to utilize this ability, and after a short time, the bird learns to fly. After some time and guidance from its parents, the bird masters the art of flying and soars with grace and perfection. This is unlike some humans that you may have seen who even after decades of walking remain clumsy and can be seen stumbling about."

"You are not like that, Sensei," young Kenjiro replied.

Akutagawa smiled, holding up a finger. "This is because I have learned to banish the ego, Kenjiro. Ego is involved in almost everything we as humans do, and that is sometimes the reason we stumble through life. We want to look perfect when we walk, we have to sound extra intelligent when we talk, we must behave this way or that way. I am not, however, implying that we just do whatever we wish and say whatever comes to mind without tact, but it is often because of ego that mastery escapes us."

Sensei looked at his student. "You must strive for perfection without ego, young one. Such a task at your age would be easier than as an adult. You are rare, Kenjiro, but you will discover that there are others not unlike you that are on a similar path to self-discovery."

"I don't understand," Kenjiro said.

"You will, in time. For now, train without ego, train for the goal of emptiness and selflessness. Only then will you truly be able to master yourself."

A few years following his and his master's walk, Kenjiro was given the task of forging his own sword. Weeks of failed attempts passed until he was able to successfully forge a simple sword, but the master was not satisfied. "Not bad," Akutagawa congratulated.

"This sword will serve you well for now, but in the real battles to come, you will need a sword far stronger than that one." Kenjiro, looking even more confused, tipped his head in inquiry.

"Sensei, people say that the Age of Technology will return and that there is no need to fight in battles using swords and physical fighting; those are the times of the past. Machines will do it all again as they did before. Why do I have to forge a stronger sword that was only used in a time that we read about in school and that people say will return soon?"

The master chuckled and replied, "Live on, my young student, live on."

After three more years of hammering and smoothing, healing small burns and squinting from the bright light of the molten coals over which he worked the metal that would be his sword, Kenjiro had finally realized his life's greatest achievement. He had forged the strongest blade seen in generations. The master inspected the weapon carefully. The curved blade was weighted perfectly, and as sharp as if a laser had tuned it during the times of technology.

"Excellent work," the master observed. "As strong as I have ever seen. I could never have forged such a sword. This one will serve you well, Kenjiro. More than just steel was used to create this. A bit of you and much more went into the conception and creation of this weapon. You would do well to name it and forever keep it by your side."

The young student looked at his new sword with a wide, gleaming smile of pride. "I told you," Akutagawa scolded, "simply do. Do not involve ego or all of your efforts are lost."

Kenjiro responded with a nervous nod, and looked at his sword once again. "Its name is … *Kenzo*." He looked to his master barely in time to see the startled look that came over his teacher's face before it was quickly replaced with a smile of approval.

"Very well," said Sensei with a bow to the sword. Kenjiro gently laid the sword atop its stand, stood up, and did the same.

As he lost himself in his remembrance of those past days,

Kenjiro had not noticed that his sister had left. He chuckled as he looked in the direction that Akemi had last been standing. How ironic it was that one of the very people the master had referred to as having similar abilities would turn out to be his own sister. He eventually had come to realize that in some ways, Akemi's abilities exceeded his own. He felt no jealousy or envy. He was happy that he had such a strong sister—even if she was a ninja—and that they could fight side by side. He would have had it no other way.

5

As she made her way up to the peak of Mt. Yamanake, Akemi reflected on her own training. Her teacher always seemed to know exactly how to incorporate the correct training methods to complement her abilities. As a girl, she had been capable of so much more than her classmates, and the master knew this. He'd been training Kenjiro for three years before she began, never once implying that she was actually exceeding her older brother's progress.

Sensei had been adamant about her performing without ego, which he'd constantly tried to hammer into her head. She'd always had a comment or a question about everything, and she never hesitated to say how she felt. Akemi laughed when she recalled the time when Sensei realized that she had a thirst for battle. Many times had the master scolded her for fighting with a devious grin on her face, while her opponent would struggle to maintain a solid footing amidst the barrage that was the little soon-to-be ninja.

"Akemi!" Sensei would say. "Do you forget that battle is a last resort? A measure taken only when all efforts for peace have been exhausted? You have a love for the martial arts and the martial way, and I commend you for that, especially at such an early age, but be mindful of your insatiable desire for the fight."

"Sensei," the young girl asked innocently, "is there anything else in life? All people do is fight. We always fight, but in different ways. Some people fight in school, some people fight in war, my parents always fight to make money for us to live in a nice home. They don't fight for real, but they sometimes don't look very happy when they think we do not see. Don't we all just fight in different ways?"

The master looked at his six-year-old student while hiding his amazement. *First her brother names his sword after the legendary ancestor he has never known, and now his sister at this age has developed a philosophy on her own!*

"Part of what you say is true," Akutagawa said, his face a mask of calm. "But you must remember patience. Your love for battle is fed by your lack of a challenge. When you meet someone who is better than yourself, will you then retain this vigor and hunger for the fight that you have now? That may be a question you will have to answer one day."

I doubt it, the girl thought, but kept those feelings to herself. The truth was that she had never met a person aside from her brother that could challenge her. Not even the senior students of the class could match her skill. She remembered one sparring match that she'd had with a twelve-year student. It was a typical medium-contact match, and all in class expected for the senior student to prevail, given the age and size gap.

"Akemi," the master had announced. "Today you will fight Tanaka in a medium-contact match."

Tanaka, one of Sensei's senior students, was seventeen years old and very skilled. He stood five feet seven inches tall with a slender frame. Being one of the most skilled students in the master's class, he restrained his curiosity at the decision. He dared not speak back to the master or question his judgment, but Tanaka couldn't help but wonder why he was being matched against a student who was only eight years old, had only been learning for two years, and was also female.

The master, seeing the concern in his student's face, added, "Underestimation of your adversary is most dangerous."

Unconvinced, Tanaka bowed respectfully to the master and then to Akemi, who did the same. They both took their customary stances.

Once the match began, Tanaka came in at Akemi with a simple right-handed open palm thrust, which Akemi avoided easily with a simple side step. Tanaka, expecting the evasion, followed up the attack with a right-legged sideways kick, which the ever-quick young girl simply slapped aside. The two stepped back, eyeing each other. After a moment, Tanaka frowned and glanced down at his ankle, which was red and stinging. *This girl is only eight years old. It's impossible for her to have this kind of power!* He was drawn from his thoughts by the master's voice.

"Akemi!" Akutagawa's voice was stern. "Concentrate, pay attention, and be serious!"

Tanaka looked back in amazement and fury when he saw the small girl, standing several feet in front of him, her face so wrinkled from fighting back a smile that she looked as if she would burst into laughter. Although the master disapproved of her attitude, this did little to repair Tanaka's wounded pride.

He moved in quickly with a series of open palm thrusts and stiff-handed chops that would have easily defeated more than half the students that sat watching in amazement. Still grinning, Akemi avoided every attack.

Her smile did vanish, however, when Tanaka caught her in the ankle with a foot sweep, tripping her to the floor. As soon as she was up again, the senior student was on her with a barrage of forward knife-hand strikes, one after another, driving the girl back on her heels. He snapped his foot up, catching the younger student under the chin and re-depositing her to the floor. The blow hurt a bit more than it should have, and it was then that Akemi realized

that her opponent was no longer holding back. Her superior attitude had been injured by her now-stinging chin. Now it was Tanaka's turn to stand and smile.

The master watched in silent disapproval. He would let them
learn this lesson on their own, though he did smile inwardly at his
students' wonderful progress.

Akemi stood up and faced her opponent, who towered over her
by more than a foot and a half. She shifted into a left-legged
stance, putting her right leg forward. This caught Tanaka by
surprise. He had not fought a left-legged opponent before, and now
both of their front legs were facing each other. The arrogant girl
smiled again when she saw the concern on her opponent's face.
Several seconds passed.

Finally, Tanaka decided to attack, but every time he made a
move, Akemi's rear foot snapped out and tapped Tanaka lightly on
his shin. He could hardly believe the speed of the little upstart. She
was clearly mocking him, but it was the ease with which she did it
that infuriated him. He doubled his efforts, again producing the
same series of forward knife hand strikes. This time Akemi dodged
every attack without retreating a step.

Tanaka followed up with a high roundhouse kick, then a lower
one. Akemi dodged both kicks and then, in a blink of the master's
amazed eye, Tanaka was on his heels.

Akemi was on him in a flurry of punches, knife-hand strikes
and reverse roundhouse kicks that had the older boy skittering
backward. He managed to block and evade for a moment, but in
short order Akemi landed a series of palm strikes to his midsection
and then three dizzying kicks to his chest, depositing him to the
floor in a breathless heap.

Swelling with triumph, the little girl stood tall and scanned the
room at her astonished classmates. Her smile melted away,
however, when her eyes fell upon her teacher, standing with his
hands clasped behind his back, looking out the window opposite
the sparring floor with his back to the class and to Akemi and

Tanaka in particular. "Class is dismissed … thank you." As the students quietly filed out the door, a compulsion that she could not name held Akemi where she stood. After all the students had gone, the master turned just enough to face the door, and exited the room. Akemi stood alone, feeling defeated instead of victorious.

How long ago that had been. Akemi had never forgotten the feeling of failure she had felt on that day. It was also the day she'd learned the most about herself. Three years after she had completed her training with Sensei Akutagawa, Akemi had become a member of the Azuma Ninja Clan and quickly rose in the ranks to become one of the most valued and feared demon hunters. Now, years later, Akemi was a lone ninja and demon hunter.

* * *

ONCE SHE REACHED HER DESTINATION, Akemi found an open area and set up a small portable shrine. The first time she'd used the shrine was to charge *Sekimaru*, the sword that she forged when she was seventeen years old. The master had waited two years longer than he did with Kenjiro to ensure that she was mature enough to forge the weapon. He had no doubt that she would create a powerful sword, which she did, but he wanted to be certain that she wouldn't become overzealous.

Akemi sat down in front of the shrine, back erect, legs crossed, and drew *Sekimaru*. It was a single-handed sword, two feet long, light, and perfectly balanced. The scabbard, as well as the double-braided hilt, was black as night and simple in design. Though she had forged it, the sword was mysterious to her. Whenever a creature from the abyss was near, she could feel a presence from the sword, a hunger to feed on the blood of a demon. She felt the hunger of *Sekimaru* today.

With the sword in a reverse grip, she held it out in front of her and put her left hand behind the right, all fingers curled except for the middle and index fingers that were pressed together and pointing upward. She closed her eyes and began to meditate. As she sank further into meditation, she felt power emanating from the blade. As she descended further, she felt the connection between her and the sword. Its hunger signified the presence of abysmal creatures in this world.

The air began to stir, growing more intense until the branches of the trees bent and swayed, and the leaves on the ground swirled around her. The wind howled as if it were a banshee, protesting its awakening. The blade of *Sekimaru* glowed with a golden hue. The sword and its wielder became one, and at that moment everything stopped and the ninja opened her eyes, her glowing sword held before her. Her disheveled hair rested on her shoulders and over her face. For a time, she sat and stared at the weapon. Then her eyes narrowed and there was a brightness, a zeal that shone in them. When she spoke, it was a loving whisper. "Sing, my sword."

6

After a light practice, the two friends were on their way back to Kenyatta's house. They'd enjoyed sparring in Capoeira together since childhood, and had often been called by Kita's father to stop after dancing all day and into the night. Of the many forms of martial arts they'd learned, it was Capoeira, part dance, part game, and part martial art, that the two friends enjoyed the most.

With music and dance, the villagers trained and played and laughed. The dance of Capoeira involved the body leaning forward, and the dancer stepping to the left with the left leg bent forward and the right leg almost swinging to the left. Then the motion was repeated in the opposite direction, with the right leg coming forward and the left swinging to the right. Within this rhythm, mostly kicks would be used, by means of standing, lying on the ground, or even balancing on the hands. Capoeira was a treat to watch, and even more of a treat for the practitioners.

On the way to Kenyatta's house, the two friends traded jokes and laughed while catching up on the current events in each other's lives.

"Hey Ken," Kita said. "You remember my girlfriend Benita?"

"Yeah, man, she's a cute one. Better be holdin' on to dat one for a while, ya?"

"Too late," Kita feigned regret. "She says that I practice martial arts and come to see you too much, and that I neglect her. She thinks it would be best if we just be *friends*." Kita said that last word with exaggerated distaste.

"Dat so?" Kenyatta snickered.

"What's so funny about that?"

"Oh nothin', me jyas tinking dat maybe since you're not with her anymore, I'll be givin' her a call." Kita shoved him, and they both laughed. "Don't be getting all swollen about it, man," Kenyatta said.

After he thought about it, Kita rolled his eyes. How could Kenyatta possibly call the girl when phones hadn't worked in well over two hundred years? Finally they reached Kenyatta's house, and the two friends sat down for some tea.

Kenyatta leaned on the table and took a sip of the cool, fruity tea. "So whatcha tinking 'bout dis energy? I feel it a lot stronger now dat I'm not concentrating on not knocking you unconscious."

Ignoring the sarcasm, Kita just shrugged and took a sip. It was an excellent blend of several different types of fruit that was just sweet enough with a tinge of tanginess to balance it. "I don't know what to think of this. Maybe we're just imagining things because the only people we've been able to fight in months are each other."

The two friends leaned back in their chairs, enjoying their tea. "I'll tell you this, Ken. I've been having an urge to get my weapons and start practicing again. I don't know why, but I think something big is gonna happen. Mostly though, I've been thinking about my staff."

Kenyatta leaned forward in his chair. "You mean the one dat you use only when we have a real fight? The last time you used dat, we both fight in a standoff between a band of samurai and ninja. Dat was a real fight man, more ninja and samurai than we ever seen in one place."

"Well," Kita responded, "I have a feeling that we're in store for something bigger than any of the challenges we've faced before. In fact, I think that all of our previous encounters will seem small compared to what's coming."

A grim look came and went across Kenyatta's face so quickly it might not have ever been there. "Ya, man," he chuckled, brightening the mood. "Maybe dis time we gettin' a challenge for real. It's been a long time, ya know. Truth is, I've been having the same feelings as you, and before you got here, I had been practicing with me swords for about a month now. I even make a new attack." Kita sat up, interested.

Taking Kita's interest as a cue, Kenyatta continued. "It's a move where ya charge in low, with da left shoulder down. You ram into 'em, push 'em off balance, and den bring da sword in da right hand to slice down." Kenyatta's eyes glittered. "Then bring in da left one and slice upward, allowing da power to pull ya all the way up. If done correctly, it could be a devastating maneuver."

Kita arched an eyebrow and nodded.

Seeing his friend's doubt, Kenyatta grabbed his swords and motioned for Kita to follow him outside. He walked over to an old, dead palm tree that was infested with ants. The tree looked to be over seventeen feet tall and at least four feet around. Kenyatta stood several spans from the tree and lowered into a crouch. Sand sprayed behind the islander as he charged the tree, slammed it with his shoulder so hard the tree shook, then slashed low with his right sword, then high with his left. True as he had said, the second swipe of his sword launched Kenyatta almost to the top of the tree and split it in half, bottom to top.

Kita was impressed as he watched his friend in the air, turning as he descended back to the ground. "Not bad if you're looking for a flashy way to make firewood."

"What?" Kita's offhandedness had Kenyatta incredulous. "Ya tinking ya can do better?"

Kita snickered at his friend then reacted quickly, catching the sword Kenyatta had suddenly tossed at him. Kita snorted, then laughed aloud as he turned his back on the oath-swearing Kenyatta, who hopped and danced about. Once inside, Kita turned and leaned against the door, still laughing at the sight of his friend, hopping and yelping and fidgeting as the resident ants from inside the dead tree crawled all over him.

"Hey," Kenyatta yelled. "Instead of standin' der, why don't you get a bucket of water. These ants are trying to eat me alive!"

"Maybe they're angry at you for destroying their home. They're avenging the tree."

"Ta hell with da tree! These little bastards are tryin' to suck the blood outta me! Get me some water or something or I'm gonna come jump on you and we can both squirm." Kita laughed all the harder, avoiding a charging Kenyatta, as he went around the house to find a bucket.

* * *

"SOMETHING BIG IS about to happen, Ken," Kita said, after his friend had finally found relief from the effects of the fire ant assault. "I have a feeling we'll be fighting again, but this time it'll be different."

"How so? People don't jyas throw off powerful energy. They don't emanate forces dis strong from their very being. We cyan't even do that."

"There's something else out there," Kita replied. "And I don't think we're gonna like it."

"And that's why you come here now," Kenyatta surmised.

"Yeah." Kita stared at the palms of his hands as though they held the answers he sought. "I can feel something inside me. Like something coming awake. My vision is clearer, I feel stronger, and my mind is sharper than usual."

Kenyatta nodded as Kita spoke. "Same for me. And me tink it's time we talk to someone else about it."

Kita looked up. "Your sister?" he asked.

"Don't look so excited, man," Kenyatta said, narrowing his eyes. "She don't fight like us because she don't see it as her way, but she is very powerful. In fact, she's one of the most powerful women in her village."

"I believe it," Kita said. "Whenever I'm around her I could feel this power coming off her, like a presence infinitely larger than the person standing there. I feel like I can fight pretty well, but there's something much bigger about her. Something that is far beyond a sword or an arrow."

Kenyatta's still narrowed eyes bore into his friend as Kita talked. "Yeah, man. I'm sure you felt all warm and protected around her, ya? I'm sure you're standing in awe and admiring her 'big' presence?"

Kita snorted and looked away. "Quit being ridiculous, I'm serious."

"Uh huh," Kenyatta muttered, leaning back. They had grown up together as brothers, after all. There was little they could hide from each other.

"So when were you thinking we would take this trip all the way to your sister? It's not like we can just jump on one of those planes my great grandpa used to talk about."

"Wasn't plannin' on that," Kenyatta replied. "There's a mental link between us. We can feel it when one of us needs the other. Taliah can do this thing she calls *skimming*, where the space around her warps and creates some sort of opening for her to step through. The way she tell it, every dimension has a sort of energy vortex that acts as a conduit to other dimensions. She can use them to travel great distances in a short amount of time. It's not like what you would think—ya don't go through a dark portal of blackness like they did in the movies … when there *were* movies." They shared a quiet chuckle. "The way she tell it," Kenyatta continued, "Each dimension exists somewhat parallel to ours.

"The heavens and the hells are not so much as above and below us, but alongside us, sitting a bit higher or lower. She says it's all about vibration. The demon realm vibrates slowly, whereas the heaven realm vibrates extremely fast. Apparently, the gods blessed her with the ability to briefly, very briefly, raise or lower her body's vibration to travel through either of these dimensions to get to a faraway place, since the laws of nature there don't really work the same way as here."

"If she can travel through either dimension, why in the world would she choose to travel through the abysmal realms?"

Kenyatta shrugged. "She says there's just as much risk trying to travel through the heavens, something about enticement, and how very few humans could handle it."

"Why did she leave in the first place?" Kita asked. "Couldn't she study here?"

"No," Kenyatta answered. "In order to develop, she travel to where her teachers live. Apparently, Ghana is one of da few places in da world with a number of people touched by da Gods in some way. From what she says, there aren't many people in da world who've been touched by da Gods, and dem that are, are never close together. Ghana have more than a handful of people she calls *Ascended*. However powerful she's become, dem well beyond her, hard as dat is to believe."

Kita rubbed his face. "This is all a bit over my head."

Kenyatta nodded. "Mine, too."

"So how do we contact her? You just think about her and she'll come?"

Kenyatta rubbed his hands through his long, thinly twined locks and sighed. "Taliah once tell me dat siblings who are very close could establish a bond so strong, dem feel each other's presence. With her abilities, she can communicate with me telepathically. Only problem was dat I was not born with da same abilities as her, so me have to clear my mind and tink of exactly what I want to say to her. If my mind is clear enough, she receive whatever thoughts I'm directing at her."

"Well you better get at it then, my friend," Kita said. "I feel like we don't have a lot of time."

More than half the day had gone by after their conversation before Kenyatta successfully established a telepathic link with his sister, and an hour after that, she was on the island with him and Kita.

Taliah was almost Kenyatta's height, with flowing, thick black hair neatly combed and freely hanging past the middle of her back. From her body radiated a power that seemed to glow just beneath her smooth brown skin. Her eyes, although round, came to a slant at the ends, and the whites of her eyes were as bright as any Kita had ever seen.

Taliah wore a beach dress that was made of linen and was tied at the waist on the left side. The dress was a beautiful blend of white background with brown palm trees and pale pink flowers. To Kita, everything about her was exotic. Even her smile was a blend of gentleness and ferocity that could be likened to a panther. When she walked, she moved with the same grace as the mystical cat and exuded an aura that was just as beautiful and dangerous. The most distinct feature about her, however, was what separated her from her brother. Although she was Jamaican, she lacked most of the Jamaican accent that Kenyatta had. Having spent most of her life in different countries, and a very long time in Ghana, her native accent had faded to no more than an occasional spark of her islander lingo.

After a while of catching up, they spoke of the strange emanations that Taliah said were coming from the direction of the Edge of the World. "I been feelin' the energy for a while now," Taliah said. "For a few months, I thought it might come and pass, since it was so random. But in the last few months it's been getting stronger. It wasn't until just a few weeks ago that it became so strong that I was able to understand it."

She sighed. "Some fool is summoning a powerful demon. Maybe more than one."

Kita and Kenyatta looked at each other and then back to Taliah.

"Someone is summoning a Quentranzi demon," she continued. "The most powerful of all the fiends in the dark world."

"Demons?" Kenyatta frowned. "Someone is summoning demons?"

"That would explain what we've been feeling," Kita said.

"This presents us with even more of a problem than a simple demon," Taliah said. "If this person, whoever he or she," Taliah paused, "or *it* is, can summon a Quentranzi, that means two things. First, this person has the ability to summon lesser, yet incredibly powerful demons in large numbers, but is also formidable themselves. I think you both will have more than your hands full in dealing with this. You're going to need help. You have gifts given from the Gods, but this is beyond what you two could handle on your own."

"Who could possibly be helpin' us?" Kenyatta asked, his tone darkening.

His sister looked at him and laughed. "You two are special." As she made the statement she glanced at Kita, who blushed. "But you are not the only ones with gifts. There are others who have similar talents. The only chance you have against what is coming is to align yourselves with people who have similar gifts as your own. You have some time before the fun starts." Her full lips curved into a smile. "Despite the power of the one who is summoning these fiends, it is going to take some time for it to fully control the things, much less a horde of other lesser dark ones."

Kita seemed to snap out of the trance he was in, staring at Taliah, and looked excited and concerned at the same time. "Sounds like fun, but how are we supposed to find these other people?"

"I can help you with that," Taliah replied. "Give me a little time to connect with someone who helps me from time to time. She has been my guide, and it was on her advice that I was sent to Ghana as a child. I will find answers for you."

"Sounds good to me," Ken and Kita answered in unison.

Taliah smirked at them. "Just like brothers," she muttered.

The sun was sinking below the western sea when Taliah came back with the news that she had indeed connected with her guide, who agreed to help her in finding the others who could aid the two friends in their journey.

"Ya know, one ting bugging me," Kenyatta said. "I mean, I know huntin' demons is just a barrel of fun, but I'm not sure me wan step out on a journey pickin' a fight with some of the most powerful evil in the dark world."

Taliah gave him a look. "So what you're saying is that when the job is done and Kita has fought and come back, you will be content having sat back and done nothing?" She paused and looked at Kita who smirked at his friend. "That *is* what you're saying, right?"

"Right," Kenyatta replied with a snort.

"You know you want this as much as I do, Ken," Kita taunted. "Quit cryin' and listen." Kenyatta stiffened, but let it go when he saw the devious smile on his friend's face.

"I've been given the general area where you can find the others," Taliah went on. "It should be within about ten miles of where they are currently located, but it should not take you long to find them. There are two of them, and they live in the hills at the base of Mt. Yamanake in Japan. I was also told that one of them is an experienced demon hunter, and that her role in this will be crucial."

"Still sounds like a small number of people, considering what we're up against," Kita remarked.

Taliah raised an eyebrow. "Perhaps there are others, perhaps not, but this was all I was given." Her face brightened. "The second thing. Your weapons will need to be charged with Daunyanic power. Normal weapons from this world will do no more than irritate the lowest of demons, but with the essence of the Daunyans, you can send them back to their own realm. Your weapons will be infinitely stronger than they are now once I have charged them."

"Well, what about the two in Japan? How are they supposed to fight demons without this charge?" Kita asked.

"And what is Daunyanic power and what are Daunyans?" Kenyatta added.

"Worry about yourselves," Taliah answered, avoiding Kenyatta's question. "Trust me when I say that they also have resources."

Kita shrugged. "As you say. So should we get our weapons then?"

"No, but when it's time, I will find you." Kita and Kenyatta looked at each other in confusion. Now seemed as good a time as any, but they didn't argue the point.

"Well, I guess dat's it," Kenyatta said as he clapped his hands together. "So, why don't ya jyas whip up a quick shortcut to Japan for us and we'll be on our way."

Taliah shook her head. "Oh, ya don't think it's going to be *that* easy now? I'm sure you two plan on doing some training, right?" The two friends nodded hesitantly. "Then," she continued, "the perfect time to do it is on the way to Japan, so why don't ya both just hike it."

Kenyatta's mouth fell open. "You suppose we strokin' across da ocean to get der, or are we rowin' a boat the whole way?"

Taliah shrugged helplessly. "I told you. You're going to need to be strong, which means no easy rides for you. You need to survive the elements and hardships of the world without assistance."

"And why is that?" Kita asked, arms crossed.

"Because the elements themselves are part of what you will face when you *do* begin the fight," Taliah answered. "Some demons can manipulate the things around them, and you should be prepared for anything. Also, there are many dangers that will come your way between here and Japan. That will be your training. If there is one last thing I can say to prepare you, it's this: When demons are brought from the abyss, they inadvertently awaken a lot of evil that already exists in this world. You will encounter these things along the way and it will prepare you ..." she hesitated, "...somewhat, for what's to come. You will get a taste of what these things are capable of. You must trust me on this. If you were to fight a demon right now, you would not be prepared for it. They are like nothing you've seen before."

Kita looked at Kenyatta. "I don't like it, but she's right." That brought a groan from his friend, but no rebuttal.

After some light conversation, Taliah decided to stay in Jamaica for a while and visit. She spent some time alone, probing her thoughts and feelings. Although she felt that the fighting that her brother and Kita did was not her way, she still could not deny an inner desire to take part in the fight. She did not want to stay in the background and play a subtle part. The young woman wanted to be at the front of the fight with her brother, to stand beside him and his closest friend in what would be the greatest battle the world had ever seen, and ironically, few on this world would even know about. They had missed too much in each other's lives, she and Kenyatta. Their grandfather had sent her to the Caribbean to study with her aunt over the summer. When she returned, she was told of what happened to their grandfather, and where Kenyatta had been taken. Fortunately, Kita's father had left information with a trustworthy neighbor so that Taliah could find him.

Now they were together only to be separated again, with those two off on another adventure, and she only helping from behind. With a sigh of acceptance, Taliah went into her brother's house to have a cup of his famous fruit tea. She sat sipping her tea and gazing out the dining room window at the ocean. *Humanity has been given another chance that so many are unaware of. Now this.* She closed her eyes, feeling the ocean breeze sighing through the window to caress her face. Could they protect this world they had nearly destroyed, or would it be destroyed by the abyss itself?

7

B rit stood unmoved in front of the fourteen-foot-tall monstrosity. He wouldn't give the thing the satisfaction of seeing any type of emotion.

"Who summons me?" the demon Kabriza rumbled.

"My name is Brit, and I have summoned you. I wish to enlist your assistance in a goal that might prove of mutual benefit."

The hideous creature cocked its head in amusement. "There is nothing a vermin of this dimension could offer that would be of interest to me."

"Is that so?" Brit countered. "I know of your kind …" He paused, deciding whether or not to mention the thing's name again, for Quentranzi demons had been known to break the strongest barriers in a fit of rage at the mere mention of their names. "Human souls are of no interest to a Quentranzi," he continued. "You have different interests."

"Do we?" Kabriza asked slyly.

"You desire to wreak havoc on this world and tie it to your own, giving you a larger world to plunder and increase your power. The goal of a Quentranzi is unlimited power and destruction."

"Is it?" Kabriza asked once again, its voice dripping with

sarcasm. Brit, however, knew the game of dealing with a dark world creature and maintained his patience. "Perhaps we merely want to rip apart those who have the audacity to summon us for their own small and pathetic conquests."

At that moment, Brit felt a mental attack more powerful than any living thing from this world could be capable of. He had anticipated the assault and held his ground, but eventually fell under the overwhelming force of his foe. Kabriza would have destroyed his mind, but his servant had been hiding in the shadows, waiting for the right time to help his master. Zreal's species, the Zetsuan, possessed the ability to shield their minds from attack. If another was close enough, they could be shielded as well. Zreal, sensing the battle, entered the fray.

He slowly, carefully, slipped a mental barrier between Brit's mind and the Quentranzi. For what seemed like hours to Brit, but was no more than seconds, his power combined with Zreal's, held the demon at bay.

"Impressive," the fiend congratulated. "Your mind seems to be a strong one." Brit noted the fiend's choice of the word *seems*. Dark world creatures of this nature were difficult to outsmart, and this one was no different. Brit knew that a time would come when Kabriza might try to test him again. "Perhaps something different," the monster suggested, and with a thought, the small flames in the corners of the octagonal seal flared.

Brit could see that the demon was energizing the seal in an attempt to overload it and break free of the barrier. The seal was flawless, however, and held the demon in place. "If you have had enough of the games, Kabriza, can we move on to business?"

Flames of barely contained rage danced in the demon's eyes at the mention of its name. It narrowed its dark red eyes at the Drek. "You walk dangerous ground, little one," Kabriza said.

"As do you, demon," Brit replied. Although his seal was strong enough to hold the creature, he still had to be careful. It still might be possible for it to shatter his barrier in a fit of rage.

"Speak your reason for disturbing me and be done with it, mortal Drek," Kabriza growled.

Brit crossed his arms. "I wish to enlist your assistance in the destruction of Takashaniel."

"Takashaniel," the fiend repeated. It stared at Brit and repeated the name as though tasting it. "Hmm, Takashaniel."

"Don't play with me, demon," Brit growled. You know of the place, and I have all the time I need to keep you right here." Kabriza adjusted its gaping maw in what could have been a mocking smile or a hungry sneer and repeated, yet a third time, "Hmm, Takashaniel."

Brit understood full well how Quentranzi liked to toy with the patience of their summoners as his was beginning to erode.

"You talk of such a place as if it were the most powerful in this world. Surely it would take more than my help to bring down such a place. Do you wish me to help you in some negotiation? Perhaps a bargain? They let you rule the world, and you let them have all the free food they want. A fair deal, so what do you need …?"

"You stretch my patience too far, demon," Brit interrupted, and Kabriza again managed something that looked like a smile. Brit began to chant a spell that the fiend apparently knew, and did not like.

"If you finish that spell I will destroy you over the course of three centuries," Kabriza threatened.

Brit smiled. "You underestimate me, Quentranzi." He lifted his hand and projected an icy blue mist at the demon. Kabriza looked at the mist and then at Brit. As the mist enveloped him, the fiend roared in agony, staring daggers at the Drek.

After a few moments, Brit relinquished. "I warn you, my friend, I will not be toyed with or betrayed." Kabriza continued to glare at the earthly creature, eyes narrow red slits.

"You say *betrayed* as if we've already struck a deal," Kabriza remarked. At that same moment the entire fortress began to shake, bottles burst and pillars cracked. Parts of the roof began to crack and fall, and the floor split into giant spider web cracks beneath their feet. Zreal looked around in alarm. Despite Brit's confidence, he was starting to doubt the sanity of this plan.

"Destroy my fortress," Brit said in a threatening tone, "and wonder how long it will be before you look upon this world again. Humans would not think of summoning one of your race, and after I release you to your abyss, it may be thousands of centuries before you see this light again! I can always find another way to achieve my goal. You, on the other hand, have no way to visit this dimension without the assistance of another." His words had the desired effect, for the quakes ceased.

"And if I were to agree to your terms, you can rest assured that I would not eviscerate you at a whim," Kabriza offered.

"I will try to contain my relief," Brit responded dryly. "I think you may find me a bit more durable than a human."

"Oh? Then I had better be careful what I say to the mighty Brit."

Brit maintained his calm. "If you are unable to help in the destruction of Takashaniel, I will call on another."

Kabriza smirked. "Takashaniel is a big job, surely even the mighty Brit would prefer assistance since the tower is made of the stuff channeled by the cursed Gods."

Zreal shook his head. The fiend seemed content to spar with Brit indefinitely. Because both minds were touching his shield, Zreal could feel them. Brit's was calculating and calm, straining to maintain patience. Kabriza's mind was pure hatred and disdain mingled with amusement. It was also playing for time while it scanned the octagonal seal for a flaw.

"Takashaniel, it is said, was created by the Gods to control the negative and positive energies so that neither one would dominate over the other," Brit explained. "The tower is not invulnerable. With our power combined, we could destroy it, and you and your kind would be able to travel to this dimension with more ease than you can now."

"And what are your plans, oh great one?" Kabriza mocked. Brit ignored the sarcasm. "My plans are my own. But what I'm offering here is for us to work together in a mutual interest."

"I am elated to know that you are so kind as to help me and my brethren come to this world and achieve our modest goals to bask in the sunshine and flora and fauna of this goodly wholesome world you have here. And I am sure the thought of us swarming this world warms you inside." The Quentranzi general looked the octagonal seal over and chuckled. "So do we shake hands, or is there some other way you want to seal our deal?"

Brit looked at the creature with resentment. "Although your encouragement and overwhelmingly loyal demeanor make me so comfortable, I will need a bit more from you to ensure that we will be working with the same goal in mind and that this will not become more than I desire."

Kabriza tilted its head and eyed Brit. "You seek to probe my mind, Drek?" It made a sound that could have been laughter. "Surely you know that such an effort could only amuse me." Brit turned and walked away, stopping halfway across the room to glance over his shoulder.

"I don't think there should be any problems between us, for now." He turned back and left the room. At that moment, the powerful demon realized that it had been outsmarted, and that Brit had simply distracted it while a subtler method was employed. After a moment, the demon bared its jagged teeth. The Drek could not have used his mind to probe from two different directions; it was impossible. There had to have been someone else nearby that was helping him. That would explain why his summoner was so confident. Brit may know Kabriza's intent now, but that could change in an instant. Kabriza grunted in respect of the Drek's cunning. *In time I will show him what power truly is.* The barrier to the demon realm suddenly released, and Kabriza stepped back into the abyss.

Zreal, still hiding in the shadows, was able feel some of the demon's thoughts after Brit had left and the barrier melted away. He would have to warn Brit immediately, but surely his master would not be so foolish as to trust a creature from the abysmal realm, especially not a Quentranzi! The Zetsuan decided to tell his master of his findings anyway. Zreal had no idea how this could end in anything other than disaster, but it was not his place to question. Zreal may not be as powerful as the Drek who had brought him to this world, but Zreal was a survivor. If Brit was successful, all the better, but if he failed, Zreal would ensure that he was not similarly pulled into a foolish death.

* * *

ON THEIR WAY to the port, Kenyatta and Kita reflected on their time living in the Philippines. Having grown up together as brothers, they'd lived in the same house, shared chores and worked and played together.

"Hey, Ken. You remember that time when we got stuck in the tree trying to spy on Aunya?"

That name brought a chuckle from Kenyatta, as he remembered their obsession with the older girl when they were boys. Many a day, he and Kita tried to get away from the house to be around her, or at least watch her from afar. "Dat tall one up the hill from your house? Ya, man, how could I forget? We get stuck for an hour after she left. I remember how hard your dad laughed when him see us up der. Didn't help us down either."

"Yup," Kita laughed. "And then you fell six feet before you were able to grab onto another limb and swing up."

"And ya laugh so hard at me," Kenyatta replied, "ya fall and get hung upside down by ya leg. All dat screamin' and hollerin. 'Me foot's hung!' I'm tinking me goin' def from all dat screamin'!"

"I still managed to pull myself up and untied my leg from that vine," Kita argued.

"Ya, den fell past me and landed in an ant-infested patch of poison ivy." Now Ken was laughing. "I tink ya found a new dancing rhythm. Da way you hoppin' and yelpin', I thought ya comin' up with some kinda new dance I never seen." Kita shoved his friend, but couldn't help sharing Kenyatta's mirth at the long ago memory.

"So ya tink we're facing some pretty powerful enemies, ya?"

"I hope so," Kita answered. "I could use the practice, and if your sister is right, we'll need all the practice we can get before the real deal hits. I wonder what these things look like anyway."

"Who knows? Dem probably six feet tall with a pointed tail and a pitchfork with horns."

Kita smirked. "Or maybe half a foot tall and land on your shoulder and nip at your ear telling you to do bad things."

"You ready to get under way, or you wantin' to hug the land beneath your feet a while longer?"

The two friends turned to regard a short, pot-bellied man with a thick mustache and a shaved head. He had his thick hairy forearms crossed over his large barrel chest.

"We're ready when you are, Captain Barum," Kita replied. "You know this isn't our first voyage."

The captain snorted. "How long you ever been aboard a ship, boy? Couple days? A week or two? Ain't no voyage. When you've seen the sun rise and fall at sea so many times you lose count, then you got a voyage under your belt." He spat in the sand and covered it. "*Siren's Song* breaks port in two hours. I suggest you get all your landlubber business done." The burly captain turned back toward his ship.

"Why do ship captains all seem the same?" Kita asked, staring after the departing Barum.

"Same reason everyone else seems the same to them and their crew, I'd imagine."

True to his word, Captain Barum had *Siren's Song* stocked and ready to break port inside of two hours. Kenyatta and Kita climbed aboard and looked back at the island, each wondering when they would see the island again. Neither had fought a demon before, and being honest with themselves, they felt a bit detached. How could one appreciate the gravity of such an unbelievable situation?

"Tink der's really demons crawling around out der somewhere?" Kenyatta's voice was quiet, thoughtful as the boat drew farther away.

"Who can know?" Kita replied. "They may always have been there, causing trouble since the first time man came into being. Maybe they are the reason there has been so much evil and chaos in the world for so many thousands of years."

Kenyatta just stared at the slowly diminishing island. "I never met a demon, but I've seen evil in men, and I've seen good, too. Both do what dem do because of who they are, not what someting else make 'em into."

For a time they watched as the island of Jamaica grew smaller and smaller until finally, it was no longer visible. The two friends turned their attention to the endless ocean before them, and the equally endless possibilities beyond.

8

S *ekimaru* awakened once again, Akemi made her descent down the mountain, allowing herself to enjoy the lush greenery, plants and trees, the insects, birds and the numerous animals and other forms of life that inhabited the mountainous forest. She came to a cliff overlooking a vast crevice partially hidden in a gray mist. On the other side of the crevice, the mountain continued in its rolling, hilled pattern. She admired the plant life that had the strength and resilience to live on the edge of the mountain its entire life as opposed to the ease of living on flat land. She thought about the hidden blessing of such a location. Although the plants and trees were living a harder life on the side of the mountain, they weren't shadowed by taller trees and denied sunlight. They were never trampled and were less likely to be eaten by a vegetarian animal in search of a meal. Akemi always contemplated the subtle lessons hidden in plain sight.

She often wondered what the chattering birds' conversations were about. Perhaps they were warning their friends that she was headed in their direction. Being in the mountains brought a smile to Akemi's face. She'd been born a warrior and had drawn her sword more times than she could recall, yet she still felt the need to stop and realign herself with nature.

As the ninja made her way around a bend in the path, she noticed that the birds had stopped singing. She went still, scanning her surroundings. A feeling of wrongness crept up her spine and the tiny hairs on the back of her neck stood on end. Suddenly her intuition screamed at her and she looked up just in time to see a tree branch falling from directly overhead. She leapt backward, narrowly avoiding the branch as it crashed to the ground, blasting her with dirt and leaves. She landed in a crouch and waited, one hand on *Sekimaru's* hilt and her other hand across her waist, slipping her fingers in a small pouch on her right hip. Again she scanned her surroundings. When all seemed clear, she went over to inspect the tree branch. It didn't take much inspection to see that the limb had been severed. What amazed Akemi was how something could cleanly shear through a branch that was at least eight feet long and larger around than she was!

She suddenly ducked, avoiding the swipe of a sword aimed at her neck. She spun on her heels, simultaneously drawing her sword to deflect another blade aimed at her heart. She could feel the presence of the sword quickening in her grasp, and knew the nature of her enemy. Finally, she saw it, a shadow wielding twin blades shaped like two slithering snakes glared at her with a face that was composed only of a pair of glaring eyes.

A smile crept across her face. "Now surely it has to be more than you who's been causing me all this anxiety."

The shadowy figure came at her again, and Akemi met it. Only wielding one weapon, she worked doubly hard to keep up with the quick pace of this new foe. In less than a few moments, she learned the creature's patterns and began to match every attack, left to right. The shadow leapt back and thrust its swords forward in a one-two motion. Akemi rotated *Sekimaru* between the two blades with inhuman speed and knocked them wide, following up with three equally fast sideways kicks to the thing's face. It staggered backward and then she was on it, driving the creature back on its heels.

Even with two blades, the figure was still hard-pressed to match the speed and ferocity that was Akemi. Holding *Sekimaru* in a reverse grip, she swiped the sword left, then right, forcing the creature to lean away or lose its head. Smirking, she executed a right turning spin and stabbed backward to her left side. As she'd expected, the shadow had deflected her first attack, but as it did so, she'd slipped a smaller blade out of her waistband, and stabbed it in the hip. The thing hopped back and stared at her. Akemi glanced over her shoulder and smiled. She finally got a better look at her attacker and saw that the blades it wielded were actually part of its arms. Her smile widened as her eyes narrowed.

The dark figure analyzed its intended prey. It narrowed its red eyes, but it clearly held a bit more respect for the woman. The smaller blade did nothing to injure the creature, as it was not from this plane of existence, but it was still surprised at the woman's skill. It glanced down, then up at her. The lack of pain from the little knife imbedded in its abdomen gave the demon more confidence. Though it could feel power emanating from that sword, it had not the intellect to reason out the difference between the two blades. One of its sword-arms reformed into a normal arm and hand, and it snatched the knife free and discarded it. It then stalked toward the woman, arm reverting to the wavy blade once more.

Akemi sent a shuriken spinning into its left eye. It stumbled back a few steps, more in anger than in injury. It removed the shuriken just in time to feel the sharp and intense pain of its essence being siphoned from its abdominal area. As it looked down on the incredible woman, it saw her embedded sword feasting upon its energy. The Kalistyi let out a hiss as it faded into oblivion. After the creature dissipated, Akemi held her sword before her eyes. *Sekimaru* had the power to completely annihilate a lesser demon. Though she had forged the weapon many years ago, she still felt that she didn't know everything about it.

She took a deep breath and looked around. Everything seemed to return to normal, but she wondered where that thing had come from and how it came to this world. She had heard of the shadow demons called Kalistyi, but had never actually seen one. She would be a fool not to see this encounter as a sign. Akemi returned *Sekimaru* to its sheath and looked around. After she was sure that there was no more threat, she recovered her dagger and shuriken.

"I think that was a warning."

Akemi glanced in the direction of her brother's voice, and saw Kenjiro leaning against a tree a few feet behind her. "Yes, it was," she answered. "There will be more. I take it you heard our little disagreement?"

The samurai nodded. "I heard your swords clashing when I was moving through the woods not far away, so I thought I would come see what was going on."

"You still move swiftly," Akemi teased. "I guess age hasn't taken its toll. You didn't come to help?"

Kenjiro stared at Akemi. "I was unaware that a few years' difference would put me at such a physical disadvantage, little sister. And what would I have done if I did come to help? That was a lesser demon and if I had interfered in your fight, I would have ended up taking the creature's place, would I not?"

Akemi didn't hear the question. "That demon was not a major demon, but it wasn't a lesser one either. Kalistyi cannot come to this realm unless there is something causing imbalance to the veil between this world and theirs." She ran a hand through her coarse black hair. "Lesser demons slip past the barrier between our two worlds from time to time, which is what keeps me in my primary line of work. If Kalistyi are roaming about, there is something more going on. And we need to find out. This situation will only get worse."

"We will need to go and see Sensei Akutagawa," Kenjiro said, pinching his chin between thumb and forefinger. "He may have some insight to all of this."

Akemi couldn't imagine what insight their teacher could have. He had trained them as warriors, but he was no demon hunter. Still, they had no other options. "Let's go now," she said, and the siblings set off back down the mountain.

They moved through the trees, the young ninja preferring the higher vantage point of leaping branch to branch, while her samurai brother moved quietly on the ground. When they rounded a bend and came to a steep hill, Kenjiro stopped at the sight of Akemi crouched on a high branch, staring intently at something. The ninja looked down at him and jerked her chin in the direction just over the hill.

Quietly, he made his way near the top and peeked over. About twenty-five feet below and in front of them were six dark figures. They looked exactly like the one Akemi had just fought. The six shadowy demons moved as if they were snakes slithering across the ground. Kenjiro signaled for Akemi to make her way around to the back of the group while he made his way in front of them. She slipped back out of sight and leapt from tree to tree, tracking her prey. The group froze, and Akemi suspected they had sensed the two humans were near.

The leading shadow looked around, then up. Kenjiro noticed a very subtle flick of light in his peripheral vision, and knew that Akemi was signaling to him that she was in position and ready. The samurai stepped out into the open in front of the demons. They eyed him hatefully.

Kenjiro drew his sword and held it before him, waiting for his enemies. He was samurai, a legendary warrior from the ancient history of Japan that had resurfaced since the End of Technology. The code of Bushido demanded that the samurai was to live, fight, and die with honor. Kenjiro wanted the group to see their deaths and give them every opportunity to defend themselves fairly.

That sight brought a groan from Akemi, as she just watched and shook her head in exasperation. She was a ninja, and though her clan was trained with some similar principles as the samurai, they, like all ninja, specialized in stealth and assassination. Akemi would have dropped on top of the group, killing several before they knew what was happening.

"I grew tired of waiting for you," Kenjiro stated as he eyed the group. He wasn't even sure they understood what he said, but it mattered little. The important question was whether or not these fiends were pawns of some bigger and stronger monster.

He received a hiss in reply, and the demons rushed at him. Behind them, Akemi leaped from the tree in pursuit. One of the shadows stopped abruptly at the realization that the one running next to it had suddenly dissipated. The group skidded to a stop and turned to see Akemi standing behind them amidst the dissipating black mist. She had *Sekimaru* at her side and ready. And then Kenjiro was there, and the two warriors were on them.

The Kalistyi quickly morphed their arms from the elbow down into steel wavy blades, identical to the ones wielded by the shadow Akemi had killed earlier. The ninja came in at the Kalistyi at the back of the group with a horizontal slash at the demon's throat. It leaned back, then countered with a forward stab with its right sword arm. Akemi sidestepped, at the same time blocking a right-handed sweep aimed at her back. She then stepped into the shadow's reach and punched it in the face. It took a step back and looked at Akemi as if wondering why she would even bother. That split-second pause was the instant Akemi needed to thrust *Sekimaru* deep into the shadow's midsection. It hissed as it began to dissipate, and she turned and deflected another sword-arm coming for her neck. She then hopped over a low swipe at her legs. This new threat came in at her in a fury of stabs, thrusts, and swings in unusual and fast combinations that drove the ninja back on her heels.

* * *

KENJIRO FARED WELL against the shadow that challenged him.

Although the beast came at him with well-placed thrusts and swings, they were telegraphed, and the samurai had learned its patterns. The Kalistyi stepped forward inside of Kenjiro's defense and attempted to use an upward thrust straight through his chin. The samurai spun to the right and slashed down with his sword. The fiend rolled forward to avoid the blade, then sprang back in Kenjiro's direction and executed a series of one-two stabs. Kenjiro's sword was a blur as he deflected the stabs each time, winding and twisting his blade to meet every thrust. As the Kalistyi pressed him backward, another fiend ascended from a shadow on the ground and stabbed at his back. The ever-alert samurai sensed the presence behind him and in the last instant, brought his sword around in a powerful two-handed parry, causing a ricocheting effect in both weapons.

The Kalistyi in front of him was temporarily stunned by its vibrating weapon. Anticipating the force created from the parry, Kenjiro used the ricochet to spin him around to block the new attack at the rear. The force knocked the new attacker off balance just as the stunned demon recovered. Kenjiro leaped into a roll, and came back to his feet in a counterclockwise spinning block with his sword, deflecting all four of the sword arms directed at his upper torso. The two demons tried to overwhelm the samurai with their two-to-one advantage, but Kenjiro's sword flashed fast and true.

* * *

AKEMI GLANCED over her shoulder and smiled as she saw her brother gracefully dance with the two demons who looked as if they could actually be breaking a sweat, if that were possible. She returned her full attention on the unfortunate Kalistyi in front of her that must have begun to realize it was outmatched. It ducked a high swipe by the ninja and countered with a thrust with both its sword-arms that was becoming repetitive to the ninja.

Akemi snickered as she jumped over the attack in a forward flip and kicked the demon in the back of the head as she passed. As it stumbled forward, Akemi's feet touched the ground and the hard muscles in her legs flexed and propelled her backward toward the fiend. The shadow demon's head fell back and it hissed in agony, then looked down at its dissipating torso. The last thing it heard before it succumbed to oblivion was one sweetly spoken word. "Goodbye."

* * *

KENJIRO HAD no such luck in seeing his younger sister's amazing skill, for he had his hands full holding off these two shadows while devising an attack. The shadow to his right jumped to the side and moved in diagonally in hopes of catching the samurai off guard. Its partner came in with a series of low swipes at his feet, forcing him to adjust his stance, which put him off balance. The strategy would have worked had Kenjiro reacted a split second slower. Instead, he leaped to the right, avoiding the low strike and flying past the other shadow's diagonal stab. As he passed, he brought *Kenzo* around in a one-handed backward swing and decapitated the demon. Kenjiro understood little of the power that coursed through his sword, but he knew that it was somewhat different in nature than *Sekimaru.* While a killing strike from the latter would completely obliterate a demon, a similar strike from Kenzo would not destroy the demon, but simply send it back to the abyss.

Caring not at all for its defeated comrade, the remaining Kalistyi came at the samurai with savage high and low one-two stabs. The fiend was sloppy and predictable, and the samurai easily avoided the attacks.

The demon then delivered an unexpected kick to Kenjiro's stomach. The samurai accepted the blow but stumbled backward, bent over. The shadow, believing the fight over, proceeded to remove the human's head from his shoulders.

As its stroke fell, Kenjiro brought his sword up to block with so much power that it severed the shadow's left sword arm. It skittered backward with a hiss and looked in disbelief at its severed arm, then at the human who was stalking toward it. The fiend recovered and attacked with its remaining weapon.

The angered samurai simply walked forward, all the while parrying every attack. The demon attempted to stab at him, but before it could draw its arm back, he stepped in and to the side. With a vertical chop, he severed the remaining sword-arm of the Kalistyi.

Its agonized hiss was cut short, and the world started to spin. Finally the spinning stopped, but now everything was sideways and it was on the ground. It glanced to its right to see its dark body dematerializing back to the dark world. The now independent head narrowed its eyes as it too sank back into the abyss.

Kenjiro heard a voice over his shoulder.

"Not bad. You handled those two whole Kalistyi all by yourself."

Kenjiro ignored his sister's japes and walked right by her. "We need to get to Sensei as soon as possible."

Akemi shrugged, used to her brother's stern demeanor and trotted to catch up. She was elated at the idea of an adventure after all this time. The thought of a battle alongside her brother, whether they triumphed or died together, excited her.

9

Three weeks into their trip at sea, *Siren's Song* had made brief stops on small islands along her route to replenish food and supplies as well as trade in fabrics and spices with the locals. The first days at sea were filled with fun and laughter as the ship encountered no threats from weather or other vessels. Their second week brought a storm that had buffeted the mid-sized ship and set it off course for several days till the clouds gave way and they were finally able to look to the heavens to find their path once more. Finally, after a long and tiring month, *Siren's Song* arrived off the shores of Korea.

"I'll make sea dogs outta you two yet," Captain Barum declared heartily once they made port. "Over a week we got slapped by that storm and not a once did you lose your meals over the side of the ship!" Kenyatta felt no need to admit that indeed he had almost lost his dinner on that first night.

"Our thanks, good captain," Kita said. "Best wishes to you and the crew."

"Yeah, man," Kenyatta agreed. "We won't forget your kindness."

The captain waved them away. "I always ferry lubbers like

yourselves across the big pond. And you were more like part of my crew than the usual land lovin' cargo. Next time you need to sail, you've got friends in the crew of *Siren's Song!* I'll always have you aboard."

Captain Barum returned to his ship, and the two friends looked around at the unfamiliar surroundings. It was the first time they had ever been to Korea, and they wished they had more time to explore the country. Kita and Kenyatta took in the many sights, sounds, and smells as they traversed some of the nearby villages and occasional cities that so effectively utilized the surrounding natural resources without exploiting them. Since the End of Technology, all civilizations were forced to start over. People had been resourceful in adapting already existing houses and buildings to the new age. Kita and Kenyatta had always found it interesting to travel to distant lands and see how cities around the world had recreated themselves.

Most places reverted back to the villages of the old times, utilizing nonfunctional devices from ages past in new and creative ways. Some places had actually taken on new names in place of old ones, while others adopted old names that had been changed during times of conquest and colonialism. Some of the major cities, however, retained their original names. Seoul, for example, was one of those major cities. Even after the End of Technology, the city had retained its original name.

Although there was an obvious absence of moving cars, buses, planes, and other signs of technology, the place still buzzed with the daily activity and bustle typical of a large city. In these times, only large cities remained while smaller suburbs throughout the world branched off and split into sections to become their own autonomous dwellings. Without technology, it was difficult for a large city to exist, and many fractured into smaller cities within the larger ones.

Kenyatta and Kita looked at all of the old skyscrapers, buildings, strip malls and freeways. Ironic that they still served the same functions they had during the Age of Technology, if in a more primitive fashion. As they ventured toward the outskirts of town, things were a bit different. Fast-food restaurants were converted into homes and neatly refined shelters. Office buildings were converted into living space to accommodate the thriving population. Restaurants were modified into places of celebration, while some of the strip malls were converted into schools of martial arts. It was in the villages outside the cities, however, where the best martial warriors could be found. Just as during the Age of Technology when many preferred to live in the country, away from the hustle of city life, many people chose life in the security of buildings and structures of the Old Age, and the major cities provided that illusion. In the villages, however, people relied on their ingenuity, wit and skill to survive the elements. The warrior class that existed outside of major civilization was of the best quality since the village's safety and existence depended on the ability to defend itself.

Another ironic byproduct of the new age was the city's cleanliness. Without technology there were less wasteful materials created and discarded irresponsibly. The world was changing, and people were changing with it.

Walking along the streets, they noticed the often-friendly, often-curious stares they attracted. Since there were no planes or vacation ships, foreign visitors were rare.

"Man, look at all dem people starin' at us. Dem act like dey never see a man wearin' a black shirt before."

They continued on in search of an inn. After traveling at sea for weeks with crew and supplies, they were ready to find a place to rest.

"I think we can spend the night there," Kita said, pointing at a triangular seven-story building with tall windows on each floor. The glass of the first two floors reflected the bright sun, while the higher windows were dull and unkempt. Not unlike the other structures throughout the city, only the lowest levels were maintained, as the absence of electricity and vehicles made it impossible to clean the higher buildings without considerable risk.

"I think that would be a good spot to rest. We can sleep higher up, and see everything coming from outside the city."

"Ya, man," Kenyatta replied. "We won't have to worry about keeping a night watch since dem lift boxes in da walls don't work anymore."

"Also, we can rig the door to alert us if anything tries to come in," Kita said.

"Right," Kenyatta said. He started toward the building. "We set up for the night in dere."

* * *

IN NAGASAKI, a man stood in front of his window, gazing at the placid lake outside. He was an elderly gentleman in his seventies, but in his eyes burned the fire of a warrior less than half his age. His face was serene, his features soft and kind. His black eyebrows could be likened to a cluster of razor-tipped needles fashioned neatly above his eyes. His face showed not a wrinkle, and his goatee was a mixture of black and gray, and was well groomed. Atop his head lay neatly cut and styled 'salt and pepper' hair. His frame, still retaining some of the hard and detailed muscles of his youth, was concealed within his loose-fitting robes. The old master stood with his hands behind his back and enjoyed the beautiful scene in front of him.

"My children are coming," he said quietly to himself. "It will be good to see them again after so many years." He walked to his small shrine, with a single incense stick burning next to a candle in front of a plant. He swiped a hand in front of the candle and put out the fire, then knelt, closed his eyes, and fell into meditation.

10

K ita stood in front of the window of the office. It was dark outside, and the stars were thousands of pinpricks illuminating the pitch-black sky. Since electricity had been gone for generations, darkness rode the heels of the retreating sun to conquer every city, and in the absence of artificial light the stars shone undisputed over countryside or city alike.

"You know," Kita said, "even though it's been hundreds of years now, it still feels funny to be in the city that we've heard so much about. All of the lights and cars and night stuff."

"I tink it's called *nightlife*," Kenyatta corrected as he set up his bedroll. "A welcome change. I, for one, like it much better dis way, man. Wit'out technology, people find less ways ta act a fool, ya know."

"How would you know, since we've never even seen any of this stuff work?" Kita turned to look at his friend, now sliding into his sleeping sack. "And I wouldn't say there's less ways to act a fool, only less creative ways to act a fool now."

"Hopefully," Kenyatta yawned as he rolled up some clothes to make into a pillow. "Better put ya head to rest, man, we got a long way ahead of us tomorrow."

"Yeah. And I'm guessing that since you're all bundled up in your little roll there, I'm stuck with rigging the door."

Kita barely finished what he was saying before Kenyatta lifted his head at the sound of a loud crash. He looked at Kita, who dropped to the floor and looked over his shoulder out of the window.

"Ya hear dat?" Kenyatta asked quietly.

"No. I always drop to the floor for no reason. What was that?"

Kenyatta pointed to a window over Kita's shoulder. "Ya wanna see what it's about? We can get by with a bit less sleep."

Kita's devious smile was all the indication he needed, and Kenyatta was up in a flash. They gathered their gear and within minutes, the two friends were on their way back down the stairs and sprinting for the woods.

* * *

"KEEP THE TORCHES LIT!" the man told the wide-eyed dusty-faced boy, who nodded his head anxiously. "Make sure we have plenty of light. We're depending on you!"

The boy nodded again, and he led a group of boys and girls off to attend to the many torches lit throughout the village. The man made his way to the edge of the village to join his friend, whose scowl was embellished by the flickering firelight as he scanned the gates. What should have been a quiet night was instead a cacophony of battle cries and arrows whistling in the wind, cries of pain and triumph. And death.

"We have to keep the entrance guarded. They can't be allowed to pass!"

A young warrior named Seung Yoon moved to the front of the battle line. Despite her age, the woman's abilities knew no rival among the villagers of Kyu. The assembled warriors formed an arc-shaped line in front of the village entrance as their final stand.

The light from the torches flickered on each of their grim faces as they waited for the next assault.

"They seem to be stronger this time," Kim remarked once he had reached Seung.

"Much stronger," the woman replied. "But not smarter."

Her companion grunted and Seung smiled at him. She loved her friend's courage. She and Kim fed off of each other, each challenging the other, one-upping each other since they were children. She returned her attention to the edge of the woods where eighteen lumbering figures emerged. Each of the nine warriors steadied their stances and readied their weapons. They were outnumbered and overpowered, but to a man, they would stand or fall beside her.

As the hulking figures approached, the light revealed hairy, bear-like creatures. Each had hands as large as a man's head, equipped with talons that reflected the torchlight. Their bodies were covered in black-brown fur that reminded Seung of the old stories her aunt used to tell her of the tall hairy ape men in the woods. These vicious creatures were something else. Even their eyes were different. Where her aunt had told of big round black orbs that shone kindness and wariness, these monsters had yellow-green eyes that shone with bloodlust. The creature in the front opened its gaping maw, revealing rows of sharp teeth, and let out a blood curdling roar. The warriors held firm, and met the roar with their own battle cry. Both sides charged and met in a flurry of swinging blades and slashing claws.

Seung Yoon wielded a double-edged weapon with a long shaft. At each end was a wide flat blade resembling a more curved broadsword. From the corner of her eye, Seung noticed one of the beasts charging at her back. She turned while spinning her weapon, and at the last moment went down on one knee and brought the weapon to waist level, creating two dead creatures out of the one. She brought the weapon up to block a descending slash over her head, then spun and brought her weapon around and down to shear through the new attacker's right leg. She rose, ignoring the blood that had spattered all over her, and whipped her mighty weapon around, decapitating the beast in one powerful swipe.

Kim had dispatched one monster and was battling another. He wielded a remarkable katana that had been passed to him by his father. The beautiful weapon had been crafted from good steel, passed down through fifteen generations. Kim was a master swordsman, second only to Seung, but with an equal thrill for battle. Kim avoided slash after slash of the hairy creature's claws, scoring tiny nicks and stabs until an opportunity for a killing blow presented itself.

The monster reached out to grab the small, annoying thing that was Kim, only to find that its claw was no longer attached to its arm. It shrieked and stumbled back, flailing its arms and slamming into one of the other village warriors. The man was launched into the back of another of the beasts and crumbled to the ground. He rose on wobbly legs and turned to face the monster, who was also regaining its footing. Seeing one of his comrades dead at the monster's feet, the middle-aged warrior shouted and charged, driving it back inch by inch in a wild fury.

The beast did indeed give ground, but Seung could see that the man's fury couldn't sustain him much longer. She started in that direction, but he was already beginning to tire, and she would not make it in time.

In that instant, a figure dropped out of a nearby tree and slammed his shoulder into the beast's lower back. It stumbled toward the tiring warrior, who sidestepped the creature as it fell on its side, landing near another warrior who seized the opportunity and stabbed the creature in the neck. Seung readied her weapon as she glanced at the warrior who, after giving his sword a quick twist in the monster's neck, retracted the blade and readied himself. They were still outnumbered, but they now faced thirteen beasts thanks to Kim's apparent victory over two more of the things, and this new stranger who had just assisted in the defeat of another.

After defeating the second monster, Kim scanned his surroundings. They had killed five of the things, but thirteen remained and three of his men had fallen. Kim was taken from his thoughts by two more oily black abominations coming at him from both sides. The two monsters slashed at him but only struck air as the quicker warrior ducked the attacks and smashed at their ankles. They hopped back, more angered than injured, and tried to position the human between them. Kim saw one of the monsters moving around behind him, and slowly turned, keeping them both in his line of sight.

Seung ran to aid her friend, but two more hulking black-brown monsters confronted her. She skidded on her heels and settled into a defensive stance. She had decided to attack when she heard an unfamiliar voice yell at her.

"Watch ya back!"

She hadn't fully understood the words, but she knew a warning when she heard one. She turned and hopped aside, narrowly avoiding a slash at her back by a third monster. Her situation now worse than his, Seung was forced to leave Kim to fight on his own.

As she glanced about, she saw that all of the defenders were engaged. Their new ally was also confronted with another beast, which he put down with three rapid cuts to the throat. Seung barely registered the movements, the thing was dead before it hit the ground, its purple lifeblood pooling beneath it.

Seung was starting to believe the battle was turning in their favor until she saw Kim barely matching the ferocity of the two monsters he battled. Kim ducked and leaped, and spun away from slash after slash in an impressive dance of evasion and counterattack.

He turned to the right and avoided a sloppy slash of a claw, but the second monster slashed in from behind, tearing his shirt and leaving four red lines of blood on the warrior's back. He growled away the pain and dropped and rolled away, quickly returning to his feet. He lifted his sword and a hot streak of pain from his back nearly buckled his knees. As the two beasts closed in, one of them fell to its knees and grabbed at the back of its suddenly bleeding neck.

Ignoring its fallen comrade, the second beast charged in at Kim. It slashed high and he ducked low, at the same time stabbing up and under the monster's arm. He cursed the pain in his back at the same time the monster recoiled. Then it arched its back, waving its hairy arms and frantically reaching over its shoulder. Kim didn't take the time to consider what was happening—his sword was a blur in the fire-lit night as he cut the thing down. After it fell, he saw a man that looked about his age facing him.

"Come on," the brown-skinned man yelled. "Two of them made it into your village." Kim understood only a bit of the western tongue, but he comprehended just enough of those words to send him sprinting beside his mysterious ally back into the village.

* * *

SEUNG HAD her hands full fending off the trio of sloppy yet dangerous monsters that that didn't seem to tire. They tried to close in, but she backed away in a graceful turn, spinning her weapon and dealing grievous damage to one monster, and dealing superficial injury to the other two. She leaped forward, swiping low and grazing the shin of one, then turned and spun the weapon vertically, removing the clawed hand of another that reached at her back. As the beast in front of her stumbled from the wound, the third knocked it out of the way and slashed at her.

As she leaned away from the attack, Seung caught another glimpse of their new ally, who was obviously a skilled warrior but was possessed of an unorthodox fighting style. He swayed left, then right, then left, and right again as the monsters tried in vain to catch him. His constant movements confused them, and every time they went to attack, he would nick them with one of his swords.

The old warrior smiled at the monster's frustration, and even laughed when one charged him.

He half-ducked, half-danced under a right-handed slash and came up with a vertical cut to the creature's right side. It grunted and stumbled backward, gripping its side. The brown-skinned warrior laughed again.

"I hope ya got better strategy than your friend over der. Him not very graceful." He half turned as the second beast charged.

Seung had to push the strange foreigner out of her mind and finish her own fight, but the strange foreigner dodged every attack, while clanging his swords together in a particularly catchy rhythm; dodge, *cling-clang-cling*, dodge, *cling-clang-cling*, dodge.

Both monsters slashed and grabbed and kicked, wanting nothing more than to rip the human apart. The second creature circled to the left and charged straight in, attempting to impale him with its razor-like claws. At the same time, the monster in front charged in, clawing at the brown warrior's chest.

He dropped to one knee and at the same time, stabbed his left sword in front and the right sword behind. The second beast impaled itself on his left blade while the other blade stabbed through the clawed hands of the first monster. It stepped back and grabbed at its bleeding hand while its comrade was being cut down, slash by slash.

The monster behind him distracted, Kenyatta went on the offensive. He hopped to his feet and began systematically slashing left, right, up, and down. He cut the beast high, then low, then high again in a blur of combinations that left the watching villagers in awe. The overwhelmed beast was backed into a tree and was held up only by the unrelenting barrage of those two swords. Abruptly the warrior turned his attention to the first beast, leaving the second leaning lifeless against the tree, covered in its own purple blood. It was dead before it fell to the ground.

Seung ducked and turned, skipped aside and countered, all the while whirling her weapon to keep the monsters at bay and dealing damage at the same time. One of the beasts grabbed at her with one huge, clawed hand, only to feel the bite of her weapon in the left side of its chest. It recoiled, reflexively grabbing at its chest with the nub where its left hand should have been. The creature to its left charged while the other circled, attempting to flank her.

The tactic was crude and obvious, and Seung gripped the shaft of her double-edged weapon, both hands close together. She spun the weapon vertically like the blades of the ancient airplanes her aunt used to tell her about. As she spun the weapon, she turned her body in place, bringing the spinning weapon left to right and cutting the monsters from groin to chin. The monsters were caught before they could react, and their purple blood spattered over the third monster who had foolishly waded into the fray.

Kim was more than a little curious about his foreign ally as they sprinted into the village. He was obviously not Korean, as his features were very different. At first sight, he was unsure, as the farmers of the village tended to be dark of pigment from the many hours working in the sun. Up close, however, he could see clearly that this friend was brown from heritage.

They followed the trail of screams and broken statues and fountains. One home had been completely demolished, but no sign of the family was found. That was a small relief, at least. They stopped abruptly as they heard the roar of one of the monsters coming from their right. They turned and sped toward the east end of the village and soon found that two monsters were chasing villagers while being hit by rocks and spears. The assault did little more than irritate the savages, but it bought Kim and his new ally enough time to reach them. The two warriors entered the area, enlarged by the destruction of yet another home, and Kim worked his way to the left while the other warrior moved to the right. He nodded to the newcomer who leaped directly at the beast closest to him with enough force to knock it off balance and wedge his staff between its legs, dropping it sprawling in the dirt. Seeing that the stranger had things under control, Kim rushed the second monster that was stalking toward him.

Kim hopped to the right, then back to the left, confusing the slow-witted creature. Before it could make out his pattern, he feinted left, then went right, dealing a heavy slash on the monster's left shoulder. When it reflexively turned away from the injury, opening its chest to the warrior, Kim stepped in and stabbed it in the chest. The brown warrior was on it in that instant, stabbing it in the side with his long spear-tipped staff, and then sweeping it from its feet. Kim spun and charged back at the fallen beast, leaping upon its hairy chest and driving his sword into its throat.

The other monster finally recovered and came stomping after Kim. It leaped into the air and was descending on him when the brown warrior came in beside him, impaled it on the blade of his staff, dropping it to the ground where it thrashed in a death frenzy.

* * *

BLEEDING HEAVILY from a gash in the middle of its chest, the hairy beast climbed slowly to its feet. Another had already fallen to Seung's blade, and the third was in serious trouble as she backed it away from its comrade.

As she twisted and spun her mighty double-bladed weapon, she continually walked toward the beast, backing it away until it finally lunged at her in frustration. She brought the spinning shaft around and under her arm, stopping it mid-spin as she dropped to one knee. The lunging beast impaled itself in the abdomen, and she stood, pulling the blade free and spinning it low to sever the monster's lower right leg at the knee. As soon as its back was on the ground, Seung brought the blade around and into its throat.

The last monster seemed to hesitate, and indeed it turned as if to flee back into the woods. The young warrior was on it before it had taken three strides. She leapt upon it and drove one of the blades of her weapon into the back of its neck. She hopped off of its back as it crashed to the ground and stalked away, leaving it lying on the ground quite dead.

She saw the newcomer crouching next to one of the hairy things, inspecting it. The other defenders were tending to their wounded and fallen comrades while Kim and another brown warrior, with the help of some of the other villagers, dragged the last two beasts out of the center of the village. They left the carcasses next to the others, where they would later be burned.

The defenders and the newcomers turned their attention to each other. Seung studied them. One was slightly darker than the other, with long black hair twisted together in a fashion similar to braids but thicker and smooth, and tied back from his face. He was actually only a bit taller than her, about five feet eight inches. The other warrior looked a shade or two lighter, but still considerably darker than her or any other native of her land. His hair was cut relatively short, only a bit longer at the front, and his build was more similar to Kim's. The two brown warriors gave each other a knowing look and one of them, the lighter one, spoke slowly to them in the western tongue.

"We figured you could use a hand."

11

The valley of Takashaniel was one of rolling hills, fields of green and yellow grass, and surrounding green mountains that had never seen the footprint of humans. South of the center of this valley stood a tower with magnificence beyond the skill of mortal hands. Inside the tower, gazing at the fields beyond, was its guardian.

Iel scanned the forested mountains that stretched beyond the green and golden rolling hills. The fields of Takashaniel were places of refuge for goodness and purity, where the innocence of nature was cherished and nurtured. Takashaniel, the Tower of Balance, stood as a beacon of love and light created by the hands of humans filled with the loving power of the Gods who would see the balance of the world maintained.

"You thinking of the Drek," a young woman's voice said from behind him. It wasn't a question.

The guardian turned to look upon his student and closest friend. He'd lived on this world for more years than he could count and had always looked upon humans with a kind appreciation for who and what they were. His human student had surprised him from an early age and had grown into the powerful and beautiful woman standing in front of him now.

"What?" Mira frowned playfully at him as she moved several strands of silky black hair from in front of her face. She stared at him with light brown, almond-shaped eyes. Her smooth, golden brown skin was both beautiful and an anomaly to the Ilanyan. Her full, round lips twitched as she regarded him. Iel felt a pang of guilt, for he knew the young woman would have had many suitors to choose from, had he not coaxed her into the life she now led. "You're not going to answer my question, Master Iel?"

Iel smiled. As always, Mira put on a mask of confidence to hide her anxiety. "Fear is the barrier between us and our potential, Mira. While danger is indeed a real thing, it is mostly fear that prevents us from exceeding our limitations. Remember that one must do what one fears, and that fear will disappear."

Mira sighed. "But what good is not being fearful, if you face an enemy you cannot defeat?"

Iel nodded. It was a good question. "In some cases, even one who is very powerful may need to enlist the help of another in order to achieve a new goal or overcome a struggle. If that person was able to put personal pride and fear aside, this could help the person to achieve their goals. The Drek is one such individual. Although extremely powerful, he has seen the limitations of his plan if implemented alone. Enlisting the help of a powerful ally has greatly increased the likelihood for success."

Mira looked at her teacher in disbelief. "Surely you don't think that an alliance between a Drek and a Quentranzi demon would hold together longer than the time it would take for the thing to be released to this plane?" If Iel had eyebrows, the young student was sure he would be raising one of them at her.

"Don't underestimate him, Mira," Iel replied. "Better to err on the side of caution, especially in dealing with one as powerful as Brit."

Mira could not deny her teacher's wisdom. In her teacher's

library were fascinating texts that spoke of many different species, both kind and malicious. The Drek species was one of the latter, and unfortunately, one of them lived on this world.

One of the kinder races in the texts were her teacher's species; the Ilanyans. Highly regarded among his people, Iel was a warrior-cleric from Ilanya, a world that her teacher had described from time to time when she pressed him, yet he never spoke of where the world existed. On his world, the Ilanyans possessed innate abilities such as telekinesis and the manipulation of energy waves. Even among his people, Iel was considered powerful. Coupled with his wisdom and insight, Iel had made an attractive candidate to be an ambassador to this world. It had been their hope to prepare humans for the day when the two races would meet.

Iel had thought his task would be easier than he had anticipated, for the Age of Technology had already met its end, and humans had once again resorted to using the skills and intuitions this beautiful world had supplied them with. He had believed that a being from a different world would be intriguing, but not as much of a shock as it would have been in times earlier. It was five years after his arrival on Earth that the Ilanyan traveler met his future student and closest friend Mira, to whom he had spent the passing years teaching the ways of the Gods; the Daunyans.

Mira was born in a village on the smallest of the islands that were once known as Hawaii. After the End of Technology, the island had undergone many changes, and its inhabitants, having never completely abandoned the old ways, easily reverted back to the way things were done prior to "modern" times. Mira was born to a family of four living in a village along the coastline. While giving birth, her mother felt little pain in comparison with the average childbirth, and once born, the infant did not utter a sound. Initially, the family believed her to have been born mute, but after looking closer, they noticed that her little eyes were scanning her surroundings as if she fully comprehended everything she saw.

As each member of the family of now five looked at the new

arrival, the child's eyes fixed upon their own as if to return the greeting. As she grew older, Mira began to discover just how different she was. As a child, she'd found that she could manipulate things with her mind. As she grew older, her abilities sharpened as she learned control. By young adulthood, she was able to not only manipulate physical objects, but also alter them. Even in the difficult years of adolescence, her heart remained pure and good natured. Mira would never be found harming any form of life, whether large as an ox or small as an insect.

She'd first encountered Iel while tending her orchard. The disconcerting experience of a voice speaking into her mind told her that a friend would soon visit. Panicked but having no one to talk to about it—she'd learned quickly that others questioned her wits when she spoke of her experiences—Mira had tried to shut out the voice, and for a time, it ceased.

Once she'd begun to let her guard down, Mira started receiving visions. A being from a world very different from her own would find his way close to her homeland. He needed her help. The message had been filled with so much love that her fear evaporated, and she knew that the voices did not originate in her own mind, or from something that meant her harm. Amid tearful pleas to change her mind, Mira—who was now at the beginning of womanhood—said goodbye to her family and departed on her quest to meet the friend she had never seen.

Mira cherished the memory of their first meeting. The Ilanyan had encountered a beautiful short-tailed albatross, and was intrigued by the bird. As soon as she'd lain eyes upon him admiring the bird, she knew he was the one who'd spoken into her mind. She had contentedly watched as the bird, equally curious, watched the strange man. She'd never seen an albatross let anyone come so close before. Sensing her presence, the visitor turned and looked into her eyes and smiled. Thus was the friendship born.

Mira regarded her teacher and friend. He was a bit shorter than she, about halfway between five and six feet tall. His skin was a marble gray and black color that gave him a statue-like appearance, and he had kind, green eyes filled with the firmness of experience, but the softness of wisdom.

"Do you think they'll be able to reach us?" Mira asked, a bit of concern in her voice.

"I do not doubt it," Iel answered.

"That's why you are calling to the Children of the Gene?" Mira moved to stand beside him, looking out at the surrounding hills. "Do you think they will be enough? So few to defend Takashaniel against a Drek, a major demon general, and most likely a horde at its command."

"That is not for us to know. The only future that is absolute is that when we leave these vessels we inhabit, we are rejoined with Daunyans, the loving Gods."

Mira frowned. "Why would they allow this to happen if they love us so much?"

Iel placed a hand on her shoulder. "It is my goal to help you one day answer that question for yourself, Mira. Every living thing has been given amazing abilities. Some have realized their potential, some have not. Those who are unconscious to it have inadvertently created realities that are blissful, and some that are hellish."

She looked at him. "So you're saying humans created the Drek and the demons? Is that what you mean?"

"The Drek, no. He is a being that was created by the Gods just as you and I. His species largely turned from the light. Demons were not created by the Gods, but by thought energy."

"Thought energy? How can something living be created by thoughts? That's not possible, is it? I can't understand that. I don't know if I can believe such a concept."

Iel smiled and gave her shoulder a squeeze. "Indeed."

12

The abyss was nowhere for Zreal to be. He had traveled through the dark plane before, but this was different. In times before, Zreal would pass through this realm using various gates that would make his travels much shorter and easier. Although traveling through the hells was dangerous for a human, Zreal was far less fragile. As long as he moved quickly without attracting any undesired attention, he could pass through this horrible place without incident.

This time, however, the Zetsuan was given the unfavorable task of traveling to the abyss not as a shortcut, but to seek out the most powerful of the Quentranzi. A demon known as Grala was the leader of the powerful fiends and resided within the deeper levels of the lowest pits of the dark world. The fifth hell.

Zreal had seen the thing from the comfortable safety of Brit's scrying mirror, and even then, the mere presence of the thing sent waves of fear coursing through him. He had no desire to personally encounter such a magnificent and terrible power. But then, to refuse Brit would mean a similarly terrible fate, if only a bit less creative. Zreal had no choice but to obey his master, but Brit was not totally without mercy.

He'd equipped his underling with a clever device called a teleportation orb. This orb was useless in the higher planes, but when traveling to the dark realms, the wielder could use the magic from this orb to teleport back to the world of light. The only drawback was that the user must be strong, as the orb siphoned its wielder's energy.

Zreal would have to be especially careful not to anger the fiend or be injured in any way. What worried him more than this was the fact that a demon, even of the lower class, didn't need anger as an excuse to torture anyone or anything in its path. Zreal was not a human, but he was not a resident of the dark realm either.

As he descended lower and lower into the abyss, cold, heavy mists drifted about like roaming ghosts. There was no darkness on the earth plane equal to that of the abysmal realm, which is why the denizens of the lower plane referred to all others as light dwellers.

Zreal shifted his vision, his eyes dilating and becoming as black as two onyx orbs. Now more comfortable, he moved on. Savage and horrifying sounds came from every direction, and it was all Zreal could do to block it out while keeping a wary eye on the creatures around him.

Dark forms hovered and darted from place to place, while stronger fiends devoured lesser creatures. The hissing and tittering of unseen furies drifted to his ears and Zreal was quick to find a hiding place. If humans knew how real some of their myths were.

...

He remained concealed behind an outcropping as the pack of cat-like horrors scurried across the distance, followed by a group of hulking creatures that regarded him with too much interest. He forced both of his hearts to slow their rapid beating while cursing himself for his lack of caution. The body of any living being not from the abyss radiated light like a beacon. If he weren't careful, he would find a grotesque death here. He concentrated on his body, cooling his temperature to radiate less warmth, and subsequently less light. Satisfied, he continued.

His descent stretched from minutes to what seemed like hours till he came upon a chasm that descended into thick blackness. With a sigh, he extended all four of his dragonfly-like wings and leapt into the pit, and toward Grala's lair. An ear-splitting screech spun Zreal around just in time to avoid a slash at his back by yet another resident horror. A Bachattta.

The creature looked somewhat like a twisted combination between a mosquito and a hellhound. Its foul, leathery skin was as black as coal, with wings protruding from its narrow back. Zreal was not fooled by the way its arms and legs hung limply as it flew. Its hound-like head was long and narrow, with a deep maw designed for gripping and tearing. The bat-winged creature descended upon its intended prey with hunger in its black eyes. Bachatttas could be dangerous in groups, but a single one was no match for the zetsuan. Zreal smothered his fear and batted the wicked thing aside with a right-handed swipe.

The creature tumbled head over heels through the air, and Zreal flew after it. They crashed into the wall of the chasm in an explosion of rock that tumbled into the darkness below. Zreal tore the wings from the screaming Bachattta and hopped away from the wall, his four wings beating to keep him hovering in place. Assuring himself that there was no more threat, he discarded the ruined wings and continued his descent. Glowing eyes watched him from every direction as he glided ever downward, but the savageness with which he'd dealt with the Bachattta afforded him some measure of respect.

Not taking any chances, however, Zreal increased his speed. He weaved his way around the many Bachatttas and other creatures of the darkness until he finally came to the floor of the chasm. Fourteen stalagmites stood as tall as the remaining skyscrapers of the human cities.

Foreseeing the possibility of Brit ordering his journey into the abyss, Zreal had taken it upon himself to study their demonic allies. There was a tome in the Drek's vast library named The Chronicles of the Order of Nyrr. Within the pages of the book, there was a detailed account of a conflict involving the lord of the Quentranzi. Grala had been narrowly defeated in a battle against another major demon and was forced to find another place to dwell. In a fit of rage, Grala had leaped into a large pit that descended to an unknown depth. The Quentranzi hit the ground with such force that it sent shockwaves throughout the dark plane and actually pushed the platform down to an even greater depth. The end result was this throne room and the fourteen huge stalagmites that had punched through the ground. Zreal didn't know which was worse, the thought of a raging Grala, or that there could be another fiend more powerful than the Quentranzi lord. Zreal had an overhead view of the throne room, but as he neared, the stalagmites began to grow and curve inward, forming a dome that blocked his entrance. Zreal altered his course and landed at the base of the stalagmite dome and a safe distance from its keeper. The Zetsuan stalked up to the impressively large creature that barred his entrance. Zreal first took it to be some sort of twisted hydra, but the thing had four legs and the faces of each of its ten heads had sharp teeth and eyes and looked grotesquely human. Zreal stopped before the twisted horror and declared his business.

"I wish to meet with the mighty Grala."

One of the ugly heads lowered in front of him and he could smell its hot foul breath as it breathed in his scent. "Are you afraid, mortal creature?" Its gurgling voice sent shudders through his body. "The deeper the fear, the sweeter the meat."

Zreal whipped out a hand and sank his claws into its scaled neck. "You might make a meal of me, but you will have just enough time to enjoy my taste before you drown in your own blood." Zreal's raspy voice was unwavering. "You will grant me entrance now, or we will discover how quickly I can rip out every one of your throats." He yanked his claws loose in a spray of blood.

The hydra recoiled and hissed at him, the injured head moving away to hide behind the others. Zreal knew his threat had been taken to heart, and so he waited. He didn't have to wait long, for the hydra backed away and let out a gurgling low-pitched growl as it shifted its bulk aside.

Taking a deep breath, Zreal stepped past the hydra, not bothering to look at the monster as he turned his back on it. Confidence.

Once inside the throne room, he looked around to see wicked and twisted depictions of suffering and agony beyond anything his imagination could conjure. The glowing black floor was decorated with carvings of symbols and etchings that emitted evil so strong it was almost overwhelming. Even the stalagmites had been carved with such horrific detail, it could be achieved only by overworked slaves.

As Zreal neared the center, he saw what looked like the images of souls that had been carved into the slate of floor that stretched the length of the room to the steps of a disturbingly large throne. As Zreal looked closer, he realized to his horror that they were not designs at all, but actual souls that had been captured and imprisoned within the floor to forever squirm in their rocky, living tomb. Zreal shuddered. This was no more than decoration for the twisted pleasure of the lord of the Quentranzi.

"Do you like my arrangement?" thundered a voice that echoed from everywhere and nowhere at the same time. Shockwaves rippled through Zreal's body. He turned this way and that, but there was no sign of the speaker. He turned back to the empty throne again to the sound of a deep, mocking chuckle, and his mouth dropped open. His black eyes opened wide and he staggered back at the sight of the fearsome twenty-five-foot-tall monstrosity that sat before him on a living demon throne.

13

A few days following their fight with the Kalistyi shadow demons, Kenjiro and Akemi made their way across the heavily wooded hills and passed through the villages that dotted the valleys at the base of the mountains. The landscape of Japan had changed much since the passing of the Age of Technology. Nature had returned and put humanity to the test of survival. Some score of years after the End of Technology, underwater volcanoes had erupted beneath the surface of the ocean; gushing rivers of molten magma flowed into the water alongside the island. In time, the magma cooled and hardened, and Japan had increased in size. During the passage of two centuries, quakes had shaped the land even further. With intense rains and the absence of human interference, beautiful forests emerged and blossomed.

The siblings had not been born to experience the beginnings of the rapid changes in the world, but there were numerous books and verbal accounts passed on through the generations that chronicled these magnificent and frightening times.

"Is that Sand Dragon's Valley?" Akemi asked her brother once they'd stopped for a break at the top of a tree near the middle of Mt. Funikoshi.

"About an hour or two and we should be there," Kenjiro answered.

"So are we to set camp in that valley or move through it?"

Kenjiro noted his younger sister's tone. Akemi did not like the idea of passing through a valley named after a dragon.

The enormous mythical beasts had only been heard of through legends and stories in the past, and in traditions that had survived countless years throughout many parts of the world. There had always been two known types of dragons in the stories told around the world. The first was the Asian dragon that was said to have been as short as a hundred feet or as long as a mile. This dragon, the dragon of the east, was known to be the symbol of strength, honor, and wisdom.

The other was the fabled evil dragon of the west, a cunning beast that resembled a huge reptilian animal with wings. This dragon was said to live in vast underground caves or underneath mountains and sleep atop massive hordes of gold and other treasures that it stole from surrounding villages and cities. This great wyrm—as it was called—was said to breathe fire and wield various types of powerful magic, depending on the individual creature's species.

Although no one claimed to have ever seen a dragon, Akemi didn't relish the thought of passing through a potential dragon lair. The old stories told that dragons were majestic and magical by nature and could not be defeated by any mundane weapon. They were also intelligent, cunning, and ruthless. Some said that the most difficult and unsolvable riddles were created by the dragons.

"Don't tell me you want to travel around this big valley, Akemi? Surely a bit of adventure wouldn't deter you."

The sound of her brother's voice pulled Akemi from her thoughts. Kenjiro gave his sister a blank look with a hint of humor in his eyes as he spoke.

Akemi glared at him. "I don't let fear control my decisions and you know that."

"So you do not deny the fear, little sister," Kenjiro teased.

Akemi breathed a barely audible sigh. "Only an insecure coward would deny having any fear. Fear, when controlled, helps to keep our senses at their peak when we are in danger. It can keep us on our toes instead of marching bullheadedly into an impossible situation. Most men do this."

Now it was Akemi's chance to turn a sly look on her brother. "And there has *never* been a time when you marched bullheaded into a fight you could not win, has there, Samurai?" A flicker of irritation came and went across Kenjiro's face and she knew the remark had stung.

"We will pass through the valley at first light tomorrow while the air is still cool and the winds blow to the west, away from the cave. If indeed there is a dragon in there, and I doubt this, it will not catch our scent in the air."

Akemi frowned and turned to face the sprawling valley that waited in the distance. The hills were few, and the landscape was virtually barren, save the trees that dotted the landscape. If there was a dragon in that valley and it came to find them, there would be no place to take refuge.

IT HAD BEEN three days since the attack on Kyu village, and the villagers, including Kenyatta and Kita, were just finishing the repairs and cleanup. A fair number of people were injured, and some were killed, but the casualties were low. Still, the loss of every person was felt.

Kenyatta noticed the leader of the defenders sitting quietly at the edge of the town, her mighty weapon lying across her lap. She had not said much over the past few days, and he suspected it was because of the loss of life. She had lost three warriors in that fight and mourned every one of them in addition to the other villagers.

"You ok?" he asked.

The woman continued to stare into the distance, and he could see by her frown that she was concentrating to understand his accent.

"I don't know," she answered. Her voice was unlike any he had ever heard. It was like melody was laced in her every word. She glanced at him and slid her hand along the long black hair that clung to both sides of her head. "So many people have never died before. We have fought many times and against many enemy, and almost every time, there were more of them than us. This time was unlucky."

Kenyatta sat down next to her. "Ya got to remember da circumstances, ya? Dem not jyas a buncha people running in to rob and kill. Dem someting else, and I cyan't say I know what. Never seen anyting like 'em."

Seung looked up at the Jamaican, her dark-brown eyes studying him. "You talk strange. Does every person in your land talk the same?"

Her tone lightened a bit, and Kenyatta seized the opportunity. "Me wonderin' when you ask me dat. I'm surprised you understand me as well as you do."

She smiled. It was a sad smile, but he enjoyed it nonetheless. "Your friend a little bit easier to understand, but when I try, I understand you ... mostly." Kenyatta gave her a big, exaggerated smile, showing bright white teeth. To his delight, she laughed. He laughed with her, and for a time they sat, studying each other.

"Some people talk like me, some of them are worse. Because us travel so much, I'm a bit easier to understand, but if you go to my homeland, you never understand unless you stay toward the coast where the visitors come."

Seung looked into his eyes and found kindness. It was the same with the other man, who seemed more like his brother than his friend. From Kim's account of the one named Kita, the other warrior was just as skilled as the man sitting next to her with his smooth dark skin and thin, twisted hair that he called 'locks.' "Outsiders call them 'dreadlocks,'" he'd told her.

"You both are far from your homes," she commented. "You, farther than your friend."

Kenyatta shrugged. "We on our way to Japan and had to cross tru here. We stop for da night in one of dem old buildings in da city, but when we hear fighting, we decided it be more fun to come find out what was going on."

Seung repressed a giggle as she watched the Jamaican struggling to speak slowly and clearly enough for her to comprehend. "You both fight very well. I never see anyone fight like you two."

"Aside from yourself, ya mean."

Seung did not answer but continued. "I have train for nearly fifteen years now and I never see anyone fight the way you do. Those things were not much problem for you."

"Ya handle dem tings well too, lady," Kenyatta replied. Her smile was warm and genuine, and he felt a friendship forming.

Back in the village square, Kim and Kita had finished helping the villagers clean up the last of the debris from the attack and the rebuilding. Through the tireless efforts of all, the only indications of the conflict were the homes in repair and the detritus littering the ground.

"You fight good, friend," Kim said slowly, taking care with every word. "Only Seung fight as good as you and your friend. I think maybe you were meant by destiny to fight with us. You fight very …" He paused, looking for the correct word. "Differently," he said, jerking his head as he sounded out the word. Kita listened with patience, smiling as the man spoke as though his skills were less than noteworthy. Kita knew better. He had seen Kim fight, and knew this man to be a formidable warrior.

"I don't know why we are able to fight the way we do. My father told Kenyatta and me that one day we would find out why we move faster, jump higher, and are stronger than others. I have a feeling that we are close to our answer."

Kim looked at Kita assuredly. "I think so, too, but do not waste your time to try find them. I think there not many in the world, and if there are more, your paths will be crossing. There is no … how to say?" He looked askance at Kita for the correct word.

"Coincidence?" Kita offered, and Kim nodded and snapped his fingers.

"Co … incidence," he repeated. "You and friend and Seung are here in this world for reason."

In short order, children were playing in the streets again and life was returning to a bit of normalcy. Kita and Kim found Kenyatta and Seung talking just outside of town. When the newcomers had arrived, Kenyatta jumped to his feet and walked over to meet his old and new friends.

"How tings goin' in the village?"

Kim looked at him with a frown, incomprehension covering his features. When he looked to Kita, who seemed on the verge of laughter, he shook his head.

"Actually things are getting back to normal pretty quick," Kita responded, glancing at Seung to see her response. "It's only been a few days and things are getting back to normal. You and your people certainly are. It's no surprise you all have survived this long out here."

"We have good leaders," Kim responded.

"And they have good warriors," Kita added.

Kenyatta rolled his eyes. "I'm gonna drown in all this mush if you guys don't quit it already."

Seung and Kim exchanged confused looks. "Mush?" they repeated in unison?

* * *

A FEW DAYS after the last of the repairs and cleanup was finished, the two travelers gathered their belongings to take their leave.

"Thank you for the supplies and food," Kita said. "I have a feeling we'll need it all."

"What is ours is yours, good friend," Kim replied. "I do not think our village would have been in as good condition as now if you do not come when you did."

"And those watchtowers we all built will help you to keep a better view outside your village."

Kim nodded in agreement, looking over his shoulder at the wooden towers they had begun erecting over the course of the week.

"What's goin' on?" Kenyatta yelled from further down the hill. "Whatcha talkin' bout over der?"

"Not very much, friend. I just thanking Kita for your help in repairing our village."

"Yeah, man." Kenyatta said. "And you repay us with food and supplies, makin' our road a little easier, ya know."

Kim looked to the western end of the village. It was early morning and the sun had just surfaced from the east to wash the waking village in its golden warmth. "West is the way you go." Kim pointed over his shoulder in the direction of the rising sun. "Japan not much far from here, and with the horses you will reach coastline quickly." Kim seemed to struggle with the last word.

"Um," Kita hesitated. "Japan is east," he pointed in the direction Kim had indicated. "That is east, not west."

"Yes, yes, east," Kim quickly agreed with a helpless smile. "I mix words."

"No problem."

"Are you sure you must leave now?" Kim asked. "You are welcome to stay with us as long as you like."

"They must leave as soon as possible," came Seung's voice from behind. The three turned to see the woman standing with her arms crossed in front of her chest.

"I feel something strange in the air and I understand why they hurry. There is some very big power somewhere, and it does not feel close. I think it is a trouble that they travel to ..." She paused, looking for the correct word. "Confront?" she asked, and Kenyatta nodded with a smile. She smiled back. "Keyatta tell me last night, and so now they hurry." Kenyatta repressed a chuckled when she stumbled over his name.

She turned those brown eyes on him again. "I can come with you to help with your fight. I have a feel ... feeling?"—again he nodded encouragingly—"Feeling you will need as much help as you can get."

Kita looked at his friend, who was still smiling at the generous offer, and looking as though he would like nothing more than to have the beautiful woman along.

"You have a village to help protect," he replied instead. "I don't doubt your second in command here," he nodded in Kim's direction, "but I'm thinking the village be needin' the both of you."

"He's right," Kita added. "Your village can't afford to be without either of you right now." He nodded in the direction of the woods beyond Kyu. "Not with those things lurking in the forest."

Seung pouted in resolute agreement and offered no dispute.

Kita saw that expression and glanced at his best friend, who seemed unable to stop smiling. "Hey, Kim. Can you help me with the last of the provisions before we go?"

"Provisions?" Kim repeated. Then he glanced at the other two and his eyebrows rose knowingly. "Oh, yes, I help."

After Kim and Kita had gone, Seung turned to Kenyatta. "Come with me; there is something I want to show you before you go."

"Lead da way," he replied. As they walked through the back of the village, Kenyatta noticed the landscape seemed to have a different look about it. Although the rest of the village was well kept, it could not begin to compare with the sights that surrounded him now. The trees were lush, bright, and almost pastel green with branches that reached far into the sky and to the sides as if to join in dance. Their multicolored leaves shone in colors he'd never seen.

The bushes and shrubs looked as if a master landscaper had trimmed them. Some even displayed bright luscious-looking berries, green, blue, orange and purple. Even the grass seemed to stand tall and show off its bright green color proudly. Spotted butterflies bounced through the air, maneuvering between little glowing spheres of light that danced around them. Beauty was everywhere, and it was almost overwhelming to the islander.

"What is dis place?" Kenyatta breathed. "I never see anyting like it."

Seung smiled at his amazement. She too had been in awe the first time she'd come here. Even now, after coming here for years, she still found it breathtaking.

They stopped at a waterfall, enjoying the sight of the water crashing down upon the lake. Seung hopped several large rocks until she reached the base of the waterfall. Kenyatta found a rock a few feet away and to the right.

Seung giggled and leaped to a farther rock. Kenyatta was startled by the jump, clearly about ten feet away. He crouched and leaped high into the air.

Seung looked in surprise as he glided with a look of superiority on his face. She also noted that he'd misjudged the distance, and watched as he glided right into the water between the step she stood on and the one in front of her. She quietly laughed behind a hand as she crouched to the edge of the rock to get a glimpse of her submerged friend. When she looked past her rippling reflection, she saw multicolored fish darting this way and that, disrupted by the intrusion.

"This pond's a bit deeper than I was thinking it was."

Startled, Seung spun on the voice behind her.

"Whoa, easy girl," Kenyatta said, holding up his hands up in surrender. "I'm not trying to scare ya dat bad."

"You swim fast and quiet, friend," she observed as she watched him slide his drenched locks from in front of his face. Seung produced a cloth from a little sack on her waist. She extended it to him and when Kenyatta reached for it, she spun her hand around his and pulled him closer. She wiped the water from his chin with a second cloth that she had produced seemingly from nowhere. Kenyatta was drawn in to those light brown eyes. She tilted her head to one side and poked her bottom lip out. "I'll need a bigger cloth for your hair." He shook his head, spraying her with water.

Seung yelped and fell backward, bouncing on her backside. When Kenyatta began to pull himself out, she raked her hand through water, blasting him in the face.

"Ah! You little...."

She laughed aloud as he slipped back into the water, then screamed and hopped away when he grabbed the rock and launched himself out. He chased her around the pond, hopping from rock to rock until they finally came back to dry land.

"No no," she pleaded, hands up in surrender. "Okay, I stop now!" Kenyatta stared at her a moment, then flicked water off his fingers into her face. She wrinkled her nose and shoved him away, wiping her eyes.

"I guess we'll call it even," he said. "Even though I should be dunking you in der." He nodded at the water to the side.

"Even?" She frowned. "What do you mean, even?"

"More slang," Kenyatta said. "Da western tongue have a lot of slang. I mean to say, ya spray me with water and I get you, too."

Seung thought a moment, then nodded, finally catching his meaning. "I understand you. Look." She pointed at the cloudy sky where several rays of sunlight penetrated the puffy white ceiling. "So beautiful. I love!" Kenyatta stole a glance at the woman as she stared up at the sky. Only several days ago they fought and killed together, now she stared at the sky with childish wonder. He'd never met a person who radiated such love for nature. It was captivating.

"This place called *Eiliki*. It mean *serenity* in a language from the Old Age. I have train since I was old enough to walk, and fighting since I was ten years old. I was youngest in my group, but able to keep up and sometimes, do better than some of my older classmate.

"My parents bring me here to help calm my mind after so much fighting. I don't know how I survive if not for them. They watched over me and make sure that I was not sickened by fighting at my age."

"Ya mean death and suffering," Kenyatta said.

Seung nodded. "I helped to keep the village safe; they kept *this* safe." The young woman tapped a finger on the side of her head.

For a while they stood in silence, basking in the tranquility of Seung's favorite place. She moved closer to Kenyatta, and her hand brushed against his. Smiling, he took her hand, and she inspected it while he enjoyed her soft touch.

"You and your friend have seen many battle together, but your hands are soft and smooth for a man."

He smiled and then reversed the hold, now her hand in his. "Me family make a special kind of oil that we put on our skin. It's made from a nut in Jamaica and it help keep the skin tough but smooth, and helps heal scars."

He gave her palm a squeeze. "How ya keep *your* hands so soft, little lady? I'm sure ya get a few scars here and der in a fight or two."

Seung smiled and pushed up against him playfully. "A similar thing, I am sure. We have special oil for same purpose." She smirked. "I don't have to use them much as you."

"Why is dat?"

"Because my hands fast enough not to get hit."

The islander raised an eyebrow. "Good answer."

* * *

AMONG OTHER THINGS, Kenyatta most admired this woman's balance. They had led similar lives, yet she retained an innocence that was long dead in the islander. The harshness of life had hardened the young warrior, and though his lighthearted and joking nature kept him in generally good spirits, Seung seemed to be able to let the past slide off her back. He wondered if it was a conscious decision she made every day or if it was a part of her nature.

Seung grinned at him. "You look like you going to say that you wish you do not have to leave?"

Kenyatta lips compressed. Indeed, that was almost exactly what he was going to say.

Seung laughed, recognizing the surprised, calculating look, and gave him a gentle peck on the cheek. She then rose to her tiptoes and whispered into his ear. "*Nintali*. It means *destiny* in the Old Tongue." That melodious voice filled his ears. When she spoke the western tongue, or her native language to her people, her voice carried a musical sound that was both beautiful and otherworldly. When she spoke these words that she called the Old Tongue, it sounded as though she sang the words. "Concentrate on the fight ahead, Keyatta. Maybe we meet again."

A few hours later the village held a gathering for the two friends, and soon after, they were on the road heading for the coast. Seung and Kim watched until the two warriors were out of sight, leaving a trail of dust in their wake.

"We will see them again," Kim said, noting the empty solemn expression on his childhood friend's face. Now that the foreigners were gone, they could speak more easily in their native tongue. "I believe fate brought them here, and I don't believe our meeting was just in passing. They will return, or we may find them one day."

Seung said nothing. She moved close to Kim and put her arm around his waist, hugging him sideways while she stared into the scenery before them. Kim held her with one arm as an older brother would hold his younger sister, and looked down at her with a sigh. He could not think of much to say to comfort her, so they stood for a time, watching the scenery before them and listening to the silence. Life was a strange thing. Predictably unpredictable.

14

K enjiro and Akemi made their way into the valley and
passed through the wooded hills that marked their final
descent to the bottom. They moved swiftly and silently through the
trees, stopping occasionally to listen for sounds of any threat, or
pursuit. Nothing seemed amiss from the surface of things, but
when Kenjiro looked at his sister's expression, he saw that she
wanted to put this valley behind her as quickly as he did.

Kenjiro scanned their surroundings. The bowl-shaped valley
held no tactical advantage, no retreat, and no way for the warriors
to elude a large airborne enemy, such as the animal from which the
valley was given its namesake. Kenjiro silently berated himself for
even considering the existence of such a creature, but the things
they'd seen in the world made it difficult to deny the possibility.

Akemi sensed her brother's concerns and kept a wary eye on
their surroundings. Sunja trees, a new species that lived only in hot
and desolate environments, grew in leaning patches of two and
three across the cracked and sandy ground, their leafless branches
reaching toward the scorching sun like the fingers of a demon
clawing its way out of the abyss. Groups of shrubs dotted the landscape as well, but otherwise, not much else lived there. Strangely

enough, however, it was an exotic-looking glen, desert-like, yet quite peaceful in a way she couldn't place.

They saw an area nearby at the southern edge of the valley that looked like it could have been a dried up lake. They nodded to one another, each guessing the other's thoughts. They would start from inside that lake, below ground level and out of view. Kenjiro started to move, but Akemi held her hand up. She pointed to a deep trench on the far left that stretched almost the length of the valley and would leave them with less than a quarter mile to travel in the open. Kenjiro looked at the path and nodded. They looked at each other, took a deep breath, and moved on.

* * *

BACK ON THE ROAD AGAIN, Kita and Kenyatta enjoyed the rushing of the wind and the multicolored blur of vegetation that raced past on either side. After hours of riding, the air was beginning to cool, and they slowed their mounts to a trot so that all could enjoy the soothing breeze. "We're close to the beach," Kenyatta said.

"Yeah," Kita agreed. "Just beyond that thick patch of forest."

Kenyatta eyed the woods before them. "We should let the horses go. We can travel on foot from here."

Kita noted the change in his friend's tone as they dismounted and turned the horses in the direction they had come from. With a pat on the neck and a slap on the rump, they sent the animals on their way.

Once the horses were out of sight, the two friends turned and faced the wall of forest that stood between them and the coast.

Kenyatta scratched his head. "We could go around and take an extra half day of travel. I don't tink I would feel like a coward. How about you?"

Kita frowned at him and they shared a nervous laugh. He shook his head at Kenyatta's attempt to relax the tension. "Let's just go straight through and get this over with," he said. "It's just a forest.

We avoid predators and we'll be fine." It was only talk, though. Both could feel that it wouldn't be so simple.

* * *

THE SIBLINGS TRAVELED across half of the valley without incident, Kenjiro making little sound, his ninja sister making none at all. They refrained from speaking, instead using various hand gestures to relay their intent. Although neither had actually seen a dragon, they had grown up hearing the stories and legends about them. The dragons of the east were fearful but mostly unthreatening. It was the fabled dragons of the west that were to be feared. It was said that these greedy beasts could sense the absence of the smallest trinket from their enormous hoards of riches. Although he and his sister were far to the east of where these beasts lived—if they existed—it meant nothing to the winged creatures who were said to be capable of flying great distances.

More than halfway across, Kenjiro was beginning to feel foolish for believing such a mythical beast could actually exist, when the temperature grew warmer and the air became still and dead. A grim feeling passed between the two warriors and they increased their speed.

As they neared the end of the trench, a hill was visible, along with the rimming outer mountains beyond. They would be safe once they reached the wooded mountains.

A few hundred feet from the trench's end, the ground began to shake, and at that moment Akemi looked ahead to see a huge chunk of the ground simply fall away, creating a chasm at least a hundred feet across. Instinctively, she began to slow; but at that same instant, her older brother grabbed her wrist and pulled her forward. Once confident that she would keep pace, Kenjiro released her wrist and pointed behind them. Akemi glanced over her shoulder and her eyes widened with horror before she recovered and nodded at her brother.

The dust from the crumbled earth made it impossible to see, yet their instincts told them that to leap outside the trench would be suicide. Kenjiro slipped a silk handkerchief from inside his cloak and tied it across his eyes while his younger sister did the same. The dirt and grit would have blinded them and disrupted their focus, so they would instead rely on their other senses and instincts.

As Akemi flanked her brother, she could feel the presence trailing them, pressing in. Dust and pebbles and grit bombarded them as they ran straight through the sandstorm. They didn't see the edge of the drop, but they felt it and leapt forward, disappearing into the dust cloud.

They called upon the endless hours, days, weeks, months, and years of training, as they glided into the stinging sandstorm. Instead of leaping up, they leaped to opposite walls of the chasm. Tiny granules of rock and sand cut at them as they leapt from the left wall to the right, crisscrossing the distance using momentum, timing and strength.

They hit solid ground and rolled to their feet in one fluid motion, racing out of the trench and straight for the grassy hills. They removed their handkerchiefs and tucked them back into their cloaks, all the while never breaking stride. Now that they were on relatively safe solid ground again, Akemi took the opportunity to glance at their backs. A worried frown creased her forehead as she saw the dust following them in the form of a four-legged reptilian beast as large as a horse, closing in. Its wings looked to span thirty feet from tip to tip. Kenjiro looked in surprise as his younger sister pulled ahead. The samurai didn't need to look behind him to know that whatever was behind them was getting closer.

They crossed the distance from the trench to the hills and passed into the woods, darting in and out of the dense foliage, leaping over bushes and jumping through the trees.

They ignored their labored breath and burning legs and climbed the hills until they'd put a comfortable distance between themselves and that valley. When they slowed to catch their breath, Akemi dropped to her hands and knees, panting. Her legs felt like they were made of both pudding and lead, and air could not fill her lungs quickly enough.

They'd come to rest in a clearing of trees, and the ninja turned and plopped on the green and yellow grass, leaning back on her elbows while her brother simply fell face first in the grass. "It warms me inside to know that my sister wouldn't have left me behind," his muffled voice said.

Akemi never looked at her brother, but continued to gaze back at the ominous valley. "There was no time to talk and I knew you would follow." She grinned. "Don't pout. We made it, did we not?"

"Barely."

"What do you mean?" Akemi asked.

Kenjiro turned his head to look his sister in the eye. "Something entered my thoughts just as we made our way out. It was like something was speaking to me through my subconscious, telling me that we were strong and would be granted passage only if we could make it to the hills. At that same instant, I felt a power on my back like nothing I'd ever experienced." He stood and took one last glance at the bowl-shaped valley. "I don't want to ever look upon this place again and I won't be comfortable until we are long gone from this place."

* * *

THE ISLANDERS HAD BEEN MOVING through the safety of the trees for an hour when Kenyatta felt it was time to get their bearings. He got Kita's attention, then pointed to a giant of a tree just ahead.

Kita nodded and leapt from limb to limb until he reached the highest branch, then climbed to the top. He nearly fell from his perch when he saw that they had at least three more miles till they reached the coast.

He descended and started to explain when Kenyatta held up a

finger to his lips. He pointed to the ground beneath them, and Kita leaned forward to peek over the side of the thick branch. He spotted a conspicuous looking shape next to a tree stump. Kenyatta whispered very quietly into his ear. "Some kinda shadow creatures creeping around down there. Looks like they been tracking someting."

Kita knew that devious look. A smile brightened Kenyatta's eager visage until he saw that Kita did not share his enthusiasm. "Whatcha worrying about, man?" he whispered.

"We have miles still, before we reach the coast," Kita whispered back. "And the forest only gets thicker and darker."

Now was Kenyatta's turn to look worried. He had thought they were close to the end of their trek through the woods, but to hear Kita tell it, they still had a long way to go. Now they were being tracked. "Should we take them out right now or try and elude them and stick to the trees?"

Kenyatta glanced down again. "Someting tell me we should get outta here fast as we can. I don't like dis place too much."

Kita agreed wholeheartedly, and they continued on, careful not to make a sound while keeping an eye on the forest floor. They stopped on the limbs of a giant oak to scan the area. The forest was still and quiet, the atmosphere tense. No chirping birds, not a single grasshopper or cricket seemed willing to chance a serenade to one another. Not even a breeze.

Kita and Kenyatta waited. Nothing happened, but they knew something was wrong. Kita was just about to indicate that they move on when a shadow on the side of the tree detached from the trunk and descended upon them.

They leapt backward to a nearby branch, their weapons at the ready before they landed. They glanced at each other and then at the strange shadow creature as its arms began to change shape. A frown creased Kita's brow as he looked around Kenyatta at the shadowy figure that now possessed two long, wavy blades where its arms once were.

Kenyatta glanced down and noticed five more shadows slithering about the bushes. He signaled for his friend to look beneath them. Kita glanced down, then back to Kenyatta, seeing an excited gleam in his eyes. Kita grinned.

The humanoid shadow figure leaped at them with its arm-blades whirling in a blur. The three glided past each other, clashing blades. As planned, the two warriors now stood on the larger branch and in a more advantageous position. As soon as the shadow landed, it turned and leaped at them again. The two warriors cut it apart before it landed, and Kita delivered the killing strike, decapitating it. As the head dropped from its shoulders, a score of thin appendages seeped out of its neck and wrapped around the head. Kita and Kenyatta stared as it was lifted and replaced back on the shadow's shoulders.

Kita glanced at his equally dumbfounded friend and then slashed the thing repeatedly while Kenyatta scanned the area once more. The shadow dissipated under Kita's onslaught, and they thought the thing was surely dead, when their instincts screamed at them and they spun and deflected two descending strikes aimed at their heads.

The shadow creature had reformed behind them and came in with a flurry of stabs and arcing strikes, all deflected by the two fighters. They drove the shadow back and worked both its arm-blades out wide, then simultaneously severed both arms and kicked the shadow from the tree to the ground below.

Not taking the time to look at the result, they leaped through the trees, swinging and vaulting from limb to limb.

"Got any ideas why dat ting won't die?" Kenyatta asked. He grabbed hold of a limb the size of his arm with one hand and swung his body under, releasing and landing on a branch a few feet below.

"Remember what your sister said," Kita answered. "Our weapons must be charged with some kind of power that can fight demons."

"So they're demons, then? Dat would explain it, but I wish me sister was here now. It would make tings a lot easier."

Four shadow demons appeared in the trees in front of them, and both warriors stopped and darted in opposite directions, Kita to the right and Kenyatta to the left. The group of fiends separated and pursued.

Kita glanced over his shoulder and noted two of the things trailing behind him. He leaped straight up, and his pursuers followed.

Once they reached the top of the tree, their intended prey was nowhere to be found. There was a glimmer of light, and the two shadow fiends found themselves staring helplessly at the ground rushing to meet them until the appendages from their necks began replacing their heads back on their shoulders.

15

Kenyatta moved among the trees with a different strategy in mind. As the two shadows followed, he deliberately led them in a straight line. Trusting his instincts, he darted to the right. He turned to see his pursuers dissipating into a black mist in front of a third creature who had formed out of a shadow in the tree and accidentally struck them instead of Kenyatta. After seeing that first one form out of a tree, he figured the creatures might plan such a trap.

The mood of the forest seemed to darken, as if the whole environment was coming alive around them. Deciding on speed in place of security, they dropped from the branches and sprinted on. To his right, Kita noted many dark figures flanking them. Kenyatta saw a similar sight to his left. They looked at each other and realized at that moment that they could not afford to stop. No matter how far and how fast they had to run, they knew they must keep their pace or die in this wicked place.

A shadow dropped in front of them and Kita jumped forward and cut it to pieces with his sharp-ended staff before it had fully stood upright. Kenyatta looked back with a surprised smile. They would be long gone before that one would be able to put itself back together. The woods continued to darken despite the fact that it was barely midday. Something or someone didn't want them to leave these woods.

Kenyatta darted to his left just enough to avoid a swipe aimed at his shoulder. In one fluid motion he jumped forward, turned and delivered a horizontal slash followed by a diagonal upward cut with his opposite sword, leaving the shadow behind him in three pieces. He was gone as soon as his feet touched the ground, never falling out of step with his friend.

"We need to get out of here," Kita panted. "These things are everywhere."

"Dis whole place is evil, man," Kenyatta replied. "It feels like we been running forever." The words had barely left Kenyatta's mouth when they saw two shadows descending from overhead. They couldn't dodge far to the left or right without falling to the countless shadows that paced them, nor could they stop, or the fiends at their backs would overtake them. With less than a second to react, they leaped forward into a roll, passing under the sweeping sword-arms. They came out of the roll and sprang even farther ahead and then leapt into the trees once more.

Below, the ground was no longer visible and all they could see was a virtual sea of shadow creatures. Just one mistake would bring their adventure to a deadly halt. Kita pointed in front of them at yet another problem. The demons had now risen to the branches in front of them, and in rather discouraging numbers. On top of that, the patches of fading sunlight penetrating the dark forest canopy indicated that they were nearing the end of the woods, and daylight.

Kita and Kenyatta shared a look, the latter smiling deviously. "Almost just like when we were kids, ya?"

"What do you mean *when* we were kids?" Kita panted while managing a grin. "We still are kids, my friend." And with one last burst of energy, the two fighters dove into the mob of shadows.

They cut down every fiend that came within striking distance, darting left and right, severing a shadow head, deflecting a blow and severing a sword-arm. It was a blur of swords ringing against swords, and shadows being split apart and regenerating. The two warriors blazed a vicious trail through the army of shadow demons blocking their path out of the forest.

Finally, the end of the trees was near, and they redoubled their efforts. Kita looked ahead and his spirits dropped as he saw the end of the forest seemingly moving farther away as they drew nearer. "I don't think we'll reach the end of this damn place on foot this way!" He pointed overhead and Kenyatta nodded.

To their own surprise, they made an unbelievable leap out of the treetops and glided branch to branch toward the end of the forest. While in flight, Kita glanced over his shoulder to see his best friend slashing at a score of long, shadowy appendages wrapping themselves around his legs. In mid-flight there was nothing Kita could do except watch in helplessness, as his friend was pulled back into the forest.

"KENYATTA!" Kita screamed as he glided away. As soon as his feet touched the warm soft sand where the forest and the beach met, the enraged warrior dashed back into the trees, kicking up sand as he ran.

Kita used the sounds of clashing steel to guide him through the trees as he cut down every shadow demon in his path. Sparks and flashes lit the unnaturally dark forest enough for him to see his friend in the midst of at least ten shadow monsters. Kenyatta's swords were a blur, but he succeeded only in cutting them apart to reform again.

Kita crashed into the group from behind slashing and stabbing, even hurling some over his head to land into others. The sight of his friend brought a new surge of energy in Kenyatta and his swords danced even faster. Although the demons could regenerate not long after being struck down, the fierce warriors were still able to put them down long enough to gradually work their way toward the edge of the forest. One particularly brave monster leapt toward

Kita and was instantly cut in half. Kenyatta parried a blow aimed
at his side so hard that it actually shattered the creature's sword
arm. The powerful block was not without a price, however, for it
sent waves of pain and then numbness into his already tiring arm.

They fought toward the light against worsening odds, and both
were receiving nicks and cuts, not as grievous as the wounds they
dealt, but still enough to slow them down. Kenyatta took a cut to
the arm, but since it was the same arm that was still numb, he was
able to ignore the pain. Kita saw the blow out of the corner of his
eye and a wave of panic and rage rose within him. With a roar, he
pressed the shadow demons back, whirling his blade-ended staff.
Fiends went sprawling in every direction.

Three last shadow demons blocked their path to the end of the
forest. The evil creatures could not know that the adversaries
charging them were completely taken by a battle rage that was
brought on by the sheer determination to survive. All three creatures were cut down in an instant, and the two warriors leaped out
of the dense forest and rolled onto the sandy beach. They heard the
loud hissing of their angry pursuers but none ventured outside
the woods.

So they cyan't move in the light after all, Kenyatta thought with
more than a little relief. *Not unless there are shadows for them to
hide in.*

After they were sure there was no more threat, they crawled
several yards farther away and lay on their backs, still never taking
their eyes from the most difficult journey they had ever experienced.

"Man," Kenyatta panted, "dem tings fight like nothing I ever
seen before." He looked at his friend. "Thanks, man."

Kita gave him a tired smirk. "Of course. What else would I
have done? I'd get bored on this little road trip without you
buzzing in my ear about nothing in particular, most of the time."

Kenyatta glared at him. "If I would have made it out, I would
surely have left...."

"Right, right," Kita interrupted nonchalantly, and they shared a much-needed laugh.

After Kenyatta shared what he'd learned regarding the demons only being able to move about in darkness and shadows, and that night was near, the two friends took a quick snack, mended some of their more serious wounds, and set a brisk pace down the western coastline for a few more hours. Once dusk had fallen, they decided they had put enough distance between them and the forest and it was safe enough to rest for the day. After setting camp—well away from any objects that could cast any type of shadow in the moonlight—they were soon asleep.

As Kenyatta drifted into slumber, he reflected on the battle not many hours ago. The more he thought about it, those demons—if they *were* demons—were not very skilled at fighting, but their numbers and the fact that they could regenerate and travel from shadow to shadow left him uneasy as they camped in the middle of the night. Could those things step out of darkness itself? There was no way to know until it was too late. Fortune was with them this night, as no demons materialized out of the surrounding darkness. The cool salty breeze pushed the clouds across the dark sky, leaving them and the surrounding sands awash in the pale moonlight.

16

Z real was paralyzed at the sight of the demon. The Quentranzi must have stood over twenty feet tall and radiated evil. Its hard, leathery blue skin covered boulder-like muscles. Tiny orange flames danced in malicious eyes that seemed as if they could lash out at Zreal at any moment. Pointed ears like razors stood out on either side of its head. Surprisingly, it did not possess the huge jagged teeth contained in a large gaping maw that one would expect, but a regular-sized mouth containing four fangs almost as long as Zreal's forearm.

From six long fingers grew claws that looked more like daggers. Perhaps the most remarkable feature of the fiend were wings that hung to its ankles like a flowing cape. Zreal knew this thing could utterly destroy him at a whim.

The enormous Quentranzi sat upon his awful throne and enjoyed the fear as only a demon could. It then leaned forward, as if waiting for the diminutive little creature to speak.

"I ... my name is Zreal of the House of Brit—"

"Do not come here and declare your house to me!" the demon thundered. "If you wish to even exist, you will never declare a house of power that is of no concern to me."

Zreal could feel every ounce of energy coursing through his body and collecting at his legs and wings. He was fast, very fast. But was he fast enough to make it out of here alive? Surely those giant wings would take time to get that towering body in the air.

Grala leaned back and eyed him. "Thinking of making a fast escape, little one?" it taunted. Zreal once again felt frozen with fear. The demon narrowed its eyes and chuckled. It was a bone-chilling sound.

"You look to be fast, little insect, but in this world you could not escape me if you moved at the speed of your own thoughts."

In that instant, Zreal spun to the sound of another booming chuckle behind him. Indeed, at the speed of its own thoughts, the demon had disappeared and reappeared behind him. Zreal wanted nothing more than to leave this place and face his master in failure. Zreal would rather die at his master's hands than in this place of indescribable horror.

He forced himself to remain calm, and faced the demon squarely. "I am here to speak of terms my master would extend to you in exchange for—"

Grala's ominous chuckling interrupted him again. "Speak just one more declaration, little insect. Speak one more, and I will devour your soul."

Zreal tried to reorganize his thoughts before the demon became bored with their meeting.

Grala looked down on him with a derisive smirk. "It is not wise to keep one such as I waiting. I might interpret your silence as a personal offering and devour you right now."

"My humble apologies, great one," Zreal said in his usual raspy voice. "My master has spoken with your general in regards to an alliance against Takashaniel."

"I am aware of this," Grala responded, bored. "I am aware of everything. You forget that Kabriza answers to me."

"Of course," Zreal responded quickly.

"Takashaniel is an ambitious undertaking. It would require quite a bit of power to bring that cursed tower down."

Zreal chanced a smile. "Yes. An ambitious undertaking indeed, but if we succeed, the balance could be shifted to our favor. Your favor. We would stand unchallenged."

"And once this is accomplished, what would stop us from destroying you and your master, who number only two?" Grala's face twisted into something of a sardonic grin.

At that expected question, Zreal reached into a pouch at his side and withdrew a flawless crystal. Zreal held the crystal before him so that the demon could see the brilliant orange glow radiating from the gem. The Quentranzi king looked into the crystal with moderate interest as it began to shift in color. After a few seconds that seemed like hours to Zreal, his master's image appeared.

"My greetings, mighty Grala," Brit declared. "I trust my assistant has begun discussing our plans with you." Grala crossed his thick arms and continued to stare into the crystal. "I hold no words from you," Brit continued, "and I speak with no deception. It is true that I would like to enlist the aid of your brethren to bring my plans to fruition, and in exchange, offer the Quentranzi the ability to walk this plane of existence with more ease and frequency."

"This grows entirely too boring for my interest," Grala interrupted. "I am already aware of your plans and how we supposedly fit into them. I do not care much for your schemes or your alliance. If the time comes when I wish to inhabit your plane, we will come."

"And how would you accomplish this, mighty Grala?" Brit pressed. At that last statement, Zreal felt as if his life were being determined by a human game of dice. He wished his master would handle this unpredictable fiend with a bit more care.

"As things stand," Brit continued, "it is impossible for any who inhabit your plane to come to this one at will, so long as Takashaniel stands. Even if summoned, your time here is limited, as well as your power. If I were to destroy the tower by my own means, which is possible, I assure you, nothing could stop me from creating a similar forbidding to keep you where you are."

Brit spread his hands. "I propose to make both of our interests more easily achievable by working together in common interest. Your kind and mine have more similarities than you know."

Grala smirked. "Such confidence."

Now it was Brit's turn to look bored. "As long as the tower stands, no one, not even I, have the power to summon an infinite number of your kind to this plane. And you, Grala, would not be able to walk upon this world so long as any number of your brethren are here. I may be able to sidestep Takashaniel's balancing influence, but your presence would push the balance too far. You or your minions would be promptly expelled."

The lord of the Quentranzi withdrew within his thoughts. "And what would make you keep your end of the deal?" came the skeptical reply. "Your bargaining chips hold little value. Even one of my chiteras could open a gate to your world without being summoned."

"That much is true, I admit." Brit smiled. "But with my help, it could be done much simpler."

The demon's growl rumbled in its throat. It knew what "simpler" meant. Chiteras could only open a weak gateway to the earth realm with Takashaniel gone, which meant that this Brit creature could destroy it and any of his brethren unlucky enough to be caught between worlds. The consequences were … undesirable.

After a few moments of consideration, the Quentranzi king regarded the crystal once more. "Grala agrees to your proposal."

Zreal noted the glowing flames dancing in the demon's eyes, more fierce than before. "But if you betray me, I will come for you." As it spoke, the entire throne room and the surrounding area rumbled as if trembling with fear.

"You have my word," Brit replied. Zreal reached into his pouch once again, and as he did, Brit spoke. "My assistant has brought a

Gezar crystal. It has energy-siphoning properties, but in your world, it could be used to devour souls. I thought you might find it … useful."

The crystal levitated from Zreal's hand and floated across the throne room to stop before the fiend, who took it with lustful delight. At that, Brit's image in Zreal's crystal faded and he replaced it in his pouch. He then turned and quickly and quietly departed from the throne room. Once he was at a safe distance, Zreal pulled out yet another small orb from his pouch. It would draw from his own energy, but deliver him away from this forsaken world.

He held the black orb in front of him and channeled his energy into it. A green mist surrounded him, and within a few short moments, he found himself back in his master's fortress. Zreal opened his eyes to see the Drek standing over him.

"Well done," Brit said

17

After traveling the coast for half a day, Kenyatta and Kita came to an old pier where a few small boats bobbed lazily atop the rippling water, their brown rusted motors long since fallen into dysfunction.

"Ages ago dem use a liquid called gasoline for these things," Kenyatta said, giving one of the boats a kick. "Now we use blood and sweat, rowing all the way to Japan."

"Yeah, well in many ways it's a good thing," Kita replied.

Kenyatta shrugged. "No complaints outta me. Let's pick a boat and get to it. I don't relish the idea of crossin' da ocean at night."

"Yeah," Kita agreed, pulling out a map that had been given to him by Kim, back at Kyu Village. "There's no telling what's lurking in the ocean in these times." They studied the map in silence for a few minutes till Kita found their location. "According to this map, we are on the coast of Pusan." He slid a finger along the map. "If we head southeast, we will be a bit farther south, but we'll reach land sooner."

"South is fine with me," Kenyatta agreed, "so long as we're not in da water any longer than need be."

After finding a seaworthy boat, the two friends acquired the best oars they could find with two to spare and turned southeast, toward the coast of Fukuoka, Japan.

* * *

THOUGH THE WATERS WERE CALM, the two friends spoke little as they rowed across the Korean Strait, conserving their energy as much as possible.

"The distance seemed a lot shorter on dat map of yours," Kenyatta said, squinting at the distant Japan.

"Times like this I wish there were still motorboats," Kita admitted.

"Whoa," Kenyatta teased. "Not mister 'in many ways it's a good ting.' I thought you were enjoying our little trip—"

Kita held up his hand and motioned for his rambling friend to look far out to the rear of the boat. Kenyatta strained to see what his friend was pointing at. A few heartbeats passed, then a spiked fin rose about six feet out of the water and gently dipped beneath the surface.

Kenyatta dropped his sandwich and grabbed an oar. "Whatcha still sitting there for?" he asked as he got into position. "Grab your oar. I don't want to see how big dat thing is!"

Kita grabbed his oar and they braced their feet. Once they had timed a rhythm between them, they increased their speed. By now, the ripple of water was steadily closing on them. Kita and Kenyatta gritted their teeth and pulled on the oars with everything they had. The cool sea air blew through Kenyatta's locks, and the mist from the water covered both men in a soothing spray. But the gentle caress of the ocean breeze was lost on the companions as they raced against the unseen horror that chased them from beneath the waves.

The front of the boat lifted as it climbed over the ripples, and the rear left a streaming wake behind it. Moving inside the wake, however, was the silhouette of a body at least twice the size of the modest boat. "I see … two sets of dorsal fins … that are about eight feet apart from each other," Kita gasped in between pulls.

"Then row harder and quit talkin'," Kenyatta growled. The muscles in his chest clenched like steel cords with each pull of the oars.

Eyes squinted closed, teeth clenched, their only concern was to outrun their large pursuer. Kita stole a glance over his shoulder and his eyes lit up. "Ken, the shore is not far, less than half a mile!"

"Oh ya? Good ting I'm not getting *tired*!"

The duo had been rowing at a feverish pace since the halfway point between the two lands without slowing, and now their muscles were on fire.

"Don't think about it," Kita said. "We're almost there!"

"You tink I'm gonna give up?" Kenyatta replied. "I got no problem with dying, man. But me got a big problem with being eaten!"

* * *

ON FUKUOKA BEACH, a little girl and her older sister were playing in the sand when she looked out to the ocean and saw a boat riding in on the waves.

"Look! There's a boat coming this way!"

The older girl came to stand beside her sister. "There is something big following them." They looked at each other and then back to the scene not far from the shore. The older sister bit her lip. "I hope they make it."

"Whatever is chasing them looks pretty big," the younger girl observed.

"Don't you ever listen?" her sister snapped. "I just said that!"

They watched as the boat neared the shoreline, the waves of the beach aiding its escape from something that they now could see was twice the size of the boat. Having reached shallow waters, the thing slowed and rose slightly above the surface of the water as if to get one last look at the prey that had eluded it. Just as its yellow eyes and huge gray body was visible, it abruptly turned and swam away beneath the surface, its tail slapping the water violently before it too, disappeared beneath the waves.

The boat slid past the watching girls all the way into some nearby rocks. The boat hit the rocks in a loud crack of broken and splintered wood.

18

K enjiro gazed at the sky, unable to believe their luck. Not only had the weather held up for the entire day, but on their path, they came upon a running stream that spilled into a lake about thirty feet below, nestled in the center of a sleepy meadow.

Smooth multicolored rocks lined the riverbed, giving it a rich pastel hue. The water in the lake below was so clear, the siblings could see to the bottom.

Akemi knelt beside the stream and tasted the water. After a few sips, she filled her water pouch while her older brother scanned the area. "Why are you so tense?" she asked. "You've been uptight for a few days now, ever since we passed through that valley."

"The world grows more tense," the samurai responded.

The ninja stood and looked around. "I've felt it, too."

"Then you've felt the twisted wrongness of it," Kenjiro replied. "Like something entering this world that doesn't belong here."

Akemi arched an eyebrow.

"Demons," the samurai said.

"Then this will be more fun than we expected!" the ninja responded brightly.

"Speak for yourself, sister," Kenjiro said.

Akemi walked to the edge of the stream and peeked over the drop, grinning. "This place is perfect for a swim."

Kenjiro frowned at her. "Has your mind fallen over the edge of that stream? We still are at least two days from Kyokoza and our mission has not even begun. We have much ground to cover and not much time to do it in. We have even less time to waste splashing around in a lake when we have not even reached Toyotomi yet."

Akemi straightened and eyed her annoyed brother. "Look, we're going to have to compromise a bit." She smiled, which brought more than a few worry lines in her brother's forehead. "OK, I'll skip the swim and we'll head straight for Toyotomi now."

"And?" Kenjiro replied, knowing his sister all too well.

"*And*," the ninja said with an even bigger smile. "We will spend one full day in Toyotomi and leave for Kyokoza the next day."

The samurai considered this for a moment, then conceded. "I suppose an extra day will be fine if we are closer to our destination. We will stay in the village for one day only, after which we set out for Kyokoza before morning light and stop only for a brief rest and continue until we reach the city. I accept your terms only if you accept mine."

Akemi nodded patronizingly through her brother's terms as he spoke. "Why are you samurai always so uptight?"

Kenjiro narrowed his eyes at his sister, then closed them and took deep breath. "If you were anyone else...."

"I know, I know." Akemi started away. "If I were anyone else, you would not tolerate my insolence and cut me down, or some such. Lighten up, big brother. Life is already grim enough without you constantly walking around like a samurai in full armor. I must believe that even those of *your* class know how to have fun sometimes."

Kenjiro just shook his head and made a sound that could have been a snicker. "What karma am I balancing from a past life for the Gods to have given me a ninja sister? Akemi, you are my life's test."

Akemi responded with a devious smirk. "You could learn from the Gods, Kenjiro. They have a sense of humor, too."

* * *

FOR A LONG TIME, Kenyatta and Kita lay in the sand underneath a tree; their broken and splintered boat not far away. Their travels from Kyu Village took most of a day, ending it with a narrow escape from a demon-haunted forest. Now, after having crossed the Korean Strait and barely outpacing some unknown monster, they had finally reached Japan. And here they lay, underneath a beach-side tree and wanting very much to sleep.

"Ugh," Kita groaned, "my whole body is on fire."

"Mine, too," Kenyatta replied. "Me arms most of all. It feel like I'm all tied in knots. I cyan't relax me arms and me stomach wants to cramp." He arched a curious eyebrow at two young girls who stood a short distance away. The younger girl bowed and spoke to Kita first.

"*Konnichiwa*," she chirped hesitantly.

Kita had almost forgotten that they had finally reached Japan. He smiled and returned the greeting. Kenyatta smiled and waited patiently. After a few short words—with the girls keeping their distance—Kita introduced himself and his friend. Kenyatta smiled and greeted the two girls in the common language of the land, which brought surprised smiles to the two bright faces.

For a while they talked, the girls smiling yet keeping a safe distance, and the two travelers making no move to close the space between them.

"How far are we from the nearest city?" Kenyatta asked with a smile, speaking the dialect as if it were his own.

"Our village is near here," the younger girl quickly responded, after which she received a poke in the back from her sister. The two friends recognized and silently applauded the older girl's sense of caution. Kita then spoke softly to the older sister.

"We mean not to intrude in your lives or your village. We have come a long way and are looking for the city of Kyokoza. Have you ever heard of such a place?"

The girl nodded. "It is that way," she answered. "Uncle always takes that path when we go to Kyokoza."

"Northwest of here," Kenyatta said, looking in the direction the older sister pointed. "Do you know how far?"

"No," she responded. "But when we used to ride with Uncle in a caravan, it would take two days. We used to always stop and get Moon Cakes brought from the land of Ba Guo along the way." Her smile faded. "We don't go there much anymore. Our parents say that the times are not in favor of a trip so far from home."

Kita moved a few strands of hair from in front of his eyes. "Your parents are wise and you should listen to them."

He turned to his friend, who stood looking at their boat. Kenyatta pointed at the craft and looked at the girls. "Did you see what was chasing us?" he asked. Both girls nodded.

"We couldn't tell until the last minute, but we know it. That fish lives in the sea where you crossed. It usually sinks any smaller boat that travels through there, but you made it. No one has ever beaten it before. Everyone knows not to travel across the water there."

"How big is that thing?" Kita asked, staring at the thing as though he thought it might jump out of the ocean at them.

"Our father said it is as big as a whale, but with long, sharp teeth. If it would have caught you, it would have eaten you both."

"I have a feeling it would have done more than eat us," Kenyatta remarked. That brought a shudder to the two sisters.

The younger girl stepped forward and smiled. "Maybe you can

ride horses there. It would be faster that way." Kenyatta noticed the look of worry on the older sister's face and smiled.

"You are both very nice, but we could not take anything from your village."

The older girl noticed twin blades crossed behind the islander's back, and the small knife tied to his friend's waist. "Are you two warriors?" she asked.

Kenyatta and Kita smiled at each other and nodded. "I believe you could say that, little one," Kita answered. "From very far away." The younger sister lit up with excitement.

"Where are you from? We knew you were not from here. How far did you go to come here?" Kenyatta rocked back as they were barraged by the wave of questions. "I am from Jamaica," he answered. "A small island that way."

"And I am from an island called the Philippines," Kita said. "Actually, my home is not very far from here at all."

The older sister became a bit more curious. "How can you speak to us? Our mother says that people from other places speak different languages than here."

Kita smiled at the little girl. "We have been here before." He glanced down at the cinnamon brown-colored sand, and then back at the inquisitive little girl in front of him. "Probably before you were born." The older girl stared into the warrior's eyes, then smiled.

"My name is Aiko," she said, then indicated her younger girl. "And she is my sister Rimi."

"Nice to meet you Aiko and Rimi," both men said.

Kenyatta attempted to help them to pronounce his name, but after seeing the trouble they were having, he just laughed. "You can just call me Ken if it is easier for you." As it turned out, pronouncing Kenyatta's name broke the tension in the two girls and Aiko finally agreed with Rimi that the two friends should accompany them to the village.

"Yamada Village is not far from here," the older girl said eagerly. "We can take you there now and you can meet our parents."

Kenyatta and Kita exchanged concerned looks. They were unsure how the parents of these two girls would react to the generosity of their daughters to two weapon-clad foreigners who just rowed onto the beach.

"Well?" Kenyatta looked at his friend. "The most they can do is run us outta town."

Kita just shook his head at his friend's logic, then bowed his head to Aiko. "Lead on."

* * *

Hours after their stop at the waterfall-fed lake, Kenjiro and Akemi cut a trail through surprisingly dense foliage. Vegetation and wildlife flourished as it never had before, and although they would have to be wary of the lesser demon spirits that were becoming more common, they also remained wary of some of the more dangerous predators that lived higher on the food chain than themselves. When traversing open fields, they hastened their pace, but when they passed through the more thickly forested areas, the ninja usually traveled ahead in the trees to get a better look at their surroundings. With fiercer animals populating the lands these days, she felt the trees were still the safest route.

Akemi called for a stop, and made her way to the top of one of the taller trees in the area to get a panoramic view. The woods were not that dense, and they would pass through at a reasonable pace. She slipped a compact spyglass out of her sack to have a closer look at the land outside the woods. Once satisfied, she descended back to her brother.

"I can almost make out a small rural city that I believe is Toyotomi. We should reach it before night."

Kenjiro nodded at that news. "Then let us leave now."

"I agree. I'm looking forward to having my first hot bath in so long." Her older brother merely grunted and turned to move on. Akemi sighed. "I suppose comfort isn't part of the samurai code," she muttered.

19

A few hours before nightfall, the samurai and his ninja sister came upon the village of Toyotomi. It was large for a village; almost a city, in fact. A brick wall ran the perimeter, giving at least some protection from outside elements. The main entrance was enclosed by a tall, narrow gate slightly higher than the wall itself, and was flanked by two statuesque guards.

Akemi sniggered at the two men. Their armor was well-crafted and brightly colored steel that looked to have never seen an instant of battle. The vests were embroidered with gold and bright green trim, while the pants were also gold with green trim and edged with black at the seams.

Thick strips of leather lined with bright silver studs covered their armored legs, and their boots were also lined in gold, green and black. Bulky, impractical, and altogether gaudy, the guards nevertheless wore their uniforms with pride and confidence. To her ninja sensibilities, Akemi found such synesthetic use of color was unnecessary and dangerous. One could not easily conceal them-selves in their surroundings with glittering burnished gold and silver shining from their body.

As they approached, the guards stiffened and took a step

forward. The guard facing Akemi held a tall Naginata. The shaft was made of strong, treated wood and was painted gold. The base of the shaft was made of iron and was blunt at the tip. The top of the weapon held a long thin blade that looked to be sharper than the wits of the man holding it.

The guard facing Kenjiro was armed with two katanas bearing gaudily embroidered hilts strapped to both sides of his waist. The stone-faced samurai moved up to face the guard, who met his gaze while slowly moving his hands to the hilts of his weapons.

Kenjiro almost laughed. Wielding two weapons was a skill that not every master possessed. He doubted this man could properly wield one of those shiny swords at his waist. Kenjiro judged that he could have the man disarmed in seconds.

"Do you greet every guest to your village in this manner?" the samurai asked, smiling.

Ignoring the sarcasm, the guard shifted his gaze to Akemi—mistake number one—and then back to him. "Where do you come from?" the guard demanded.

"A good distance from here," Kenjiro answered. "We have been traveling for days now and seek rest within the walls of your kind village."

The two guards glanced at each other—mistake number two—and back to the travelers. "You have not answered the question," the other guard persisted. "Where do you come from?"

Kenjiro never shifted his gaze, but answered as non-threateningly as he could. "We have traveled from the far away Mt. Yamanake, and would enjoy rest, more than banter."

The guards were shocked at how far they had traveled. The siblings could see the question in their eyes. Why had they come so far, and why stop here in this small village when Kyokoza was not far?

Akemi could see the skepticism plaguing the guards and attempted to ease the tension. "As my brother has said, we are tired travelers who wish to stop in your kind home to rest and buy supplies before moving on our way. We mean not to stay long."

The guard frowned down at her. "Where is your destination?"

"That is not your concern," the samurai shot back, but Akemi raised her hand and continued.

"We travel to the city of Kyokoza," she answered. "The city is not very far from here," the guard replied skeptically. "Why not press forward and not delay?"

"Why not rest and be better prepared for the duration of our trip by stopping in a village that lies between us and our destination?" Akemi countered.

"If it is supplies you wish to acquire, it can be arranged for them to be brought to you here, including portable tents for you to set for camp."

"Money that could be more appropriately used to buy more food and supplies instead of a tent that would be used temporarily," the samurai replied in a low, dangerous tone. "You believe us to be a potential threat to your village. If our intentions were ill, your intestines would already be lying on the ground the instant your eyes left mine to look at your friend."

At this bold statement, both guards took a ready stance, mistake number three. The guard facing Kenjiro reached to his katanas, but a flash of Kenjiro's sword had them lying in the dirt to his sides.

Kenjiro shrugged. "My apologies. You looked uncomfortable wearing those fancy swords, so I took the liberty of disarming you."

"We mean no trouble here," Akemi said. "We wish only to rest, buy supplies, and move on. May we please seek shelter within your walls?"

With the humble request of the female traveler, and the other traveler's obvious effort to conceal his nausea for his sister's humbleness, the two guards grudgingly stepped aside and allowed the travelers to enter. Kenjiro noticed the pained look on the two men. They really had not much choice and they knew it. Kenjiro could have had one of them dead in an instant.

Akemi smiled and tipped her head to the guard and entered, followed by her irritated brother. "What happened to the gentle tolerance of the *samurai*?" she teased.

"I follow no lord," her brother responded.

"And so that reduces you to a *ronin* bandit? What of Bushido and honor?"

"What of it?" the samurai quipped.

"Was that honorable, back there?"

"That was necessary," Kenjiro answered. "And as far as the way of the ronin is concerned, perhaps I will educate you, but not today."

"I look forward to it, brother," Akemi said.

Kenjiro grunted.

* * *

ADMIRING the beautiful landscape of the constantly changing world, the two friends moved about the foliage and the open fields on a fast trek toward the city of Nijika. Riding on horseback gave them a much-welcomed rest after the trials they had faced while crossing through Korea and the race to the shores of Japan.

"Hey, Ken," Kita called from behind. "How far do you think we have until we reach this place?"

Kenyatta shrugged. "The man at Yamada who give us these horses say that it take a full day with their caravan. Witout the extra load and pushing straight tru, we should make it by night."

"That's fine by me," Kita replied. "I'm wiped out. Besides, we can replenish our food and gear."

At dusk, the travelers came to the front of the city of Nijika and stopped at a tree line sprinkled with large rocks. It was small for a city and surrounded by a wall over a dozen feet high. At the front stood two tall double doors made of solid iron, and flanked by four guards. At the edge of each end of the walls stood single watch-towers with two men in each.

The travelers looked at each other and back at the well-guarded city. They knew that the chances of talking their way into an obviously wary place were slim.

"I think we should consider slipping in," Kita recommended. "The place doesn't seem ready to welcome outsiders."

"Looks paranoid," Kenyatta agreed as he watched the guards. "We should wait for night, then slip in from one of the far ends away from the front."

Kita nodded and they set camp, awaiting nightfall concealed in the trees.

* * *

THEIR SEARCH for a suitable inn brought the samurai and his sister to an old western-style tavern. The common room was spacious and open, furnished with western style wooden tables and chairs. Neither of the two warriors cared much for the place, but the location was prime because of its view of the rest of the village, and the proximity to the gates.

"I hope you are happy, sister," Kenjiro remarked. "This place reeks of lust and the trifling existence of sheep being led by their day instead of leading it themselves."

The young ninja shook her head and sighed. "Always the sharp observer. Let's just enjoy our stay and rest. These people have no business with us, nor we with them." She walked over to her brother and laid a hand on his shoulder, smiling like the devious little girl that had been such a challenge to keep out of trouble. His brow creased. Akemi laughed.

After securing their room, and arguing with Kenjiro about sharing a room for efficiency instead of having separate ones, Akemi put her hand on her stomach and prodded the samurai with an elbow. "Come, let's see if this quaint little village has some decent food."

With her brother in tow, the woman descended the stairs and filtered through the crowd toward the door. Although every man in the tavern moved aside and gaped as the soft and smooth material flowed across her seductive figure in a dance all its own, one pair of eyes seemed to concentrate intensely on the young warrior. Kenjiro sensed that they were being watched and was sure that his sister felt the same.

As they neared the door, a bulky man stepped out and barred their way. It was obvious to Akemi from the start that he could not be from anywhere local, as he was rotund and sloppy, and had on dirty denim pants and a leather vest that was too small for his girth.

He stood over six feet tall and seemed just as wide, and wore the scraggly beginnings of a beard, and had long greasy black hair tied behind his back. Underneath his vest was a tattoo that looked as if it wrapped across his chest to his back. The little she could see from the front was of a serpent preparing to swallow a smaller animal, of which kind Akemi was unsure. She stopped a few feet in front of the giant and eyed him. So crusty were his black denim pants that they looked as though they could stand on their own without the wearer. His black boots were surprisingly shiny and clean.

"You are a round one," Akemi said. "Couldn't find a shirt big enough to fit, hmm?"

The barrel-chested man took a step forward. "Who you are?" he demanded in a ragged voice, and it surprised the ninja that he actually spoke her language, despite where he might be from. "None seen you here before and we don't welcome strange ones like you passing in and out of here."

"We are merely travelers passing through and not wanting any trouble." She glanced over her shoulder at her brother, whose sword hand had gone very still. "If we may, please allow us to pass."

The mountain of a man looked down on her and smirked. "Maybe your friend there won't mind if I charge a price for your passage."

"Name it," Akemi agreed.

"You come to my room and—" He stopped short at the woman's cold, smiling stare. The one behind her, who was not so subtle, was now gripping the hilt of his sword despite his casual stance.

"I would take careful consideration of my next words if I were you," the woman cautioned. The fire that burned in her eyes and the happy tone in her voice were not lost on the big man. After a bit of consideration, he scanned the bar and noticed that every gaze in the tavern was fixed on the three of them.

"Quite a position you have created for yourself, my giant friend," the ninja remarked. "You have a dilemma, don't you? On one hand, you can stay there and we will cut you down like a boar. On the other hand, you can step aside and live, but with damaged status as the big tough boy in here." She tapped her smooth, pointed chin and let out a half smile. "Decisions, decisions."

Kenjiro glared up at the large man. "Step aside while you can still walk."

At that ultimatum the giant man reached to his right and pulled what looked like a club from under his chair with a mighty swing. Spectators grabbed their drinks and cleared away to give the trio plenty of room. Before everyone had gotten a safe distance away, however, the round giant dropped to his knees and slumped over, clutching his groin as the two warriors stepped around him and out the door.

20

L ife began to stir in Nijika just before dawn. Because it was so large by the standards of a village, businesses had to be competitive just as in a larger city. The predawn blue of morning slowly brightened as the sun crested the mountains far to the east. The streets came alive as children scurried off to schools, and adults tended shops, perused the marketplace, and foreigners milled about.

Kenyatta stood on the balcony of their room and watched the place come to life. It reminded him of home and his life as a child with Grampa.

"You're not gonna get all teary eyed on me, are you?" Kita said from across the room. Kenyatta glanced over his shoulder to see his friend chuckling as he slipped on a pair of sandy-colored moccasin-style shoes.

"Why don't you find some business of your own and stay outta mine, ya?" Kenyatta shot back.

"Hey, easy now," Kita laughed. "No harm meant, just joking."

"Ya, man, I'm knowin' that. I'm kind of edgy today, that's all. Last night my sister came to me."

Kita's eyes lit up. "What did you talk about?"

"Hmm." Kenyatta eyed his friend suspiciously. "Looks like me gettin' your undivided attention now, ya?"

Kenyatta sat down on the corner of his bed and ran his fingers through his shoulder-length locks. "She say she gonna visit us when we get to Kyokoza and that is where she's going to deal with our weapons."

"Ok," Kita replied. "So why the distressed look? I would think that should be good news." Kenyatta looked over at his friend from the window.

"She also said that she's going to fill us in on what's going on and that when we leave Kyokoza our mission will truly begin. She says that everything up to now was just a bit of training and was nothing compared to what's ahead of us."

At the sight of his friend gathering up a small pack and a few concealed weapons, Kenyatta raised an eyebrow. "Where are you planning on going?"

Kita smirked. "I don't plan on missing the chance to mingle and enjoy our little stay before we take to the road again."

Kenyatta's mood brightened at the mention of fun. "Ya, man, count me in."

They strode through the streets of Nijika, buying supplies and gear, as well as a few trinkets that may or may not have possessed the properties the vendors claimed.

"Amazing how times have changed from when we were little," Kita said. He eyed a piece of armor that was light and thin, but sturdy. The shop owner explained that it had been created from a new species of tree that had a smooth and flexible bark, but was also as tough as steel and resistant to harsh weather conditions. The best part about the process was that one tree could be used multiple times. The bark need only be stripped away during the summer months so that the tree would have time to grow more for the cold seasons.

"Hey, Ken," Kita asked. "What do you think about this armor?"

Kenyatta inspected the unusual piece. It was flexible yet tough, as the shop owner had said. He turned it in his hands, marveling at the sturdiness of the material despite its wood origin. It would turn aside a blade as effectively as most armor, and so much lighter.

"Looks pretty good to me," Kenyatta replied. "Strong, too. I tink it serve us much better than what we have now, and it's not too flashy either. Get one for me."

While paying for their wares, Kita felt an odd vibe and glanced over his shoulder, but there was no one behind him. He stuffed their new armor in a sack the shop owner had given him and looked around. Kenyatta was busy bargaining over items in another shop.

Kita frowned and glanced over his right shoulder to accidentally make eye contact with the most out-of-place person in the city.

A beautiful woman seemed to glide across his path. Her presence was both overt and subtle at the same time. Her lips were thin and sharp and slanted in a half smile that hypnotized every male shopper she passed. Although she had an undeniable allure about her, Kita's instincts warned that there was more to this woman than his eyes could see.

"C'mon, man," Kenyatta teased. "Why don't ya jyas go tell her what you're really tinkin' and see if she don't slap your face off your head."

The woman stopped in front of them. "You are not from here," she said in the native tongue of the land.

"You aren't either," Kita replied.

The woman offered a smile in response, then pointed west of the village. "I am from west of here, a very far place in the mountains."

"What brings you so far from your homeland?" Kita asked.

"I have business to tend and people to seek."

"Well," Kita said politely, "I wish you luck."

"You haven't told me where you and your friend are from," the woman persisted.

"I appreciate your interest, and your trust in me, but I cannot return it. It's true, we are not from here, but our place of origin is of no importance either."

"Only a warrior would be so aloof."

"Perhaps," was all Kita offered. "I think my friend and I should move on now. We have much to do and the day moves on."

The woman smiled and tipped her head. "I'm sure we will meet again."

"Perhaps."

Throughout the conversation, Kenyatta felt a necessity to remain quiet and observe his unusually reserved friend. "Did I miss something back there?" he asked. Kita glanced at him.

"There was something about her that I couldn't place. There was more there than I could see, but I'm not sure what."

Kenyatta shrugged. "Maybe we'll find out if we see her again."

Kita nodded, but the thought of seeing that woman again put him on edge.

21

K enjiro waited at the edge of his patience for his sister to return from the village square. She had insisted on going to see what type of merchandise would be sold, but the samurai preferred to avoid the crowds. He looked up from his tiny cup of sake to see the heads of seemingly every man in the general area turn in the direction of his sister. With some effort, he put away the reflexive desire to cut down every one of the lusting heathens.

"Put that look away, Kenjiro," Akemi chided. "I have seen desire in the eyes of many women when they gaze at your handsome, if not rigid, visage."

Kenjiro grunted. "Did you find what you were looking for so we can move on?"

Akemi sighed. "You really must learn how to relax, brother. We have one day, remember? I will enjoy every minute of it before we depart."

"You insist on wasting time here?"

"I insist on us having some time to relax and unwind before we endure the trials of the road," Akemi replied. "Quit trying to hide it. I know you like this place as much as I. When was the last time we were able to enjoy the quiet of a nice village such as this one?"

Kenjiro grunted again, but complained no more. Akemi accepted that as a small victory.

* * *

As the afternoon turned late Kenjiro followed his adventurous sister through the village that could be called a small city, observing every sight and exploring every bar and social establishment that Toyotomi had to offer. One such place was The Eagle's Eye, the very tavern where they'd rented their room.

The place earned its name because it towered over every other tavern in Toyotomi and was also positioned in a corner overlooking the town square. The Eagle's Eye was four stories high instead of the usual two or three, and three times as large as any other in town.

"Quite a big place, this is." Akemi glanced at her brother, who continued to scan the huge common room and the many throngs of people who mingled about.

"What are you talking about?" he frowned at her. "We spent the night here."

"It looks bigger to me at a second glance," Akemi said.

"There are too many people from different parts of the world here. This tavern has mimicked the western ones too well, and even most of the patrons are from those rowdy lands. A fight could start from any corner of this place."

"Are all samurai as intense as you, my beloved brother?" Akemi smiled. "Come, let's have a drink. I'm sure we can find something we've never had before in such a grand tavern as this one."

Kenjiro, still looking confused at why his sister spoke as if it were their first time here, shrugged and followed. Many eyes fell upon the two warriors as they moved across the large room. Some —many, in fact—were present the night before, when the two siblings had so easily dispatched the absent burly troublemaker. None challenged them this time, but stared sidelong at the two as they made their way to the bar.

It seemed every inch of the big western-styled establishment was made of wood, and the place glowed in the golden brown light of the candles on the walls and in the chandeliers that reflected it from the shiny plywood finish. There were two elevated dance floors, and a bar that stretched the length of the room. Customer after customer would yell out an order and one of the six bartenders would prepare the drink and send it sliding down the counter toward the caller. The atmosphere was filled with the loud chatter of patrons that were filled with the energy of the place, and at least two mugs of the house special blend.

Oddly enough, contrary to Kenjiro's words, there were none of the customary bar fights that one would expect to occur in an establishment such as this. Akemi smirked, attributing the lack of violence to the six guards who stood at each corner of the common room.

An hour later saw the duo in the farthest corner of The Eagle's Eye, Kenjiro slumped in an alcohol-induced stupor, and Akemi enjoying the sight. "What is this mix, brother?"

"Don't know," Kenjiro slurred. "Bartender recommended this as the house special mix. I thought we might try it."

Akemi nodded, grinning inwardly at the change in Kenjiro from just an hour ago. "Quite a lively place isn't it?"

The samurai nodded in agreement, giving the area another look. "We've attracted a bit of attention, little sister," he drawled.

"We have," she agreed. "I felt it ever since we walked through the doors. Many who look to prove themselves as fighters come to places like this one." Akemi leaned back in her chair and took in the raucous atmosphere until her gaze once again settled on the armed guards. "And what of the six champions of the Eagle's Eye, standing at each corner?"

Kenjiro snorted. "I place them not much higher above the others. They stand with the pride and arrogance. I doubt their skill reaches outside the boundaries of this village."

Akemi laughed. "Perhaps we'll assist in broadening their experience, before the night is done."

The samurai eyed his sister, then took another draw. "I'm up for it!" he declared, slamming the mug on the table.

* * *

"GOOD VIEW, ISN'T IT?" Kita said, as he and Kenyatta viewed the nightlife of the village from atop a water tower, a high point in the village that was second only to a huge tavern toward the middle and rear of town. They had climbed the water tower in order to get a panoramic view of the place at night, as well as the general surroundings outside. Ever since their tree-climbing days when they were boys, the two friends had learned the value of having an overhead view of their surroundings during the day and at night.

While Kita watched over the village, Kenyatta concentrated on establishing a connection with his sister. He had been trying since they had first arrived in Nijika, but all of his efforts were in vain.

"Still nothing," he said.

"I wouldn't worry too much," Kita said. "If there's one thing I know for sure, it's that your sister always has a reason for everything. When it's time, she'll contact you."

Kenyatta's eyes popped open. "Kita, you feel that?"

Kita concentrated, then shook his head. "Feel what?"

"I feel a strong presence in this place. When we first got here I felt it, but now I'm feeling it again. There is someone, no, more than one person here who is strong, I can feel it."

Kita concentrated. "I'm not getting anything. You don't think it's that girl that we met in the square earlier today, do you?"

"You mean the girl *you* met in the village square?" Kenyatta replied. "Well she did throw off a weird vibe that I couldn't place." He concentrated. "No, I don't think it's her."

Kita resumed his watch. "I know what you mean. That woman had a really strange presence, and it didn't exactly fit her. He looked back at Kenyatta, who was now running his fingers through his locks. "This is gonna sound weird, but I think that girl—"

"Wasn't human," Kenyatta finished, and Kita nodded grimly.

* * *

THE SAMURAI TOOK the last gulp of the house special and looked at his two sisters sitting to his right, both staring at him and smiling. "What are you smiling at?" he demanded.

"Oh nothing at all, brother. Just a samurai still pretending that he can out-drink his little sister."

"Bah." Kenjiro slid his mug aside. "I have no need for useless competition with you."

"Of course not," Akemi said sweetly as she watched him slump in his chair. She wondered if he would ever realize she always managed to start after he'd already had a mug or two, and wasn't paying attention that she didn't drink as much.

Her attention was pulled from her inebriated brother to a man making his way to their table. He had long black hair tied back from his face by a golden ring. He wore a purple jewel in his left ear that gleamed when the light hit it just right. His goatee was neat and well-trimmed, giving him an almost sinister look. No, not sinister. Cunning.

Akemi took special note of the skintight shirt that finely displayed every muscle in his arsenal, and also served as a thermal garment to protect the wearer from the cold. Over the shirt, he wore a dark brown vest that fit him perfectly. His pants were loose fitting and altered to provide ease of mobility, and his shoes were of a thin material and fit the contours of his feet.

The man's utilitarian style spoke of an experienced traveler, but there was one thing about him that drew the ninja's attention. An odd sword hilt—the likes of which the ninja had never seen—hung over his left shoulder. She stared at the hilt for a moment, then blinked in surprise. It was almost as though she could feel the weapon, as though it touched her mind.

With considerable effort, the ninja wrenched her attention from that curious sword back to its owner. Nowadays, most travelers were armed in some way, be it crossbow, bow and arrows, or sword. This man made an effort at looking the part of an ordinary traveler, but Akemi knew better. From his stride to his perfectly designed clothes to his overall appearance, this one was definitely a seasoned warrior, not a simple armed traveler.

She smiled politely and crossed her arms, her left hand positioned under her arm and only inches away from *Sekimaru*. Her tipsy brother remained slumped in his chair, gripping his mug and eyeing the approaching man from the corner of his eye, his right hand resting on the hilt of his sword.

"I don't think that will be necessary," the man said politely. He smiled and glanced at her left hand, still hovering above her sword's hilt.

"Who's to say?" she replied.

"Let me assure you that you have no enemy in me, ninja." He winked. Akemi kept her expression neutral despite her surprise, then realization hit her and she knew with whom she was dealing. Only one warrior other than a samurai could recognize a normally dressed ninja on first sight. He was a Neo Strider, one of the most mysterious and respected warriors in the world. Very little were known of striders by the general populous, but ninja and samurai knew well of them. Indeed, striders were feared and respected for their incredible skill, and although Akemi had never met one, she could feel by the presence of this man that their reputation was well-earned.

"And what business do you have with us, strider?" she asked carefully.

"My name is Shinobu." He crossed his right hand over his chest and bowed. "I know of your mission and wish to talk with you, if I may."

Kenjiro lifted his head and straightened himself in his chair. "And why, or rather, *how*, would you know anything about us? Our business does not concern you."

Shinobu glanced at the chair to his left and then back to the two siblings. Akemi nodded her head, and he sat.

"Two days ago I felt a powerful evil that seemed to be coming from the far reaches of the world. Yesterday I sensed the same thing, but also a lighter presence. Strong, but not evil." He winked again. "And here I find two of you. I would like to talk of your intentions, if we may?"

Kenjiro took note of the strider's words. He had found *two* of them. Who else was in this cursed village?

* * *

A SLENDER FIGURE materialized in front of Zreal and instantly he knew that it was Szhegaza. "Is there a reason why you chose my chamber to return, *zeNaga*?" he snapped.

Szhegaza frowned. *ZeNaga* meant untrustworthy in Zreal's home tongue. She and Zreal's species were related, but bitter rivals, which was the source of the zetsuan's distrust of her and their tense relationship.

"I thought I would pay you a visit before I went to see the master with my report," Szhegaza answered, turning her frown into a grin.

Zreal glared at her. "And what do you have to report?"

"Oh, you will know in time Zreal. You need not worry."

Zreal's narrowed his eyes at the Zitarian shifter, for her physical appearance was not the only thing that could change. Everything about Szhegaza and her kind was deceptive, including her cryptic response.

He watched as she reverted to her true form. She was almost as tall as he, and her two sets of wings were transparent and similar to a dragonfly. Her arms and legs were long, like poles, and her entire body was dark green with white stripes.

Each of the four fingers of her hands housed retractable claws about half a foot in length and sharp enough to slice cleanly through bone. Her face was slender and long, and housed mischievous yellow eyes and a small variety of tiny white dots, giving her face a speckled look.

Unlike Zreal's species, Zitarians had hair, and Szhegaza's was tied above her head with a cylinder that she had stolen from the village she had just returned from. It hung to her waist in a long, orange ponytail.

"I do wish you would leave," he said.

Szhegaza moved closer to her untrusting ally and smiled. "Oh that's just rude, Zreal. Your mistrust is breaking one of my hearts. What have I done to earn such contempt?"

Zreal snorted. "It would take more than me to break either one of your hearts, Szhegaza."

"Perhaps in time you will see me as a worthy ally, my friend."

"It is not your worth that I doubt, but your motives. I have never known a Zitarian to work for the better of another without a hidden purpose." Zreal waved a hand. "The master expects you, I'm sure." Now was his turn to grin. "Unless you plan to keep him waiting?"

Szhegaza turned for the door. Halfway out, she stopped and smiled over her shoulder. "I have never seen anyone with abilities such as yours who is so humble. It is I who value your alliance."

Zreal pondered those last words long after she had gone. Szhegaza would be aware of his capabilities, given their related heritage, but did their master undervalue him? He narrowed his eyes at the closed door. This was the main reason for his mistrust of the Zitarian. In but a few minutes Szhegaza had planted a seed of doubt in his mind about his relationship with Brit. If he was not careful around her, Szhegaza's poisonous words would surely lead to his demise.

L egs crossed, hands resting in his lap, Iel sat in the middle of a clear room that by all appearances had no walls, no ceiling and no floor. His skin color fluctuated between its natural gray and black, to blue and gray, while his eyes glowed green, then shifted to blue.

Descending ever deeper within himself, Iel delved his own consciousness until there was nothing but himself, then he pushed outward. The Drek was bringing an unimaginable evil to the world, and humans would not be able to stop him.

As his consciousness traveled farther out, crossing through the many dimensions of creation itself, he felt a familiar presence, like a smile touching his mind. In this state, Iel was formless, and could see in every direction at once. Now he floated inside what seemed to be an enormous colorful cloud. He sent his thoughts out to contact the ancient being, and his old friend.

"My friend. It is good to be in your presence. It has been too long since last we've spoken, but I fear I must be brief. I seek your council." In less than a heartbeat, Iel received a telepathic response.

"Your visit is welcomed as always, my Ilanyan friend," the

entity greeted. *"You are troubled ... this concerns of your world, does it not?"*

"As always, you are correct," Iel answered. *"The power of the abyss is being gathered for an incursion to my world, and I fear for the future."*

"Is that not why Takashaniel was created?"

"Yes, but the situation is complicated. A small army of the most powerful demons to walk the dark world is being gathered at this moment. I have felt it."

Iel felt surprise from his formless friend. *"Who or what on such an infantile world as Earth could have the ability to summon an army from the forsaken realm while Takashaniel stands?"*

"A Drek," Iel answered.

"A Drek inhabits your world?" the presence was calm, but incredulous. Several moments passed and Iel waited patiently. He knew the entity was seeking answers for him.

"You have more to battle than you can imagine, my Ilanyan friend. The union of a Drek and an army of Quentranzi is worrisome, yet you do have allies." Iel felt it smiling at him. *"Your unwitting allies will be enough. Alongside your resources, you can together repel the Drek."*

Iel wasn't so sure. *"They are powerful, for humans,"* he replied. *"I know they are the Children of the Gene, touched by the Daunyans, but they are too few against what will be a legion of demons. An army of five hundred thousand humans could not stand against ten Quentranzi."*

"You are correct, Iel, but they are unlike the rest of their species, as you will see when you meet them. Two of their number carry weapons capable of dealing enough damage to banish a demon back to their lightless world. Within Takashaniel, you can replicate this power and charge the weapons of the others who come with them. They will need you, my friend. You must trust in the abilities of these humans and stand beside them."

Iel tried to swallow his apprehension. *"I have no doubts of your knowledge, my friend, but how can a fragile human battle denizens from the dark plane?"*

"They are special warriors who have been given rare gifts," the entity answered. *"They know that they are different, somehow, but they have not grasped their true potential. Each of them has abilities that reach beyond their limited perceptions of themselves. Soon, however, one of them will discover more of her inner talents. With these warriors by your side, you have an incredible force to stand against the Drek and his army."*

Despite the entity's reassurance, Iel still had more questions. It spoke again, as if reading his thoughts.

"You must understand, Takashaniel is a magnificent creation and was erected for the purpose of balancing the negative and positive forces of your world. The Children of the Gene will come to you. Trust in them, for they have been entrusted by the Daunyans, though they do not know it."

Iel hoped the ancient being was right.

* * *

AFTER HIS MEETING with his ancient formless friend, Iel and Mira began preparations for the defense. Minor demons could be dealt with easily, but to fight the more powerful fiends, the Ilanyan turned to the magical creatures of the earth.

Spawned from wild magic, these beings were not subject to the same laws of nature as were physical beings, making them more durable and their defeat less ... final. Through his expressed wish to avoid harm to the wildlife of the fields surrounding the tower, he had been able to persuade these beings to come to his aid.

"What you have experienced so far," he said, addressing his student, "is nothing compared to what approaches. But you are ready."

"It truly has come to this," she said. "The tower that was

created to balance the world will be the center of the darkest battle the world has ever seen."

Iel put a comforting hand on her shoulder. "It is unfortunate but necessary. Where light exists, shadows are cast. Opposites are what make up the physical world."

As he spoke, Iel moved his sorrowful student to a transparent wall overlooking the forest. "It is how your kind learns and grows. Humans learn through personal physical experience. The Gods are always with us, and oblivion should be your last concern." He smiled and Mira noticed his color changing from its normal dark gray and black to marble gray, which signaled affection and love from her teacher, and closest friend.

"Worry not," he said. "There are others who have yet to assist."

Mira looked up at her teacher, her eyes shimmering with repressed tears. Iel felt, more than saw, the warm aura that surrounded the young woman. Even during her adolescent years, the girl had always had a strong affinity for nature and despised conflict.

"Never lose your love and passion, my student. It is the force behind your power."

"I will do my best," she responded.

"As always," Iel smiled.

23

S zhegaza watched Brit standing in the center of the dark room. He had been in meditation for half the day, standing still as a statue, preparing himself. The only light present pulsated from his glowing, red-purple eyes. Szhegaza, although notoriously eccentric and oftentimes impatient when it came to ritual of any kind, knew well not to make a sound in the Drek's presence. After an hour of waiting, the light in his eyes dimmed and Brit turned to regard her.

"Thank you for your patience, Szhegaza," he said.

"I would wait an eternity if that be the master's wish," Szhegaza replied.

A chuckle came in response. "Your loyal appearance is noted and appreciated for what it is, Zitarian." His naming of her devious race was not at all lost on Szhegaza. She stepped forward and presented Brit with a black orb, which he took from her and held in the palm of his hand. After a moment it began to hover.

"I encountered two interesting humans." As she spoke, the Drek eyed the orb as it began to show the details of Szhegaza's visit to the human town.

"Interesting," he said. "There is some unusual power about those two."

"I don't see any reason to be concerned about them," the Szhegaza remarked, waving a dismissive hand. "How would they know of your plans? They are only humans, after all. Could there be a more limited perception than that of a human? They are oblivious and totally powerless to stand against you alone, much less your new allies."

Brit never lifted his gaze from the orb as he responded. "Underestimation is a deadly adversary. The power I sense from those two is far greater than any homo sapiens I would expect to inhabit this world. It would surprise me if they were not involved in the defense for Takashaniel."

Szhegaza let slip a raspy-sounding guffaw. "In my travels I have heard nothing of a rising defense for the tower. You believe that there will be—"

"It is you who is oblivious, Szhegaza," Brit interrupted. "There is never a battle without a defense. If you believe that the most powerful structure on this world is completely oblivious of our mounting offensive then you are more fool than naive. These powerless humans that you speak of may have innumerable shortcomings, but they have survived through many ages."

Szhegaza lowered her eyes in response to the insulting but correct observation. Harsh words or not, Brit was right. Takashaniel was the most powerful structure in the world, and it was absurd to think that it would be unprepared to stand against an assault.

"Come." Brit opened a set of tall double doors. Zreal spun about as the two entered and immediately dipped into a bow, sparing a covert glare for his counterpart.

Brit glanced between the smirking Szhegaza and Zreal. "Put away your nonsense and come with us." The Drek led his two subordinates to yet another set of double doors.

Brit, Zreal and Szhegaza stepped out onto a semicircular balcony overlooking the largest horde of demons either of them had ever seen. Brit smirked as the shocked pair stared in disbelief, entranced at the sight of so many dark world denizens in one place outside of the abyss. Fiends of many different kinds flooded an area bordered by what Zreal guessed to be more powerful versions of the same seals Brit had used when first he'd summoned Kabriza.

"Master," Zreal ventured. "I have no doubts of your wisdom and power, but is it a good idea to align ourselves with such a vast number of unpredictable fiends as these?"

"I must admit my similar curiosity," Szhegaza added. "This is a large variety of fiends in one place and could prove difficult to control."

Brit eyed the two of them. "You need only fear me," he responded. "Be assured that I am prepared to deal with any … issues. The management of these 'guests' falls to one of their own wretched species." Zreal and Szhegaza looked at each other, still concerned.

At that, to the left of the nervous Zitarian, a black portal opened, and out stepped a mighty figure, fourteen feet tall with clawed hands hanging close to the ground. The horns protruding from its forehead hooked upward and ended in razor-sharp points.

As it emerged from the blackness, Szhegaza carefully backed away, staring in shock at the hideous thing. Her blade-like nails extended by pure reflex to the horror that towered over her. Although Zreal had seen it before, he felt no less intimidated by the frightening demon.

"You have done well in assembling the forces," Kabriza observed. "Perhaps it may be a bit more difficult to dispose of you than first I thought." The fiend managed what appeared to be a grin.

"You are amusing, Quentranzi," Brit said, his dark face a mask of calm. "One day we may see who is the stronger, but now is not the time for small-minded challenges." The red fire in the Quentranzi's eyes burned bright while Brit's entire body began to glow.

Zreal and Szhegaza slowly backed away from the face-off until they were out of the room.

"Zreal," Szhegaza whispered once they were alone. "I think we should put our differences aside, at least for now. If we are to survive this, we'll need to combine our efforts. I believe Brit would be able to defeat that thing, but we would be fools to think that he will extend his protection to us. I doubt Brit has given much thought to our lives outside of his plans. If we are to survive this alliance, we must work together."

Zreal considered her words. "You're right. We will put our survival above our differences. That mass of demons would rip us apart in the midst of battle no matter what side we are on. I would sooner add to their number of casualties than become one."

Szhegaza responded with a wicked smile.

* * *

KENJIRO STOOD at the edge of their campsite, enjoying the sunrise while Akemi finished packing the last of the breakfast supplies.

"Next time *you* cook," she complained. "I hate having to clean up everything while you get to enjoy the dawn."

"Have you forgotten who stood the first and longest watch while you slept most of the night?" Kenjiro smiled at her, and Akemi nearly fell over into the hot embers of the campfire. She hid her surprise and gave herself a silent pat on the back. It had been a good idea to rest in Toyotomi after all. The stern samurai seemed to be actually enjoying himself since their stop in the village.

"We should move on soon," he said, turning back toward the sunrise. "Our destination is not far from here and we can reach the city before dark."

The ninja woman nodded and secured the sack to one of the two horses they had bought. "I have a feeling that Kyokoza will be the place where many pieces to this puzzle will be filled in." Akemi looked moved beside him. "Wouldn't you agree?"

"I do. There is more at work here that we haven't discovered yet. I think there are more players in this game."

The ninja tied the last sack to her horse and mounted, turning toward the road while her brother did the same. "Then let's get back in the game and see when these players reveal themselves."

Kenjiro grunted. "The pawn never sees the player. We know little and less, yet are compelled by some unknown force. Warriors are rarely the players in the game of war." He looked at her. "Are we the pawns, or the players?"

Akemi shrugged. "At this point, it matters little. Aside from dispatching a few demons, we've seen no strings tying us to the fingers of any would be puppeteers."

Again, the samurai grunted. "Like the pawn, the puppet never sees the strings that move *his* body." Before Akemi could express her exasperation, he changed the subject. "What do you think of the strider?"

"Tough to say," she replied. "He seemed genuine, yet cryptic as to his intentions. But he's a strider. They're not known for being even as social as he was, let alone explaining anything to anyone."

"Striders. They have existed for as long as the samurai, yet I have never met one. I have a feeling we will see him again."

"Time will tell," Akemi yawned.

* * *

KITA TOOK the lead on the narrow trail across the ravine leading into a patch of forest.

"I've seen *this* before," Kenyatta called from behind. Kita shuddered at the thought of passing through another forest. Their narrow escape from death in the previous passage still fresh in their minds, neither man was eager to pass through any place that had more than a handful of trees. Their weapons were not yet charged with this demon-fighting enhancement that Taliah promised, which meant that the most they could do was slow the shadow creatures. Both prayed they did not encounter anything else unnatural before they reached Kyokoza.

Once inside the forest, they slowed their mounts and proceeded to a nearby stream. While the horses drank, the two warriors had a snack of cheese and bread.

"You feel that?" Kenyatta asked, swallowing his last bite. "Someone's nearby."

"You think so?" Kita replied.

"Don't you feel it? It's like that same feeling back in Nijika."

Kita rolled his eyes. "You mean *Toyotomi*." His voice dripped with sarcasm with the reminder of the two-named village, as they'd come to learn.

"Yeah, right," Kenyatta said, equally sarcastic. "It can be pretty confusing to folks not from around here when locals call it by two different names. Thought we were in da wrong place when first we got der."

"Nijika to the country folk, Toyotomi to the people who actually live there." Kita shook his head. "What the hell is all that about, anyway?"

"Forget it," Kenyatta said. "A pointless stumble along the way. Nothing more."

"And back to the other point," Kita said, "someone is following us for sure, but what I'm *not* sure of is whether or not they know they are following us." Kita pointed to the path they had just traveled. "This road hasn't been easy for horses to travel. If someone was pursuing us with purpose, they would have caught up to us a while ago."

Kenyatta stared back at the trail. "Good point. But I still won't feel any better about dis ting until we find out."

"Guess we'll find out when we do." They saw that the horses had finished their drink and were now lazily grazing next to each other. "Let's get moving." Kita said. "I've had my fill of forests."

* * *

MILES FROM HUMBLE TOYOTOMI, Kenjiro and Akemi came to a forest where they were forced to move at a slower pace, mindful of the shadow dwelling Kalistyi. On instinct, they dismounted and scanned the woods. The forest was eerily quiet and the horses began to whicker and shuffle nervously.

They took defensive stances with the horses between them. A dark figure dropped from the trees and landed in a crouch so low, its knees were side by side with its shoulders. Akemi moved around the horses to stand beside her brother. No one said a word, all waiting for the other to make the first move.

The figure slowly and deliberately straightened into an unorthodox stance, its right foot in front and facing the two warriors. Its left leg was positioned directly behind the right, with its foot also facing forward. From the shadows of the dense foliage, the two warriors could not see much of the stranger, but it seemed to be analyzing them.

"We are travelers passing through this place," Kenjiro began. "If you wish us to leave you need only step aside—"

Before the samurai could finish, the figure darted backward into the shadows and disappeared. An instant later, both warriors leapt in opposite directions just as a large disc with four long straight blades sliced into the ground where they had been standing.

Kenjiro and Akemi turned as soon as they landed, only to find that the weapon was gone, and there was no sign of the attacker.

A high-pitched sound cut through the air and Kenjiro ducked as the vicious weapon sliced through the space where his head had been only an instant earlier. The samurai rolled to the left and crossed his sword before him defensively. Again, there was nothing there.

Akemi had watched the attack, but it happened so fast she was barely able to follow. Her instincts screamed at her, and she rolled to her left just as the bladed disc sliced through the ground from

behind. As soon as her feet were under her, Akemi spun and
released a dozen shurikens in the direction the disc had come.

She couldn't believe her eyes when she saw every one of the
blades deeply embedded in the trees in the distance. The ninja did,
however, catch a glimpse of the strange chain-like cord that the
disc weapon was connected to. The cord bent into a wide arc and
pulled the disc into the air following the dark figure that glided
through the air to land between them.

This guy is good, Akemi thought. She could see by the look in
his eyes that Kenjiro was having similar thoughts. Anyone who
would intentionally land between them and put himself at a disadvantage was worthy of their respect. The dark fighter stood
between the two warriors, not facing either of them, but merely
standing in that strange stance as if waiting for them to make the
next move.

Now granted a closer look, Akemi could see that it was a male
barely above five feet in height. He wore nothing more than a
thick, tattered loincloth covered by old shredded strips of leather
hanging from his waist. His brown skin contrasted sharply with
shoulder length hair that was so black it looked blue. His small
frame was covered with lean, rod-like muscles.

This fighter had the frame of one who lived his life in the
jungles and used wit and skill to survive. Akemi was pulled from
her consideration of the man by a nod from the samurai, and both
warriors dashed in for the attack. To their surprise, the warrior did
not leap away from them as before, but held his position while
parrying and dodging every attack. They had never seen such technique before. This man, whoever he was, fought with unorthodox
but tremendous skill.

Kenjiro delivered a short vertical strike, which the dark fighter
avoided by leaning backward. Akemi smirked as she struck horizontally at his head. To her surprise, he ducked the attack with
impossible speed and agility. Both warriors hopped back and
watched him.

"I can think of a more friendly way to test your skill, strange one," Akemi remarked. The dark fighter slowly turned his head to face the ninja. His eyes could not be seen through the wild hair that hung over his face. "Now it is time for you to make a choice." She winked.

Kenjiro charged forward and Akemi leaped backward high into the air. While the samurai came in fast, the sky rained with shurikens. Kenjiro delivered a combination of horizontal and vertical strikes that the warrior avoided, rather than parried. With the storm of shurikens within a few feet of their mark, the wild fighter darted away to safety, and in the same instant, Kenjiro rolled backward, and the descending shurikens passed over him.

His escape was not complete, for one of the airborne blades had found its mark in his shoulder. The samurai ignored the pain as he parried every attack the incredibly fast fighter delivered. Kenjiro was in disbelief at the speed and strength of someone so small. After his first round with this thing—he wasn't entirely sure it was human—he knew he was in trouble. The samurai would have to find an opening to strike or retreat before his adversary overwhelmed him with speed.

Akemi, still gliding backward, grabbed hold of a branch and propelled herself back toward the fight. She launched another handful of shurikens to distract, just long enough for Kenjiro to gain some distance and recover.

The fighter leaped backward, all the while bending and twisting in every direction to avoid the barrage of shurikens. After dodging the last of the airborne missiles, the warrior froze, then ducked to avoid a horizontal strike at his head. He then spun to the side to avoid a vertical swipe that followed. With untiring agility and speed, the fighter leaped forward and launched his weapon at the two siblings, who dove to either side.

As soon as his feet touched the ground, the small warrior rolled to the side to avoid an overhead descending blow from the trees. Akemi and Kenjiro looked on in confusion as this unusual fighter now matched the fury of two new fighters, blow for blow. One of the warriors was almost the same complexion as the wild fighter, but larger, while the other was lighter in complexion but with a similar build.

It was an awesome display of skill as these two newcomers battled the wild fighter. With a nod to each other, Kenjiro and Akemi leaped into the fight in attempt to overwhelm their foe. Against all that seemed possible, this one fighter defended against all of them!

The two new warriors were clearly skilled, yet this wild fighter fended off every attack. The fighter with the spear-tipped staff stabbed forward, which the wild fighter spun around while ducking a cut at his head at the same time. The new dark fighter with the two swords slashed horizontal, then vertical with each weapon and struck only air. The wild fighter planted his feet and gripped the disc in his hands. His arms were a blur of motion as he blocked every sword or staff that came at him.

Just as the wild fighter seemed to be moving even faster, over-whelming them all, the new stranger with the two swords snarled and increased his own speed. For the span of a heartbeat, it looked as though he was gaining the upper hand, then the wild man ducked a cut aimed at his head and brought that bladed disc around for a diagonal slash downward, bringing the weapon back up for a horizontal spin, driving all four warriors back and stirring up dust and leaves. In the next instant he was gone.

Kenjiro, however, caught a glimpse of a few leaves falling from above and knew the fighter had retreated through the trees.

The four warriors instinctively leaped back and faced off. At first, no one spoke. Then the dark warrior spoke.

"We are not enemies."

"Who is to say?" Akemi asked, hiding her surprise that he spoke their language.

At that comment, all warriors straightened and, watching each other, put their weapons away.

"You are not Japanese, yet you speak perfectly," Akemi observed.

"When you spend some years in a place, you learn the language," the warrior responded in a friendly tone. He moved a few short locks of twisted hair from in front of his face and smiled.

24

A kemi examined the strangers while her brother took note of their surroundings as if expecting another attack.

"See something you like?" the darker of the two asked with a grin. The ninja cut him a sharp look, irritated with herself for heat that was rising in her cheeks at the comment.

"You fight well," the samurai remarked. "Where could two such as yourselves acquire such skill?"

"Many places," the lighter foreigner answered. "We have had the opportunity to travel to many countries throughout this ever-changing world and come away with a variety of skills."

Akemi eyed the man who spoke. "Why did you help us? We did not request help nor did we require any."

"I'm sure," came a facetious reply. "Under normal circumstances you may have turned on us for interfering in your fight, but you offered no resistance to our aid."

The ninja noticed the darker warrior take note of her brother, who visibly stiffened.

"The truth is," he continued, "we encountered that strange individual a while before you arrived and neither myself nor my friend here believe in coincidence."

"And what coincidence are you referring to?" Akemi asked.

Securing his spear behind his back, the foreigner pointed down the trail from which they all came.

"We could feel someone behind us and we're not having anyone at our backs that we don't know. Then our friend from the trees came and gave us the toughest fight we've have had in some time, possibly the toughest fight we've *ever* had." He smiled as he studied the two siblings. "I don't think you would disagree?"

"And now," the other interrupted, "maybe we could reverse the conversation, if you don't mind?"

Akemi cut the other man a sharp look. "We follow no one," she stated. "You happen to be traveling the same trail as us. We have no more business with you than you with us."

"I'm not sure of that," the man replied. She narrowed her eyes and he raised his hands, palms out and shrugged his shoulders. "Coincidence is a convenient excuse," he said, "but fortune is a better explanation. The web of life connects everyone in different ways, and I have a feeling that the strands that connect us are longer than a brief meeting after a fight with a mysterious opponent." He smiled, and Akemi found it to be a rather handsome smile. From the derisive sigh from her brother, her features must have betrayed her thoughts.

"My name is Kenyatta," the dark man with the twisted locks said. "And this is Kita," He indicated the man next to him. "As you have already figured, we're not from here. I am from the island of Jamaica and he, the Philippines." Without any further pleasantries, Kenyatta knelt and studied the trail. It was dry with only a hint of moisture making the ground a bit soft. At one time the road had been heavily traveled, but that was long ago. The wear was ages old it seemed, and there was no sign of any recent use by horse or cart.

"What takes you to the city of Kyokoza?" the samurai demanded, ever suspicious. Kita gave a sidelong glance at the road in the direction they had all been traveling.

"What makes you believe that is our destination? And even so, your companion here has already informed us that we have no business beyond this soon-to-be brief meeting."

A hint of a smirk showed on the samurai's face. "Your friend has taken an interest in the road that leads directly to Kyokoza."

"That is because he possesses some tracking skills," Kita answered just flatly.

The smirk deepened. "If that be the case, the world must be a much safer place with him around, for I know of children who could tell that this road has not been used in years."

Kita narrowed his eyes.

"It would be even safer," Kenyatta interrupted from a few paces away, "if these children could tell that this road was traveled last night, and by a score of unfamiliar creatures if these odd impressions in the ground are any indication. Something is wrong here, and I have a feeling the wrong will do as it always does." Kenyatta looked over his shoulder as he and Kita stated in unison, "Multiply."

Akemi's looked past Kita to the trail. She then looked over her shoulder at her brother and nodded. "He is right. At least a score of Kalistyi passed through here. Now that I am focusing on it, I can sense it." She frowned. "And there's something else that I cannot identify."

Kenyatta moved to join her, all apparent sarcasm aside. "What is strange is that the trail is moist, but only here." He glanced to the left and right of the dirt road. Nothing showed a hint of moisture. Plants were dry, not a blade of grass shimmered in the sun. "There has been no rain in this area, and the trail carries the stench of … wrongness."

Akemi met Kenyatta's gaze. "Ren," she breathed.

Kenyatta thought he detected a bit of glimmer in the woman's eyes at the discovery.

"If I may ask," Kita said while eyeing the ninja, "what are Kalistyi and Ren?"

"Kalistyi," Akemi answered, "are from the dark world. They are not as powerful as many other denizens of the abyss, but they can still be formidable. They have the ability to shift the shape of their arms—"

"Into long blades," Kita interrupted.

"And they look like walking shadows that regenerate as soon as they're injured," Kenyatta finished.

"So you have met them," Akemi said with a bit of surprise. She glanced at Kenjiro, but the samurai was busy studying the surroundings without much interest in their conversation.

"Yes, we have," Kita replied. "We were ambushed in a forest at the edge of Pusan Beach in Korea. We found out the hard way that these things can't be defeated by conventional weapons."

"And what about this *Ren* you spoke of?" Kenyatta asked.

"It's short for *Renkosheznieran*. Demon of the Red Fire." She grimaced at speaking its full name. "You are fortunate that you did not meet this fiend with the shadow demons. If you had any difficulty in dealing with them without the spirit charge," she noticed Kenjiro looking over at them with mild interest, "you would not have survived an encounter with a Ren."

"You called that thing 'Demon of the Red Fire,'" Kita said. "That word is not Japanese."

"It is an ancient language that deals with creatures from the different planes of existence. There are books, forgotten tomes that describe these monsters."

"Actually," Kenyatta said, latching on to their previous conversation, "this spirit charge that you spoke of is why we travel to Kyokoza."

"We are less than a day away," Kenjiro stated.

Kita looked at the samurai and then back to the ninja. "It would seem that we have a common destination, and enemies who wish us not to reach it. Although my friend and I do not possess the spirit charge you speak of, we can still aid each other in our journey." Kenjiro looked Kita squarely in the eyes while Akemi did the same with Kenyatta. They were trying to decide whether or not to trust them, and the two islanders politely endured the dissections. Finally, they relaxed.

"I am Akemi, ninja of the Azuma." She inclined her head politely.

"I am Kenjiro, ronin samurai." He stood erect with his hand on the hilt of his sword and bowed slightly at the waist. The two islanders glanced at each other before responding.

"Our service in this country has landed us a place among the Shikata clan," Kita said. "Although our services generally have been nomadic, we served the Shikata for a few years and thus were adopted."

The siblings glanced at each other. "Shikata," Akemi echoed. "The Shikata are a scattered band of vagabonds who take miscellaneous missions for the right price. Sellswords." She eyed them warily.

"Unfortunately," Kita replied, "the Shikata have acquired a partially inaccurate reputation." He motioned to the road. "We would happily tell you the story, but I think we should get to the road before those things find us."

"We should get moving," Kenyatta said. "We already know they're after us. No need to provide a sitting target."

The samurai raised an eyebrow. "What makes you think they are looking for all of us and not just the two of you?"

Kenyatta frowned at the ever-wary samurai. "When I discovered their trail, you didn't appear to be surprised. You can let go the suspicion, samurai. We're all being hunted and you know it. Our best bet is to work together."

Akemi gave Kenjiro a slap on the back. "They are right, brother."

With that, the four warriors mounted and set a hard pace for the grand city of Kyokoza. The trail in the woods was fairly smooth, with ruts on both sides from frequent use by carts in the past. Grass carpeted the trail now, and the group of travelers had to keep an eye on the road so as not to veer off course. Towering evergreen trees lined their passage, while scattered oaks embraced the heavens with bright, leafy limbs.

They rode close together at a fast canter, with Kenjiro in the lead. Kenyatta and Kita looked over their shoulders, then at each other. Whatever was hunting them was on their trail, and they would have a better chance of a strong defense if they could clear the foliage and fight on open ground.

Akemi looked back at them and offered a slanted smile. "Kalistyi prefer to fight where there is cover. Their existence almost solely depends on the shadows they inhabit."

"What about that Renkoshi ... Ren?" Kenyatta asked.

"The Ren was sent to lead the Kalistyi," came the response. "The presence of the red demon strengthens the weaker ones."

The samurai called over his shoulder, "We are close to the end of the forest." An unspoken need for silence passed between the group at that announcement. They lowered themselves in the saddle and rode on, the only sound being the thud of the horses' hooves upon the grass-covered ground.

Kita felt the tiny hairs on his neck stand on edge. He looked over at Kenyatta, who looked uneasy. Danger was near and everyone could feel it. The question was if they could reach open ground before the fiends were upon them. The forest was eerily quiet, even the trees seemed to be stiff in anxiety.

Kenjiro signaled Akemi to take the lead and then fell back with Kenyatta and Kita. "How well-trained are the horses you ride?"

"The best stock and most well-trained the stableman had to offer," Kita responded.

"Hope that they follow our horses out of the forest," the samurai stated. Kita and Kenyatta exchanged confused looks but nodded. Kenjiro sped up to catch his sister. Whatever they talked about, neither of the two friends could hear.

* * *

KENYATTA LOOKED AT KITA. "Dem right on us," he said in a low voice, using the western tongue. Kita nodded glancing over his shoulder from time to time. The horses, too, must have sensed the danger, for they increased their pace unbidden by their riders.

Akemi continued to scan the surroundings, wrapping her fingers around *Sekimaru's* hilt as her horse thundered up and down the snaking trail.

When she glanced back at them, Kenyatta saw the excitement in her eyes, as if they were glowing. He also noticed the samurai, who had moved one of his hands from the reins to the hilt of the sword. Kita was crouched low in the saddle, and Kenyatta realized that he himself had taken a similar position. The horses clearly sensed the danger and were now in a full run, and the riders let them have their heads.

Kenjiro's arms and legs tensed with his agitation, and the horse underneath him, sensing his tension, snorted and stretched its neck out, pounding down the trail.

The wind rushing across her face was invigorating, and Akemi's blood started to run hot as the demons neared. Her lips parted in a smile.

Kita stared at her. He barely had enough time to wonder at the crazed look on her face when they rounded a bend and the ninja shot straight out of her saddle like an arrow, and in that same instant a hand the size of Kita and his horse combined, burst from the ground, pulling up a tree in its massive grip.

The horses, including the one with no rider, sat down on their heels as they skidded to a stop. The terrified animals reared and whinnied, the whites of their eyes showing their terror as their riders struggled to bring them under control. Kenjiro and the two islanders abandoned their saddles and found refuge in the foliage.

The horses scattered as the ground lifted and broke apart. Hidden in the brush, Kita searched but couldn't see the others. He looked back to the road and could hardly believe what he saw.

The ground burst open to reveal an arm as wide as an oak tree, covered with white speckles and pulsating blue and green veins. A bulky shoulder rose from the hole, followed by a head that was half the size of Kita's body.

Its eyes were as black as night and the warrior could not tell if they were two big black orbs with no irises, or if they were just two empty sockets. It finally climbed out of the ground and rose to its full height, which looked to be halfway past a dozen feet. The veins in its body pulsated, and its chest heaved as its deep, ragged breaths fouled the air. Steam crept from its body, then they heard what sounded like a spark, and the monster's body lit aflame. Kita could feel the heat emitting from the towering fiend, and he wished they had exited the forest in time. Nearby trees and bushes began to whither. He was unsure if it was from the heat that the beast emitted, or the foul presence of the thing.

It made a growling sound, its tongue darted in and out of its mouth like a snake. Those pitch black eyes made it difficult for Kita to tell if it was looking at him or the others.

Was this just a minion? If this was a glimpse of what was to come, what would their true foe be like? He felt a sense of dread, yet excitement at the same time. Although the demon was unlike anything he had ever seen, something inside him quickened, and anxiety gave way to a spark inside.

* * *

FROM OVERHEAD, Kenyatta watched in disbelief as the fiend climbed out of the ground and burst into flame. *I guess all the talk about 'the devil's going to getcha' wasn't jyas to get me to be good when I was little,* he thought. Movement from above caught his attention and he saw what looked like two pieces of a shadow falling to the ground. Both pieces dissolved before they hit the ground.

Akemi descended from the sky toward the fiery demon, who stomped aside to avoid the stroke of the ninja's sword. With each footfall, the ground cracked and broke. The demon hunter landed in a crouch, studying the slow-moving demon.

"I'm guessin' the time for hiding has passed," Kenyatta said when he saw Kita leap onto a branch above Akemi's right side. He focused back on the ninja, who seemed unaffected by the stifling heat and evil that the demon emitted.

"You look as if you have done this before," Kita remarked from overhead. If the ninja had heard him, she gave no indication as she circled the demon and kept turning to face it.

Once the fiend's back was to him, Kenyatta started to attack, then ducked as a horizontal swipe that came from the shadow of the trunk of the tree next to him.

A shadow demon slid from the tree and swiped at him again. Cursing, Kenyatta dodged, then retreated to a branch not far from where the shadow now stood. His instincts saved him once again, and he dove from the branch as five more Kalistyi fell upon him from above.

He rolled to his feet, then dropped to one knee and deflected a one-two attack from yet another Kalistyi that leapt from a shadow in the ground. After parrying the strikes, he thrust his hips back and twisted around a stab at his midsection.

The shadow demon swiped high, then low, and Kenyatta ducked and jumped into a backward flip to avoid the lower sweep while simultaneously delivering a kick to the shadow's head. The kick did little more than buy him a couple seconds to recover before the demon was on him again.

The five other shadows were closing in, and he would be hard-pressed to survive the onslaught. From the corner of his eye, Kenyatta saw three shadows falling in half and dissipating.

Kenjiro appeared beside him and met the other two. With a surge of exhilaration, Kenyatta came at the remaining Kalistyi, but somehow it seemed to be stronger and faster than those he had fought before.

It swiped low with one sword arm, then stabbed with the other.

Kenyatta hopped to avoid the low strike and stopped the stab with a crisscross block of his blades, lowering the stabbing sword arm. He then ducked to avoid a horizontal swipe at his head, bringing one of his swords up to block another stab while simultaneously delivering a successful stab of his own to its midsection. It hesitated for an instant at the blow, and in that time Kenyatta stabbed it with the other blade, and then ripped to both sides, cutting the demon in half.

All of this happened in little more than a few seconds, but he wasn't finished. Before the severed body could land, he spun and struck horizontally, sweeping the head clean from its shoulders. Kenyatta stood and watched, chuckling mirthlessly as dark, smoky tendrils began reconnecting the body.

* * *

THE DEMON THREW its head back and let out an unearthly roar. Akemi charged, then darted to the side and attacked at an angle. Kita was about to spring forward, but he stopped. He needed to study the thing, yet he did not want to leave the ninja unaided.

Akemi came in close and brought forth *Sekimaru*. She could feel a hunger within the blade. The ninja swiped and slashed while the lumbering demon grabbed at her. Thin claws as long as sword slid from its fingers as it slapped and slashed its burning hands at her. Akemi ducked, then rolled to the side to avoid its pounding fist.

Seeing how it moved and the patterns it used, Kita finally joined the fight. He jumped from his perch, spinning the staff above his head, and brought it around. To his surprise, the demon actually avoided the attack. Only a moment ago it moved like a slow and lumbering thing. Now, the beast retreated and lunged, slashing at him whenever he missed an attack.

Even the demon-hunter had to take note of the sudden speed of it. She rushed in and the two warriors teamed on the flaming demon. Kita swiped horizontally at its midsection, and as it stepped back, Akemi glided over Kita's head and struck down, slicing into its arm. That drew a wail of pain and the demon exhaled a gust of hot wind that blew Kita into a tree and Akemi out of sight.

Kita came to his feet and shook away the haziness in his mind. The ninja was nowhere to be found and the fiery demon was stomping toward him. It drew its arm back, lining up its claws for a killing stroke.

Kita's first instinct was to bring his weapon up to block, but at the last second, he rolled aside instead. The demon's claw drove into the ground down to its shoulder, then ripped its arm out of the ground with little effort and slashed in Kita's direction.

He had already gotten to his feet and leaped into the air while once again spinning his staff above his head. The demon looked up just in time to see the blade of the staff driven between its eyes.

* * *

KENJIRO DUCKED and parried as the two remaining Kalistyi came on him in a team effort. The samurai was surprised with the improvement of the shadow demon's tactics. Only days ago they were hardly much of a challenge. What had changed?

One shadow leaped completely over his head and delivered a downward strike from above. The other shadow swiped horizontally with both sword arms at the same time as the overhead strike. A well-seasoned fighter would have fallen to such a well-coordinated attack. Kenjiro was more than a seasoned fighter.

The samurai parried the double swipe while spinning toward it to avoid the downward strike and putting his back to the demon. He whipped his hand out and sent two throwing knives spinning through the air and into the airborne Kalistyi's torso. He ducked to avoid yet another swipe as the shadow behind him hopped back and attacked.

Kenjiro spun away, avoiding the sword and the other falling shadow demon. It fell in front of the other, and before it could recover, Kenjiro stepped in and took its head with a clean swipe of his sword, turning with the motion and stabbing backward into the other Kalistyi's abdomen. He turned as he pulled the sword free, and brought it around in one motion to lop of the head of the remaining fiend.

With the shadowy bodies dissipating around him, the samurai turned his attention to the larger confrontation. A shower of sparks lit area, a howl rent the air, and Kenjiro broke into a run.

* * *

HAVING the misfortune of landing in the trees, Akemi was immediately set upon by a group of Kalistyi. A Kalistyi attempted a sweep of its sword at her neck, then stabbed low as she ducked. She spun sideways and down to avoid the sweep ending the motion on her back.

She kicked up and out, using the muscles in her stomach and thighs to flip back to her feet and simultaneously avoid three blades that stabbed the ground where her head and chest had been. As Akemi landed on her feet, she slashed upward, driving one of the demons back. In the same motion, she spun in a circle back to the ground while cutting outward, and severed the legs of one of the shadow fiends. As it fell sideways she brought *Sekimaru* around to finish it.

* * *

THE FIERY DEMON's head had snapped back from the force of the staff that Kita had driven into its head. Slowly it recovered and Kita could see its eyes focus on him from his position, hanging from the embedded weapon. It opened its mouth to reveal not teeth, but dancing flames within. Realizing the dangerous position he was in, Kita flipped himself onto the top of the shaft and leaped upward, barely escaping a thin stream of fire the monster spat at him.

As soon he landed back on the shaft his feet slipped, and he was barely able to grab hold of his weapon to avoid a high drop. Fortune was with him, for his descending body weight was enough to yank the weapon upward, slicing through the top of the demon's head. As he fell, Kita brought the staff back around and thrust backward with all his strength, driving the blade home into the monster's abdomen. He grunted through the pain as his arm snapped straight from the weight of his falling body.

The demon lurched, and Kita curled his body inward, then thrust his feet down, then repeated the motion, creating enough momentum to cut through its abdomen and dislodge the weapon again. This time he faced the monster, and once again drove the weapon home into its torso. Each stab should have dealt the creature grievous injury, but the staff had done no real damage.

From his previous encounters with the shadow demons, Kita suspected as much, and was able to land on the ground and retreat a safe distance without being burned to ash by the already recovered Ren.

KENYATTA SAW the fight from the corner of his eye, but had his own problems. Though this shadow demon was a lot stronger and quicker, it was still no match for him. It didn't matter, Kenyatta knew. He was not equipped with the proper weapon to deal with the demon and would eventually tire. He had severed its arms and legs several times, but it simply regenerated. Sooner or later it would get lucky.

After avoiding another swipe and coming around to sever the demon's head, the islander realized something. It took longer to reattach their heads than any other part of the body. He also noticed that the range and type of movement of their sword-arms was limited.

Kenyatta blocked two parries, knocking one sword-arm low. He then stepped on the weapon, causing the demon to bend over and expose its neck. Kenyatta shook his head, then delivered the stroke. Before the angry demon began to reattach itself, he hurried off to help his friend against the fiery monster.

* * *

KITA DODGED JUST in time to avoid the huge fiery fist that crashed through the ground where he'd been standing. It ripped its arm free and swung left, then right, knocking trees over and leaving a heat vapor in its wake. Kita knew that if he caught one blow from that flaming arm, the fight would be over.

The beast lurched forward, then tried to reach over its shoulder with both arms, not in pain, but in annoyance. As it spun this way and that, Kita saw his friend hanging from its back by one of his swords.

Kenyatta drove the second blade through its back and then used his feet to push away from it. He landed in a roll, cursing as he hopped and stamped his smoking feet.

Swallowing a snicker, Kita waited as the fiend turned toward his smoking friend, then stabbed it multiple times in the back and slipped his staff between its legs. It snarled and rounded on him, but as it did, its legs tangled in the staff and it crashed to the ground.

Kita slipped the staff free as the enraged demon climbed back to its feet and released a flare of heat energy that blasted both warriors away.

Smoking and lying on the ground, Kita waited for his sight to return, then groaned as he saw that yet again, the demon was standing over him, poised to strike. He rolled backward, ending in a crouching position, his staff in front of him. The demon reared back, opened its mouth and spat another stream of liquid fire that was as big around as Kita's body.

He lunged toward the demon, just beneath the fiery stream, and whipped his staff around. The blade severed part of its leg, and as it started to fall, it went into convulsions. From behind, Kenyatta slashed at its back with blinding speed, driving home blow after blow all the way to the ground.

Kita spun his staff vertically and leaped at the beast, slicing across its chest to its face. While in the air, he swung the staff down onto the top of its head with all his strength. As he started to fall, Kita brought the staff around in a two-handed vertical chop to the side of its face, using the force to propel himself away.

Kenyatta had severed one of its arms by then and continually hacked at the slithering appendages as they tried to reattach the limb. The demon tried to climb to its feet, but the lack of a complete right leg made its efforts clumsy. Still, it managed to swing its remaining arm at the troublesome warrior.

Kenyatta jumped above the arm, as Kita thrust his staff into the demon's face. At the same time Kenyatta spun in midair and brought both his swords down on its neck, severing its head.

They watched, chests heaving, as the fiery body regenerated itself right in front of them. They gripped their weapons firmly, slowly backing away from the thing and readying themselves. The large beast of fire rose once more while continuing to reform its lost limbs. Kita stood in front of it, trying to devise some strategy. Kenyatta stood at its back, waiting to see whether he or his friend should initiate the first move.

The whipping sound of a handful of shurikens caught Kenyatta's ear just before they found their mark in the demon's back. It stumbled forward, then spun a circle, grabbing at its back. That was the first time it appeared to be in any real pain as far as the two warriors could see.

From behind the islander, the samurai sprinted past the howling fiend and cut a deep slice across its thigh. Its roar shook the ground.

The ninja descended from above with *Sekimaru* in a two-handed grip. She sheathed the sword to the hilt in the top of its head, holding on with her hands, and her feet firmly pressed against both sides of the hilt. "Hurry!" she called to her brother.

The samurai was there, cutting deep gashes into its arms and midsection as it lunged at him, while also trying to grab at the ninja whose sword was feeding on its very essence. It dropped to one knee, and Kenjiro plunged his sword deep into the demon's chest.

There was a flash of red light, and the monster emitted even more heat, then howled in agony. It grabbed at the samurai's sword, only to have its hand seemingly stung by the power of the weapon. In moments, it was over, and the hellish creature was overcome by the power of the two swords. It began to dissipate into a red mist, and then to nothing.

Akemi stood for a minute, holding her sword in her right hand. She could feel power radiating from *Sekimaru*. Finally, the sword calmed and went still. The ninja replaced it in its scabbard as the others did the same.

Kenyatta waved a hand over the last of the dissipating carcass. "So was that the Ren-thing you've been talking about?"

* * *

IT WAS NOT FEAR that drove the warriors on, but the urgency. Their horses had run off during the fight with the Ren, and they needed to avoid any more delays on their way to Kyokoza. Obviously someone or something didn't want them to reach their destination.

"You fight well," Kenjiro remarked. "Your skills complement each other effectively."

"As do the two of you," Kita replied. He nodded at the path farther ahead. "Do you think the horses made it?"

"Ours did," Akemi answered, a bit smugly. "Yours may have if they followed ours."

"I have a question," Kenyatta said. "That thing scorched everything it touched but nothing burned."

The ninja looked at Kenyatta evenly. "The fire of a demon scorches and chars and burns, but it creates fire only where it wishes. The reason it didn't revel in burning the forest down was because it was more concerned with us."

"Nice," Kenyatta replied.

Once they reached the end of the forest, they stopped short and examined the surroundings from behind the tree line. The landscape was open and clear, with brown rolling hills with patches of green grass. They climbed one of the hills for a better view.

"The horses are there," Kenjiro pointed west of their position.

Kita was surprised. "It's as if they know where Kyokoza is and are taking the path in anticipation of us catching up to them."

"They are," Kenjiro replied. "The stable where we purchased our horses assured us that they have seen the road to Kyokoza many times and could find their way to the city without us. Your horses simply followed ours. Come, we will follow them and when the wind is right, they will catch our scent and wait." The samurai's words proved true, as the horses had indeed caught their scent and waited safely atop one of the hills, grazing in two pairs, head to back.

If horses could look relieved, Kita and Kenyatta's mounts looked just that. When the four companions reached the animals, Akemi's horse came straight to her and nuzzled her with its nose, to which the ninja responded with a gentle rub on the flat of the animal's forehead.

Once mounted, the four companions set out once again, only stopping to allow the horses to graze and drink. The hilly brown and green landscape seemed so peaceful on horseback, as they cantered along the winding trails between and over the smooth and rocky mounds of earth. They slowed the horses to a walk and

Akemi let her head fall back and closed her eyes, enjoying the gentle breeze that sighed across the fields.

"We should reach our goal before night," Kenjiro announced, pulling the ninja from her reverie. The samurai pointed to a high patch of hills in the distance that looked to be about another ten miles away. "Just beyond those hills is Kyokoza," he said.

"It's been some time since I've been there," Kenyatta said. "It'll be interesting to see what changes have taken place since my last visit."

Akemi glanced at him. "What brought you this deep into our land, Shikata?"

"A brief mission," Kenyatta answered, though he suspected she already had guessed at the answer before he spoke it. "The city is large as you know, and a guild of assassins had decided to make a base out of an area close to the main building where the governing body convened. It was suspected that they planned on eliminating the local government in order to establish themselves within this building. It was not a power move, but the structure was a prime location for any organization, and the local government was simply in the way."

"And why were you invited to take on this 'simple' mission?" Akemi inquired.

"The assassins knew of every form of protection the government employed," Kita answered, "and where they were located. No one from their organization could get within five blocks of the base without risk of being cut down. We, on the other hand, were foreigners. The last thing the assassins expected was 'imported' help. And they expected even less, that Shikata would have done so."

Akemi scrutinized the two friends before speaking again. "What was the name of the assassins?"

Kenyatta glanced at Kita before answering. "Kenzuro Clan," he answered. Akemi said no more, and returned her attention to the road ahead. Kita and Kenyatta glanced at each other and let the subject drop.

As they rode on, Akemi silently reflected on what she had learned. The Kenzuro clan was indeed a guild of assassins, but unlike any other. This guild had a specially trained elite faction called Shadow Dancers, who were undisputedly the most deadly assassins in Japan. No one would think of challenging them unless they were tired of living. Even those that lived outside the city and in the countryside knew of the Kenzuro and their Shadow Dancers.

Akemi knew them well. At one time the Shadow Dancers had tried to recruit her before she became a ninja. Refusal meant death, but she was one of the few to survive the invitation.

News had spread swiftly across the country of an unknown ally of the local government that had defeated the Kenzuro with remarkable efficiency. She had always wondered who could have been able to do this, and now the answer was riding next to her. She couldn't imagine how they had survived the wrath of the Shadow Dancers—who endured to this day—after the fall of the Kenzuro. Regardless of the answer, the fact that her new traveling companions were still alive to tell the tale was proof enough that they were formidable allies. Assuming these foreigners were telling the truth, she had a newfound respect for them.

25

The four travelers reached the lands just outside Kyokoza just as the sun began its descent toward the western horizon. Their journey had been uneventful since the attack in the woods, yet an uneasiness had taken hold of the group.

"What is it?" Akemi asked when Kenjiro pulled his horse to a stop at the base of a hill.

"Do you smell that?" he asked, staring in the direction of the sprawling city. "It smells like fire."

"Is that unusual?" Akemi frowned. "Yes, it does smell like fire, but...." She prodded her horse up the hill to get a better view.

The city below was littered with billowing smoke and dancing flames. Tall buildings had been knocked over or simply burned to the ground, while smaller structures were completely leveled.

"What's happened?" Kita asked, moving his mount beside hers.

"Fire," Akemi answered. "The city is scorched by unnatural fire." A sense of foreboding fell over the group as they looked at each other. "Whoever or whatever is trying to stop us knew that we were coming here."

The ninja dismounted and snatched a shuriken out of a pouch on her waist. "I had a feeling we were being watched, but I was unsure until now." She held the shuriken close to her face and closed her eyes.

Several heartbeats passed when she drew back and loosed the shuriken high into the air.

"Did I miss something?" Kita asked, watching the tiny weapon's ascent.

"That," the ninja answered, pointing. A screech rent the air as the shuriken imbedded itself in an unseen object above. A winged blue creature suddenly appeared in the sky, fluttering as it struggled to maintain control. "Bachattta," she spat.

"So we've been spied on," Kita said watching the wounded creature.

"Had we guessed this sooner, the city might have been spared," the samurai said.

"You can't know everything," Kenyatta replied.

Akemi readied another shuriken while the Bachattta flopped toward the ground, then let fly, hitting the creature again.

"They can bend light around their bodies to appear invisible," she said, "but only for a short time. That one probably flew higher into the sky when not invisible, so we didn't notice it." She watched as black tendrils of the demon's essence leaked from its body until it hit the ground and broke apart. She turned away as the creature dissipated back to the abyss.

"They may not be very tough compared to some of the stronger demons, but that one trait makes them useful. I should have known that was the reason the Ren and Kalistyi knew exactly where to find us!" They turned back to look at the smoldering city.

"A whole city," Kenyatta said lamented. "Destroyed to stop the four of us."

"There may be some people alive down there," Kita said.

"This will sound heartless," Akemi replied, "but we have not the time. We need to find cover somewhere long enough to think about what we do now."

Kita didn't like it, but Akemi's words were true. "Fine," he said. "Let's just go, then. I'll feel better away from here."

Kenyatta sighed. "We'd better get moving now. With things like that on our trail," he pointed at what was left of the dissolving Bachattta, "we don't want to endanger anyone else nearby."

Kita waved a hand toward the broken city. "What's left to endanger? Everything is destroyed!"

"He's right," Kenjiro said. "If there are any survivors, we would give them a better chance if we leave. We will figure out a course of action once we've put some distance between us and Kyokoza."

And so they left, each of the four warriors gazing one last time upon the ruined city as they turned their mounts west.

* * *

THE SCRYING mirror showed only black smoke now as the Bachattta dissipated into nothing. Brit stood for a while, absorbing the last images he saw of the four humans. They had been brought together by forces more direct than just fate alone. Szhegaza was right in her suspicions about them. *Kalistyi are one thing, but no human should be able to bring a Ren down, not even twenty humans.* He had never seen a one of the fragile creatures move that fast. The female seemed unusually adept at battling dark world creatures and this made the Drek even more curious. These humans had definitely earned his attention.

"Should I have another Bachattta sent to retrieve their trail, master?" Zreal asked from behind. Brit never turned to face him.

"No. They would be aware if we sent another. We must stop them now, before they reach the tower, although I am unsure if they even know what they're looking for. I believe that many of the answers they sought were in that city, but there is no way to know exactly what."

"Perhaps we could completely level the city and any chance of them finding whatever it is they seek there," Zreal suggested.

"No," Brit answered again. "I doubt they will enter, not now that they realize the possibility that they could bring danger inside its walls. If they were able to discover their invisible pursuer, then they are aware that someone is against them. They will move on, and there is no need in wasting valuable resources. I'm sure they know that something is happening, but I don't think they have figured out what. What does concern me is that the female is somehow able to sense demonic energy. The presence of these unique humans is not coincidence. I am sure they are involved in the defense of Takashaniel, even if they do not yet realize it."

"They do not know or they would have made straight for the tower," Zreal offered."

"Yes, that's true," Brit responded. "Unless they do not know where it is."

Now he did turn to face Zreal. "Inform Kabriza that there will be a change. I wish for the Kalistyi to observe these warriors instead of ambushing them. I believe that further ambush would result only in further diminished numbers. I don't think there are enough of them in this world yet to defeat these four, and I don't want to waste time or resources. What I do want, however, is to know where they are going and what their plans are."

A worried look crossed Zreal's green, ridged face. "It will be done as you order, Master." He gave a deep bow and turned to exit.

"Do not worry, my friend," Brit said at length. "Kabriza will not bother you, not now anyway, for I have wards that protect those that I favor. Do keep in mind, however, that the wards I have set over you and Szhegaza will only hold within the walls of this fortress."

"I understand and thank you my lord." Zreal turned and left. *This is quite unusual,* he thought. *Why send humans, no matter how capable they are? No human could be powerful enough to survive what is coming.* Though he truly believed that last thought, it brought him little comfort. Brit was not one to underestimate anyone or anything, and he knew that there was more to these mysterious warriors than flashy sword techniques and speed. There was something more about them, but in order to eliminate this new annoyance, he would have to discover exactly what these humans were capable of.

26

K ita pointed across the grasslands toward a copse not far off. "I think we should stop there and collect our thoughts."

"Yes, we should," Kenjiro agreed. Once they'd dismounted and picketed their horses—who immediately commenced to grazing—the four warriors sat in a circle, each buried in their own thoughts.

"I don't think we should leave just yet," Kita said. "I can't speak for you two, but our main purpose for even coming to Japan was to reach Kyokoza."

Kenjiro looked back toward the billowing black smoke in the distance. "We also had very important business there."

"We've been blinded," Akemi said. "We know not where to go or what we are doing. I think perhaps we should double back and take the risk of seeing if there are any survivors in the city."

"And with us," Kenjiro added, "we bring the possibility of attack to any survivors who remain."

Akemi frowned. "What choice do we have?"

"There is always a choice," said a disembodied voice.

The warriors spun into back-to-back positions—all except Kenyatta, who smiled—with their hands over the hilts of their weapons. Not far from the group, the air began to shift, as though bubbling. The space warped and swayed, and out of the seemingly liquid air stepped a feminine figure that practically glided from the light. Recognizing the figure at once, Kita relaxed and straightened, trying not to look surprised next to Kenyatta. Seeing the other two at ease, Akemi and Kenjiro relaxed, but only a bit.

"Nice of ya to catch up with us after all dis time," Kenyatta said. "Me wondering when ya come see us again."

Kita snickered to himself at the confused looks on Akemi's and Kenjiro's faces. Understanding the western tongue as a second language was a task alone, but understanding Kenyatta's version of it was another matter.

The wind blew through the copse, rustling leaves and swaying tree branches from side to side. Taliah slid a few strands of hair from her face and smiled. "Me watchin' the both of you for some time now and I admit I'm impressed."

Akemi and Kenjiro looked even more confused. The way her accent came and went made comprehension nearly impossible. It was like hearing information in pieces.

Kenyatta huffed, a smile slanting across his face. He walked up to his younger sister and they shared a long hug, followed by Kita, who seemed to enjoy the hug more than a bit, the ninja noticed with amusement.

Kenyatta stood to the side and motioned to their two new companions, who were still trying their best to decipher the thick accent of Kenyatta and the lighter one of his sister. Kita was the only one who seemed to be fully understandable. Kenjiro glanced at his sister. *Perhaps our way of speaking the western tongue might be just as strange to them,* he mused.

"Taliah," Kenyatta introduced with an open hand in the direction of the samurai. "Our new traveling companions—"

Taliah walked over to them before Kenyatta could finish, and offered a slight bow at the waist. "Samurai Miyamoto Kenjiro and

Ninja Demon Hunter Miyamoto Akemi," she greeted. "It is a pleasure and an honor to meet you. Your reputations precede you." She smiled. "I am Taliah, Kenyatta's sister." She looked over her shoulder at her brother. "I am sure he has told you all about me." Kenyatta shifted uneasily, suddenly taking interest in an imaginary trail in the grass. She smiled as she noticed the strained look of the two siblings, both of whom were struggling to understand her words. She shifted to the native language of the land.

"Perhaps now you can understand me better, as my accent is much less present in your dialect. Our grandfather and aunt made certain we were well versed in as many languages as possible, and your tongue was one choice to learn." The siblings visibly relaxed.

"How do you know who we are?" the samurai asked. Taliah held back her amusement at the huskiness in his voice.

Akemi noticed too, but she was less hesitant to laugh at her brother. This Taliah was quite a rare and exotic sight for the samurai, who made a great show at not noticing her fine qualities.

"Partly through hearing of your exploits and partly through watching you up till now," Taliah answered. "There is someone who knows quite a bit about you. All of you." Her smile deepened at the expected puzzled expressions, and a glimmer of light flickered across her eyes. A few heartbeats later, the air began to bubble again, and another figure stepped out. Akemi's mouth fell open but no sound came.

Although he showed no outward surprise, Kenjiro was also taken aback by the emergence of their teacher. He smiled as he dipped into a humble bow. "Sensei Akutagawa. We are relieved that you are well."

All four of his former students quickly moved in front of the man and dipped into respectful bows.

"Sensei," Kita said. "We are relieved by your survival of the attack on Kyokoza. We came as quickly as we could …."

Sensei Akutagawa held up a hand with a gentle smile. "Say no more, Kita-san. I know you've all come as quickly as you could, and I am fine." He looked his four students over with fatherly pride. "I am glad you have found each other." The four looked at each other and then to Akutagawa.

The subtle creases at the corners of his eyes deepened as he smiled at the questioning looks. "You should know by now that coincidence is not an answer for happenings such as these. I am sure that you discovered that you were traveling to the same place for important business, yet you were unable to see that you all have a common goal against a common foe."

"Yes, my young students. You began your training with me when you were but children, and now have returned to me together, for you are my most capable students."

"Why did you not tell us that there were others like us?" Kenyatta asked.

Sensei turned his smile on the islander. "Does the tree tell every robin of others who have roosted on its branches? What reason would I have had at that time? Each of you possess different talents that you will discover in time. All I have done is guide you in your beginning years and keep you from destroying yourselves or anyone close to you. You now have the control and the will, which had marked the end of my duty years ago. I can see within each of you, experience and strength that I always knew you would attain."

"Sensei," Kenyatta asked. "Do you know what's going on and why we've come here?"

"So," Sensei replied, feigning hurt. "You did not come to see how your old teacher was doing after all these years? Always coming back for answers to difficult questions?" Kenyatta shifted uneasily, stuttering an apology. Sensei winked at Taliah and continued, wrapping an arm around his embarrassed student.

"Do not apologize, *Kenyattasan*. Even your old teacher can have a sense of humor." He looked at the others. "You have felt strange energies about the world lately and that is why you are here." He turned his gaze to the dark black smoke rising from the city in the distance. "Before I tell you of what is happening now, you must know how the world came to be the way it is, and how each of you fit into this puzzle."

Dusk had arrived, and the sky took on the familiar fiery orange hue. The wind whispered through the trees as if sharing secrets that only they knew. Squirrels and other small inhabitants combed the ground in search of nuts to store up for the night and the winter yet to come, while birds made their final flight to run chores before the dark arrived.

Kita started a campfire for the night, while the others prepared the provisions. They would have a filling meal this night, as Taliah had brought plenty of food from wherever she'd arrived. The horses were fed and watered and now stood at rest, back to front, heads hanging low as they napped.

Sensei Akutagawa and his students sat around the campfire talking and laughing and remembering old times they shared with their teacher. Taliah circled the campsite, creating wards against any type of unnatural creature that might find them, and setting alarms that would warn them of any impending danger.

Once finished, she came to sit with the others. Akutagawa took a sip of hot green tea and sat staring at the fire, looking into another place.

"Several hundred years ago, the world experienced a drastic change, and has been changing ever since." Everyone listened quietly as the master spoke, like children hearing a campfire story. "As the histories have taught you, the Age of Technology was a fast-moving time in human civilization, and corruption had become commonplace."

He took another sip of tea and sat the mug on the ground, still staring into the fire. "There were many wars of many different types. People fought each other for a multitude of reasons, and solutions were not forthcoming. Masses of people died for religion, cultural differences, in appearance, economic power, and most of all, money." Sensei seemed to have spat the latter of the reasons. "The value of life seemed to be constantly diminishing. The pursuit of wealth had overshadowed value of life and respect of the ideals of those long gone." None of the students really knew how old Sensei Akutagawa was, but it was rumored that his lifestyle and meditations had not only blessed him with a long life, but a youthful body as well. Perhaps this was why he seemed to know so much about the Age of Technology while he looked no older than his mid-forties.

"Many died because of the disagreements of a few," Sensei continued. "Technology was a wonderful thing until it had been taken too far. Cures for diseases were found and used, but for a price. There were even machines created that could graft new skin to diseased or burned areas of the body, but for a price. Even lost limbs could be recreated and reattached. Technology had brought many wonders, but with them, high prices."

Akutagawa looked over his students. "It is as I have always said, my students. Positive and negative cannot exist without one another in this world. When there is light, dark is not long behind."

"Some few countries enjoyed many luxuries, but many other countries, some of which produced these luxuries, starved and suffered. The imbalance of the world was beyond what any of you can begin to understand."

He leaned his head back and looked to the sky, closing his eyes, then opening them to stare at the dark, starry sky. "All times must end, and so they did. Only half of what I know is from memory. To my great fortune, my family had a library of books and a passion for boring their children with stories and advice about the world." The master let out a self-deprecating chuckle.

"History has recorded that in one sudden, cataclysmic moment, technology died, and with that, everything not created by nature. Cars no longer ran because gas and oil could no longer be created or harnessed. Machines no longer created each other. Every luxury that people took for granted was gone, and no one knew why." He took another sip of his tea.

"Because of the times," Taliah said, picking up the story, "people believed that God had decided that humans were incapable of using their advanced tools responsibly."

"God?" Kita looked at her questioningly.

Taliah made an impatient sound. "Did either of you study anything as children? Oh, you're still children. Never mind. Sometime before, and during the Age of Technology—"

Kenyatta snarled at his sister's tone, which suggested she was speaking to someone slow-witted.

"Most of the population of the world believed there was only one God. Wars were fought over beliefs such as these. The knowledge of multiple Gods is an ancient belief that has come around once more."

She addressed the group again. "All knowledge of the creation of technology had seemingly been stripped away from humanity at large. There were even people who spoke of still possessing the knowledge of recreating some of the inventions of the past, but feeling as though the knowledge was just outside of their mind's reach."

"How do you know this?" Kenyatta said, looking at his sister as if he had just met her for the first time.

"That is for another time, Kenyatta. Suffice it to say that I have access to the recordings of all knowledge, in the non-physical dimension."

She laughed at Kenyatta's glassy-eyed look. "According to these records, it is believed by people from every part of the world that the Gods sought to simplify the lives of humans before they could destroy themselves and the world they inhabited, along with all other life that shared this world...."

Kita frowned. "I agree with what you're saying, but what about the benefits? Many vaccines and medicines were made using technology. My granddad used to say that people who were born handi-

capped, or invalid, were able to move about easier with the help of
machines and motor-powered chairs. Families could even talk to
each other over great distances with clever ear devices."

Taliah nodded patiently. "Many did suffer and die as a result of
the lack of advanced technological medicine. But there were long
term effects. You are all examples of the long-term advantages of
this drastic change. You have impeccable health, because the air in
our cities is pure. You have less chemical imbalances in your
bodies because your food was grown naturally. You never went
hungry because all you needed was to raise your food on your own
land without fear of toxins in your water."

She looked at the ground in front of her. "That is not to say that
the change didn't come without new and different problems, or
new manifestations of old problems.

"People from lands that had been living without the luxuries of
technology went on conquests against the stricken lands after the
End of Technology, feeling that they had been chosen by the one
God." She shook her head. "Always has humanity been slow to
learn. Unfortunately for some of these self-righteous peoples,
punishment by the Gods was not the case, and many nations had to
learn a costly lesson.

"There are numerous books about this time of upheaval that is
referred to as the Neo Feudal Times. When technological warfare
was no more, the sword was raised once more to replace the gun.
The martial warriors of old arose once more and these warriors
took their place back at the front lines of their nations, defending
their people and using the skills passed to them through the blood-
lines and teachings of warriors long past.

"In many societies, honor annihilated greed, and nations
reestablished themselves with a higher degree of tolerance and
unity that was unheard of in times past. Illnesses and diseases were
overcome by old medicine, and people began to realign themselves
with the natural order of the world. The ancient sages were no
longer thought of as wandering, mumbling frauds, but instead were

more widely sought for their wisdom and aesthetics. During these times of upheaval, the true frauds sprouted from everywhere, but were also more easily discovered by people who had been manipulated time and again, and were forced to finally listen from within themselves, to find truth.

"For uncountable years, nature has been waiting for humanity to return to it, and with a greater return to a value for life, the majority of humanity had begun to shift in thinking and action, moving toward better lives." Taliah turned to Sensei Akutagawa, who now continued.

"As humans became healthier once again, so too did the world around them. People found that they became sick much less because they did not sit in place to allow disease to find them as easily. That is not to say that sickness disappeared, but it is much less common than before, as people had evolved to be stronger even before the change.

"People found that different types of edible and medically beneficial vegetation arose and become plentiful, though these plants had always been there. Technological remedies were replaced by more effective natural ones. It was as if the world itself had breathed a sigh of thanks for the release of the bondage that humankind had held upon it."

"But as it has proven throughout the ages," Taliah continued again, "humans would resort to other methods to achieve their conquests. There is always a flicker of evil in every society." Kenyatta noticed a glimmer of disappointment in his sister's eyes.

"Humans recovered long lost knowledge, including the ability to summon denizens of the dark world, as well as the use of magic for ill purposes. Because of humanity's continued disbelief in the existence of magic, practitioners good and evil reappeared in the world virtually unnoticed, and the use of magical weapons arose unchecked. The dark realm watched with delight, knowing that humans still didn't completely understand the different types of magic and their sources. It was only a matter of time and patience before denizens of the dark realms would roam this world in greater numbers than ever before."

Now was her turn to look to the stars. She ran her fingers through her shimmering black hair. Sensei Akutagawa fixed them with his gaze. "Only one of you knows what you are," he said. "And the rest of you must learn."

27

T he camp sat in silence for a time, sipping tea and digesting the information. Sensei Akutagawa looked over the group thoughtfully, then spoke to Kenyatta's sister. "You are the only one who understands who you are, and soon, I believe you will discover that you are capable of far more than you believe now." He looked over the other four. Sensei could see the question in all of their faces.

"Each of you are unique. You were born faster, and stronger, and your vision and hearing reaches beyond that of others. You are more in tune with the world in nearly every way. Unfortunately, my knowledge of why this is so extends only as far as this young lady has taught me." He smiled at Taliah, who spoke again.

"I, as well as the four of you, have been born with a special gene that was indirectly given to us by the Daunyans, the Gods. Being all-knowing and possessing all wisdom, they knew that when technology was no more, humans would resort to other methods to achieve their goals, good or ill. Technology was gone, and with it, all knowledge associated with its creation and exploitation. Human beings began to turn to nature in every form. The practice of magic reemerged, and with it, the use and creation of powerful spells and potions, some for good, some for evil."

Taliah settled her attention on her brother. "A special gene was implanted within a number of people around the world. What that number is, I don't know. This gene had no effect on the people who carried it. However, this person would pass the gene on to their children, whereupon it would become active. I'm sure all of you remember being the fastest kid in your village, or the highest jumper, and you learned things faster. We *all* did.

"It is believed that the Daunyans blessed us with this gene and with it, the burden and honor of being the highest level of human protection the world has ever known."

Taliah swept her gaze across the four warriors. "It is you who have broken apart dangerous organizations. You are the ones who protected the remaining pieces of government that were not corrupt." That last statement brought a skeptical grumble from the group, and Sensei chuckled. A half smile crossed Taliah's face and she continued. "Battles of the sword were waged once more for the protection or destruction of civilizations." She swept her arm over the group, indicating three of them, minus the ninja. "You were at the front of those lines of defense, and with your courage, battles were won."

She then looked to Akemi and smiled deeply, a smile of pride from woman to woman, sister warrior to sister warrior. "I do not make light of any of the accomplishments of the others, but it is you and others like you, who have done the greatest deeds in protecting our world. Although most people live their lives oblivious of the darker perils of the world, it has not gone unnoticed that you are the most skilled demon hunter in the history of the world.

"It is you who have hunted and destroyed some of the most elusive and powerful fiends to ever taint the ground they walk upon, an undesirable yet admirable job. Your knowledge and skill will lead this group to the Drek named Brit and his powerful ally, the Quentranzi general Kabriza." Akemi winced at the mention of the powerful fiend. She had heard that name before and had no desire to come face to face with it.

"*Kabriza,*" she breathed. "If ever there was a day that I wish would never come, that would be the day."

Kenjiro's face was a mask of calm, but a flicker of shock lit in his eyes. Never had Akemi hesitated or avoided a fight, human or demon. "You know of this thing?" he asked.

"Yes," she murmured. "It is one of the most powerful demons among the most powerful race of demons of the dark realm."

She looked at her brother with the closest thing to fear in her eyes that he had ever seen. "That thing is capable of more than you can imagine."

"And so are you," Taliah answered. "All of you. You still have not discovered your true power and you still have not reached your physical potential."

Kenyatta's eyes glazed over as he looked into a place far from where they all sat. "There are others like us," he said. Taliah raised an eyebrow at him.

"That's what I said. Are you thinking of someone in particular, brother?"

Kenyatta cut her a sharp look, not answering the question. He knew that one of his sister's many abilities was to see things, no matter his distance from her. She was obviously referring to someone that he felt close to, someone he had recently met. Judging from the smirk on his best friend's face, Kita shared her suspicion.

"You will find that your friend is unique in more ways than you think," came Taliah's cryptic reply.

Kenyatta made a rolling motion with his hand, bobbing his head impatiently. Kita choked back laughter.

Seeing that her brother wished to be removed from the spotlight, Taliah continued. "There is a tower made of light energy, and its creation is beyond the scope of your imaginations, though few humans know of its existence. Every animal in the world is intuitively linked to it, however. Since the majority of humans have not evolved enough to fully appreciate the tower without attempting to exploit it, they remain oblivious to its presence. Animals, on the other hand, are innocent in the ways of conquest and corruption. They do what they must to survive and nothing more than that. It is this simplicity and innocence of life that allows them to retain their intuition given them at birth, the same intuition that humans lose after a short number of years, and must re-learn later in life."

Taking control of her surfacing disappointment at that last fact, she continued. "The tower is the strongest structure on this world and was created by humans infused with the knowledge of the Daunyans to build it."

Akemi straightened. "I know this place. I had a dream of a tower that pulsated bright, colorful light energy. I thought it nothing more than a dream, but the vision of that place gave me a sense of peace that I'd never thought possible. I had the dream more than once and every time, I felt refreshed and more alive once I awoke."

Taliah passed a knowing smile on her. "That is because of your profession, demon hunter. No one can fight demons as you do without it taking a toll. Your dreams were anything but. While you slept, your non-physical essence, your true self, separated from your body and visited the tower to replenish and purify. You were allowed by the Daunyans to visit the tower because of the necessity of your work and the effects it has on you.

"The tower was created to balance the positive and negative energies of the world," Taliah continued. "Good and evil are kept in balance opposite each other, and humans continue to grow and evolve as a species. In our current stage of development, we still learn our best lessons through negative experiences. It is the physical experience of life on this world that humans learn their greatest lessons."

The group sat in silence, digesting the information. Kenyatta was stunned at his younger sister's wisdom. He decided to talk to her at length about it later, but for now he listened.

"The Drek and his Quentranzi ally seek to destroy the Tower of Balance, and thus the barrier between the abyss and this world. By his very nature, the Drek siphons energy from the land around him. While Takashaniel exists, he cannot drain enough energy from the earth to become powerful enough to deal with humanity at large. If he tried, his power would be nullified once he reached a certain pinnacle of strength."

Her features darkened and she gazed into the campfire, looking into a very dark place. "Ka …," she hesitated, not wanting to speak the demon general's name. "The Quentranzi wishes to destroy the tower so that more of its kind can roam this world freely. Brit has found an ally of like mind. At least for now."

Kenyatta ran his hands across his face. "So where do we go from here? Do we go to this tower and wait, or do we try to find the Drek and stop him first?"

Taliah bit her bottom lip. "Even now they march. Somehow, they have found a way to weaken the tower's defense just enough for them to bring in more of their kind. The Drek is powerful and has been able to manipulate the tower's own defensive power to his advantage. How he has done this I am unsure, but I suspect that instead of attempting to nullify the energies of Takashaniel, he bent the energies for a very short time and then pulled a score of fiends here, to this world. He would have to have done it quickly."

She took a sip of tea. "I suspect even Iel was unable to stop it by himself."

"Iel?" Kita asked.

"The guardian," Sensei answered. "He is of a peaceful race called Ilanyans, who remain apart from others of this world, and this kind being has served the tower at the behest of the Gods."

Taliah cradled her mug in her hands. "The Drek is smart and has planned carefully."

"He definitely knows of our existence," Kenjiro stated. "We

believe it was he who sent minor demons after us on a few
occasions."

"You call that last fiery thing we fought minor?" Kita asked.

Taliah nodded and looked at Akemi. "It is good that you
destroyed the Bachattta before you made any other move.
Although it served as his eyes, Brit could also hear your talks and
plans through the creature."

Kenyatta finished his tea and addressed his sister. "What do we
do now, and what part do you play in all this?"

"I have a rather indirect role," she answered solemnly. "It is
you who will stop them. If I were to interfere, then you would not
gain the experience necessary to prepare you for what lies ahead.
That is why I had not charged your weapons, or did you forget?
Your speedy trip through the forest was partly my help, for I aided
your horses' steps with speed and endurance. It took some time for
the Ren and the Kalistyi to find you and when they did, you were
already at the edge of the forest." Kita could see the pain in her
eyes. She opened her mouth several times, but managed no words.
Sensei Akutagawa moved closer and wrapped an arm around her.

"I do not make light of your mission, my students, but the
hardest task is to watch over a loved one," he looked down at the
young woman, her head down as she wiped tears from her cheeks.
"Or in this case, to watch two people that you care deeply about,
and not help in any way, regardless of how grim or impossible the
situation may seem."

Akutagawa's smile was filled with love. "She could not interfere because you needed to make it on your own. If you had died
on your trek, it would have been a more desirable death than one at
the hands of Brit or the Quentranzi." He patted her on the shoulder
and offered her a sip of tea, which she brought to trembling lips.
Kenyatta could see the misplaced guilt in her downcast eyes.

"There is no amount of training I could have given you to
prepare you for this," Sensei continued. "The only way was by
coming here on your own without any help, and you did a magnifi-

cent job. I could not be prouder. Now," he gave Taliah's shoulder one last squeeze and stood. "Come with me. I have something for each of you, now that you're ready."

Everyone stood and followed Sensei away from the campsite. Kita bent and gave Taliah a hug, then continued on. Kenyatta stopped and knelt beside her. "You getting all mushy on me, ya?" he whispered. She looked up at him and hiccoughed a laugh, shoulders bouncing. Kenyatta's lips wrinkled at the sound, and they both broke into quiet laughter and hugged each other, rocking side to side. "How come you always know everyting? You always make me proud, Taliah."

She looked at him and for a moment, and he saw a glimmer of that baby sister who had depended on him for so long when they were kids, before she left home.

She shoved him away. "It's because girls are smarter. Get over there, you fallin' behind, as usual."

Kenyatta smiled and jumped to his feet, racing off to catch up to the others. Sensei had already started Kenjiro and Akemi on a new technique for each of them, and was now walking toward his best friend. Kenyatta had just trotted up beside Kita when the master reached them.

"You two must know how difficult this was for Taliah. I had expected her to come to me before your arrival, but she came much earlier." He looked at Kenyatta with sympathetic eyes. "She needed me to keep her strong enough to not help you. When the two of you were ambushed in that forest on the coast of Korea, it looked very bad. We were unsure that you would survive." He stared at Kenyatta and shook his head slowly. "When you fell back into the forest alone, she nearly intervened to save you and I had to stop her.

"It was because of that incident that you both discovered more of your abilities. She wept even after you made it out safely, constantly questioning the wisdom of her stance in all of this." He looked at the woman, staring into the campfire. "She began to question herself as a good sister and a good friend, and I had to stop her from that, too. We need all the strength we can hold for each other. Come, I need to teach you a few techniques now."

Bathed within the light of the campfire, they practiced the new techniques that Sensei taught them well into the night before having a bit more tea and then retiring. Kita was the last to settle down, but as soon as he laid his head on his travel pack, he was fast asleep. It seemed only seconds after he was asleep that he was awake again.

He opened his eyes to see that he was no longer at the campsite. He stood in the middle of the most vividly colored garden he had ever seen. Fish swam in the streams that snaked along the sides and underneath the path he walked, which seemed like polished marble beneath his feet. Trees of every kind towered over him, many with bright colored leaves and berries shining in iridescent colors like nothing he had ever seen. Kita felt a sense of ease he'd never before experienced, and wished he would never have to leave this place.

With some effort, he wrenched his gaze from the sights around him and looked down the path. In the distance, he saw a magnificent tower that looked to be made of pure light. It glowed in clear iridescent colors, brighter even than its surroundings. The magnificent tower stood high over the trees, pulsating light and energy.

In the presence of the structure, Kita felt lighter and more connected to everything around him. A waterfall came into sight at the right of the path. He closed his eyes and leaned his head back to enjoy the mist that beaded on his face. The environment had a life-giving feel that surpassed anything he could have imagined. He looked further down the path and saw Taliah waving for him to join her.

Kita trotted down the path but seemed to move faster than he intended. In an instant, he was in front her, and stumbled to a stop. The others where there as well, Kenyatta, Akemi and Kenjiro, with only Sensei Akutagawa missing. As if she had read his thoughts,

Taliah explained that Sensei wished to remain behind to watch over the group. *Watch over the group?* he thought.

"This may feel like a dream," Taliah continued, "but it is not. The fact that you are all here together is proof enough." Everyone looked at each other and at their surroundings. Everything about the place was heavenly.

"You stand before the Tower of Balance. These surrounding lands," she swept her hand out to encompass the vast fields, "are a representation of the purity of this place of those who created the tower. Only the best is wished for us while we inhabit this world, and the Gods take every step in assuring that we are able to learn what we are here to learn and experience all that we must, but at the same time, not directly interfering unless absolutely necessary."

"It would take too much time to explain everything, and time is what we have little of."

On their hike to the tower, they came upon a slender figure waiting in the middle of the path. So peaceful was the presence of the woman—for once they drew nearer they saw that it was indeed a woman—that none of the warriors felt the need to be on their guard.

"Nothing will harm us here," Taliah said, again as though she had read their minds. "Our true selves, our spirits, are in the presence of Takashaniel. In the realm of light, nothing evil can exist."

"Who is that?" Akemi asked pointing up the winding path.

"Her name is Mira," Taliah answered. "She is the student of the guardian of Takashaniel."

"Try saying that three times," Kenyatta whispered to Kita, who sniggered.

Mira walked to the group and met all of their gazes with a smile. Kenjiro, composed as always, gave a polite bow. The other two men, however, smiled back with boyish grins, and Taliah and Akemi both rolled their eyes.

The young woman gave a graceful bow and introduced herself.

"I am Mira and I welcome you to Takashaniel. My teacher has been awaiting your arrival and has much to discuss with you. If you would follow me?"

She led the group to the base of the tower where they entered, and the group marveled at the sights around and above. Words could not describe the magnificent colors that radiated from every part of Takashaniel. Even the smallest corners of the tower emitted pure light energy. The inside of the tower was transparent. Every floor or set of stairs or wall was see-through, and made of pure iridescent light energy. Some walls, although made of the same light energy, were solid. Mira explained that privacy was only a thought away and if one did not want to be seen for any reason they need only to think of a solid wall and it would appear.

She led them onto a platform of colorful light that was as thin as paper but felt as sturdy as normal ground. She said and did nothing, but the platform began a slow ascension. "I thought I would choose a slower speed so that you can see everything." She smiled innocently as the four companions' heads turned in every direction as they took in the remarkable surroundings.

"So you are the four my teacher speaks of," she said. "He says that you will be the deciding factor in the future of this world. I admire your fortitude, in the face of the burden you all share."

"We all share the burden in different ways," Kita responded. "You do your work here in this tower that we have come to know as the most important factor in the balance of the world."

"Yes, but ultimately it is *people* who stand and hold the strands together in this web of life that we are a part of. People such as you, are why the tower can stand."

"And also why the tower is necessary," Kenjiro added in a bit of a sour note.

Mira dropped her gaze. "Yes, that's true as well. But despite out many faults as a species, there is always hope." She smiled.

Akemi and Taliah rolled their eyes again as they let out a sigh of disgust at the men, smiling idiotically. "I hope they don't taint the place with their lust and get us thrown out."

Taliah giggled. "He would just throw them out, not us."

Beaming, Mira turned her attention to the next floor coming up. The platform stopped and the group stepped into the room. Just as the other rooms, the walls were transparent, giving it a feeling of vastness.

What appeared to be a man with marble-gray and black skin stood at the far wall, looking out at the sweeping landscape.

Mira led them into the room and bowed. "Teacher, they have arrived."

"Thank you, Mira," the man replied. The serenity of his voice matched perfectly, the tranquility of Takashaniel. "If you wish, you may remain with us."

"I have some matters to attend," she said, "but I will return." The teacher gave her a nod and she left the room.

Kenyatta shook his head in disbelief, watching through the floor as she descended to the bottom level of the tower.

"My name is Iel," the strange colored man said. "And I offer greetings and gratitude to you for coming."

Taliah bowed in response, and the others followed suit. "It is we who are honored to visit you and behold the grace of the tower," she replied.

Iel smiled, and Akemi thought she noticed his gray and black color shift ever so slightly with his smile.

"There is much to discuss and not much time," the guardian of Takashaniel said. "I hope I do not appear rude, but we must speak at once."

"We understand," Taliah assured him.

Not long into their talk, Mira returned with a clear iridescent tray with seven glasses of the same fashion. She offered a glass to each of them, then to Iel, taking the remaining glass for herself.

Kita took a sip and was instantly invigorated. He looked

around the group and noticed the same response. Whatever the drink was, he wanted more.

"As you already know," Iel began, "the Drek has aligned himself with the Quentranzi demon, Arritezmeshezbreandokabriza, or Kabriza, as you know it. Together they have raised an army of fiends from the dark realm and set them on a path directly here." At a look of uneasiness from the group, the Ilanyan continued.

"In the past, there was an attempt against the tower by a mage who had foolish plans of subjugating an entire civilization and establishing a new order of magic wielders under his rule. Although he was quite accomplished in the practice of dark magic, he could not get by the tower's first defense, which is its invisibility to human eyes. You see, Takashaniel cannot be seen by humans, only nature, and some beings of this world can see it. The majority of humans are too infantile in their evolution to be in tune with the tower.

"Unfortunately, denizens of the dark world can see the tower simply because they exist on a different plane than our world. Although they are evil, they still perceive more than humans are capable of, which is why they are able to see the tower. What keeps them from attacking, however, is that most demons cannot get close enough without being destroyed."

Kenyatta noticed Iel's color darken. Did his complexion reflect his mood?

"Quentranzi," the guardian continued, "can penetrate the protective ward. Other demons cannot enter because they cannot wield magic. Quentranzi, however, can wield magic better than the most powerful mage."

Kenyatta frowned. "Back in the forest when we fought some of those shadow demon-things, it looked like they were using magic to me."

"Demons, by nature, have many innate abilities that are beyond many species of the prime material plane, our world. Magic does not number among those abilities for the average fiend."

Taliah leaned forward, interlacing her fingers. "If I am not mistaken, not more than one Quentranzi can exist in this world at one time."

Iel nodded. "According to humans' summoning abilities, yes. But the Drek could summon more than a score of Quentranzi to this world. The simple fact that he was able to summon one of the most powerful of them all is testament enough."

Iel looked over the group. "I cannot emphasize enough, the importance that you use caution when dealing with this evil. Quentranzi are the smartest of all known demons, and some are especially adept at peering into one's mind and toying with whatever they find there. You will be tested to your limits."

For a while everyone sat in silence, absorbing the Ilanyan's words until he spoke again. "I understand that you have encountered a number of Kalistyi and one Ren." The group nodded.

"Then you have an idea of what to expect." The four warriors glanced uneasily at each other. A nervous smile crept across Kenyatta's face. Kenjiro looked tense, and Kita merely closed his eyes and shook his head in resolution. Akemi sat virtually unmoved concentrating on the Ilanyan's every word.

Iel regarded the ninja and her brother. "The two of you already have magically charged weapons, but you will need more." He turned his attention to Kenyatta and Kita. "You will need to have your weapons charged for the first time. I am sending Mira to assist Miss Taliah in the task."

Some time passed as Iel discussed his plans, and the group detailed their experiences leading up to their meeting in the woods outside Toyotomi. As the group stood to take their leave, a small and incredibly beautiful woman entered the room with a tray to collect the glasses. She wore a cloak that hung to her ankles, with a hood that hung at her back. Her curly shoulder-length hair was a dark sandy-brown color that seemed to glow.

Kenyatta discreetly eyed her as she passed. There was something peculiar about her. She had smooth yet angular features, a slightly pointed chin and a petite nose. Her eyebrows came to sharp points at the tips and at the top, giving her facial features a sleek appearance. Much like her hair, her golden brown skin shimmered in the soft light. She was like nothing he had ever seen before, tiny, almost fragile, but with a hint of some inner strength.

After the unusual girl—or small woman, for he could not tell—had collected the glasses, she turned to leave. Even her stride was unusual, as if she glided rather than walked. As she moved away, a few locks of her hair fell behind her ear and Kenyatta noticed that it came to a point at the tip. He dismissed the sight, thinking the strangeness of this tower and its inhabitants were getting to him.

A sharp poke in the ribs jarred him from his admiration, and he turned to see his sister staring at him with narrowed eyes. Behind her, Kita's shoulders trembled with repressed laughter.

Kenyatta smiled timidly and jabbed a thumb in the departing woman's direction, about to explain, then decided better of it.

"These sacks are filled with water from Takashaniel in this dimension," Iel said, handing one to each of them. "Although they are physically smaller than those you carry now, they hold three times as much liquid. A few sips will renew your energy, but your body will feel as if you've had a full night of sleep. I do caution that this will not replace solid food, and anything in excess is unwise. Allow your bodies to recharge naturally, but use this drink to help speed your physical bodies' return here."

The Ilanyan moved to stand before the group, taking each under his gaze. "There is more that I would tell you, but we've not the time. I must send you back with well wishes and know that I will be watching your progress. When we meet again in the physical plane, it will be as allies against the darkness. From this day forward you will always be able to sense where the tower is and be able to see it with your eyes. I must tell you, however, that only you can see and enter the tower. Anyone else, whether they are with you or not, will be unable to see or enter it. You must not attempt to bring any other human here."

The Ilanyan closed his eyes and pointed a finger at each of the warriors. All four leaned backward, startled. A rush of information surged into their minds in an instant.

"I have mentally implanted the path of your destination. You now know the way to reach Takashaniel in the physical world. The dark horde has already begun their march here, and you must meet them between here and the Drek's fortress."

After shaking off the shock, the companions followed Iel onto the platform and began their descent back to the first floor.

"I have looked inside each of you and I see many of the same qualities." He looked at each of them in turn. "Strength, courage, passion, indomitable spirit and," he smiled, "wisdom. Though in time, you will acquire more of the latter."

The platform stopped on the first floor and Iel escorted them to the front of the tower. "There is nothing more that I can do to assist you but to wish you well. Remember that you are not alone in this fight, and you have all that you need to see you through what lies ahead." He curled the small finger and the one next to it inward, toward the palm of his hand, and smiled. "Inyana," he said. "Power of light be with you."

As soon as they stepped out of the tower, everyone awoke with a start, realizing they were back at the campsite. Kenjiro lay still for a moment. He felt as if he had fallen, or rather, been slammed back into his body. He looked around and saw that everyone else seemed to have had the same jarring experience.

They looked around, surprised to be at the campsite after such a vivid experience. It was a few hours before daylight and the air was cool and still. Taliah and—to their surprise—Mira had already begun preparations for their work with the weapons. Mira looked over at the group with that innocent smile that made the men grin like simpletons.

"Would you bring your weapons here please? We are ready for them."

One by one, the four warriors placed their weapons on the

ground. The two women placed each weapon in a specific position and then sat facing each other on either side of the circle they had drawn.

Sensei Akutagawa was finishing breakfast when Akemi came to sit beside him. "I hope you'll enjoy this." He gave her a sly smile. "This is the last real meal you will have for a while."

Akemi smiled back at her youthful old teacher. Aside from the salt and pepper hair gray hair, he looked much the same as when she was a child.

Akutagawa smiled at her in admiration. "Keep your vigor. It is a large part of your power. No matter the situation, you have always found a way to smile through it. You have a kind of cheerful stoicism, but do not let it lead to your demise."

On the other side of the camp, Mira and Taliah sat with their legs crossed and eyes closed. The others watched, feeling the buildup of energy in the air. It continued to grow until it was almost overwhelming. Blue and silver light lined the bodies of the two women, and the air around them howled.

Kenyatta held his arm in front of his face. It was like a tiny windstorm. "How long are they going to keep *that* up?" he asked the ninja when she stopped beside him.

"Until they have gathered a high enough energy to transfer it to the weapons without depleting themselves," she answered.

"You've done this before?"

"Not exactly. I've charged my sword before, but I have never used a power as strong as this. It is beyond my capabilities."

Taliah and Mira ceased to glow, but now the weapons radiated energy.

"That feels like a lot of power," Kita commented, a hint of hesitance in his voice.

"Don't worry about it," Akemi said with a wave of her hand.

"You will find that your weapons are different than before," Mira said. She leaned on her side, spent. "Each is now attuned to the owner alone and has attributes that complement your abilities."

The four companions walked up and took stock of their respective weapons.

Kenyatta's blades glowed when he held them. They seemed even sharper than before, but lighter and somehow stronger.

Mira indicated the swords. "You will find that the cut of your weapons can now do harm to a demon. They cannot destroy, but they will banish the fiend back to their world."

Kenyatta nodded as he studied his swords. He could feel the odd power coursing through them.

Kenjiro found that his sword was also stronger and lighter. Taliah moved closer to him. "Yours and Kenyatta's swords have the least detectable changes of all, but you will discover its new traits in time."

The shaft of Kita's staff was a bit slimmer, and now had a wavy form to it, as if it molded to his hand with an ergonomic perfection that seemed impossible.

Mira smiled at him. "Your weapon needed a bit more diversity. You will find that it is retractable and its form interchangeable."

Kita regarded his weapon with the intrigue of a boy with a new toy. After studying it a moment, he gave it a twist at one end. To his surprise, the long shaft separated into a chain that fell limp to the ground. As with its staff form, the weapon ended with the same bladed tip.

"Not bad," Kenyatta said, giving Kita a friendly backhanded slap across the chest. "A chain blade will definitely come in handy. I'm almost jealous."

"You will also discover that it has one other form," Mira said as she moved away to join Akemi and Taliah.

Akemi held *Sekimaru* in front of her. It emitted a power like nothing she had ever felt from the sword. "It's a bit longer now," she observed.

"And much more powerful," Taliah added. "Your sword is the most unique, simply by the nature of its creation. It needed the least alteration, but you may find it more excitable than before. I felt a sort of …" Taliah searched for a word she already knew but was hesitant to speak. "Sentience," she finally said. "Until you have mastered it, I caution you to refrain from allowing it to feed on any demon energy. It was already quite willful, as you know. If you are unprepared to handle it now, the energy surge could be overwhelming and make the sword's power uncontrollable." The ninja nodded and replaced the sword to its scabbard.

A call from Sensei Akutagawa brought everyone to the campfire. "You must eat before you depart, but I want to say one thing before we start." He waited for everyone to gather together and then beckoned for them to sit.

"You will have to depend on each other from now on. You must trust one another and learn each other's skills, strengths and shortcomings and complement each other accordingly. It is my hope that you will become friends during your travels, as I regard you all as my children. You make me proud and I wish you the best of luck on the greatest mission of your lives."

For the remainder of the day they ate and talked, and for a time, all were able to put aside the grim circumstances that had united them. As the sun followed its arcing path across the sky, the six companions enjoyed good food and good company, trained with each other under the watchful eye of their esteemed teacher, and finally set up their bedrolls to enjoy what might be the last peaceful night of sleep for a long time.

* * *

IEL WATCHED the six humans from one of the far walls in his room. *They will be ready,* he thought with a smile.

28

The sun had yet to peer over the eastern mountains as the four companions saddled their horses. After saddling and securing their gear to the horses, Sensei Akutagawa spoke.

He eyed the six that stood before him with that same proud, fatherly smile. "Kenjiro, Akemi, Kita and Kenyatta. I have said this before but I feel it should be said again. You make me very proud. All of you have become true warriors and good people."

"With a heavy heart do I watch you depart into what lies ahead, but with a happy heart I know that you go at your best. In one night you each have mastered the new techniques I've taught you. Know that these techniques are unique to each of you. I have had the pleasure of watching you grow over the years and am honored to teach you techniques that would normally be physically impossible."

He looked at Kenjiro and the two islanders on his right. "On this mission you must trust Akemi's judgment. She is highly experienced in dealing with demons. I will stress again that you must learn to trust and complement each other's abilities as though you are family."

He turned to Taliah and Mira. "I have never had the pleasure of meeting you before now Mira, but I wish to say that you are an exceptional young lady and I can sense a power within you that you have not yet realized."

He turned to Taliah. "And you, Taliah. I have known you through your brother, and like him, you have become like a daughter to me. Though your true potential eludes you for now, you will soon discover a power inside you that is like nothing the world has seen for generations. If you ever need help or guidance you need only to come and see me." He laughed as Taliah and Mira tackled him with a fierce hug.

The four warriors looked on, smiling. Taliah and Mira were experiencing the same relationship with Sensei Akutagawa that all of them had. It was like having a second father.

Kenyatta leaned over to Kenjiro and whispered, "You aren't getting misty-eyed over here are you?" The samurai responded with an incredulous frown, but Kenyatta could see that there was a smile behind those stoic eyes. Akemi glanced at the two and smirked. The childish islander was exactly what her brother needed.

Taliah walked to Kenyatta and Kita and gave her brother a crushing hug, then turned to the waiting Kita. Kenyatta's lip curled back as Kita and his sister shared a rather long embrace.

"All right, all right, man! Let's not get carried away now! Ya wan disentangle my sister from your tentacles, ya?"

Sighing, Taliah moved to Kenjiro and Akemi, giving them each a hug. "I consider you family, now. Watch over my foolish brother, as he will watch over you." She retreated a few steps as Mira addressed the group.

"Just as he has said, Master Iel is watching you, even now. After this is done, he will watch over you and if ever you are in need, you will find help. I treasure the opportunity to have met each of you, and look forward to our next meeting."

After saying their last minute goodbyes, the four companions mounted their horses, and in minutes had disappeared beyond the hills.

"They have quite a challenge ahead of them," Sensei said, breaking the silence. "There is no way I could fully prepare them for what lies ahead, but I believe they are ready."

"They will be fine, I think," Mira said.

"Come," Sensei Akutagawa said. "Let's clean up and return to Kyokoza. There may yet be survivors we have missed."

After cleaning their little camp, Taliah created a gate in the air as she had done when she met with the four departed warriors, and moments later, the three were gone.

inspired that muscle, and its tissue, and of appeared beyond
medical

The Lieve put in being some of all pieces in that said
with I mean the sense. The disease would have pulse another
a which is also this picture devoted

I could be sure. I have hold it will

Cerest and that it was say the of their minds serving
he says there were the supreme. We have learnt

The disease hell had come latish could speak to the to
disease diagnoses as to the the life days, then the
the institute, a once described

29

The companions held their mounts at a strong canter and blazed a trail straight across the open landscape. There was a silent tension about the group as everyone mentally replayed their teacher's last words before they'd left. Finally, they knew who and what the enemy was, but that only left them with more questions. The guardian had hinted that there was more, concerning their abilities, but he hadn't spoken of it further. In their private thoughts, each wondered if the Ilanyan held the answer to why they were able to do the impossible.

"I can see a lake at the foot of that forest," Kita said, pointing ahead. "We should stop there." They stopped their lathered and winded horses near the lake and dismounted. While they approached the small body of water, Kenyatta hesitated. His stomach knotted and seemingly every nerve in his body tingled with anxiety.

"Wait!" He trotted up to stop the others. "Something's not right about this lake. I don't think we should get any closer."

Kenjiro caught something out of the corner of his eye and froze. The water rippled gently and then a large black fin sliced through the surface and then sank once again.

Kita was horrorstricken. "Whatever is attached to that fin is bigger than I care to imagine."

Everyone slowly backed away from the pond. Kenyatta realized how careful they all were stepping and laughed. "What are we tip-toeing for? It's not like the thing can hear us and is going to jump out of the water."

Kita shook his head. "Yeah, well all the same, let's just find another place to rest." The group moved around the lake at a distance. This time Akemi got a glimpse of the large fin, and then the larger yellow tail that followed. The tail had grotesque waving tentacles attached to it, and upon closer observation, she noticed that the tentacles seemed to wave consciously, as if they were searching for something.

"Why don't we move a bit farther away," she suggested. Upon receiving a questioning look from her brother, she pointed. "Look there, those small tentacles. Look at the way they sway in that pattern. I think they're smelling the air."

The group entered a copse a short distance away to take their rest. "According to the map Iel implanted in our minds," Kenjiro said, "I don't think we are far from intercepting the Drek's forces." He looked at Kita, who nodded.

"We should find a safe place to release our horses," Akemi said. "Demons find no better pleasure than causing pain and suffering to any living thing, especially animals that are close to humans. They know how we care for our animal companions."

Kenjiro noticed Kenyatta focusing on something outside the tree line and moved beside him. "What is it?" he asked.

"Over there," the islander whispered. "I knew there was something trailing us for some time now but it was too far away to be of any real concern. Whatever that thing is, it's getting a little close to that lake."

Kenjiro looked in the direction Kenyatta pointed to see a gray, four-legged animal of some sort walking toward the edge of the water. Even from that distance, the thing looked to be larger than a lion. Shaggy gray fur covered its hulking body, and four fangs protruded from its smiling maw. Its glowing red eyes looked as if they were filled with lava. Its claws sliced into the ground as it walked toward the lake.

"Grey Krindra," Akemi whispered as she silently crept up beside them.

"What's a Krindra?" Kita asked.

"I am unsure of exactly what it is, but it's often used by demons, higher or lesser, to track certain targets or just plain hunt them down and rip them apart." She narrowed her eyes. "It isn't very intelligent, but it can grate a tree into shreds with those claws."

A splash of water brought everyone's attention back to the lake. A long, thick tentacle shot out of the water and wrapped around the beast, and began dragging the Krindra closer to the pond. It roared and dug its claws into the ground, digging deep scars in the ground.

A second tentacle whipped out of the water and slapped at the beast before it too wrapped around the animal. After a bit more of a struggle, the tentacles lifted the kicking, shrieking monster into the air and plunged it into the water. There were a few splashes and then nothing. The pond was as still as they had found it, and it was as though the Krindra had never been.

Kenyatta looked at Kita with widened eyes. "That thing had to weigh at least twelve to fifteen hundred pounds and was yanked into the water like it was nothing!"

"The world is changing," Kita responded, not taking his eyes from the scene in front of him. "Just as Sensei and Iel said."

"I hope there are some more friendly changes taking place," Kenyatta replied, unconsciously moving backward.

The companions rested and shared their rations before mounting and setting off again. They moved slowly through the copse and later came upon a forest. The trees opened and revealed a path wide enough for them to travel two abreast. They increased their pace, no one needing to explain their desire not to spend more time in a wooded area than need be.

For a while, all seemed well, but then, the companions began to feel an uneasiness about the woods. Kenyatta could feel the wrongness in the air. He sighed. *They must know we're coming,* he thought. He sped his horse up to catch the leader and warn of the danger when the ground burst open and the horses screamed and dug their rear heels into the ground.

The four warriors leaped from their saddles and landed in a crouching defensive formation, two on the left and two on the right. Akemi and Kenjiro's horses ran into the thicker parts of the brush with the other two in tow. Kenyatta and Kita said a silent prayer of thanks for having selected such intelligent animals.

Out of the ground came a large flaming red hand big enough to grab them all. A Ren even bigger than the one they last encountered broke through the ground and towered over the group. Its chest expanded as it drew in a deep breath, then it thrust its head forward and spat a gout of flame.

The warriors leaped backward into the air, landing behind the flames. Everyone crouched, their weapons ready to strike as the fiery demon moved closer. Just as Akemi leaned forward to initiate the attack, they heard a sharp sound like a thin sheet of metal slicing through air. The Ren lurched forward and then tumbled to the ground and began to dissipate.

Akemi and the others remained crouched and ready, watching in confusion as the Ren dissipated back to the abyss. After it had fully dematerialized, they saw a slender figure standing at ease. Everyone stood and took a more aggressive stance, not sure if their benefactor was friend or foe.

"This is how you welcome an ally?" asked a voice familiar to Kenjiro and Akemi. Kenyatta and Kita remained at the ready until the other two relaxed and sheathed their swords.

"I see a strider does keep his word after all," Akemi said. "We thought you decided the better of accompanying us."

"His word is all a man has," Shinobu replied. He walked up to the group and inclined his head with a smile. "I presume you are the others from Toyotomi that eluded me," he said, turning his attention to Kenyatta and Kita, who turned questioning looks on the two siblings.

Shinobu spread his hands. "I'd sensed the presence of two others but was unable to locate you. Looks like you've met up after all. I am Farstrider Shinobu." He offered a smirk that brought an unimpressed look from Kenyatta. Kita returned the introductions and they went to recover their horses.

The strider led them to his mount, which was grazing in an open patch of grass. They rode at a walking pace for a time, comparing information and Akemi explaining their meeting at the Eagle's Eye to the islanders.

"We almost missed the place entirely," Kita said. "We were told to look for a town named Nijika. We nearly left until deciding to talk to some of the locals and found out that Nijika and Toyotomi were one in the same."

"Some people have felt the need to hold on to some remnants of an age passed," the strider said. "Nijika is the old name. You will find that many places have taken new names, as every land has done for centuries. People are divided on the subject." He shrugged as if it didn't matter. Kita and Kenyatta didn't see the point in such reasoning either, but in the end, what did it matter?

"There is a score of monsters the likes of which I have never seen before," the strider continued. "All moving east of here and destroying everything in their path. They are savage, but there is definitely some direction to their flight." The two siblings looked at each other and then at Kenyatta and Kita.

Akemi shared their recently acquired information, drawing a smile from the strider. "So you are on your way to intercept these things? I hope you have an idea of what you're up against, because not only are there a lot of them, but they're strong; very strong."

"I have a question," Kita asked. "How were you able to defeat

that thing back there so easily?" Shinobu's face took on a distant
look.

"That is a question that must remain unanswered, I regret." The
matter-of-factness in Shinobu's voice brought no further questions
in that direction, but a little less trust between the strider and the
four companions.

* * *

THE MILES FELL AWAY behind them as they crossed the grasslands,
rolling hills and fields, and jumping across creeks and ravines.
They rode without rest until the sun was directly overhead. "We
are close to them now," Akemi said, her voice going grim. "I can
feel the stench of their presence even from here." She looked at the
rest of the group. "Whatever we plan to do, it's going to be now."

"There is a patch of woods not far from here," Kenjiro said. "I
have no desire to involve my horse in this confrontation."

"Agreed," Akemi replied.

"You have quite a bit of confidence in their loyalty," Shinobu
commented.

"We should," Akemi retorted, giving her panting mount a pat
on the neck. The winded horse's sides heaved in and out as it took
in gulps of air. "They have served us well."

"I see," came the smiling response, which drew an annoyed
look from Kenyatta.

Once they reached the woods, everyone dismounted and unfas-
tened their gear. The horses were turned loose to graze and rest in
safety. "How fast do you feel?" Shinobu asked the others. "If we
set a quick pace, we can be on them in less than three hours."

"Then let's get moving," Kenyatta said while fastening a water
flask to his waist.

Akemi nodded. "We need to reach them before nightfall. I'd
like not to fight demons in the night if it can be avoided." That
statement had everyone ready to leave in a matter of minutes.

The group sped across the open fields, stopping only to peer at their quarry from atop some of the higher hills. "There," Kita pointed out three Bachatttas gliding in the sky far in the distance.

"Scouts," Kenjiro said with disgust.

"And they can probably see us even from this distance," Akemi added.

"I know this area," Shinobu said. "There is a canyon between us and them that stretches for miles in both directions. The good news is that it's narrow and we could cross it without those things seeing us from the sky. The bad news is that we would be quite vulnerable climbing out."

"We have few options," Kenjiro said. "We must cross."

"Then we start now," Akemi said.

* * *

STANDING in front of his scrying mirror, Brit watched with amusement as the group headed for the canyon. "Courageous of them to try to cross that canyon so close to our forces, don't you think, Kabriza?"

The Quentranzi general looked into the mirror with little interest. "Would you consider those five humans such a threat that you would have them eliminated?" it asked with that low, rumbling voice that made Zreal's wings want to shrivel.

"You may yet learn, Kabriza, that I leave nothing to chance. Better to overestimate than to underestimate. No one has or ever will defeat me because I was unprepared."

The demon narrowed its eyes and smiled at the double meaning in the Drek's words. Brit could feel the fiend's eyes burning into his side, but showed no concern. He had Kabriza's respect, somewhat, and he must remain unmoved and strong in its presence. "I won't waste valuable resources on humans, but I will take no unnecessary chances either. I will send three welcoming parties to them, each headed by a Krindra."

Brit and his Quentranzi general stepped through a dark portal and were transported not far outside of his fortress. "I must say again that I admire your style in surroundings," Kabriza said. "It almost reminds me of home."

Brit ignored the comment and concentrated on summoning the creatures of the edge of the world, vile grotesque living monsters that were only found in these lands and were rarely mentioned save for old stories and campfire tales. Three Krindras appeared from the brush, and soon after, three groups of hairy brown beasts with glowing green eyes joined them.

Kabriza made a sound that could have been a chuckle. "Those are the same type of Chimsura as the score you lost track of not long ago. Are you feeling luckier in using such mentally dwarfed creatures?" Kabriza glanced at its summoner. "Perhaps you use them because stupid creatures are easy to outwit and easier to control?"

Brit spared a glance at the mocking demon. "That's why you're here, pet."

The fire in Kabriza's eyes danced wildly at the insult.

The three Krindras and the other monsters backed away from them, growling warily. Brit, most of his attention on his slow-witted but fierce beasts took note but once again showed no concern of his unpredictable ally's irritation. A few moments later he produced a dark portal and the three groups departed.

* * *

THE NARROW CANYON stretched as far as the eye could see in either direction, but for however long it was, the distance across its width was quite short. The four warriors positioned themselves behind a bolder, and Akemi took a quick peek around the side.

"What do you see?" Kenjiro asked.

"More than I can count," the ninja answered. "At least several

of every kind of demon you could think of, except the Kalistyi."
She shared a look with her brother, then took a longer look.

"Five Ren, the three Bachatttas we spotted earlier, three Pit
Demons, and other demons the likes of which I have never seen. I
hope you're ready for a fight. What concerns me is not their
numbers, but how powerful this Drek thing would have to be in
order to summon this many of *those* kinds of demons to this world.
They're bad enough, and they aren't even Quentranzi. Not a one!"
She looked back around the boulder and then once more to the
others. "Fighting him might be more difficult than that army."

"No sense in prolonging this," Kita said. "Let's cross the
canyon and get to business." That brought a smile to the ninja's
face, a sigh from the samurai, and an amused look from Shinobu.
After peeking around the boulder once more, she held her hand up
to the group and after a moment longer, signaled for everyone to
make for the canyon.

"This reeks of a setup," Shinobu said in a bored tone. "I'm
almost positive we will be attacked as soon as we reach the floor of
the canyon."

"Then why don't you jump across it," Kenjiro retorted.

Akemi glanced at them. "We have no choice but to cross from
the bottom. Whatever happens, we will deal with it or this will be a
short mission."

Without hesitation, they dropped over the rim, hopping from
one level to another, one boulder to another. Halfway down, they
spread out and stopped, scanning the surroundings from the
concealment of the scattered trees and boulders that littered the
canyon wall.

Kenyatta crouched next to a slit in the wall, watching. A hiss
drew his attention, and he froze, moving only his eyes to meet
those of a colorful and deadly canyon snake, coiled and poised to
strike. He remained perfectly still, but never took his eyes from the
snake. "Maybe you not wantin' me visiting your house, ya?" The

snaked snapped and hissed again. "Me jyas passin' by, my friend, no need coilin' up like that, ya know."

Kenyatta could see the others continuing their descent, and knew he would need to move on. The angry snake, perhaps impatient with waiting, struck at his face. Kenyatta's hand snapped up and caught the serpent. He held it by the head, and its tail twisted and wrapped itself around his arm. Carefully, he removed the snake from his arm and placed it on the ground, still holding its head. After moving to the edge of the cliff, he released the snake and dropped over the side, following as the companions zigzagged from rock to rock, ridge to ridge, all the way to the bottom.

After a short time, the five warriors reached the floor of the canyon and moved toward the other side. Almost halfway across, two red dots of light appeared on either side of them, then elongated while turning and widening. They faced back-to-back in a circle and drew their weapons. From each side, a Krindra stepped out of a portal with ten Chimsuras in tow. There was an unmistakable glow of hunger and malice in those eyes. These monsters weren't demons, but it was clear who'd sent them.

"We need to get those things between us," the strider said.

"What do you suggest?" Kenjiro asked, holding his sword before him.

Shinobu was thinking fast, taking in the area as the monsters closed in.

"Everyone move to fight the ones facing Kenyatta first. When the other group catches up to us, on my signal, circle around and reposition behind them on both sides—" he gave Kenjiro a dark, triumphant look "—and slaughter them!"

"Go, now!"

The five warriors charged the group of monsters closest to the wall of the canyon, the howling creatures pounding the earth to meet them. Akemi drew forth *Sekimaru* and swiped one monster across the chest, shearing through flesh and bone and nearly cutting it in two. She shuddered at how easily the sword had cleaved through the beast. An instant later she rolled to the side to avoid a downward slash at her head, and a Chimsura's claw dug deep into the ground. It drew back with an agonized howl as part of its arm fell to the canyon floor. Akemi didn't need to finish the monster, for Shinobu came upon it with zigzagging slashes across its back. It crashed to the ground, quite dead.

The strider glanced over his shoulder to see that the second group of monsters was near. "Now!" he called, and he and Kenyatta leapt backward, landing behind the charging group while Kenjiro, Akemi, and Kita leaped forward and landed behind the first group. The monsters stumbled and slashed each other before realizing that their quarry had gone.

The beasts were crammed together, surrounded by the master warriors who put them down with merciless efficiency. Claws slashed and were severed, swords found their marks in the backs and midsections of hairy bodies. One Chimsura attempted to leap at Kenyatta and smother him under its heavy bulk. The Jamaican warrior brought both his swords up and stabbed the beast three times before stepping aside, and the instant the beast slammed to the ground he spun and slashed another beast across the throat with his right, then left blade, and then completed the motion, stabbed the fallen beast with his left blade.

Kenjiro avoided a right-armed slash from a Chimsura, then a descending claw from behind. He shifted left and right, working for a more advantageous position, but the two beasts matched his steps without giving any ground. The samurai held his sword in front of him and jumped straight into the air in a spinning front flip. Both monsters staggered away, grabbing at their ruined faces.

Kita stabbed one beast in the chest and withdrew the staff, jamming the butt of his weapon into the face of a monster behind him. He spun the staff over his head, forcing the monsters back, then launched it at a Chimsura and grabbed the end of it at the last second. The tip of the staff found its mark in the beast's throat, and at the same instant, the shaft separated and Kita yanked free the whip-chain and flung it back across him to wrap around the neck of another of the hairy creatures creeping behind him. He yanked the whip back, the razor-tipped chains slicing into the monster's neck. It fell to the ground in a pool of its lifeblood.

The sound of thin steel slicing through the air spoke of Shinobu's mighty blade as it passed through monster flesh like a knife through silk. The other four warriors could not help but be impressed at their new ally's skill, and the strange weapon that he wielded.

A particularly large Chimsura came at the strider with heavy yet quick slashes in every direction that would have surely had any average fighter meeting death instantly, but the strider hopped back and ducked under the sloppy assault.

To Akemi, it was as if he was actually dancing with the beast. She could see a hint of a smile on his face as he avoided those claws, and knew that he could have ended the fight the instant the beast attacked. Finally, Shinobu dealt the monster another zigzag cut, and it fell dead to the ground.

Akemi cut down a Chimsura and stole another glance at Shinobu. The strider practically sheathed the blade after every attack. Once or twice, Akemi saw that when he held the blade for longer than usual, it seemed to become insubstantial, as though it was made of light. She mentally shrugged the possibility away. The reflection of the sun and the din of battle played tricks to the eyes, no doubt.

After felling yet another of the hairy beasts, the ninja focused her attention to the sky. The three Bachatttas that had been miles away were now flying low and circling the battle, no doubt spying for their master.

I'll give them something to report, she thought. She drew a handful of shurikens from a pouch and launched them at the winged fiends. Every one of the small blades glided true and hit their marks with deadly accuracy. Without watching to see them flop in the air, she returned her full attention to the fight on the ground.

* * *

THE LAST THING Brit and Kabriza saw was the earth rushing toward them, and then nothing. The Bachatttas had disintegrated before they hit the ground.

"It seems that your minions are not much more useful than mine, Quentranzi." Brit turned a blank look on the demon general.

"What of the third group of beasts you sent?" Kabriza replied. "Perhaps they possess cowardice to complement their intelligence. Bachatttas can be summoned infinitely, but how many of those powerful four-legged meals can you spare?"

Brit had to admit that Kabriza was correct, but he would not give the fiend the satisfaction of saying so. Instead, he turned to Zreal. "Bring Szhegaza. I wish to meet with her."

"As you wish, Master," Zreal said with a bow, and left the room.

"Whether they perish in the canyon or out of it is of no concern, but they will perish, and once the tower is destroyed, we will attend to our own business."

The fires in Kabriza's glowing red orbs flared. "So we shall, tether."

* * *

THE CHIMSURAS WERE FALLING ALMOST in a pile within the circle that the five warriors had formed around them. Aside from being outmatched by the warriors on equal terms, it was hard for the monsters to get a solid foothold when stumbling over the dead carcasses.

A roar split the air, and the remaining seven Chimsuras suddenly were hurled in every direction away from the circle. The three gray Krindras stood crouching as if to attack, eyes flaring, fangs bared. "Be ready," Akemi said. "They are much faster than their size would tell."

The warriors assumed a defensive formation around the snarling monsters. Kenyatta glanced over his shoulder. All of the remaining Chimsuras lay sprawled and broken. Kita and Akemi faced one, Kenjiro and Shinobu faced another, leaving Kenyatta facing the third.

"Think you can handle that one on your own, islander?" Shinobu asked.

"Think you can be quiet, just for a while?" Kenyatta snapped.

The three Krindras charged, and the warriors met their attack with skill and grace. Akemi leaped aside and stabbed a Krindra in the flank while Kita leaped straight into the air and stabbed down between the huge beast's shoulders. He landed on its back, then leapt to the opposite side from Akemi.

* * *

SHINOBU RAN straight to the beast, and at the last second when it lunged forward, he slid underneath it, cutting the beast as he passed. When he rose to his feet, the gray monster whirled to face him, not showing any signs of pain despite the pool of blood forming at its feet.

Kenjiro suddenly landed on its head, sword first, thrusting it down to the hilt through the thick skull.

* * *

KENYATTA ROLLED to the left as the Krindra passed him in a cloud of dust. He then rolled to the right as it spun about and charged him once again. When he came to his feet he met it face to face. *She wasn't jokin' bout 'em speed or agility,* he thought. It lunged forward and slashed horizontally, catching the warrior across the front and leaving three shallow red gashes across his chest. If he had been any slower, Kenyatta realized, his entrails would be spilling at his feet. The Krindra lunged again, snapping its jaws, but this time Kenyatta was quicker. He hopped backward while delivering a right-handed outward slash, cutting it across the nose. It reared back at the painful cut, then stood on its hind legs. Kenyatta took a step back, completely covered in the shadow of the now thirteen-foot-tall beast.

* * *

THE TWO WARRIORS kept to the Krindra's flank, pacing it as it tried to turn to face them. It spun and slashed at Akemi, almost scoring a deadly blow. The ninja stepped back at the last second, then countered with a horizontal cut. The beast withdrew its huge claw and was about to lunge when it stumbled forward, now favoring its left hind leg. Akemi saw its wounded leg when it struggled around to face Kita. She darted in close and hamstrung the other leg, and the thing howled. It tried to stand up on its hind legs, but instead tumbled to the ground in a cloud of dust and gray fur.

To its credit, the Krindra was fast. She had barely scored another cut to its flank before it had already regained its feet. She crouched, waiting for the inevitable lunge, when a whip-chain wrapped around its neck, forcing it back. This time it did manage to stand on its hind legs, and seeing the opportunity, Akemi brought *Sekimaru* up and went in straight, plunging the sword deep into its belly. She twisted left, then right, then withdrew the sword and followed the motion with another slash to the front of its hind legs. It stumbled backward and then fell forward, barely holding its bulk up on all four legs.

Kita, who had been flung in every direction, held on then landed on the creature's back, still holding the whip-chain wrapped around its neck like a leash. With all his strength, Kita yanked once, then again, and the razor edged links of the whip-chain sliced through the bulky neck of the monster. It lumbered several more steps until it finally fell to the ground and lay still.

After her foreign ally had finished off the beast, Akemi glanced down at the sword in her hand with a bit of apprehension. She could feel a hunger in the sword, and wondered if it had to do with the drained feeling she was experiencing.

* * *

SHINOBU SLICED both the monster's front legs, then sliced it across the face. Kenjiro withdrew his sword and leaped to the side. While the blinded monster thrashed about, he ran forward and slashed downward and then up. Kenzo sheared through flesh and bone, and the Krindra half stumbled, half fell, struggling to rise as its entrails spilled onto the canyon floor.

Shinobu arched an eyebrow. "A little sloppy, but impressive."

* * *

THE KRINDRA STALKED toward the small human, teeth bared and claws ready to strike. Before it could react, Kenyatta rushed forward, arms pumping as he stabbed the monster innumerable times in the midsection.

He drove it backward, but the beast managed a desperate swing, grazing the warrior across the shoulder and drawing yet a few more lines of blood. Kenyatta leapt away and put his hand to his chest. As soon as he saw the blood on his fingers, he became aware of the stinging wound. He looked up at the Krindra and smiled.

The others were taken aback at the sight of the dark anger that flashed across the islander's face before that wicked smile he now wore. The gray Krindra charged, and Kenyatta crouched, still smiling, and also charged.

"What in the abyss is he doing?" Kenjiro asked, staring at the crazed warrior. The samurai looked over at Kita, who had no answers. He had never seen this before and was equally surprised. Then, as he watched Kenyatta lower his left shoulder, he knew what his friend had in mind.

The monster tore at him, kicking up rocks and dust in its wake. As impossible as it seemed, Kenyatta, who seemed so small in comparison to the Krindra, slammed into its foreleg and sent the monster stumbling onto its belly as Kenyatta rolled aside.

Snarling, the Krindra regained its feet and stood on its hind legs, and Kenyatta took advantage of the movement and charged again. The others thought he was surely dead, for he leaped straight at the beast, slamming into its belly. To their surprise, he knocked the beast back into the canyon wall.

As soon as his feet touched the ground, Kenyatta cut downward in a diagonal swipe with his right sword, severing the beast's right leg at the shin. While crouched he reversed his grip on his left sword and launched himself straight into the air, slicing the beast up the middle of its body all the way to its head. Once he cleared its head, Kenyatta spun in the air, and as he descended, he turned the grip on his left sword and cut the beast across the throat. The islander landed with his back to the monster and started toward the others, who stared at the bloody Krindra, leaning against the wall, lost in the void of death.

Kenyatta sheathed his swords as he walked, unmoved by the ground-shaking thud when the monster finally crashed to the ground. The others stared at him in disbelief until the strider finally spoke. "Those things were pretty fast for their size, but they weren't that fast." Shinobu indicated Kenyatta's injuries. "I hope you just slipped on a rock, or perhaps lost your footing. Otherwise you may not make it through this mission."

Kenyatta looked at him for a moment and then walked by, toward his friend. "If you have questions about my skill, strider, come and test them for yourself."

Shinobu regarded the warrior for a moment. *Was he joking or was that an invitation?* Kenyatta never turned to look at him, but simply stood with his back turned, as if waiting for a response. When there was none forthcoming, he shrugged off his pack and began sifting through it. *He really was serious,* the strider realized. "Perhaps those little scratches have made you a bit edgy, friend, but do not be angry. They are the result of a mistake that you survived, barely."

Kenyatta slowly turned to face him. "What would be more interesting is to see if you are able to survive the mistake you are making now, questioning my skill and calling me friend in the same breath. You are not my friend, for I do not know you. Second, I tolerate criticism from no one but my teacher and my family. I do not doubt your skill, or make light of it, but if you wish to use your tongue to joke another day, you best rest it now or carry it in a sack for the remainder of *our* mission that you have included yourself in."

The strider slowly reached over his shoulder for his weapon. The characteristic smirk was replaced by the dark look he gave the islander. Kenyatta met that stare, waiting.

"Perhaps you both could take the greater challenge of acting like *silent* children instead of loud ones," Akemi scolded, stepping between them. "Children have very short attention spans, and since you have obviously forgotten about the mission on the other side of this canyon, let me remind you. We have no time for nonsense. Put away this ridiculous confrontation for a time when you both have nothing else stupid to do and let's get this business done." Both warriors nodded, still staring until Akemi sighed and grabbed Shinobu by the arm. The strider smirked at her and let himself be led away. Kenyatta glanced at his friend, who stood quietly to the side, and noted the concerned look on his face.

Kita smiled nervously at his friend retracting his weapon and securing it to his back. "You all right?" he asked, patting Kenyatta on the back.

Kenyatta took a deep breath. "Yeah, man. I don't know why, but every time he opens his mouth it gets under my skin."

"Let it go," Kita replied, giving him another pat and stepping past him toward the canyon wall. "There's plenty of demons to fight."

Kenyatta followed after his friend. "Yeah, man."

Minutes later, the warriors reached the top of the canyon. In the distance they could barely see the horde of fiends blazing a tainted trail toward the tower of balance. "They have a good start on us." Kenjiro said, "We'll have to move quickly if we're to catch them before dark." After checking their gear and fastening all straps and belts, the warriors ran after their quarry.

* * *

"THEY MADE easy work of those things, but that band of monsters they're racing to catch is like nothing I've ever seen. Either they are true masters, or suicidal would-be heroes." Kim glanced at their leader who continued to stare in the direction of the departed group.

"Neither," she said. "They know what they are up against and will see it through to the end."

"How can you be so sure?"

Seung turned to face her second in command. "I just know, Kim." She saw the concerned look in her friend's eyes.

"You don't understand," she replied. "It's not wishful thinking. I can't explain it, but I know they will succeed. I can feel it, and I wish to accompany them. Somehow, I feel an intangible bond that I can't explain."

She turned and looked back at her companions, who stood amidst a score of scattered Chimsura carcasses and one Krindra that she herself had felled.

"Do you wish to follow?" Kim asked.

Seung smiled and kissed him on the cheek, which instantly

went red. "I have no doubt that you would follow me into the depths of the dark world itself," she said. "But this is not our fight. We have played the small part in this that we were meant to play, and now we return home."

"You knew there would be more in store for those two, didn't you?"

Seung looked back in the direction of five warriors, now gone from sight, and her face softened. "I don't know why I chose to find them, or how I was able to track them down. I just had a feeling and went by it."

There was more, Kim could see it in his best friend's eyes. He said nothing, though. Whatever the outcome, and whatever the future might hold, the web of life would reconnect them at a later time if so it should be. The small band of village warriors recovered their grazing horses and turned toward the sea, toward their home across the ocean.

30

Hot on the trail of the demon horde, the five warriors passed through patches of forests and dark woods, fighting their way through bands of skulking Kalistyi. The shadow fiends were no longer a challenge since their weapons had been imbued with the power to banish them back to the abyss.

After hours of pursuit, with brief rest stops, the companions finally caught up to their quarry. They stopped at a plateau overlooking a valley, and alongside the horde passing below. "We have the element of surprise in our favor," Shinobu said.

"In addition to an advantageous position," the samurai added.

"We waste no time here," Akemi said, her eyes glowing with anticipation. "We end this now." The ninja was not the only one whose eyes glowed with excitement. Though Kenyatta and Shinobu showed casual interest, Kita could see the eagerness about them. The samurai, however, remained stoic and ready to be done with this business, as was Kita himself.

Without hesitation, they dropped from the edge, hopping from level to level toward the valley floor. From their vantage point, the surrounding hills and distant mountains could be seen. The countryside was an expanse of rolling hills of grassland, and scattered clumps of trees and outcroppings.

To their left, a herd of slender golden-brown animals with curved antlers crowning their heads ran and jumped in the distance. As Akemi drew *Sekimaru*, she knew why it was so important that they must stop the Drek. The world they inhabited was vast and beautiful, rich with life. This Drek would see her precious world forever darkened.

She wondered how humankind could have allowed themselves to become so detached. How could they not marvel at the countless wonders of the world, and in their arrogance, manipulate, exploit and destroy what they themselves did not create?

It was no wonder that technology and all knowledge of it was taken. In response to the valuable lesson, humans did begin to turn to nature once more. More often than not, however, it seemed humanity was still determined to exploit its surroundings to suit itself. Wars and conquests still raged, and the threat they faced this day, although not wrought by humanity, was still an example of humankind's inability to understand who they were. Humans did indeed summon denizens from the dark realm, although much weaker than Quentranzi. Humans still had not learned the lesson that the Gods had been trying to teach them; they had not evolved.

The young ninja thought back on the many adventures she'd had in her short years of life. How many demons had she extermi-nated that had gotten loose and slaughtered their summoners? Time and again it was the same, a foolish person with some degree of skill brings a demon to this world only to die at its hands. And time and again, Akemi or some other demon hunter would come to send it back to the abyss. No demon could ever enter this dimension without a tether to summon it, and for centuries innumerable, there was always a willing tether to try, and ultimately die.

Would this forever be the future? Would it be she, with her brother by her side and perhaps the others, stepping up to the responsibility of cleaning up the mess that humankind seemed to constantly create? She smiled to herself. If not for the mess of humanity, she would have to take up another profession, and the ninja couldn't imagine what that might be.

In a flash of blinding light and streaks of energy, one of the Ren fell and began to dissipate. Each warrior landed atop one of the larger demons and quietly sent it back to the dark realm. Suddenly, as if the horde operated on one collective mind, they turned to face their attackers. The group stopped short and quickly analyzed their situation. For the first time they truly realized their enemy for what it was and what they were up against. A score of Ren stood before them, as well as a vast number of other demons that no one in the group had encountered before.

Several slimy green beasts lumbered toward them. Their long tails were connected to the lower part of their backs, which were covered with plated scales. They made a grating, hissing sound, spreading scaly arms that were twice as long as a human's body. Two sets of eyes glared at them from beneath a single horn in the middle of their foreheads. The drool that seeped from their hungry maws blackened the ground that it touched.

A group of short, silver creatures stood to either side. They had no distinct features other than being humanoid in appearance. Despite the warmth of the day, the air around the diminutive fiends was misty, as though freezing. They stood at ease, their blank stares leveled at the newly arrived humans.

Kenyatta heard a snapping sound and turned to see two demons approaching, snapping together what looked like giant crab-like pincers. Within each pincer were jagged, spikes, no doubt designed for tearing and ripping. On their heads were horns that curved downward toward their elongated jaws.

Akemi saw several nightmare demons within the horde as well, having received their name because of their ability to peer into the minds of their victims and twist what they found into horrid images and sounds. These fiends were as black as pitch, and had narrow yellow eyes. They had no mouths, for they communicated telepathically. On each of their shoulders was one long, metal-like spike that curved upwards.

Four pit demons stood at the rear, towering over the entire horde at near to eighteen feet tall. Two horns also grew atop their heads, curling backward and then forward to stop at the lower jaw, similar to that of a ram sheep. Their eyes were dancing red flames that matched the ominous red glow that pulsated in their scaly hands. A host of many other types of fiends that not even the ninja woman had seen before completed this medley of evil, and the five warriors hesitated, studying the intimidating force.

"This is gonna be good," Kita muttered, voice dripping with sarcasm.

"I've never seen anything like this," Kenyatta said in a low voice.

"Don't tell me you're afraid," Shinobu teased.

"Only that you will continue to irritate me," Kenyatta retorted.

"Not now!" Akemi snapped. "We face a powerful horde of demons and you talk nonsense!"

Kenjiro leaned closer to his sister. "Why don't they attack us? We have hesitated too long already."

"I think they knew we were pursuing them. The major demons are much more intelligent than the lower ones and I suspect that their mission did not include engaging us. They wait for us to make a move."

"When have you ever known a demon to think like this?" Kenjiro asked. The ninja shrugged.

"What do you think of our chances?" Kita asked, not taking his eyes from the abysmal creatures.

"Tough to say," she answered. "Some of those things are not that powerful, but I have never fought a pit demon before. Those things are more wicked than anything I have ever personally laid eyes upon, and there are four of them."

"Those other things don't look very eager to come and play," Kenyatta commented.

"I would rather face a score of Ren by myself than four pit demons," Akemi said. "Take care with them. Nothing fouler has ever walked this plane."

"Yet," Kita added.

"I wonder if the Drek knows of what he summons," Kenjiro said. A glimmer flickered in Akemi's eyes and she drew *Sekimaru* close. She could feel the hunger in the sword and was reminded of Taliah's warning. She glanced at her weapon. The twisted, grotesque fiends hissed and gurgled, but did not attack. The pit demons stood erect at the back of the horde while the Ren stood crouching at the front. "I don't think they will wait for us to conceive a plan," Kita remarked. Kenjiro nodded.

"We better do something while we can." Shinobu said. "We should split into pairs."

"We are not fighting Chimsuras and Krindra," Kenjiro remarked.

"That's true," Shinobu agreed, "but we have to even our odds somehow, and this seems the best way."

"Let him do what he will," Akemi said. "We don't have time to debate."

"Maybe he's right," Kenyatta said. He looked over the group. "Kita, you should team with Kenjiro." He then looked at the ninja with a nod. "And I with you."

"Agreed," she said. "We will push straight through the middle and the other two will flank them on the right side and cut through the middle behind us and then straight across to the left." She looked at Shinobu. "Do you have a plan, Strider?"

"Yes," he answered. "I will flank them on the left and meet Kita and Kenjiro when they cross the middle."

"Fine," she said, looking at Kenyatta. "You should be in front and try to cut through the center while I protect the rear. Just don't push through too far ahead." She regarded the others. "Try to keep your distance from the pit demons long enough to kill everything else first. We must fight the pit demons together."

The five warriors faced the now slowly approaching horde. The ninja stood low, with *Sekimaru* in a reverse grip in her right hand. Kita held his staff in a firm grip, its bladed tip angled toward the advancing demons. Kenjiro stood with his hand resting on the hilt of his sword, head held high in defiance of the evil approaching.

Kenyatta drew his swords and crossed them in front of his legs, tips facing the ground, waiting for the Ren that was closest to him.

The strider stood to the side of the group opposite Kenjiro, with his arms crossed over his chest, smirking. The exotic blade on his back glowed brightly in its scabbard. "Let's get this done," he said.

Akemi nodded at Kenyatta and they charged into the midst of their enemies.

The ninja lunged forward and cut the Ren a deep gash across its abdomen. She turned back to follow up the attack, but to her surprise, it had already begun to dissipate. She turned to face the second Ren who slashed at her midsection. She hopped back just as Kenyatta glided over her head and split the flaming beast in two.

* * *

KITA AND KENJIRO sprinted around the right side of the horde, then ran up the side of a mound and leaped at the closest demon Akemi had identified as a ripclaw. It snapped at them with one of those spider-like claws, but Kita batted the scaly arm aside and Kenjiro, right behind him, severed the limb. Kita drove the spear end of his staff into its chest, and an instant later it began to dissipate and return to the abyss. A second ripclaw came in, slashing and hammering the ground, and in short order, also began its descent back to the abyss.

* * *

SHINOBU MANAGED to defeat a number of the lesser demons as he moved to take his position. He stopped in front of two of those icy blue creatures and smiled. "At least you two look somewhat human," he said, and rolled to his left to avoid a shower of ice spears that flew at him. Once he came to his feet, the silver demons stood with what looked like ice swords in their hands. They made not a sound, but charged at him, freezing the ground with every step.

* * *

KENYATTA FELLED another Ren and a score of lesser demons in the middle of the horde so that only the more powerful ones remained.

Sekimaru left streaks of light in the air as it passed, cutting through every demon in its path. Two Ren came from the rear and attempted to flank Akemi. She launched a small handful of shurikens at the fiend on the left, while leaping to the right. The instant the shurikens struck the Ren on the left, she slashed the leg from underneath the Ren on the right.

As soon as her foot touched the ground, she launched herself in the opposite direction, hurling another handful of shurikens at the fiery demon on the right just as she plunged her mighty sword into the belly of the recovering Ren on the left. The now one-legged Ren on the right received a chest full of shurikens and had just enough time to see the other Ren dissipating from behind the human that now glided at its face. An instant later, its head was dissipating in midair along with its body.

"Nice moves back there!" Kenyatta yelled from the distance.

Behind Akemi, five of those smaller silver demons tumbled and dissipated, and then her brother and the strider darted criss-cross through the path, passing each other in the air. The last Ren stomped in front of her, then split in two and dissipated, and she saw Kita in the wake of smoke and ashes. He darted to the right and stabbed a nightmare in the head and then the midsection.

Across the battlefield, she saw the strider's strange sword moving like lightning as it sliced through the air with a *shing*.

The path behind them was cleared save the last few lesser fiends that Kenjiro had eliminated, and when the ninja turned, she saw that Kenyatta was facing two Tasarien. Their crab-like pincers snapped and clanked as they moved closer. Kenyatta backed away until he stood beside his ninja partner. "So do we each take one, then?" he said.

"Why?" came a hideous reply. "Are we too much for you, human?"

"They understand us?" he whispered.

"Some do, yes," she replied. "Now how will you respond?"

"With these," he said with a smirk, holding up his blades.

The Tasarien in front of him sneered. "Human with such confidence find himself scattered across the valley, yes?"

The four adversaries charged each other, Akemi on the left and Kenyatta on the right. The Tasarien, although they stood better than ten feet tall, were surprisingly fast and agile. Several times Kenyatta was almost cut in two by a quick snap of one of those pincers.

* * *

KENJIRO AND KITA faced the four silver demons, but when the samurai saw that Shinobu came face to face with two nightmares, he wavered. "Kita, you must get to the strider. He knows not what he attempts to fight alone. One mistake and they can destroy his mind."

"I don't doubt you, samurai," Kita said, "but how do I get past these things, and that scaly one that's moving toward us?"

"I'll hold these four," Kenjiro said. "The scaly one is your business."

Steel clashed with ice as the two warriors worked as one against four foes, then stood back-to-back when the four demons backed away to regroup.

"When I signal," Kenjiro said over his shoulder, "duck, then jump over the one in front of me."

"Ok."

The silver demons formed up again and converged. "Now!" the samurai yelled.

Kita ducked low, and Kenjiro whipped the sword over his head, taking one of the icy fiends in the neck. It stumbled backward, and in that instant, Kita leaped backward over the samurai's head. When his feet touched the ground, he thrust his staff backward, stabbing the fiend behind him, then rotated the staff up to knock away the slashing claw of the scaled demon.

"Well done!" he heard Kenjiro yell from behind.

* * *

SHINOBU SLASHED through the pitch-black demons, but they seemed to be made of nothing solid. The area that he cut would tear, then mend back together. They came at him straightforward, and the strider leaped over them and then turned to narrowly avoid a swipe at his head. One nightmare managed to slam him into the ground with its claw, then lift him and slam him again. They were surprisingly fast.

He growled away the pain and flipped back to his feet, his hand resting over his shoulder on the hilt of his sword. "Not bad," he grunted. "I was beginning to wonder if there were any among you that posed any kind of challenge." Despite Shinobu's sarcasm, he was hurt, but there was no reason for them to know that.

He ran toward the fiends, then darted to the side while slashing in a horizontal zigzag. One of the nightmares was hit several times and thrown on the defense, but the pounding he'd just taken had slowed him. Before he could react, the other Nightmare came forward and fell over him.

He held his breath and slashed. Finally, he passed through its black body and splashed out the other side, landing on his knees and curling his arms around his midsection. His pupils contracted into little black dots, and he gulped for air, shaking his head in denial of the images assaulting his mind.

As the two fiends emerged behind him, he held his head, trying to fight the excruciating pain, unaware of his surroundings. His body felt as cold as ice on the inside, but burned on the outside. His mind raced with every thought he had ever had in his life, past to present. Every thought, emotion and fear slammed into his head in an instant, combined with the bodily pain that raked through him.

* * *

KITA FOUGHT with the scaled demon and found that this one used its tail and plated scales to deadly effect. He parried and ducked several swipes, only to counterattack and his weapon skip off of the strong hard plates on its body. Suddenly, when he saw Shinobu on his knees and the two dark fiends closing on him, he twisted the shaft of his weapon at the middle, and the butt of his spear slid back to reveal a second blade.

He had no time to marvel at the surprising modification, however, for he had to duck another horizontal swipe. The demon was strong but not fast or intelligent, and Kita stabbed it, retracted, then whipped the staff down, cutting it down the face and chest. It wailed as its body dissipated.

* * *

KENYATTA AND AKEMI battled the long-limbed Tasarien without gaining much foothold. They were agile for their size, and used their long limbs with surprising intelligence.

The islander ducked, barely avoiding a swipe at his head, then hopped to avoid another swipe at his feet, only to be slammed to the ground by a third strike. He rolled aside just in time to avoid being drilled into the ground by the stabbing pincer.

The ninja demon hunter danced with her foe while *Sekimaru* radiated a mighty hunger that her savage adversary had to feel. "You know of the might of *Sekimaru?*" she asked with an edge of superiority in her voice.

"Do you know of the might of my strike, little human?" it responded in a thin, crackly voice. "Your little toy seems to have some spirit, but it will never know its thirst quenched while in your hand."

"Is that so?" the ninja chortled.

She rolled toward the demon, and drove *Sekimaru* home. The Tasarien roared in agony, then raised its huge pincer to slam it down on her head.

The sword was deeply entrenched in the fiend and Akemi could not remove it. The blow was coming but she couldn't remove the blade and would have to abandon the embedded sword.

Out of the corner of her eye she saw a figure gliding toward them, and the huge pincer fell to the ground and turned to black mist. Kenjiro landed opposite the beast and looked over his shoulder. Akemi looked around the fiend at him and nodded.

The samurai brought his sword up just as the demon rounded on him, and scored a deep cut in the remaining pincer. The blow stung, but the demon managed to land a kick to the samurai's midsection that sent him flying backward. It fell to its knees, having spent the last of its dissipating energy and succumbed to the ferocity of the hungry blade embedded in its midsection.

Akemi gasped, looking at her sword after the demon was gone. *Sekimaru* had never fed so fiercely before, and its power was almost overwhelming. Now she knew why she felt a bit drained after their fight in the canyon. She stood on shaky feet and almost tumbled over.

The ground trembled at the roar of the four pit demons. She looked up and saw that the kick from the Tasarien had landed her brother right into their midst. She jumped to her feet and sprinted in their direction only to skid to a stop. She'd forgotten about Kenyatta, who still fought the remaining Tasarien, and seemed to have given a bit of foothold.

Kenyatta saw her hesitance and yelled at her. "Stop watching me and get over there, he needs you and I don't!" He smiled at her after parrying another blow. "Besides, I don't like people to watch me fight."

The ninja said nothing and hurried to her brother.

* * *

KITA TWISTED the shaft of his staff, retracting the rear blade, then twisted the bottom part of the shaft. The weapon fell limp into its whip-chain form. He spun it from left shoulder to right shoulder, turning his body in order to build the momentum. Turning his body again, he brought his hands around and sent the blade flying through the air to pierce the back of one of the nightmares and plunge out of its chest.

It hissed and rounded on the warrior, grabbing the chain and pulling him toward it. Kita was unable to react quickly enough, and was drawn in and swatted aside. Through the dizzying pain he still managed to hold onto his weapon. Unfortunately, that instinct allowed the nightmare to yank him back once again and catch him in its hand begin squeezing the life from his body.

* * *

SHINOBU, still suffering through the torment of the nightmare, felt the presence of the demon from behind. Anger flooded into him, and his eyes snapped open. "I hope you're ready for this," he growled.

The strider hopped to his feet and in one fluid motion, turned and drew his blade. He cut the fiend in every direction, left to right, up and down and diagonal. The blows came with such speed the monster could not hope to defend itself. Pieces of it flew in every direction, and before long there was nothing left but shreds of black particles dissipating into black mist. Shinobu dropped to his knees once more and grabbed his head. Another nightmare came behind him, its yellow eyes glowing.

* * *

THE TASARIEN'S blows were heavy, and Kenyatta had to bring both swords up to successfully parry its attacks.

"How long before you falter, human?" it asked in that wicked, crackly voice.

"Funny," Kenyatta replied, especially wary of those huge razor-sharp pincers snapping at his neck. If this demon got ahold of him with one of those pincers, it would snap him in half.

The fiend drew back and launched its right pincer straight at him. Kenyatta dropped to one knee and slashed upward, scoring a long gash along its arm. It hissed and recoiled, but that split second earned it another slash across the leg. When it dropped to a knee, he thrust his swords into its midsection several times before it was able to slam him to the ground with its arm. Kenyatta blinked away the stars in his vision and rolled back to his feet, gasping for air.

* * *

WEAKENED THOUGH THE DEMON WAS, Kita still struggled in vain to break free of the nightmare's vice-like grip. Then, seemingly from nowhere and everywhere at once, he heard a voice in his head.

"Maintain your concentration. Keep your mind focused."

He didn't know where the voice came from, but it gave him a flicker of strength. For a moment, he was able to separate from the pain and concentrate on freeing his weapon. Growling, he pulled the weapon free and snapped the shaft together, twisting it into its double-bladed form. Kita stabbed the nightmare in the face till it dropped him. Then he spun the staff vertically, slicing the monster repeatedly before finally driving the blade home.

* * *

"INFINITE PAIN, despair, and torture is your fate. All that you love will wither for eternity and you will burn and freeze for all time. You will be dismembered and put back together for the pleasure of being taken apart again. Lowly human, your soul will be ripped to shreds and fed to the lowest forms of the abyss."

All of this and far worse bombarded the strider. Every path he took in his mind to escape the hideous suggestions lead to another one, for there was nowhere he could hide from the nightmare.

A sharp pain like nothing he'd ever felt pierced his chest and through his heart. His chest felt cold, and then numb, and he was paralyzed on his knees, awaiting oblivion. Despair and resolution consumed him. Isolation absorbed him and he felt dark and alone with no one to help. There was no hope, no sense in resisting. He may as well open his arms and welcome death and the abyss that was to become his new home for eternity. His foe was stronger than he and it was impossible to win.

Then he felt a fire grow from deep within, and it gave him strength. He rose to one knee. "Your suggestions would work on someone with the will of a coward," he growled. "I am no coward!"

Shinobu gritted his teeth and struggled to his feet. "You've made a fatal mistake, demon." A surge of energy rushed through the strider as he straightened. The nightmare doubled its efforts and the pain seared through every part of his being. He dropped to his knees again, but in an instant the pain was gone and his head cleared. He managed to turn his head to see Kita standing between him and the dissipating nightmare. Then he fell into darkness.

* * *

KENYATTA STAGGERED to his feet and raised his weapons. The Tasarien now had many glowing holes in its chest, and its green lifeblood dripped from its poisonous maw. "Not bad, human. But not good enough, either. You must do better if you are to best me." Then it stood tall and still, and its eyes turned milky white. The blue sparks from the tips of its horns flickered with building energy.

What now? Kenyatta thought as he watched the sparks between its horns. A surge of blue energy flew at him like a bolt of lightning, and even with his remarkable reflexes, Kenyatta was unable to avoid the bolt. He was blasted several dozen feet away and hit the ground rolling until he came to a stop, convulsing and struggling to regain his feet. Another bolt shot at him, but somehow he managed to roll away in time to avoid it. The Tasarien moved in closer, building its energy for what Kenyatta knew was a final blast of energy that would destroy him. To his right he saw Akemi standing in front of a recovering Kenjiro, and four approaching pit demons.

The Tasarien let loose another blast, and on pure instinct Kenyatta pointed one of his swords at the demon, and the other at one of the hulking pit demons in front of the ninja. The sword harnessed the energy and it passed through the blade, then through Kenyatta's body, then through and out of his other sword and shot directly at the targeted pit demon. His body vibrated but he held firm as the bolt jarred the pit demon and knocked it to the ground.

"Clever little insect," the Tasarien rasped.

Kenyatta barely registered the comment, still shaking from the bolt that had passed through him. There was an angry roar from behind, and he saw, through blurry vision, the pit demon rise and disappear, reappearing behind the Tasarien. It grabbed the squirming fiend's throat and ripped it out, then dropped it to the ground where it lay evaporating into a mist. Kenyatta backed away on wobbly legs, his swords at the ready. To his good fortune, the pit demon gave him no notice, but turned and headed back to the others.

* * *

NOT QUITE BELIEVING HIS LUCK, Kenyatta saw his friend drag the limp strider to rest under a group of boulders, then rush to aid Akemi and Kenjiro. He concentrated on steadying his wobbly legs and started after the departing fiend that had just inadvertently saved him. He was unsure if he should attack the pit demon closest to him now or wait. He'd seen firsthand what it could do and had no desire to tangle with the thing on his own. Still, the original plan had fallen apart by now, and they would have to fight one each by themselves.

Akemi dropped to one knee and began to chant in a language the others did not understand. She thrust *Sekimaru* into the ground and closed her eyes. She gripped the hilt of the sword with her left hand and held her right hand in front of her face, fingers curled downward except for her index and middle fingers, which were bent but pointing up. The pit demons struck hard at the two humans, but when they did, a transparent shield blocked them. Akemi fell further in meditation, and every time one of the massive fiends struck the shield, she staggered.

Kita sprinted toward them to try and even the odds, hoping that Kenyatta would be able to handle the straggling pit demon without any help.

Kenyatta trotted, then sprinted to catch the massive demon. He leaped at the fiend and dug both blades deep into its back. The hide was tough, and he couldn't free his weapons. He lifted his knees up and pressed his feet on its back and held tight as it spun from left to right, reaching around its back to grab at him. He pushed with his feet and pulled with all his strength until he finally freed his blades, flying backward to land hard on the ground.

Kenyatta rolled to absorb some of the shock, then came to his feet. The furious demon rounded on him, its hands glowing and yellow flames pouring from its mouth. It sent a stream of fire at Kenyatta, who darted left and right, avoiding each blast as he worked his way toward the beast.

Akemi was weakening under force of the attacks, and after two more blows, her shield shattered. She snapped out of her meditation, snatched *Sekimaru* from the ground, and slashed the reaching hand of a fiend on her side. Kenjiro struggled to his feet and moved to her side. The three pit demons encircled them and closed in.

"To the end," the samurai said to his younger sister.

"Nonsense!" came a yell from behind, and Kita raced by in a blur to slam into one of the fiends. He scored several stabs to its chest before leaping back. The sight of their new friend brought renewed strength to the siblings, and they attacked with renewed fury.

Kenyatta knew he couldn't block such powerful blows, so he avoided or parried. Still, every parry resulted in him rolling to absorb the shock of the blow, and the shock was slowing him down. He tried just avoiding the attacks altogether, which was the only advantage he had. It slammed the ground and swung right to left, then hurled a small fireball at him, which he barely avoided. Kenyatta screamed at a sudden searing pain in his ankle, and looked down to see a flaming whip wrapped around it and burning his flesh.

Akemi managed to cut many gashes in the hide of the beast, but it seemed not to notice. It continued to advance on her despite the damage she dealt it. Its hand began to glow, and a club of fire formed in its hand.

Uh oh, she thought.

It swung the club down and she hopped to the side and slashed its wrist. It looked at her with something akin to amusement in its cruel eyes, then spat a stream of fire that nearly scorched her left side.

Kenjiro had received several injuries as he worked to keep his enemy at bay. The pit demon continued to push him back with savage attacks that the samurai could scarcely avoid.

"I've had enough of this," he growled.

The demon roared and produced a club of fire in its right hand. The club descended, and Kenjiro, with a mighty yell, brought his sword up to answer the blow. Sparks of fire erupted, and the pit demon was shocked to be held at bay by a mere human. The muscles in his arms strained as Kenjiro used all his strength to hold the monster back. He felt his strength beginning to ebb, but then a warmth trickled through his body, building until a surge of power filled him and exploded outward, sending the fiend stumbling in one direction and the samurai flying in another.

* * *

"Amazing," Sensei Akutagawa said.

"Yes," Taliah agreed.

Sensei looked at her, surprised. "I think Kenjiro just accessed a power within himself that had lain dormant till now."

"If only the others can do the same," Taliah replied.

Sensei could only nod in wonder as they both looked back to the wall that showed them the struggle of the five mighty warriors, and Takashaniel's best chance at survival.

* * *

Kita parried and countered with his staff. Because of the two-handed weapon's length, he was afforded more leverage to absorb the shock of such heavy blows. The pit demon's chest glowed with red fire from the many wounds he had inflicted upon it. It seemed the fight would never end, but finally, the beast fell to its hands and knees.

It had barely fallen when Kita thrust his staff into the monster's throat. He pulled the weapon free and separated it into its chain form, whipping it around his back, then swinging it wide to wrap about the demon's neck. With a grunt, he yanked the chain free, shredding the pit demon's throat.

Kita drew the chain back and snapped it into a staff once more, and with a final thrust sent it deep into the monster's chest, sending it back to the dark realm.

* * *

THE PIT DEMON dragged him closer to it with its whip. The fire was gone now, but the pain from the burned skin was screaming at his senses. On top of that, a ring of fire now surrounded the monster, and it was pulling him into it. He tried cutting at the whip but it was made of unearthly material. In desperation, he launched his left sword into the monster's chest and it released the whip and howled, stumbling back.

Kenyatta and the fiend seemed almost to have fought to a stalemate, each injured but determined to kill the other. Just when Kenyatta had run out of ideas, the monster staggered as it succumbed to the enchanted sword embedded in its chest. He charged in and stabbed the beast with his remaining blade and then withdrew the other and stabbed continually before it could recover.

Kenyatta then brought his blades up over his head in a cross to block the descending club of fire that the pit demon had formed in its right hand. To his surprise, he was in too close and the monster had overreached, catching its arm on the blades. Without a moment of thought, and with all the power he could muster, Kenyatta pressed the blades deeper into its arm and then slid them apart.

The demon shrieked, and its body burst into flames as an expression of its fury. It tried to push the flames outward, but it was too late. It had sustained too many injuries in this world, and the fires surrounding its body died. It crashed to the ground and melted into black mist, returning to the dark realm.

Kenyatta sat for a moment, panting and looking around. He knew it was not over, so he stood once more and limped as quickly as he could to the remaining fight.

As he approached, Kenyatta couldn't help but be impressed at the power and skill the siblings displayed as they tore through their adversaries. They worked as one, even when facing separate enemies, they fed from each other's energy.

Akemi worked even harder than before in a blinding display of speed and agility. *Sekimaru* was a blur in the air as she whirled around to attack, parry and counterattack. It was amazing that such a small sword so easily matched the power of that enormous club of fire, and the two behemoths that were the pit demons who wielded them.

Kenjiro avoided a horizontal swipe by his adversary, then came up with a diagonal upward thrust with his sword. The sword left a body-length scar that stretched from the fiend's right leg to its left shoulder and sent the demon staggering away.

Kita saw the blow land and could have sworn he saw something that looked like surprise on the demon's face. It gave an angry roar and plunged its fist deep into the ground and ripped out a bed of solid rock. It hurled the flat rock at the samurai, and Kenjiro leaned forward and whipped his sword up and over in an overhead chop, slicing through the rock as if it were butter.

Kenjiro charged at the beast with a series of vertical and horizontal swipes, which it blocked with its naturally armored forearms. It waded through the assault and grabbed the samurai, lifting him up to eye level. Kenjiro could see the fire in its eyes, as well as the fire dancing in its mouth.

He needed to think fast. His sword arm was pressed to his side, but his other arm was free. The pit demon drew in a deep breath, and

Kenjiro struggled to turn the sword upward and stab the beast in the wrist. It loosened its grip just enough for Kenjiro to slip his arm free and grab the embedded sword. He pulled the sword free, reversed the grip, and stabbed the beast in the top of its hand between two of its four fingers. The fiend reflexively dropped him, and as soon as the samurai touched the ground, he shot forward and thrust his sword deep into the midsection, then with all his strength, cut out sideways and hurled himself to the side and rolled back to his feet.

The monster made an angry, moaning sound, clutching its torn abdomen. It stared hatefully at him, then whipped out a hand and hurled a bolt of fire at the samurai, who stood crouching and holding his ribs. Just before the bolt hit its mark, Kenyatta tackled Kenjiro aside just as the flaming ball passed. Kenyatta's back was singed, and he lay there, eyes clamped shut, groaning against the sting.

"Don't say I never did anything nice for you, samurai," he growled through clenched teeth.

* * *

AKEMI DARTED LEFT TO RIGHT, avoiding the pit demon's tireless assault. Although it was far stronger than she, *Sekimaru* still held true, and met every bit of the monster's power with its own fury. Finally tired of the game, the beast raised its fiery club into the air and, before bringing it down, stomped its foot into the ground, creating a small tremor.

The ninja was thrown off balance, but kept her feet as the monster brought its club down with enough force drive her into the earth. *Sekimaru* flared to life, and when Akemi brought the sword up to deflect the blow, it destroyed the flaming club.

The demon went into a fit of rage and brought its hand down to slam the ninja into the ground, but again she brought *Sekimaru* forth and ran the sword through its palm. The monster had never known such pain and tried to pull free, but the sword drained its dark life force.

Akemi was overwhelmed by the surge of dark power and her strength faltered. Just when she could no longer withstand the struggle between the fiend and the hungry sword, she heard the strider's sword slice through the air.

The demon stumbled backward and fell to the ground, and Akemi saw Shinobu standing behind it, holding his head with one hand and barely standing upright. He managed a glint of a smile before he turned his gaze back to the fiend, trying to rise. *Sekimaru* had drained a great deal of the pit demon's material energy, and it was having a hard time maintaining itself in this dimension. Black mist seeped from its many wounds, and it began to dissipate. The ninja went in for the killing blow and cut the beast deeply across the neck. Its roar turned into a sickening gurgle. Then, in dying revenge, it threw its hand in front of the ninja. Red light glowed from its palm, and Akemi drew her sword in front of her and braced her other arm behind it just as the flames engulfed her.

"No!" Kenjiro ran toward his sister, but there was nothing he could do. The monster descended back to the dark plane, and when the smoke thinned, Akemi stood with her arms crossed, *Sekimaru* in a reverse grip, and tendrils of smoke slithering from her body. Then her knees buckled and she fell to the ground.

"I'm sorry," Kenyatta said once he reached the samurai, crouched over Akemi. "I did not want to interfere in your battle so I hesitated."

"Save your apology for the day that you do interfere in our fight," the samurai responded. "She would rather die than accept help in a fight that she was confident she could win."

"Why did she not burn?" Kita asked. "The demon engulfed her in flames."

"The pit demon's flame," Kenjiro answered. "They can control how it affects this world. The fire that burns her is inside, not outside." He looked down at his unconscious sister as he spoke. "If the pit demon was not already weakened, it might have killed her. The only thing that prevented the flames from consuming her completely was quick thinking on her part. Her sword absorbed some of the energy from that thing, but whether it was enough to save her...." He trailed off, holding a hand to her forehead.

"Is there something we can do?" Kita asked.

"I know of some herbs that may help, but I don't know how effective it will be against this. Watch her," Kenjiro bade them. "I will return shortly." Kita rested a hand on the samurai's shoulder and nodded. Leaving his younger sister in the care of the other three warriors, Kenjiro left in search of the proper herbs.

When he returned, the others had laid her under a tree in the shade and placed a cool, wet washcloth on her head.

"She's burning up," Kita said. Shinobu looked up at Kenjiro, who sat and riffled through a sack of supplies. Kenyatta neither looked up nor said a word. A cloud of grief had settled over him and he could lift his gaze no higher from the ground than to Akemi.

"I would rather her anger than her death," he said solemnly.

"We want neither," Kenjiro replied, and there was a hint of comfort in his tone.

"We must move her from this shade into the sun for a while," he said at length. The others looked at him, incredulous.

"She singes to the touch and it is a hot day," Shinobu said. "Why bring her into the heat when she has too much already?"

"A different kind of heat," the samurai answered, never taking his eyes from his sister. "The sun heals and replenishes, and its rays will help burn the taint from her."

Kenjiro carefully lifted Akemi and moved her out of the shade. Her skin had turned red as if she were sunburned. He started a campfire, then boiled some water and crushed some leaves in it, then added the herbs he had found not far away.

"What is all of this?" Kita asked.

"I am making a solution made from Kokoya leaves and some

other herbs that I have. She must drink some of it, then we let the rest sit until it forms into a balm, and we will apply it externally."

Kita watched as Kenjiro worked on the remedy. Although he appeared confident, Kita could see that the man was worried. The lines in his forehead ran deep, and he never lifted his gaze from his sister except to attend to the medicine. His hands moved quickly and carefully and he always laid his hand on her head. Kita looked over his shoulder at his friend. Kenyatta had climbed a nearby hill by himself and had been there for a while. He hoped for Akemi's sake and for his friend's, that she would recover. Kenyatta would never forgive himself regardless of what the ninja wanted.

* * *

KENYATTA STARED ABSENTLY down the hill. It was not very high, but he could see for miles. He knelt and picked up a rock and let fly.

"You can't blame yourself." The strider's voice was gentle, almost comforting. Shinobu moved beside him and picked up a rock and hurled it into the distance. "It was her fight and hers alone. If you had interfered she would have been furious."

"And alive," Kenyatta added.

"She's not dead yet, my friend. You have fought beside such warriors before, and you know the reality of battle. Every time we unsheathe our swords, we expect nothing, but are prepared for anything. I would rather die defending rather than being defended."

Kenyatta slid a few stray locks from over his forehead and leaned his head back, closing his eyes and feeling the sun warm his face. "You interfered in the fight, did you not?"

Shinobu looked at him evenly. "That was to save her from her sword, not her adversary." At Kenyatta's questioning look, he explained. "I have sensed a power about that sword since first I met them, and it is a wild power. She has a measure of control over it, but she hasn't mastered it as she believes. If I had not done what I had, the power influx would have overwhelmed her."

Shinobu placed a hand on the other man's shoulder. "Whatever the outcome, we must face the future together without regret, else we might join her, supposing she does not recover. The sick are sometimes aware of those around them, so stay strong even if only for her benefit. She can likely sense our feelings and it will help her to feel our strength."

With a final pat on the shoulder, the strider left to join the others. Kenyatta continued gazing out at the open planes, but his sight was inward. The strider's words were true, but it did little to lessen the burden of guilt that he carried.

"How is she?" Shinobu asked once he had joined the others.

"Her temperature is no longer rising," Kita answered. "Now is the time to hope that it lessens."

Shinobu looked at the sleeping woman. Even in her fragile state, she was beautiful. A dangerous beauty, the strider thought. Yes, even though the ninja seemed to be resting more peacefully now, she still looked deadly, as if she could spring to life at any moment, her wild sword firmly gripped in her hand.

"The balm is almost ready," Kenjiro stated.

After a few more moments, the samurai removed the small pot from the fire and waited for it to cool. The shadows of the plants and trees were beginning to lean toward the east as dusk approached, and with it, came the gentle caress of the evening breeze. The grass and trees and surrounding hills glowed under the brightness of the orange sky as the sun made its final descent to the western horizon.

Kenjiro began gently applying the balm to his sister's face, then moved on to her arms.

"How much of this must you apply?" Kita asked.

"All except that which she must drink, "Kenjiro answered with a strained voice. "It must be applied over every inch of her body."

Both their faces coloring, Kita and Shinobu shared a look, then stood.

"We should keep watch for any danger," Shinobu said stiffly. "We'll go collect some firewood. If you need help with anything, call for us." Without looking up, the samurai nodded and continued to apply the ointment.

"Do you think our mission is done?" Shinobu asked as they walked.

"Hardly," Kita replied. "There is a lot more to this, trust me. Stay on guard and expect anything." Their arms laden with dry branches and twigs, Shinobu glanced back toward the camp at the shadowy figure of Kenjiro redressing his sister.

"I think we can go back now," he said.

"Give him a few minutes or until he calls us," Kita responded.

Shinobu nodded and they placed their burdens in piles and walked a bit further from camp.

"How's Kenyatta?" Kita asked.

"Feeling totally responsible and extremely guilty," came the response. "I feel that there is more to your friend's guilt than just this recent occurrence."

"There is, but that's his story to tell," Kita answered. "*If* he tells it." Night had fallen when they returned, and to everyone's relief, Akemi's temperature had lessened considerably. The color had also begun to return to her skin, as she slept peacefully in front of the campfire.

"I was able to suppress the effects for now, but in time the demon fire will spark again with more strength." The worried look on the samurai's face was concerning. "There is nothing else I can do to help her now."

"What then?" Kita asked. Kenyatta had returned to the camp while they were gone, and listened while he prepared the meal.

"We must get her to the tower," Kenjiro said, a glimmer of hope entering his eyes for the first time since the battle. "If we can get her there in time, perhaps they can help."

"How far are we from there?" Kita asked.

"Don't know," the samurai answered. There was a long stretch of silence as everyone considered the next course.

"I need to think," Kenjiro said, standing. He looked over Akemi once more, then disappeared into the night.

Akemi stirred to the sound of soft conversation. They had wrapped her in a blanket and laid her a bit away from the fire. She opened her eyes and rolled to face the voices. She felt tired, as if she had won some internal battle, but her foe lay in wait for her to weaken.

"Brother," she whispered. She barely heard her own words, but as soon as she'd spoken them, Kenjiro was at her side.

"I was wondering when you would decide to join us again," he teased.

Akemi smiled. For her brother to attempt a joke meant he was more than a little concerned. "I needed a rest," she responded with a weak smile.

Without a word, Kenjiro stood and left, then returned a moment later with a bit of meat and some rice. "Eat. I mixed some of the medicine in this before its composition changed into the balm."

Akemi took the wooden bowl. She hadn't realized how hungry she was until that first bite, and she devoured the contents quickly. She could feel her strength seeping back into her body.

"Careful you don't bite off a finger, little sister," Kenjiro teased, frowning.

"Not bad," she said, surprised that her brother knew how to cook anything.

"I did not prepare it," he said with a chuckle.

Akemi shrugged and continued to eat. In mid-bite, she stopped and regarded him. "Balm," she asked, her voice going flat as comprehension dawned. Kenjiro nodded, his face coloring. "You used the kokoya herbal remedy?" Akemi asked, feeling heat rising in her cheeks. "Where did you find the leaves? You brought none."

"Luckily I found some not far from here," he answered.

Akemi took another bite, not wanting to ask the next question. "And when and where exactly did you apply the *whole body* remedy, brother?"

Kenjiro stared at the ground as if the answer would sprout from the ground like the plant he'd used. "They left while I applied it, you need not worry."

Her cheeks coloring brightly, Akemi opened and looked down her blanket. Sighing in relief that she was clothed, she stood and removed it.

"Where are you going?" Kenjiro asked. "You need rest."

"I will. But I see our group numbers four, and I wish to find the one who is missing."

She found Kenyatta at the top of a hill overlooking the planes below, oblivious to the brisk night air. "Your concern is touching," she said.

"We need the extra person to keep watch for the night," the islander responded a bit too casually. Akemi smiled and moved beside him, hooking her arm in his.

"You think about the past and let it torment you in the present."

"What do you mean?" he asked.

"A bit of advice," she said, ignoring the question. "Learn from the past, but don't live in it. Misplaced grief and guilt are more dangerous than ten pit demons."

She turned him to face her, and Kenyatta saw fire in her eyes. Whatever the injuries to her body, her spirit was strong. She wrapped him a long hug and then gave him a playful punch in the chest that made him stumble backward in surprise.

"If you had interfered in my fight, *Sekimaru* would have found your chest instead of my fist." With a smile, she leaned in and gave him a long peck on the cheek, then returned to the campsite.

Kenyatta stared after her in disbelief. Finally, with a shake of his head, he followed. Of the many warriors he and Kita had fought alongside and against, none were more unusual. Never had he met a woman with such girlish charm, yet seductive maturity. Even after a flirt with death and an uncertain future, she was able to joke and smile. Determination flared in him, and he found himself smiling. *Nothing will stop us from getting her to the tower in time*, he thought. *Even if I have to carry her halfway across the world myself.*

31

The fight was endless, the enemy unstoppable. She looked to her right and saw Kenjiro struggling to hold a pit demon at bay as it forced him to his knees. She looked to her left and saw Kenyatta facing another. There was no smile on his face, no joking or taunting remarks. His face was grim and cold with resolution. His movements empty and meaningless, only serving to half-heartedly turn aside his adversary's attacks. The fire and vigilance in his eyes had given way to hopelessness.

Behind her, Kita was in the grip of another pit demon while it held Shinobu in its other hand. Both screamed in fear and agony. The fiend threw its head back and roared, basking in their torment.

She tried to scream, but no sound came. She ran to help but no matter how fast she moved her legs, she came no closer. She heard Kenjiro scream, a sound she had never heard from her brother, and then all was black.

She sat up in a cold sweat, her palms and forehead dripping. For a while she just sat, looking around. The rolling hills of the once grassy landscape now lay torn and withered. The tall proud trees and bright green and blue grass now lay twisted and charred, black with soot and ash. She felt the ground vibrating beneath her and she heard a distant rumbling. She stood and looked in the direction of the sound. Coming toward her was an endless stampede of animals.

Animals not native to the region, from bison to tigers and horses, predators and prey, all running together. The ninja had never seen anything of the sort and it was unsettling. What could make these animals flee together?

Once the stampede had passed, she saw other creatures approaching. They blazed a trail of destruction, twisting and burning, slashing and ripping everything in their path. It was an endless mass of demons varying in size and appearance. Everything they touched, every piece of land underfoot was consumed in death and darkness.

In seconds, the army of fiends was upon her. She reached for *Sekimaru* but the sword was not to be found, nor were any of her other weapons. There she stood, weaponless and without any resources to stop the dark incursion. Not that she could do much by herself.

With resolution, she stood tall and straight, her legs and palms together. She closed her eyes and concentrated on the power within. Her body began to glow, and soon she would be consumed in a powerful blaze of light, but the twisted monsters would die with her.

The harder she searched for the light within, the more it escaped her. She fell to her knees and opened her eyes, looking at her palms. Her mind and inner light had failed.

"You cannot destroy us, useless animal," a frightening voice said to her. She looked up to face a rather small fiend. It was no larger than she was, but the malevolence that it exuded was overwhelming. She sat on her knees, paralyzed by fear.

"Because of your failure, your friends and brother have fallen, one by one. We allowed each to watch the other die to the last, and now they continue their existence forever in torment."

"Liar!" Akemi shouted.

The fiend laughed at her. "What do you know, hairless monkey? Your little mission was over before it started. Your hopeless fight is ended, and you will watch us destroy the tower, and with it, every shred of hope to live in the world of light again."

The demon laughed at her. "Once the Drek was destroyed, the gate between our two worlds was forever opened and now we will rule this plane. Our mighty leader comes, and all that you know will perish. And you, will continue your infinite destruction and reconstruction. You have not known agony, primate, but you will."

The creature laughed again, a horrid, triumphant laugh, then walked on. Every one of the foul creatures in her path walked by her as if she was not there, and there was nothing she could do but watch. Again her mind was bombarded with tormenting words.

"Your brother squirmed and screamed most of all." Akemi held her head and struggled against the suggestions. "I was the one to destroy him, and at the end of his pitiful life, he begged me to allow him to cease to exist, but in reward for his cowardice, I made him my personal property. Soon I will give him to the master."

Akemi spun to face a nightmare demon standing behind her. It was tall and black as night with haunting yellow eyes. Although it had no mouth, it projected laughter at her. Then, it suddenly reached out and grabbed her shoulder and shook her violently.

"Akemi!" it shouted at her, laughing. She fought to break its grip, but it was like trying to pry iron from her shoulder. "Akemi!" It screamed again, but this time, it was not laughing; it almost sounded concerned. "AKEMI!"

She awoke and jerked away from the hand that was attached not to a nightmare demon, but her brother. She scanned the area, her eyes rolling around in her head. The others were crouched around her, and Kenyatta stood a bit in the distance, his turn at watch. The dark of night had begun to fade, and the coming of dawn was not far away.

"You were having a bad dream," Kenjiro said.

"No dream," she responded while gazing into nowhere. "That

was too real to be a dream." Akemi sat up on her elbows and drew her knees in against her chest. "I think they've entered my subconscious. It felt very real, and some of the things they said were obviously untrue, yet I almost believed them. I think there was a bit of the future in the dream though, or maybe a possible future. Perhaps they gave me a bit more information than they intended."

She closed her eyes for a few heartbeats, then opened them and sighed. "You aren't going to like this. We have been misled. When one of those things was telepathically taunting me, I caught a glimpse of their plans. That group we destroyed yesterday was not moving in the direction of Takashaniel. They were moving in the opposite direction. Our enemy has effectively distracted us and moved us farther away from our objective."

Seeing the others crouched around her, Kenyatta had returned to camp. "Has the attack begun already?"

"Not yet, but it will before we can get there." Akemi afforded them all a hopeful look. "There is still time."

"And how do we get to this Takashel?" Shinobu asked. "Were you not given mental directions to the horde, but not the tower? And who is this Eel you speak of?"

"It is Takashaniel," Akemi corrected, "and Iel is the guardian of the sacred tower. For your other question, I received mental images of their destination. The stupid thing inadvertently told me what they were about, and gave me the fastest route. It will not be happy to meet its master, once we send it back to the abyss."

"We should move now," Kita said. "We're a good distance away from our horses, so we should move."

At her request, Kenjiro reached into his pack and produced a bland-looking whistle and handed it to Akemi. "We are at least two days' ride from the tower," she said. "But we do have a bit of luck. Takashaniel lies in a path that will take us close enough to our horses to use this whistle. We will not go to get them, but when the winds carry the sound of this whistle, our two horses will come and yours will hopefully follow. We will run and they will catch us, no time wasted."

"You expect me to believe that you can blow that whistle," Shinobu, on the edge of laughter, "and our horses will not only hear from miles and miles away, but come to us?"

Akemi shrugged. "Believe or do not, it matters little. Come, we leave now."

"And what of our saddles and supplies?" Shinobu asked.

"We leave them, there is no time."

With a disbelieving sigh, the strider joined the other four warriors in cleaning up the campsite. Once finished, they set out for the Tower of Balance. Despite the labor of their pace, Kenyatta found that he enjoyed the run through the lush landscape of green and yellow hills sprinkled with trees and shrubs and flowers of every kind. They were in the countryside, many leagues outside the city of Kyokoza and headed toward the lands surrounding Tokyo and beyond. He found it revitalizing to see the earth reverting back to its natural state. It was almost as if the End of Technology marked the beginning of the earth's rehabilitation. Once or twice, he thought he saw figures watching them in the distance. Whomever or whatever they were, they made no move to intercept, but seemed content to track their progress, for whatever reason.

Kita mentally removed himself from the road and thought of home and all that lay ahead. If they did not succeed, there would be no home. And even if they did succeed, what then would become of the Earth? He was also aware of the rapidly changing world and wondered where humanity would fit in.

They passed through a city of decaying buildings and other human structures. It was once thought that concrete and metal could forever withstand any element of nature, but the earth had been given a chance and was recovering with vengeance. The buildings were wind-and-rain beaten, crumbled and disintegrating back to the earth from whence it came. The sight was almost magical when considering the relatively short amount of years following the End of Technology.

The land began a gradual incline, and soon they came upon a cliff. The five warriors seemed to think as one. No one spoke, and all trusted in each other and moved in sync, leaning left or right on their course like a flock of small birds flying in one direction and then turning abruptly in another.

As they approached the cliff they saw that it ended in a decline. Once they reached the edge they began their descent, half running half sliding while swinging around trees, hopping over rocks and sidestepping bushes. At one point the ground was so soft that it became difficult to maintain control and more than once Akemi found herself stumbling and barely avoiding a tumble to the bottom.

Difficult as the terrain was, Kenjiro watched Akemi with a worried look. She should have been able to handle this cliff with much less difficulty than she was having. The pit demon's taint must be slowly draining her strength again. He made his way to within a few feet of his sister so as to catch her in case she lost her footing.

Once they reached the bottom of the cliff, they hit the ground running. Akemi glanced over her shoulder at the others and pointed to a patch of woods just to the right of their path. At the pace they held, they would reach it within half an hour. Past the base of the cliff, the land continued to descend and the group maintained a fast pace with greater ease. Finally reaching the woods, they slowed to a jog, allowing their bodies to cool down.

After a few moments, they came upon a creek with a running stream rushing along a path that snaked through the trees. Akemi was the first to reach the stream, and dipped her hands in. She took a sip, then splashed her face. The water was cool and fresh, and leaned her head back and enjoyed the gentle breeze that blew across her wet face.

Kenjiro knelt beside his sister and dipped his hands in the

water, washing his own face. After a sip, he dipped his hands in again and drank deeply. The water was sweet and cool, and he felt refreshed.

After everyone had washed their faces and had their fill, Shinobu broke the silence. "I'm modestly familiar with this region. The terrain will be easier for our horses to navigate...."

"If they weren't so far away," Kita added, and the strider choked back a snicker.

"Yes," Akemi replied, ignoring the jab. "I'm actually quite familiar with this area. We left them that way." She pointed northeast of their location.

Now Shinobu did laugh. "Might I ask again how they are going to hear this magical whistle of yours?"

"There is nothing magical about my whistle," Akemi replied patiently. "We are about to pass through a narrow mountainous area where the winds carry sound much farther than normal."

"It's going to have to carry sound really far," Shinobu said, shaking his head.

"It is in this pass," Akemi said, ignoring him, "that the wind will carry our call a distance that would normally be impossible. After we rest here, we will enter the pass. There are multiple paths that snake through the mountain range. One of them is in the general direction our horses should be."

"If they're still there," Kenyatta muttered.

"Our horses know to wait for us," the ninja replied. "And since horses are herd animals, there is a good chance yours will remain with them."

The five companions ran off and on for the better part of the day, and the evening was a few hours away. They had traveled more than a score of miles and were on the brink of exhaustion when they decided to rest again. Shinobu reached into a travel pouch and produced a hunk of bread that he divided amongst the companions. Kita drew the remaining pouch of water that they had taken from Takashaniel. They'd hidden the other three in the woods with the horses, but Kita had felt the need to bring one, even at the cost of its inconvenience. Glad he was, that he had decided to bring it along. He still wondered how they had acquired the drink from the tower when they had not physically gone there. The only explanation he could think of was that Taliah must have traveled by portal and brought the pouches with her before the others awoke.

After sharing the bread and a chunk of cheese and some dried seaweed, they sat and talked. After some time, the group had taken a nap after a long protest in vain against Kenyatta remaining awake while the others slept. "Everyone here is capable of waking at the slightest sound," the ninja had said. "Why keep watch?"

"Exhaustion might slow your reaction," he'd argued. "Just sleep. I'm fine."

Akemi saw in his eyes that the islander would not budge on the topic, so she'd relented. After a few hours, Akemi was the first to awaken. She lay on her side, staring at Kenyatta's back. Although he insisted that he was past it, she could feel the grief and guilt in him.

"How was your nap?" He asked over his shoulder.

"Refreshing," she replied, rising. She moved beside him and stretched. "You will be able to continue? We have a great distance to run still."

Kenyatta smiled. "I will be fine. Iel spoke true. The water has a sustaining effect. I feel that I can continue without a problem." He looked closer into her eyes. They were dark black orbs that seemed to be a gateway to a void of nothingness. "It's creeping back into you. It won't be long before it overtakes you again." He saw the strain on her face and regretted bringing it up.

"I'll be fine." She smirked at him. "If I can get the rest of you to quit slobbering all over me with your worry."

The islander laughed for the first since time since their fight with the horde. "So you think you can keep this pace until the horses catch us?"

"Whether I think I can or not is no matter. I must, and that is all there is to it."

Kenyatta looked at the woman with admiration. She could be touched by a dark power and face a tortured death, yet still remain in good spirits.

The others awoke moments later and began gathering the few supplies they had brought. There was not much to clean, for their stay had only lasted a few hours and there was no need for a camp-fire. Shinobu looked up at the sky and frowned. "Visibility will not be in our favor."

"Maybe not," Kita responded, "but we have to press on. For all we know, Takashaniel may already be under attack."

Kenjiro moved beside Kenyatta. "No sign of anything?"

"Nothing," Kenyatta answered. He looked at the siblings standing on either side of him, remembering a question that he'd meant to ask some time ago. "I admit my ignorance in affairs that concern the dark realm, but I found it strange that those demons move so freely in daylight."

"Human folklore stems from truth and fiction intertwined," the ninja said. "Daylight means nothing to them, although they do prefer darkness. Quentranzi in particular are resistant to everything in this world. The hottest magma from the core of the earth would not burn them, and the coldest bite of the arctic would not freeze them. The cut of an earthly sword might remove a limb and cause pain, but nothing more. Only by the means available to us, can they be sent back to the abyss. This is why the Drek that Iel speaks of is the first to make such an attempt in so long a time."

Kenyatta looked at her and frowned. "So, someone has tried this before? What person could be capable of summoning such evil as what we've encountered?"

"I will tell you this and then we must go." Akemi looked out at the open fields, but her gaze went farther still. "Once, I was told of a powerful mage that lived before the Age of Technology. It was during this time that many different forms of life inhabited the world, and magic was more commonplace than now. This mage was the most powerful of all mages of the world, or so it has been said. In time, however, he succumbed to temptation, and the power corrupted him.

"His peers realized that he was becoming too powerful too quickly and they warned him to be careful. Growing ever more powerful, however, the mage took their warnings as a sign of weakness and jealousy, and ignored them. The more powerful he became the darker his mind grew. Soon he began to study more of the dark arts, believing them to be the source of true power.

"Every mage must study some of the dark arts," the ninja continued. "But they usually study only enough to understand them so as to be able to effectively defend against it. When one studies the arts out of personal interest and desire, that is when things go ill and the mind becomes vulnerable. This mage had walked the line between light and dark for so long for so long that his developing interest in the dark arts crossed the line. By the time the others of his order realized how far he'd fallen and decided to move against him, the mage had a fully developed knowledge of necromancy and demon summoning.

"It started with summoning an imp or two, something all mages are capable of. Then he summoned a tryte demon, a great deal stronger than an imp, but not so powerful that he could not control it. He would send these fiends on small tasks while maintaining a strong 'leash,' or 'tether' to them. After much success in using these creatures, he became more and more confident and his summonings became more and more ambitious until he was able to summon a Tasarien. Although the force of such a fiend was vastly overwhelming, he was able to hold it in the seal he had created, and that gave him even greater confidence.

"He had one day discovered through one of his imps—a familiar, as they are called—that the other members of his Order were conspiring against him. The man was amused by the discovery, and sensing his growing arrogance, the imp suggested that he summon a demon from the most powerful race of demons in the dark realm."

"By that time, he had grown to trust his familiar, since it was incapable of harming him. But in his arrogance, he forgot that an imp's power lay not in its physical or magical prowess, but in its power of suggestion. It subtly manipulated his thoughts and finally, after some coaxing, convinced him that he was more than capable of summoning a Quentranzi demon."

Akemi looked at the ground and then back to the path where she and the others now walked. "That was his undoing. Powerful he was, but no human is powerful enough to summon such a terrible monster. The imp knew this, and waited patiently as the foolish human grew in confidence and arrogance."

Finally, the mage summoned a Quentranzi, and although it was among the weakest of its brethren, the beast was still far more powerful than the dark mage could have imagined. Its presence was overwhelming but it appeared to be held by the seal."

She smirked. "He was a fool. He didn't know that Quentranzi are adept at manipulation. This fiend was no different, and in its infinite patience it let the human plan and prepare for the destruction of his Order, all the while feeding his ego and awaiting the opportunity it needed. After some time, the mage 'unleashed' the demon on his peers, and despite the combined efforts of the mages, it destroyed them all.

"The fiend had been taxed in the fight, but was far from weak, and when it returned, it laughed at the mage's attempt to send it back to the abyss."

Akemi seemed on the brink of utter disgust. "The demon let him believe he was in control until it was ready to strike. The mage's prowess held him in the fight for a short time before the demon prevailed, torturing him in unspeakable ways. In the end, it took another faction, some ten monks from the Order of Dasha to send it back. Since then, it has been taboo to even speak of summoning a denizen of the abyss. Not even a simple imp."

Her features darkened. "The power of this Drek has all my respect. If we come to fight him, it will be our greatest challenge, and we still have not felt the power of the Quentranzi general. Compared to the one known as Kabriza, the demon the dark mage summoned was nothing."

Shinobu frowned. "How many of that horde of demons we fought were Quentranzi?"

Akemi turned a look on the strider that spoke of laughter. "The four pit demons could almost be considered equal to the lowest level Quentranzi demon ... almost."

"Oh, is that all?" the strider responded in mock cheerfulness.

"Sounds like we have our work cut out for us," Kita said. "That last fight was tough enough, and we still have yet to face a real Quentranzi?" He looked at Kenyatta. "Gods help us."

Akemi smiled and cupped Kita's chin in her hand. "If it makes you feel any better, the Tasarien and the pit demon are not much different than lower Quentranzi, only more simple-minded. Tasarien are much smarter than pit demons, but less powerful over-all. If we had fought a lower level Quentranzi, I believe the battle would have ended much the same."

"That would be comforting if our enemy was summoning a horde of weak Quentranzi," Kita said.

Akemi shrugged. "We will be ready."

Kenyatta thought about the growing taint he could see through the ninja's eyes, and his tone was uncharacteristically sober. "If you think so."

32

B rit walked to the balcony at the highest point of his fortress and looked out at the blight that encompassed the area. His thoughts were directed at that irritating tower and its unexpectedly resilient allies.

"Any more flawless plans, oh mighty Drek, destroyer of Takashaniel and conqueror of the world?" Kabriza's mocking tone seemed commonplace at the fortress for some time now, and Brit's patience was beginning to wear.

"Had I known I had employed forces that could not destroy five small humans wielding earthly weapons, I might have planned differently." Brit eyed the demon towering over him. "The only thing impressive about your brethren is how efficiently they managed to die."

Kabriza rumbled deep in his throat. "And yet the mighty one enlists such help, for he cannot achieve his goal alone."

Brit refrained from grinding his teeth at the insufferable creature. Since he had summoned the Quentranzi general, it had been a constant battle of sardonic comments and outright insults. The fiend was obviously waiting for him to lose his temper, and thus his control. *But why not openly challenge me if he thinks he can destroy me?* That was what puzzled him the most about the demon. "Is there another reason for your visit with me or did you merely come to pollute my ear with foolishness, Kabriza?"

The floor began to shake, and doors and windows rattled. Red flames danced in the Quentranzi's murderous eyes. "Perhaps I came to inform you that I have come to alleviate you of the burden of your life."

Brit turned a flat, unconcerned look on the fiend, then turned his back. "Perhaps," he replied. "But perhaps I could travel to your realm and destroy you all." He smirked. "Perhaps, but not likely, my demon friend."

"The humans move toward the tower," Kabriza growled. "If they succeed any further I shall find amusement in your improvising of this situation, *tether*." The demon spat the last word.

Brit kept his back turned. "That is not your concern. I summoned you for reasons that you are already aware of. Save your counsel, animal. I have made arrangements for every situation, should it arise."

"Of course you have," the demon chuckled, much to Brit's irritation. "I doubt not that you have thought of everything and left nothing to chance. I am sure you are prepared for anything to happen, mighty Drek. I feel lucky to have such an ally as you by my side. Us lowly ones should kneel before such a power. Perhaps if I am lucky, you may feel kind enough to show me what true power is. I would be most grateful."

Now Brit did turn, having reached the limits of his patience. The beast was gone. He stood for a moment, pondering this last conversation. Kabriza was not subtle with its challenge, and he was certain the fiend would attempt to undermine him at a very inconvenient time. Perhaps he could send it back to the abyss?

He expelled that thought before it had time to take root. The only reason he was able to maintain such a large host of fiends in this world was because Kabriza aided him. Not to mention a breach in contract with Grala would bring devastating results.

Further, if he did fight and defeat Kabriza, he did not relish the thought of living with the vengeful wrath of the two most powerful Quentranzi hanging over his head.

There was only one course of action and that was to play his plan through, and watch his back. He smiled to himself. *Quentranzi may be powerful and cunning, but underestimation has always been one of their shortcomings.* If his powerful ally did decide to oppose him, he would be prepared.

* * *

ZREAL AND SZHEGAZA entered the large circular room and dropped to one knee as Zreal spoke. "Apologies for the disturbance, Master," he began.

"No need for apologies, my friend," Brit responded. "Your return is welcomed. What have you for me?"

Surprised and wary at the Drek's uncharacteristic kindness, Szhegaza stood and moved forward. "We have done as you instructed, Master Brit," she said. The Zitarian presented a dark crystal that pulsated between green and blue. She started to hand it to Brit, but before her arm was completely extended, the orb levitated from her palm and floated to rest in his. Without a word, she returned to her place by Zreal's side.

"No need for such formalities," Brit said, eyeing the crystal. "Stand."

"Wards have been set about the entire fortress," Szhegaza said. "If even one of the smelly things decides to act against you, you will know."

Brit smiled. "You remind me of my wisdom in having you beside me, Zitarian." He then looked at Zreal who was making a great effort to mask his irritation.

Szhegaza offered a narrow-eyed smile that seemed to stretch more in Zreal's direction. "I am here to serve if it pleases you, Master Brit."

"I am sure," Brit replied, his expression hardening. The Zitarian warrior found her gaze dropping to the floor under that gaze.

"Understand, Szhegaza," Brit continued. "I know well, and appreciate the nature and talents of the Zitarian race."

At that moment both Szhegaza and Zreal felt a tremendous weight pressing down on them. The moment their knees started to buckle under the crushing force, it released. Szhegaza gasped and stumbled forward, but managed to keep her feet. Beside her, Zreal also panted, half doubled over.

"The Zitarian value alliance only with those worthy, Master Brit," Szhegaza said in response to the obvious warning in regard to her treacherous race.

"And what does Szhegaza feel about such an alliance?" Brit asked.

"Honored," she was quick to reply.

"You speak with sugar on your tongue, but poison can be disguised with sweetness." Brit turned his back, motioning for them to follow. They entered a lightly decorated room where each section of a wall held a different piece of history that happened long ago. Zreal shut the door and looked over the wall paintings, focusing on one featuring a being that looked much like Brit, manipulating some unseen force against a spear wielding foe. Once his attention was fully focused on it, the painting animated, becoming a moving historical account of depicted conflict.

At the end of the room was a tall mirror. Brit motioned them closer. "The Quentranzi believes that its Bachatttas are my only means of monitoring our progress. He is wrong. I see everything."

Zreal wondered if that statement was directed at more than just Kabriza.

They looked watched as their reflections in the mirror faded, then transitioned into the image of sprawling host of fiends the like neither Zreal nor Szhegaza had ever seen. They moved with remarkable speed toward the tower of light, leaving destruction in their wake.

"Do you think they will be able to get near the tower, Master?" Zreal asked.

"You don't know the Quentranzi, Zreal," Brit replied. "Takashaniel will hold them for a time, but no ward on earth can stop that horde from stomping that tower into oblivion. Although magic can defeat them, it takes powerful magic to do so, and I don't think the Ilanyan will be able to work fast enough to draw such a power from the tower. Takashaniel will fall soon, and then the only concern I will have will involve our *allies.*" He left them to ponder his words.

Szhegaza was just opening her mouth to speak when Brit returned, standing halfway in the door. "If the two of you are ready, I have considered sending you to the tower if things turn ill. You would do well to prepare." After he'd left again, Zreal and Szhegaza looked at each other.

The Zitarian shrugged. "I know you don't trust me, Zreal, but considering the company surrounding us these days, I am the least threat to you."

"I doubt that," Zreal retorted. "But I don't have much choice. We must look after each other in the midst of those things." His face twisted in disgust. "Especially since the master plans to send us into battle with them."

Szhegaza laughed. "You do have a point, my dear Zreal, but consider this. Why do you think he would send us into battle with such powerful monsters as those? Do you really think he believes the two of us could tip the scale any more in his favor? Of course not! Our usefulness lies on the path that crosses with those troublesome humans."

Zreal smiled as she left the room. "Pest control," he hissed. Standing there, Zreal considered his situation. *Strange times,* he thought. Never would he have imagined aligning himself with one of the most deceitful creatures he had ever known. Ironically, he trusted her more than his master's demon allies, but he knew to keep his disapproval to himself.

Although there was never much trust between Zetsuans and Zitarians, he had often wondered what it would be like to battle alongside his cousin species. He found himself excited at the prospect. *It has been a while since I have been in a good fight,* he thought. And after all, they were only humans.

* * *

THE FIVE WARRIORS maintained a swift pace for several hours, moving from open field to wooded patch and through the many hills that dotted the landscape. Kenjiro could hardly believe his eyes at the surroundings he now looked upon. So different, were these lands when he was a child. Sensei Akutagawa was right, the world was changing at a rapid pace and it seemed that in time, they would hardly be able to recognize it. As his mind wandered, he thought of the other possibilities. That huge thing swimming in the lake that had grabbed the Krindra back at the patch of woods they'd rested in some time back. The Krindra was a massive beast, but the water creature had little trouble snatching it into the water as if it were a small dog. Would animals like those come to inhabit the world in addition to the other changes? The samurai frowned. It was a grim possibility.

Akemi focused on nothing but keeping up, but dark thoughts and intentions kept creeping into her mind. It was a constant battle to push them out. At times when her mind was unclear, her judgment wavered under the weight of what seemed a great burden resting on her shoulders. At one point her eyes began to droop as a pervasive sleep crept on her. With an effort, she shook it off and increased her speed, but only for a short time before she fell back to a slower pace once again.

Kenjiro and Kenyatta noticed her inconsistent pace several times and kept a watchful eye. The taint was becoming stronger in her again, and neither of them knew what to do. Somehow, the two friends doubted another treatment like the one Kenjiro had used before would be effective this time.

Still the ninja ran on, more determined than ever not to let the evil overcome her. She looked into the distance and smiled in relief.

They were within a few miles of a canyon that stretched out to the right. From their vantage above, they could see its depths scored with ravines and trenches so deep, they gave the place the look of a labyrinth. Already they could feel the winds increasing. As they approached, the open fields were replaced by mounds and hills sprinkled with trees, shrubs, and outcroppings.

Suddenly, the wind shifted to an awkward angle and turned against them. Not only did they work twice as hard to maintain their speed against the wind, but also to remain in a straight line. The struggle became increasingly difficult as the wind constantly shifted, causing them to lean forward into it, then shifting again sideways and then in their favor, causing them to stumble at the unexpected ease.

Kenjiro stole a glance at the others. Navigating these constantly shifting winds was tiring, and they would need to rest soon. The wind gave a harsh shift, and Shinobu stumbled. With quick reflexes, the strider rolled with the motion and came smoothly back to his feet. *There has to be a better way to do this,* he thought.

Tree branches and bright green and orange leaves swayed in the howling wind. High above them, a bird glided in the cloudless sky. It looked only as big as a crow at such a distance, but crows were not known to hover in place, as this bird was doing. Gracefully, the bird of prey glided, shifting its tail subtly and allowing the wind to carry it this way and that, while maintaining control.

At the sight of the large bird, Shinobu realized their error. They could use the wind to an advantage at times, and move against it with efficiency at others. In order to prove this theory to himself, he waited till the wind shifted in their favor again, then he leaned slightly back into it, straightening a bit. Although he still kept pace, he was using less energy than before. Knowing that the wind would change again soon, he waited. As soon as he felt the wind shift against them again, he leaned forward, low to the ground. The wind passed over him more easily, and he was able to exert less energy moving against it. He overtook Kita, and then held his pace. With a nod from the strider, the other warrior watched.

Once the wind shifted at an angle but in their favor again, he straightened a bit and allowed himself to be pushed along.

Kita followed and found it much easier to accept help from the wind instead of using the same energy no matter the direction. Shinobu also used the powerful winds to his advantage by speaking in a slightly louder than normal voice to the others in front. Although no one spoke, in order to conserve energy and breath, the strider remembered the very reason they were traveling to this particular place. The winds were strong, and would carry sound much farther than normal. *Why not try now?* he thought. He spoke in a voice only a bit louder than normal, and called for the others to follow his lead and watch. To his confirmation and amusement, the others glanced over their shoulders at him in response.

He and Kita easily overtook the others and Shinobu took the lead, rising with the wind that aided them, and lowering under the wind that pushed against them. He found that the others not only adapted, but fell into line behind him, allowing each other to absorb more of the force of the pushing wind, and then spreading apart so that everyone could benefit from the wind when it pushed at their backs. Once they had established a technique, they moved like a flock of birds, shifting this way and that in unison, zigzagging across the land but still making their way to the canyon ahead.

They alternated as the head of the group, allowing the previous leader to rest behind him when the wind pushed against them. Akemi was the only exception. The others signaled for her to remain behind and not take the burden. When she did not argue for her turn, Kenjiro knew she must be struggling.

At one point, Kenyatta was at the lead and noticed that they were leaning in the direction of a patch of woods on their right. His eyes lit in alarm, for although the woods would provide ease from the harsh crosswinds, he was unsure they would be able to hold enough control not to slam into a tree if the wind shifted suddenly. When the wind shifted in favor of them again, he heard Kenjiro's voice from behind.

"No matter the shift of the wind, push forward. The canyon is close and those woods are yet closer."

Kenyatta glanced back and nodded. When he looked back ahead, he could see the rim of the canyon, and soon they would begin their descent. The canyon was deep and rocky, with no distinct shape to it. There was not much in the way of trees or plant life, but many large and small rocks dotted the walls and floor, and the smoothness of the canyon wall was an indication of the years of the harsh winds carving and polishing the landscape like a master sculptor.

He noticed a deep, narrow crevice snaking away to the east, like a giant serpent fleeing the moaning winds. Doubt filled Kenyatta's mind as he considered their plan. *I hope this foolishness works,* he thought. *I'm tired of runnin' everywhere.* He felt a burning in his legs that he was sure the others felt as well.

When they finally reached the rim of the canyon, everyone trotted to a not-so-graceful stop, and bent over with hands on knees.

After she'd caught her breath, Akemi walked to the front of the group and peered over the rim of the canyon. She pointed to the narrow crevice that Kenyatta had spied earlier. It was a mile away, more or less, and they would have to descend and cross the floor of the canyon to reach it.

"I grow weary," Shinobu said, his voice barely audible above the howling wind. "Are we to make our way to that crevice first or rest once we reach the bottom?"

Kenjiro scanned the canyon. "Time is against us. We should try to make the crevice first as quickly as possible. We can rest then."

Shinobu frowned. "I understand, but our pace will be slowed by fatigue, unless the wind lifts and carries us to our destination."

The mischievous glint of excitement that crossed Akemi's labored face made him wish he'd withheld his sarcasm.

"Does anyone feel like adventure?" she asked. Kenjiro, having known his ninja sister all his life, turned a wary look on her. Shinobu and Kita frowned incredulously, while Kenyatta shared the ninja's devious smile.

"I tink adventure what we been doing all dis time," Kenyatta replied in his islander accented western tongue. The others eyed him with confused expressions and Kita laughed. The smile on the ninja's face looked as if it belonged on a tigress, and with a raised eyebrow that the Jamaican could only interpret as seductive, she knuckled him in his side and pointed to the crevice. Excitement practically glinted in her eyes.

"Adventure! We will time the wind and leap with it." She turned to face the others just as they exploded with disbelieving laughter. "If anyone has a better suggestion, let him speak it now!" Realizing that the woman was serious, they frowned.

"Do you really believe the wind will carry us that far?" Kita asked.

"No matter how far," she replied. "Whatever the distance it will be faster than if we run."

"And what of the landing?" Shinobu said. "It may be a bit difficult to stop before slamming into the canyon wall or crashing into the ground because the wind decided to have sport with our vulnerability. And then, of course, there is the little matter of gravity. The farther we fall, the faster we fall, and the heavier we get."

"Have we not done things already that are physically impossible for any other human being?" the ninja replied.

"Yes," Shinobu said, "but none of it has included a hundred feet of free fall."

Seeing the unrelenting hesitation, she declared them timid and disgusting, then turned to the canyon and crouched.

She really means to do it! Shinobu thought. To his surprise, Kenyatta was the first to move beside her, then, rather tentatively, Kenjiro joined them, followed by an equally apprehensive Kita. With a sigh to the heavens above, the strider moved to join the group.

Can't live forever, he thought. As he peered over the cliff, the excitement contaminated him as he too crouched on the edge, waiting for the right moment. The wait wasn't long, and the wind shifted against their backs once again. As one, the five warriors leaped from the cliff. Everyone glided on the edge of nervousness, anticipating the wind to shift again and bring them to a stop, and an untimely death.

Luck was with them, and they made a gradual descent into the canyon where the wind was more consistent than above.

And so they glided, ever downward. Though buffeted by the occasional gust, or change in wind direction, the five warriors were able to maintain a measure of control as they were carried in the air toward the canyon floor.

Beautiful was the view from the air. Every child fantasized about flight, and the five companions were no different. Hardened veteran warriors were replaced by excited children laughing and giggling as they rode the winds to the ground. All except Kenjiro, who maintained discipline.

Kita and Kenyatta laughed like boys taking in the sights with a childlike sense of wonder.

Even the strider, Shinobu, enjoyed the ride. He could hardly believe the wonder of flying so high above the ground. He was reminded of the bird he'd seen earlier, and for the first time, knew what it must be like to fly high above the ground.

Kenjiro saw a light in Akemi's eyes that he hadn't seen since the fight with the pit demons. Seeing his sister enjoying herself, he relaxed a little.

Although her brother was ever the pragmatic samurai, it appeared to Akemi that he was actually enjoying the experience, and that made her smile even wider. Kenjiro noticed her elation and they fed from each other's excitement, like two adventurous siblings running to the next "trouble" they could find.

33

I el and his apprentice watched with amusement as the five warriors glided into the valley. Mira couldn't believe what she saw.

"They are amazing!" she said. "How can they find fun when facing such a future? And the ninja. She fights the dark power in her, yet she can still smile."

Iel cast a knowing smile on his student. "The future will be what it will be, but until it has arrived, there is no reason to dread it. We prepare, and we move bravely to meet it, but until we have met the future, we must live in the present."

He turned and looked out beyond the gardens of the tower to the fields beyond. "One can choose to dread a fearful future, or prepare to meet the future while living in the now."

"I envy them," she said.

"Why is that?" Iel replied.

"They possess power unlike anyone in this world," Mira answered.

"And with that power lies a heavy burden," Iel responded. "They carry a burden not many could bear. They have seen many battles, and other unspeakable things in this world that would take the sight from your eyes and the quiet from your mind. A lifetime of meditation and guidance from a remarkable teacher has brought four of them through a harsh life. The fifth warrior remains a mystery to me. He fights as they do, and his weapon seems to have some form of power to fight demons. I would like to know how that is."

Iel concentrated on the strider. "I wonder where this warrior comes from, and how he came to be." He turned back to Mira. "You speak of envy, as if they are different from you. They are not."

The Ilanyan left her to ponder his words and went to the fields to make one last check on the defensive preparations. Mira stood alone in the room, lines of confusion creasing her forehead. *Aren't they different?* she thought as she gazed at the wall that showed the five traveling warriors. *They are different from me, from everyone. What could Master Iel have meant by that?* Though she was capable of things most people were not, she was not able to jump so high, or move so fast. She could not leap from a high cliff overlooking a valley, and glide to the ground unharmed. She turned away from the wall, and it returned to its normal multicolored state.

Iel watched her in a small corner of his mind's eye. She had practically grown up in the tower and thought of all she did as normal a life as anyone would lead. She never questioned anything in life unless he challenged her to do so. He patted a unicorn standing next to him. Its smooth white coat was like silk, and its mane was wild about its head. It looked up at the Ilanyan and blew a playful snort from its nose. Iel looked at the young one, its mighty horn glistening in the sun as if polished with lacquer.

"I don't know why humans live such short lives," he said to his exotic companion. "They seem to take so long to understand things yet more often than not they fear what they do not understand. Perhaps in time we will both understand them, my friend." The beautiful animal tossed its head and nuzzled his arm in response.

He gave it a gentle pat on the neck, then walked out to the fields. Magical beasts of every kind guarded the land like sentinels, unmoving and awaiting the coming storm. *It will be a great battle,* Iel thought. *The likes of which the human world has never seen, and will probably never know of.*

IEL STRODE across the fields of Takashaniel and gazed at the many magical beings gathered to protect the precious tower. Not far away, he spotted a group of Rizanti fighters. Though every one of the magical defenders of Takashaniel was spawned from earth magic, these creations were an expression of protection. Rizanti were from wild earth magic, and only appeared for one whose need was genuine and unselfish. They were tall by human standards, each standing at about six feet nine inches. Their long heads were pointed, front to back, and their sleek, thin bodies were a blue-silver color, but with a hint of transparency.

They each carried long, oval-shaped weapons with sharp tips on each end, while the sides of the weapon were honed to a cutting edge. The grip was in the center, requiring precision and confidence since the weapon would be dangerous to the wielder as well as the adversary. The five magical fighters stood tall and passive, waiting.

Iel moved on to inspect the magical wards, making his way toward a humanoid-looking man no taller than four feet. For his stature, his shoulders were broad and thick, and his short, stout legs and arms were heavily muscled. Lines of experience creased his curly-bearded face. He was dressed in ragged brown trousers that were shredded at the ankles, and two thick suspenders held them up, each strap lined with two-inch-long spikes. The club he rested on his left shoulder was almost as big as he was and was littered with spikes. He glowed with the magical energy that sustained his artificial likeness.

"Time come er soon," he said. "We feel strong bad force come er this way fast … get here soon."

"Yes," Iel said. "And I believe we will be ready."

"Brunts always ready for fight," the short warrior said, referring to the name of his kinsmen earned as a result of them always receiving the brunt of battle. "Brunts be ready for a fight. We's just hope they're ready for a fight with us."

Iel smiled. "I think you will get your wish, my friend." The magical warrior turned with a snort and huffed back to his group that stood not far away.

The Ilanyan walked through the fields with his unicorn companion at his side, passing the many small platoons of magical warriors. In the distance he found the one he sought.

Grimhammer looked down at Iel and nodded. With the equine part of his body the size of a Clydesdale, the centaur stood head to hoof at nearly ten feet tall. His human torso was equally large and heavily muscled.

In a hand the size of Iel's head, the centaur held a six-foot-long shaft with a three-foot hammer head, a spike on each end. It was the weapon of his namesake, and quite intimidating.

Iel looked up at the mighty centaur, then at his incredible weapon, which must have weighed halfway between a hundred to two hundred pounds.

"I should be here in my true form," Grimhammer rumbled. "Not cowering behind this magical likeness."

"We could not risk losing such a mighty warrior as yourself, my friend. These are major demons, summoned from the deepest pits of the abyss." The Ilanyan offered a disarming smile. "The Brunts argued as well, but I convinced them as I did you, that magical representations of yourselves were far a better choice." Grimhammer grumbled in his deep, booming voice, and the ground vibrated beneath them.

"Magic is powerful, but it cannot copy the real thing," the centaur replied. "My real form should be here to fight with honor."

"None are braver than the mighty Grimhammer," Iel responded. "I have witnessed your prowess in our adventures together, old friend. But you must understand that Quentranzi are a different kind of monster, not born of this world or even this dimension. The world is changing rapidly and you will be needed throughout the course of its evolution. It is for this reason that I have asked you to avoid the fight directly."

The proud centaur let out a deep snort and stamped his front hoof, looking to the fields ahead. He was unusual for his kind, having two horns atop his head that grew from the sides and curled up, as if reaching for the heavens. The centaur was a mighty warrior known by many in the stories of the battles of old. Ironically, his kind were known to humans, but only in mythology.

Iel patrolled the rest of the fields, checking on the remaining wards and battalions of magical warriors. Unlike the centaurs and the Brunts, these creatures were created specifically for battle. Iel wanted to minimize the harm to any living creature, thus was he granted these magical beings through earth magic.

Despite his efforts, the guardian was concerned that it would not be enough. Once fighting, magical creatures could only sustain their form for a limited time. If the battle lingered too long, the forces would diminish.

Another concern was the centaurs and the Brunts. Grimhammer was right. These were only magical representations of the physical warriors, and were less capable than their real counterparts. Iel could only pray to the Daunyans that it would be enough.

He turned back to the tower see Mira standing on one of the balconies. With his keen Ilanyan eyes, he saw that she was looking past him at the distant sky, lines of worry etched in her forehead. He followed her gaze, and saw a sky that was dark as night even though the day was still young. The darkness was traveling toward them, swallowing everything in its path.

Iel clenched his jaw. "And so it begins."

34

The five companions were beaten and tired. Their descent into the canyon had been a rough one. The winds had carried them straight into the wall of the canyon. Unable to control their speed, it was a hard impact that sent them stumbling and tumbling to the canyon floor.

Kenyatta spat bits of gravel and sand out of his mouth from where he had rolled into a bed of loose dirt, growling curses through gritted teeth as he'd tumbled painfully over the rocks.

The others were no worse for wear. Kenjiro nursed a scar on his left arm from a particularly sharp rock that he'd skidded across. Shinobu sat against the wall holding his head in his hands. He seemed to have recurring pains from the fight two days ago.

Kita had perhaps the worst landing of all. He rubbed a bruised shoulder and forearm that had resulted from his unlucky collision into a tree. The tree that grew at an angle on the canyon wall, and he'd hit it while rolling, and was launched into the air. Once in the air he was caught in a crosswind and fell straight down to the ground. The only thing that broke his fall was that the dirt was thick and soft, but that brought little comfort to the battered Kita.

Akemi seemed to have had the most successful landing of the

group. Although she did not escape the fall unscathed, she'd managed to grab hold of a bush that was strong enough to hold her until she was able to orient herself. Long after everyone else had crashed to the bottom in a heap of dust and dirt, she'd carefully picked her way down the decline until reaching the bottom.

Now the companions rested in a cave Kita had discovered that provided relief from the violent, ever-changing winds that punished the canyon.

"How can anything live here?" Kita asked as they looked at the howling windstorm. "If these winds were just a bit more powerful, the dirt and sand could turn a building to dust and grind the skin from your bones."

"Yeah, man," Kenyatta replied. "Feels like I almost lost my skin even with my clothes." He inspected his right arm, which was raw from the chafing sand. "It's dangerous out there. I've seen nothing like it."

"We will need to cover well when we leave," Kenjiro said. "I like my bones better with skin covering them."

"I say we camp here and recover," Kita suggested, and all agreed except Shinobu, who still held his head in his hands.

"What's wrong with you?" Akemi moved to sit next to the farstrider, then flinched and fell away.

Kenjiro looked over his shoulder. "What's going on?"

"I can feel it," the ninja gasped. "It feels like the same power that I was attacked by. A different kind of dark power, but definitely demonic." She cupped the strider's chin and lifted his face to look into his eyes.

"Touched by evil," she said. Shinobu's eyes had a distant and tormented look. None understood more than her, the nature of the agony he felt. It was like a persistent sickness that slowly crept from the subconscious to the conscious, and each time she pushed it back, it returned a little stronger. There were times that she heard voices, dark suggestions that remarked on everything she encountered. She felt as if she was being drained of her energy as time passed.

When she looked into the strider's eyes, she saw a similar pain.

"It was the nightmare," he stated. "It entered my mind and thrust a lifetime of torments in my head in a manner of seconds. I've never felt such potent evil before, but after the fight I'd felt better, and thought nothing of it."

Kenjiro stooped beside him, closed his eyes, and concentrated. "The demon's incursion in your mind was more influential than you thought. The energy around you is tainted." He stood, never taking his eyes from the strider. "The power that plagues you is different. You can withstand it if your mind is strong, but until you receive proper treatment, you will be forever haunted in your sleep and will have no peace of mind … or, your mind may be ripped to pieces."

"A worthy test," the strider remarked with a wry smile.

"One that may destroy you," the samurai responded.

"This will take longer than a few days, as I thought," Akemi said, drawing everyone's attention. "The tower is still farther west, and we have not made half the distance." She stood at the mouth of the cave just out of reach of the whipping sands. "We will need to camp for the night as Kita suggested. The winds have gotten stronger, and if we make the attempt now the sands will devour us before we take a dozen steps."

Kenyatta moved beside her and looked out at the howling night. "I know you said that the winds are stronger here than any other place in the world, but there is something unnatural about this place."

Kenjiro looked over at them. Even Shinobu lifted his head as Kenyatta continued. "The winds *were* always strong, but the sand-storm didn't start until we reached the floor of this canyon, and now it is twice as intense."

"It's as if we were trapped here," Kita said, peering out of the cave entrance.

Kenyatta picked up a rock and threw it out into the sandstorm. It was ground to dust before it hit the ground. "I think our friend is aware of us."

"This costs us time that we cannot afford," the samurai said.

"And we are two or three days from our destination," Akemi added.

"We could tunnel our way out. Anyone have a shovel?" The group turned to see Shinobu leaning against the wall with a strained smile on his face.

Akemi saw the struggle in his eyes and used his conviction to strengthen her own.

"How long can he keep this up?" Kenyatta asked, waving a hand at the storm.

"If it is the Drek," Kenjiro answered, "there is no telling how long he could detain us here."

"So we could be here for days or longer?" Kenyatta chuckled in frustration.

He looked to Akemi for any possibilities, but the ninja just looked out at the raging sandstorm that was their captor. *This Drek could be a problem.*

* * *

DEEPER INSIDE THE CHILLY CAVE, the group sat around a campfire Kita had created. Fortunately, there was some old dried up tree roots lying around and he had a bit of tinder in his pouch. Akemi produced a small, flat item from Kenjiro's sack. After a bit of unwrapping, Kita saw that it was a pack of thinly sliced dried meat. She then reached into a pack that she had on her waist and produced a sack stuffed with rice.

"This will sustain us without weighing us down," she said. "If we cook it on the fire and add the water from the tower that you brought, its revitalizing qualities along with the food will last longer."

Kita reached for his sack and brought out the water skin. Kenyatta had set up a frame over the fire on which to sit a small pot.

Kenjiro gave the islander a sidelong glance. "Unless things have changed more than I thought, lone warriors traveling the road don't carry cookware with them."

"Nope," Kenyatta replied, reverting to the western tongue, "but us improvise when we be need someting we don't have. Carved wood makes a good bowl ya know."

Kita nodded with an amused smile as he looked at the dumb-founded expressions on the other three companions' faces. Although they all spoke a bit of the western tongue, they could barely decipher the Jamaican's strong accent that even he, after living most of his life with Kenyatta, sometimes had difficulty understanding. Kenyatta looked around at the others and shook his head. "Some time or another, dem have to understand me."

"You think so?" Kita replied. "You manage to speak Japanese with little to no accent, my friend. Your version of the western tongue is another story altogether." Kenyatta just smirked and continued his work.

While the Jamaican prepared the food, Akemi moved next to Kita and spoke slowly. "How long you know each other?"

Kita looked at her in surprise. It was the first time she or anyone else in the group had attempted to speak in the western language.

"Almost our entire lives." Kita offered a warm smile. "You speak the western tongue well," he said, reverting to her language. "Maybe one day I'll teach you the language of my people." The genuine smile on her face and the tip of her head told him that she intended to take him up on the offer.

"All right, done!" Kenyatta announced, sitting five wooden bowls beside the campfire. "Time to eat!"

Kita laughed at his friend's use of Tagalog, Kita's native tongue. He couldn't say why Kenyatta had made that choice, but sometimes it was better just not to ask.

Shinobu moved closer to them. "Am I going to need a linguist to understand you two?" he asked.

"Don't worry about it," Kenyatta replied, reverting back to the tongue of Japan. "We just didn't want you to know what we really think of you, is all. We don't want any tension, especially since you're a bit fragile after your bout with that nightmare a while back."

The strider arched an eyebrow at the obvious sarcasm. "You don't forget much, do you?" he said, referring to his remark about Kenyatta's skill, days ago.

"What do you think?" came the retort.

Shinobu pursed his lips. "I think that harbored aggression spawned from a casual bit of sarcasm can be a detriment to one's well-being."

Kenyatta shot him a dangerous look, and Shinobu held up his hands. "Be at ease, friend. I meant no threat. I simply mean that to harbor such ill feelings for so long is bad for anyone's health."

"When the time dictates, I use judgment and act accordingly," Kenyatta said evenly.

"Was my remark that offensive?" the strider asked.

"Would you tolerate a similar one from someone you don't know, and who doesn't know you?" Kenyatta replied. He straightened to face the strider. "I have yet to meet a warrior who would tolerate a stranger questioning his skill or ability in any way, joking or not."

"I have yet to meet a warrior who would take such a fleeting remark so seriously," Shinobu countered. "I think there is more to you than you reveal, Kenyatta, but that is not my business. I would offer this, however. Since I so deeply offended you, I offer my apology and an attempt to begin anew. We have a long road ahead of us yet, and I wish not to go into battle beside one who would watch my back for the sake of what is right and not for the sake of camaraderie or even friendship. It was not my attempt to create tension, which is what I have done. My wish now is to offer my hand to you in allegiance and hopefully in time, friendship, for I cannot think of a more capable ally to have at my side."

Kenyatta regarded him for a moment. The man was genuine, and had also taken the more honorable road by apologizing. He let out a self-deprecating chuckle. "My grandfather once told me that a friend worth having is one that you can learn from. It is not you who should be apologizing, but me for my pettiness and ill-placed aggression." For the first time, Shinobu and Kenyatta exchanged smiles.

Further toward the front of the cave, Kita and Akemi watched the two who seemed to have finally mended the tension between them. "Ken isn't quick to anger," Kita remarked, "but he can hold a grudge when he gets there. I think our strider friend has brought about a change for the better, and without a fight."

Akemi nodded as she watched them. "You are like brothers," she observed.

"We *are* brothers," Kita replied.

35

A fter a satisfying meal, the companions took their ease around the fire. Akemi was the only one who seemed discontent. "I understand the reality of the situation, but this is just too much dirt, and nowhere to wash." That remark drew a round of snickering before everyone sank back into their private thoughts.

After some time passed, four of the five drifted to sleep, with Kita having volunteered for first watch. With the exception of the violent sandy wind that persisted outside, it was a rather quiet and uneventful night. *What could get in here from out there anyway?* he thought.

He made up his mind to go sit by the fire for a while when he felt the ground vibrate. He froze, not daring even to breathe. Lately he had learned to be wary of everything. The trembling intensified, waking the others who were quick to their feet. Everyone froze, moving only their eyes to scan the cave.

"What now?" Shinobu muttered.

The trembling became more violent, and then the entire cave started to shake, pebbles and rocks dislodging from the walls and ceiling to fall to the ground. They group came together and formed an outward-facing circle.

"Do you think the cave is collapsing?" Akemi asked, looking to Kenjiro. The samurai was still studying their surroundings and didn't respond.

"Be ready to make for the mouth of the cave," he said loudly, over the tumult.

Shinobu looked at him as though he were insane. "And have our skin flayed from our bones?"

"We can try the storm, or have tons of rock fall in on us. Choose one."

The samurai had barely spoken those last words when the rumbling stopped. It was so abrupt that it was as if the quaking had never happened.

"What games is the Drek playing now?" Kenjiro muttered. The cave had gone ominously quiet. It was eerie in contrast to the endless sandstorm punishing the canyon outside.

To their disbelief, the walls started to shake again, and huge pieces of rock separated from the cave walls.

A sizable chunk of the cave wall fell away and rolled to a stop in front of Shinobu, then started moving of its own accord. Farther back, a set of green eyes appeared in the wall, then a jagged head dislodged from the stone.

Shinobu's mouth stretched into a crooked smile. "Just when I thought I'd seen it all."

The sound of stone grinding on stone rumbled all around them as arms the width of a man's body broke away from the walls. Massive legs broke free, and then a mighty torso. The ground shook as each one of the heavy-looking creatures stepped from the walls and advanced on the companions.

"We're surrounded," Akemi whispered. The warriors fell into a defensive crouch, hands at their weapons. The ground continued to vibrate as parts of the cave separated to become more and more of these rock beings who came stomping forward to encircle them.

"They are massive, but look slow," Shinobu whispered. "We should try to overwhelm them with speed and agility."

"How do we know they're unfriendly?" Kenyatta whispered. That brought an incredulous look from the group.

"Do you plan to parley?" Shinobu asked.

"They haven't made any aggressive moves against us yet," Kenyatta replied.

"That could change."

Kenyatta glanced at the strider. "How would you react if a group of armed strangers came into your house?"

"We didn't know this was their house."

"Do they know that?"

Shinobu tipped his head. "Fair point, but I still don't want to die by crushing."

The rock creatures seemed to frown at the group as they closed in. Kenyatta had slowly released his grip on his blades and spread his arms, palms facing out in what he hoped they would view as a non-threatening gesture. The others shook their heads and Kenjiro muttered under his breath, something about foolish and over trusting. The creatures did seem to relax a bit.

"You take quite a risk, my friend," Shinobu whispered.

"If you tink I'm helpless without my weapons then maybe we have dat fight later, after all," Kenyatta replied with a wink. He repressed a laugh when he saw the confused expression on the strider's face at his harsh accent.

The rock creatures facing the other warriors did not relax, however, but kept their distance. Akemi thought she saw a bit of anger in the somewhat fixed features of one of them.

"Groumber di sonosi al ti al fommo ao gerren aoi!"

The warriors glanced at each other as the rumbling voice spoke. The one standing in front of Kenyatta had spoken, and with each word, his teeth chattered. The creature seemed to be scrutinizing them. After seeing their confused looks, it spoke again, but in a broken use of the tongue of the land.

"Wise it would be if follow your friend, you do. Hurt you we will not, if threaten us you don't."

"Hurt *us*?" Shinobu muttered."

"Don't be so confident, strider," Kita whispered. "We don't know them. Just because they're made of rock doesn't mean they are as slow as you think."

The words had barely left Kita's mouth when several things happened at once.

One of the rock creatures took a step closer. Too close, apparently. Quick as a thought, the samurai ripped his sword from its sheath and whipped it around so that the blade was next to his head, tip pointed at the nearest rock creature, the cutting edge facing the ceiling.

That move alarmed the creature, and with speed that seemed impossible for its size, it batted the samurai aside.

Akemi ducked as her brother flew over her head to crash into the stone wall. She came up with *Sekimaru* ready to strike. A roar rumbled the cave, and they turned to see the creature holding its wrist. It had not struck the samurai without taking injury.

Akemi slashed horizontally at the approaching rock-like things, but hit nothing but air. *They* are *fast!* she thought.

Kita twisted the top of his staff and the shaft separated into a chain and he whirled it vertically, sending the blade end speeding forward.

Shinobu let loose his unusual sword and struck in quick, controlled forward strikes, bringing the sword back to its sheath each time. The group was careful not to break their defensive position and kept their backs at each other, but with enough distance so that they could move freely.

Kenyatta thought to reach for his swords, but then a rumble came from over their heads, and one of the creatures dropped out of the high cave ceiling. It twisted in mid-midair, straightened, and raised a hand over its head as it landed in the middle of the group with a ground-quaking crash. As it was descending, thick stone tentacles slithered out of the ground and bound their feet. Before the warriors could react to the new situation, another group of tentacles reached from the ground and wrapped around their arms, rendering them helpless. Once the humans were secured, the tentacles solidified.

Akemi glanced at her brother, lying on the ground unconscious. "Worry you need not," came the rumbling voice again, speaking slowly as it chose its words. "Alive he is. Kill we want not."

Akemi turned a dangerous glare on the creature that had struck her brother. It returned the gaze with anger. She thought she saw a bit of resentment in its hard, glowing green eyes. The one who had spoken before said something in its rumbling language and the surrounding rock creatures withdrew a bit. The one in the center of them leaped from the circle and landed a few feet away. She thought the move unnecessary and boastful, but given the size of the creature and the tightness of their circle, it could not have squeezed past them.

Kenyatta looked at the large rock creature standing in front of him. They seemed as though they could be reasoned with, though they were obviously angry.

"Why our cave you have come?" it asked. Kenyatta and the others noted that its voice did not rumble nearly as much as it did moments ago. "Our home this is, and welcome you have not been made."

Kenyatta saw Kita on his right, struggling with his stone bindings, and then he glanced to his left to see Shinobu doing the same until a few of the other rock creatures had come to stand directly in front of them.

"Well it would be, if answer me you did. Impatient with humans, the others can be."

Kenyatta looked back at the speaker. "We didn't know this was your home. We sought refuge from the dangerous sandstorm out there." He jerked his head toward the entrance to the cave, where just outside the sandstorm was still as violent as ever. The rock creature considered him for a moment.

"Deny the violent air I do not, but come to this cave why? Other caves there are. This one why?"

Kenyatta thought of several jokes about the creature's oddly arranged words, but given their current situation, he kept them in check. "This was the closest cave to us when we got here," he said. "We mean no harm to you. We just came to wait for the sandstorm to pass."

The rock creature looked at him, then back to the mouth of the cave. Then the one to its right said something in its own language. Kenyatta didn't think he liked its tone.

"Throw you to the storm, he says," the speaker translated. "Why I should not, you tell me."

On Kenyatta's other side, Akemi was still locked in a stare with the creature in front of her. She was not challenging it, but trying to understand the hatred wafting from it.

"We have nothing to gain from you, except shelter from the storm," Kenyatta continued. "What have we done that is wrong?"

"Unnatural that sandstorm is. Trouble, humans always bring."

Kenyatta nodded. There it was. These rock beings considered humans untrustworthy and troublesome. "If perhaps you can help us, you will be rid of us all the sooner."

That brought a rumbling laugh from the other stone creatures.

"Themselves, humans good at helping," one of them spat.

"Never does good come from helping humans," a particularly big one said. Its tone left no doubt that it wanted nothing more than to throw them out into the sandstorm and be done with them.

"Has our refuge to this cave upset you this much?" Kita asked. "If we knew that we would happen upon unfriendly hosts, we would have avoided it. We have no fight with you unless you make one with us."

The big one moved to tower over him. "Always ready to fight, humans are." It looked at the original speaker. "Nothing but trouble, they bring."

"We want no trouble nor do we want a fight," Kita repeated, and Kenyatta nodded.

"Attack you we did not, but draw weapons you did, and attack, that one tried." It pointed toward the samurai who was just now stirring.

Kenjiro groaned and grabbed his head. "Thing has a heavy hand," he mumbled. Before he could stand, several pairs of stone tentacles came out of the ground and bound him.

"Why come to this place, you have? Travel here, humans do not."

"We are on an important mission," Kenyatta answered, "and the long stretching crevice not far from this cave is important to our trip." Kenyatta looked over his shoulder at Akemi. She was now looking at her brother but caught Kenyatta's gaze out of the corner of her eye. "It may help if we explain," he said to her.

For the next several minutes, the ninja explained their trip to Takashaniel and how the heavy winds from the canyon could carry the sound of her whistle to their horses, miles away.

The stone creatures went into a deep discussion in their language.

"Trick it could be," the big one said.

"No," came the response of the one Kenyatta took to be the leader.

"Tower of Balance humans do not know, unless special they are."

The bigger of the two cast a condescending scowl over the humans. "Nothing but trouble do *Nyamas* bring." The one Kenyatta took to be the leader eyed him again, then turned to its larger companion.

"Truth, they might speak."

"Doubt it we do," the big one said. "Easier it would be if throw them out we did. How much good, humans can bring?"

The leader seemed to consider the other's words. It had a face that showed wisdom and experience gained through ages come and gone. Kenyatta wondered what this stony creature had seen and done in its time.

"True it is that troublesome many humans are. But not all, my friend. Chance, they must be given." With something that sounded like a grinding snort, the big rock creature cast yet another scowl over the group, then moved toward the mouth of the cave. When it passed by Kita, the ground shook in front of him.

"If we don't reach Takashaniel," Akemi said, "you will find more troublesome things to deal with than us."

"Why are you so untrusting of humans?" Shinobu asked.

The grinding sound of rocks laughing shook the cavern until the leader called for silence. It moved to stand in front of the strider. Its head was round, but with small jagged edges protruding from its scalp. Shinobu saw compassion in those green eyes. He looked the leader of these rock people over, and snickered, not in sarcasm, but at the realization that one of those arms (as wide as his body) could snap every bone in his body with little effort.

"Much harm, humans do. Take advantage of the world, you do. Destroy what you do not understand, you have. Patience and understanding you lack."

It seemed to be looking someplace far away.

"Fragile you are. Fearful you are. When once my kind show ourselves, fight us you did. When beat us you could not, use big weapons from afar you did. Defend against such things, impossible."

"Start fight, you do, then run behind big weapon like coward." Another of the rock people glared at them in barely suppressed rage.

Akemi found that she could not discount their anger. Though this was a different age, most people were educated about the Age of Technology, and the great wars waged during those times. Most human civilizations had warred with each at some point in history, but during the Age of Technology, humans had developed the means to break the world.

"Many of us left, there are not," the leader said. "Destroy us all, you tried."

To his left, Kita saw that Kenyatta was silent, a look of lament on his face. He seemed to empathize with the creatures.

"It is true," he said, "that humans have done little more than harm the world. That is why things are the way they are now. I ask you though, to look within us and judge us as individuals, not by what other humans have done to you. We regret the crimes our species has committed, but we are not all the same."

"Hard to trust those who betray trust," the leader said. "Violent and unchecked humans are."

"True," said Kita, "but if you do not trust us, monsters like nothing you have seen before will run the earth and cause problems like no human could think of."

"Know what we have seen, you do not. Hard it is, to believe that save the world five humans can do." Everyone looked to the mouth of the cave. It was the big one who'd spoken.

"What will you do with us then?" Akemi asked, growing impatient with the slow conversation. "Will you kill us by your own hand, or by throwing us out to that deadly storm? We don't seek mercy, or even help, but we have a job to do and we must finish it or die in the effort."

"Pound them into the gravel of the fallen ancestors, we should!" one of the rock beings rumbled, and some of the others agreed.

The leader held up a stone hand, each of its four fingers nearly as wide as Kenyatta's forearm. The rumbling quieted and the leader continued.

"Reminded of our pain we are, when look at you we do. Unpredictable, humans are. Hard it is, to trust you."

"Then let us redeem ourselves in your eyes," Kenyatta said. "Times are changing and so are humans. I don't deny that there are still evil humans. There are many. You will have to trust us or the world will be confronted with a darkness that is like nothing that has walked the earth before." A wave of doubt crossed the leader's face as it considered his words.

Kenyatta tried a different direction. "The guardian of the tower will be most upset if Takashaniel is destroyed because you would not let us go."

That seemed to help the leader make up its mind quicker and it spoke to the others.

"Release them," it said.

"We cannot!" the big one rumbled.

The leader shot a challenging look at what was clearly the second-in-command. The bigger rock creature seemed to shrink under that gaze.

"Leader you are not. On your shoulders, decisions do not rest." The leader spoke calmly, but the command in its tone was indisputable. By his command, the rock warriors unbound the five humans on the condition that those holding their weapons release them before they were released.

Kenjiro was helped to his feet by the very same creature that had sent him flying into the wall. The samurai looked up at the creature in surprise, and saw within the formidable rock warrior similar values that he himself lived by. There was nothing personal, and politeness was exercised, even among adversaries. After looking into the eyes of his former aggressor, the samurai found he could not look at the rock being as an enemy.

The rock beings listened as the five companions spoke of their mission and all that had happened. In time both parties began to enjoy each other's company, and the last of the tension dissolved. Kenyatta and Kita taught some of the younger rock warriors the dance of capoeira. Again, the warriors noted that the ground did not shake one time when the hulking rock creatures moved in friendliness.

Their unlikely hosts proved to be quite fun and caring creatures. Although the second in command remained aloof, most of the others, after some time, had come to enjoy the humans.

"Long has it been since talk with humans we have." It was Marblehead, the leader of the Stonecliff Clan, who spoke.

"I regret the past that humans have with your kind," Akemi responded. "When did you have dealings with humans? I have never heard of, grongolians, before."

"Many ages past," Marblehead answered. "Very early ages we see humans, and were curious. Ages ago deal with humans our kind did. In time, humans forget because not long they live. In our lifetime, many, many generations of humans come and go. Sometimes different, your children are, and changes they make." A pained, distant expression crossed Marblehead's rigid features.

"Think better than us they did. Shun us, they did. Use us as tools they wanted, until leave, we decide. After many, many years, try to make friends again, our people did." He let out a deep sigh that sounded like wind passing through a hollow tunnel. "Forget, humans do, and fear us they did. Many die, many wounded. Impossible it was to beat big weapons they had." Marblehead's bright green eyes seemed to dim. "Leave we did and never deal with humans again we vowed."

"The same others do too," came a voice from behind them. Little Granite came to stand with the group. "Many others, there are, that like humans not. Dangerous you are, and avoid you they do."

Akemi shook her head. "Everything you say is true, I cannot deny that." Marblehead tried to put his massive hand on her shoulder, but ended up covering her entire shoulder and most of her back. She stumbled forward under that frighteningly strong grasp and smiled, appreciating the effort of the gentle leader.

"Perhaps, changed your people have," he offered.

Her smile was sad. "Perhaps, but I would say that you should still be careful in dealing with humans. Some of us are accepting, but many would still strike out at you in fear."

Marblehead let out another regretful sigh. "More time," he agreed.

Kenjiro sat with two grongolians by the names of Quickrock and Grok. Quickrock had explained that he earned his name by his unusual speed among their kind. Kenjiro smiled, rubbing his still stinging head. Quickrock seemed to blush—if that was possible—in guilt until Kenjiro assured him that there was no ill feeling. Shinobu walked up to join them just as they had begun planning.

"They say that there is a way we can escape this valley and still send the signal to our horses," he said as the strider sat down beside Grok.

"Tunnel we do," Grok explained, "and help you we can. Unnatural this sandstorm is. Long, it lasts."

"We think it was created by the one that seeks to destroy Takashaniel," Kenjiro said.

"Magic, he uses."

"Powerful magic," Kenjiro responded.

Shinobu spotted the second in command and excused himself. The big rock warrior was massive, at least seven feet tall, and more than half that in width. His arms were thicker than the strider's body, and even his fingers were as thick as Shinobu's arms.

"Need your friendship, I do not," he spat. "Untrustworthy humans are, and turn my back on you I will not."

Shinobu smiled and tipped his head. "Then we have something in common."

Upon seeing the responding curiosity, the strider continued. "I rarely associate with my kind. I tend to be ... untrusting." He looked at the big grongolian. "I don't ask you for your trust or friendship, but if you are willing, I would like to at least ask you to share a drink with me." The strider pulled out a flask and held it up.

The rock man looked skeptical. "Only a drop it is."

"Only a drop you need," the strider replied with a grin.

He stiffened and looked down at the small human. "Drink, we do not."

"Every living thing has to consume something," Shinobu said, unscrewing the cap. He filled it and then the big grongolian grabbed the entire flask from him.

"Um, I don't think that would be wise," the strider chuckled.

"Fragile you humans are, tougher are grongolians!"

The strider laughed and lifted his cap to the other. "We'll see."

The big rock warrior watched as Shinobu put the cap to his lips and with a backward jerk of his head, swallowed the contents. Warily, the rock man looked at the flask and then sniffed the opening.

"Like spiced swamp scum it smells," he said, wrinkling his nose, which looked like pebbles stacking on top of each other.

"I promise it will taste more harsh, my friend," Shinobu replied.

With another skeptical look at the strider, he swallowed the drink in one gulp, and sat for a moment.

"Not so strong this drink is," he scoffed. Shinobu nodded with a smile, pretending not to notice the strain in the rock warrior's voice, and the stiffness in his posture.

"You are a strong one indeed, friend. I have never met anyone who could pretend that his insides didn't feel like they were melting as it went down." And he could see that the drink was doing its work, for the giant warrior actually laughed at the statement, although it sounded more like a rockslide.

"Bouldarius my name is. General and second in command of the Stonecliff Clan, I am."

Shinobu tipped his head. "Shinobu," he responded, "Farstrider." He glanced over his shoulder at Kenjiro and the two stone warriors sitting with him.

"Your friends say that you can help us send the signal to our horses and escape this valley."

"Assume you do, that help you we will," Bouldarius replied, a bit sharply. "Strong your drink is, but dim my mind it does not, Shinobu, Par Rider."

* * *

AFTER SOME TIME, and a lot of laughs, Kita managed to get Obsidius and Quickrock to do the basic dance of capoeira, and they did it with surprisingly fluid motion. Although the sight of big stone people moving from side to side was a bit cumbersome and silly looking, it was still quite a sight and did well to loosen any lingering tension between the two groups.

Kenyatta's two students learned quickly, and the lessons had turned into a challenge. Although they were not as graceful as their teacher, the rock warriors managed to copy some of the kicks—if only waist high—and even a spin or two without falling much. Then they challenged Kenyatta to try a few of their techniques, mostly consisting of rolls and trampling movements. To Kenyatta, they looked clumsy, but there was a tactic there that he didn't miss. The contest became so competitive that it attracted the attention of everyone in the cave. Even Shinobu and that big general came to watch. At first, Kenyatta held back, not wanting to show off in front of their new friends. After prodding from his companions as well as the Stonecliff Clan, he went into a series of spins, flips, and aerial kicks that left the stone warriors staring in amazement.

Kita leapt into the circle and Kenyatta spun to face him, smiling. They faced each other, slightly bent forward, dancing left to right, the dance of Capoeira. Kita spun backward with an inside-to-outside crescent kick. At the same time, Kenyatta ducked with a backward sweep that slid across the space where Kita's kicking foot had been. When his foot reached its highest point, Kita brought it straight down just as Kenyatta spun away. He followed with the same backward sweep that Kenyatta had just done.

Once again, with perfect timing, Kenyatta—with one hand on the ground—spun backward and whipped his leg around with a kick where Kita's head had just been. The dance went on for quite some time, and the Stonecliff Clan seemed to have as much fun watching as the two giving the performance.

Akemi watched in surprise, a smile crossing her face. Kenjiro raised an eyebrow and nodded, a glimmer of amusement in his eyes. The two friends danced left, then right, then left, then right. As if reading each other's thoughts, Kenyatta changed direction and went right again while Kita continued to dance to the left. In that instant, they both leaped into a one-handed cartwheel past each other, and then using the momentum, both did a second cartwheel using no hands. As soon as they landed, they simultaneously dropped into a pose called the 'K' kick, standing on one hand, with one leg kicking horizontally over the head, and the other leg kicking vertically into the air. They held this pose for several seconds, before falling back to their feet.

The Stonecliff Clan clapped and stomped with excitement, and the cavern shook as the grongolians fell this way and that as they tried to imitate the two warriors. The night passed in fun with the telling of stories, jokes and trading traditions. The two peoples learned quite a bit about each other that night, and even the more apprehensive grongolians came to talk and listen. Soon the five human warriors had earned the clan's trust and respect, and the beginnings of friendship formed.

"Hope for the future you bring us," Marblehead said. "In time become friends again, we hope."

"Time," Akemi said. "It will take time, but humans will change, and with the absence of technology, things have begun to change faster than ever."

Marblehead nodded at that. "Morning we will come to help, and on your way you will be."

"Thank you."

The festivities continued on for a while longer into the night, but gradually the grongolians began to retire, sinking back into the walls of the cavern. After the last of their new rock friends had gone, the five warriors stood looking around, and then to each other.

"Anyone else wondering if they're asleep?" Shinobu said, breaking the silence.

"We just made friends with a clan of creatures that we never knew existed," Kita stated as if in a trance.

"I wouldn't have believed it if I didn't see it for myself," Kenyatta said.

"I think I still don't," Shinobu said. Kenyatta and Kita looked at each other and then back at the walls, then to the mouth of the cave where the unnaturally powerful sandstorm continued to ravage the valley.

"We really need to get to that tower," Kita said, arranging a sleeping palette around the campfire.

Despite everyone's objections, Akemi took first watch. She sat only a few feet from the group, keeping her sight from the camp-fire so as not to lose her night vision. From time to time she saw that Shinobu was having a restless sleep.

Finally, he stood and moved to sit beside her, studying her face.

"You still feel the pain of our last fight," he said.

"At times my whole body feels cold, then I feel like I'm hot on the outside and cold on the inside, then the opposite. Then at times I feel some dark feelings creeping inside me." She shivered.

"I've been having some of the most morbid nightmares I have ever had in my life," the strider said. "These dreams are most disturbing, and quite real." He slid back the sleeve on his right arm to show a four-inch scar on his forearm.

"I got this the other night when fighting a strange gray and black striped beast with a mouth the size of your body. It reared and scratched my arm, and that's when I woke from the dream to find you stirring in your sleep, as well." Akemi inspected the wound.

"They try to kill you in your sleep, and me through the sickness that pit demon cast on me."

"Then we must work together," the strider said. "Before we go to sleep, we must meditate on each other and unite in our dreams.

If they can enter our dreams or use residual energy on you while you sleep, then we should be able to link in our dreams and fight together."

Akemi nodded. "Hopefully we'll discourage them and get a restful sleep soon."

With a confirming nod from the strider, Akemi left him to take watch and lay beside her brother. Whether the evil poisoning her could sense hers and the strider's resolve, or just through luck, her rest was mostly peaceful.

36

I've never seen a *night* this dark," Mira said. "The stillness is unnatural, and I feel uneasy." She and Iel stared out the window at the blackened fields. "The forces seem unmoved, though."

Iel stood beside his student, hands clasped behind his back. "It takes more than darkness to shake a warrior, my young pupil, and magical warriors are altogether unshakable. You need not worry about morale out there."

"I feel small in this," Mira said. "Like there is nothing I can contribute."

"Your contributions are dependent upon you and you alone," Iel replied. "If you feel that you should stay here, that is fine. If you wish to join in the fight directly, that is your choice as well."

Mira could tell by the expression on her teacher's face that he would prefer for her to stay within the relative safety of the tower.

"I don't know," she said. "I want to help, but I don't know how. My skill is underdeveloped, and I can sense these things that approach us now … they're stronger than anything I could have imagined. I can't deny the fear that I feel." She looked at her teacher in shame.

Iel smiled. "If you would have denied your fear, I would never have allowed you to fight." He smiled wider at the young woman's confused look. "Anxiety is a natural feeling and helps us to stay alive. If you were to go out there relaxed and unconcerned, how careless would you be? When you have no nervousness or anxiety, you are less cautious. The difference between a skilled warrior and an untested one, is not whether they feel fear, but how well they manage it. Fear holds us back until we learn to use it as an opportunity to grow. If you can summon the courage to face that which you are afraid of, then that fear will weaken."

"You don't seem worried at all," Mira said.

"He then looked back out at the darkened landscape. "Yet worry, I do...." The Ilanyan's features darkened, and he moved for the door. "They come," he said.

The statement made Mira's blood run cold and her heart fluttered. She had difficulty breathing and the room suddenly felt hot. With an effort, she marshaled her nerves and steadied her breathing again. Finally, having regained her composure, she followed her teacher out the door and caught up to him just as he was stepping onto the elevating platform.

"I'm nervous," she said. "Terrified actually. But I'm here." She stepped onto the platform next to her beaming teacher.

"You have come far," Iel remarked.

"I have a good teacher," she replied.

* * *

A FEW HOURS BEFORE SUNLIGHT, the five warriors were awake and packed to leave. The Stonecliff Clan had finished a tunnel underneath the canyon floor and had begun angling it toward the surface, a safe distance outside the raging sandstorm. The humans were amazed at the clan's ability to manipulate all forms of rock, including the ability to listen to the earth and feel what was happening to the land.

"How did you get your name anyway?" Kenyatta asked Marblehead.

The stone leader tapped his fist against the top of his head, which made an echoing thud. "On my head a boulder fell, when young I was," he said in his usual, rumbling voice that made Kenyatta's chest vibrate.

"From far up it fell, a hundred feet maybe. A long time it took me to get better, but surprised others were that survive I did. My name, this is how I got."

"That sounds like a nickname," Kenyatta observed. "You didn't have a name before that?"

"From experience grongolians give names. A year, maybe ten, fifteen could be."

"Fifteen years without a name!" Kenyatta said, incredulous. "How could you go that long without a name?"

The clan leader smiled. "Short lives humans live, and impatient you are. Many years grongolians live, maybe two hundred years, maybe three hundred. Fifteen or twenty or thirty years, a young child still." Kenyatta just shook his head, unable to wrap his mind around such a lifespan.

Behind them, conversations and well wishes were being exchanged. Kenyatta and the grongolian leader turned to see the other four humans practically surrounded by their unlikely hosts.

"I guess it's time for us to go," Kenyatta said.

Marblehead nodded. "Come."

General Obsidius, who hesitantly accepted the order given to him, explained the preparations they had made. "Already see you can, that to the surface this hole above you goes." He then pointed to Kenjiro, who stood with his back against a wall farthest from the hole. "Behind him the path of the strongest wind travels. That direction you face, when up you go." Then he pointed to a path to his right that extended into darkness. "Outside the valley that path leads, and in the direction you want, so your whistle you blow, and leave you will."

Despite his curtness and eagerness to be rid of the humans, it was obvious that the stone general had grown fond of them. Shinobu smiled to himself. He and Obsidius had become something like friends, although the big rock-man would never admit it. He offered his hand to the stern captain. "Hopefully we will meet again.

"Doubt it I do, because avoid humans we do."

Shinobu repressed a smirk. "Of course," he said.

Akemi had secured her supplies in a small pile next to her brother and stood beneath the opening in the ceiling. Next to her was Quickrock, the same young one who had dropped in the middle of them and bound them in stone tentacles. "Strong the sand winds are, and cut they do." The young grongolian's voice was much lighter than Marblehead's or Obsidius' but still carried several times as much bass as any human she had ever met. "Not long the walls will hold, so fast you must be."

"I only need a few seconds," the ninja responded.

"All you will have," Quickrock informed her. "Magical is this storm, and like razor the sand is. In seconds, wall is gone."

With a nod, Akemi and Quickrock stood next to each other. She gave him a nod, and Quickrock lifted his hands over his head. With startling speed, the ninja was lifted to the hole on a small stone platform just wide enough to hold her, and at the same time she ascended the hole, a stone cylinder rose to surround her. She withdrew *Sekimaru* and cut a slit into the wall in front of her. The intensity of the cutting sandstorm had already begun shaving the wall away. On impulse, she stepped to the side of the slit anticipating a sandy assault to come in. She laughed at herself upon remembering that the wind traveled in her favor. She slid the whistle into the slit and blew three times. It made no sound to her ears, but she knew that the wind would carry it to where the horses would hear. She descended the hole and all looked up as the stone cylinder was ground away by the storm.

"It's done," she said.

Marblehead gently stomped his way to stand before her. "On your mission, much luck we wish. Of us tell the guardian. Know us he will and visit someday he may."

After many farewells and promises to return, the five human companions departed down the dark tunnel. Trusting in their senses and the fact that they were told that the tunnel was fairly straight, they reached the end of the corridor where two of the tunneling team remained. The stone men were awash in the golden glow of dawn. They knelt and cupped their huge fingers together.

"You're going to give us a boost?" Kita asked, doubtfully.

"Throw you out, we will!" one of the grongolians said, and the two shared a rumbling chuckle. One by one, the five warriors were launched up and out of the tunnel.

"If one of them so much as thumped us with a finger," Kita said, once they had gathered, "we'd just crumble."

"You're right," the samurai said. "When that one hit me, I could tell he held back."

"You realized this after you awoke, you mean?" Akemi teased. Kenjiro didn't laugh.

"I know I have asked this before," Shinobu said, "but how are our horses supposed to find us?"

Akemi sighed. "I told you before. They will run straight in the direction that the sound came from. Since we will not deviate from our path, they will overtake us soon enough."

"That seems a bit convenient," the strider said, moving beside her. After seeing the questioning look from the woman, he continued. "How is it that our path is in a straight line from the valley, which is in a straight line from the patch of woods where we left our horses? This just seems so easy and well-placed for us." The strider looked at her skeptically. "I do not believe in coincidence, but the fact that the tower—" he did not bother trying to pronounce the name anymore "—lies in a path straight from a valley that *happens* to have a path that carries sound for an incredible distance straight in the direction that we left our horses just seems a bit strange."

The ninja frowned, growing impatient. "When this is all over you can ask the guardian, if you choose, and I am sure he would be happy to explain it to you."

Shinobu started to say more but stopped short when he saw the strained look in her eyes. She was weakening and needed all of her strength for the road until the horses caught them.

"Then let's go," he said.

* * *

GRIMHAMMER LOOKED around at his forces and the surrounding magical warriors. All stood passively and waited, unmoved and unaffected by the unnatural darkness surrounding them. The tallest and sleekest of the Rizanti stepped to the front of their diamond formation and leaned forward.

Knowing the magical creation could see perfectly in light and dark, Grimhammer watched it. The Rizanti leader lifted its disk blade and held it over its head. The other Rizanti set their feet and lowered into a crouch, with their disk weapons raised over their backs.

Grimhammer turned to his clan. "It is time, my brothers. Let these magical shells carry us into battle with the same honor as if it were our own physical bodies. The Quentranzi believe this darkness will steal our courage!" He turned toward the darkness and raised his mighty warhammer. "We will show them!" The centaurs roared and thrust their weapons into the air, rearing up on their hind legs.

The Brunts, as usual, had not said anything. In fact, they hadn't waited for a signal or to see their enemies, but were already gone into a thicket, moving from patch to patch.

Once they had decided on a formation from within the trees, Grit looked around uneasily.

"Somethin' wrong?" one of the soldiers—a rather wide fellow with big, wrinkled cheeks, and arms that looked like short logs—whispered, moving up beside the leader of the Brunts.

"This place ain't right," Grit replied. "Somethin' watchin' us from all round."

They looked around in the blackness. From the trees, they could see strange forms moving skulking about that seemed to materialize right out of the trunks and slither from tree to tree.

"Look like they try to surprise *us* for a change!" Grit said, a gleam of excitement in his eyes.

"We surrounded!" the big one next to Grit cried, thrusting his club in the air. The Kalistyi materialized everywhere, from the trees, bushes, from the ground, and even out of the sky.

"Everywhere!" Grit yelled. "Be knowin' they everywhere! More fun than we thought!"

The band of compact fighters practically hopped up and down at the overwhelming prospects.

"We do this now!" Grit shouted, and on his signal, the band exploded into action.

* * *

"THE BRUNTS HAVE FOUND BATTLE," Iel said.

Mira leaned forward and squinted at the wall of darkness. "How can you know that? It's pitch black that far out."

The Ilanyan smiled at her. "There are those that can see even in unnatural darkness. Those that cannot must use their mind's eye to see what cannot be seen by physical eyes."

He put a hand on her shoulder and her nerves stilled. "Go now, and prepare yourself. It's time."

Without a word, Mira retreated back into the tower. Her

thoughts whirled as she walked from corridor to corridor until she came to her modest room. Aside from the bed and a circular white rug in the center, the room was bare.

Mira sat cross-legged and rested her hands on her thighs, palms facing up. She closed her eyes, and within a few moments, her body began to glow with white light. The time had come, she focused her mind, and her power grew.

* * *

AT GRIMHAMMER'S SIDE, a youngling pawed at the ground impatiently, shifting his weapon from left hand to right. "Patience, my young warrior," Grimhammer admonished, not taking his eyes from the darkness before them. "No war has ever been won on strength alone." The young centaur still fidgeted a bit more, but did calm somewhat.

"I smell the filth," he said.

"So can I," the centaur leader responded. "Our time draws near, but we must be patient."

He then noted that the Rizanti had lowered into a crouch with their disks raised over their backs, he hefted his warhammer and signaled for his clan to be ready.

"Be ready, my brothers!" Grimhammer cried. The words had not completely left his lips when the Rizanti darted off into the distance, moving at a speed impossible to match by any living creature. "To battle!" Grimhammer bellowed. The mighty clan reared on hind legs and thrust their weapons high into the air. With a crash, their front hooves hit the ground and they ran into the darkness, charging after the Rizanti.

* * *

IEL WATCHED as some of the magical defenders charged into the darkness while others remained behind, serving as the last line of defense. The Ilanyan could hear everything that was happening in that blackness. The charge was met with unnerving ferocity.

Iel closed his eyes for a few moments, then smiled. Inside her room, Mira sat meditating and raising her energy level. Her body glowed in several colors. The closest to her body was white, and the other layers glowed in various colors of the spectrum. She was calmer now, sitting erect with a peaceful appearance to her face. Iel could feel Mira's power growing with every second.

"You look worried, Master Guardian," Siti said. She was one of the more powerful of the magical defenders, spawned purely of earth magic. Her bluish silver skin radiated energy, and a cold mist wafted from her body.

He imagined that if a crystal or a diamond could talk, it would sound like the exotic Siti. Iel withdrew from his thoughts and looked into her blue face, her soft, yet icy features marking her with an unusual kind of beauty. "I cannot sense the Drek or his Quentranzi general," Iel replied. "I don't think he is here."

"Is that not a good thing?" Siti asked.

"Not at all," Iel answered. "This means that he is controlling everything from his fortress and can most likely see everything from a more advantageous point of view." He rubbed a hand over his smooth head. "I had thought that he would want to have a direct hand in taking Takashaniel, but he must have faith in his army."

"Is he right to have such confidence?" Siti asked.

Iel gave her a confirming nod and looked back to the fields that were shrouded in darkness. "This also means that he may be concentrating some of his attention on the humans. It is likely that they won't arrive as soon as I had hoped."

Siti put a gentle hand on his shoulder. "Do not worry, Master Guardian. They will arrive in time to help." A mighty roar split the darkness.

"Grimhammer has met battle," Iel said.

"As soon shall we all," Siti responded.

THE FIVE WARRIORS rode as fast as their horses could take them. It had been half a day before the horses had finally caught up to them, and they had to make a few stops to allow Akemi to rest. The demonic taint was growing stronger, and it was an effort for her to simply stay in the saddle. On they rode, through copses and open fields, across plains scattered with hills and through heavily wooded paths, blazing a trail to Takashaniel.

"We're not far," the ninja yelled to her companions. "Perhaps a few hours, but not much more."

The others rode in silence, each contemplating the battle to come and what they might expect.

"I see no trace of the tower," Kenjiro finally said. "I remember it stretching toward the heavens, but I see nothing ahead."

"I can feel it, brother," Akemi said. "Our journey is near its end."

GRIT SWUNG his spiked club left to right, up and down felling any Kalistyi that ventured too close. The Brunts, true to their name, had taken the first blows early on, slamming head-on into the wall of evil. Despite the terrible odds, the sturdy band mowed through the Kalistyi forces, hacking and slashing every shadow demon in their path. What their magical bodies lacked in actual strength, they made up for with unlimited endurance. And endurance they needed, for every shadow demon that was defeated, two materialized to replace it.

"This fight not have an end soon," a fighter closest to Grit said. Dok, his name was, and he was highly regarded in their ranks. Grit made a noncommittal sound, noticing a gash in Dok's arm dealt by the arm-blade of a Kalistyi. What looked like liquid light seeped from the injured arm, and he knew that his part in the fight was nearing its end.

"Me magic is failing, Leader Grit," Dok growled. Despite his diminishing magical essence, he fought beside his beloved leader until finally, in a cloud of pale blue light, he diminished and was no more.

* * *

BACK AT THE cave in the brunt city of Brickdawn, Dok's eyes popped open and he gasped from the shock. The others were still standing, silent, eyes closed with their full awareness in the battle miles away. Defeated and angry, he stomped to the mouth of the cave where the three sentinels stood guard over their helpless physical bodies.

"First one back, eh?" one of the guards chuckled. Dok cast him an even look and the chuckling faded.

"Dammed lucky blow," he growled. "If it was me *really* there, I would still be in the fight!"

They turned to the sound of two more of their kin waking with an angry fire in their eyes. One particularly angry fellow stomped and spat, shaking his fist in the air.

"Danged things er gave me a cheap shot. I ain't done yet!"

* * *

THE CENTAURS CHARGED behind the Rizanti into battle, allowing the sleek warriors to cut a path into the demon forces before they branched into their own formation. Grimhammer was impressed by the efficiency in which the Rizanti fought. They ran in a perfect diamond formation, the leader in front cutting a trail while the others cut at the sides, sending fiend after fiend back to the dark world.

Before they were deep into the horde, Grimhammer pulled his clan up short. He looked in the distance to see the Rizanti, still blazing a trail farther into the demon forces. It was a suicidal tactic, but he knew they would accomplish their goal. No living warrior would dare such an advancement, but the Rizanti existed only for battle and would cut a path straight into the heart of the army and fight till the magic sustaining them dissipated.

The centaurs made their stand and bashed demon after demon, sending dozens of the abysmal creatures back to their world. Beside Grimhammer, the youngest of the centaur clan bashed a Tasarien in the head with his club and sent it flying away. As soon as it hit the ground, he was on top of it, pounding the big demon with his hooves until it finally fell apart and faded back to the abyss.

A ripclaw came behind him and snapped at his back with a spiked pincer. The young centaur was faster. With a mighty leap, he jumped over the dissipating Tasarien and once landed, spun to face the pursuing ripclaw.

Grimhammer swung his mighty warhammer and bashed a Tasarien in the side of the head. The demon was launched away and faded into mist before it hit the ground. A smaller, silver demon worked fast against one of the other centaurs, catching it off balance, but with one powerful swing of his weapon, Grimhammer blasted the thing apart. With a nod of thanks, his companion was away to seek his next adversary.

The Rizanti continued their advance, cutting down every demon in reach. Once they were fully immersed in the demonic horde, they stopped. As one, they turned outward into a defensive formation and continued to cut their enemies down.

* * *

HOOVES POUNDED the ground as the horses sped across the land. Shinobu was amazed at the changes to his beloved homeland. As a strider, he had traveled the world and seen many places. Never in all the years he lived in Japan had he seen so much landmass on the island, and especially so many untouched places. *Maybe the world* is *changing,* he thought.

In its descent toward the western mountains, the sun cast a fiery orange light upon the undersides of the clouds. The day was calm and serene despite the evil they raced to confront.

"Time passes faster than our progress," Kenjiro said.

Akemi gave him a sidelong glance. "It seems so, but we have no choice but to follow this path. Hold faith in the guardian. He would not lead us wrong."

"Especially when it's *his* tower at stake," Kita added. He glanced at the setting sun. "Looks like we will be fighting in the dark. Unless any of you have night vision, this is gonna be tougher without light."

Akemi responded with a strained smile. "Then your training is not yet complete." Kita could only guess what the ninja was referring to with that comment.

The five companions rode in silence for a few more hours before slowing to a walk to allow their exhausted horses to rest. The brave animals' heads hung low and their nostrils flared as they caught their breath. Once they cooled down, the companions dismounted and shared the water from the ration that Iel had given them. Despite the animals' larger size, the water did its work, and after only a few deep gulps of the wondrous liquid, the horses were energized.

"We must let them rest a bit longer," Kenyatta said. "The water does satisfy them and give them energy, but we've driven them hard."

Akemi shook her head as he spoke. "You would be correct if this was a magical potion," she replied. "But this is natural water from Takashaniel. The horses will be good to ride in a few minutes."

Kita looked into the distance in the direction of the tower. "And how long will our ride last once we continue in a few minutes?"

"There is no exact distance that I can give you," Akemi replied. "Only that it will not be much longer." She saw Shinobu's disbelieving smile from the corner of her eye. "If the strider has a better path for us to follow, then let him speak it now."

"Nothing better," he replied flatly. "Faith is not one of my strongest attributes."

"Then perhaps that is the major theme you chose to learn before you came to this life," the ninja said. That set the strider back on his heels.

Kenyatta walked up next to his friend and enjoyed the little daylight that was left. "Anodar day on the battlefield?" he said, reverting back to his version of the western language to soften the mood.

"Not another day," Kita replied soberly. "I haven't felt this type of anxiety since we had our first real fight."

Kenyatta smiled at that memory. "Ya man, you could barely hold your staff because your hands was so sweaty."

Kita shoved Kenyatta away, and the Jamaican laughed. "And you weren't shaking so hard that your swords were banging together?" he shot back.

"But me palms wasn't drippin' wit sweat," Kenyatta said, laughing louder.

Beside Akemi, Kenjiro shook his head. "They find fun before they jump from the cliff to the jagged rocks below," he criticized.

Akemi watched the friends with amusement. "Because they enjoy the life they lead during their descent to the rocks, regardless of whether or not they survive the fall. Worry is useless."

Kenjiro frowned.

Akemi sighed. "You know that I am not implying that you worry, older brother, but look," she motioned at the islanders.

"They enjoy themselves now, but have you seen a reckless moment in battle with them?"

The samurai grunted and walked away, and Akemi let it go. She was surprised that these foreign warriors had his respect so soon. Her brother would never go into battle with incapable allies. Even the strider, with his amusing but sometimes annoying sense of humor, proved to be a valuable ally.

Kita lunged with a playful punch at his friend, but Kenyatta's suddenly serious expression stopped him. "What is it?" he asked.

Kenyatta closed his eyes for several heartbeats, then opened them and started for the horses.

"We need to go," he said. "Now."

"What is it?" Akemi asked.

"Taliah just spoke to me," he said, recovering his horse. "It's started."

* * *

THEY RODE for an hour before Akemi pulled them to a stop.

"What is it?" Kenjiro asked, and Akemi pointed a trembling finger toward a group of trees to the left of where they stood.

"We are close," she said. Her voice sounded tiny. Hollow.

At the concerned look on the samurai's face, Kita looked at the ninja and saw the flickering life in her eyes. She looked aged, as if something inside of her was pulling at her life energy. Up to now, she had looked well, despite her internal battle. Now, she showed visible signs of her losing struggle.

"I don't see anything," Shinobu said.

"A portal," Akemi said, her voice almost inaudible.

Shinobu looked through a gap between two trees and then he finally understood. The tower could only be reached by a form of portal like the one Kenyatta's sister created. They would have to wait.

"We leave our horses here," Kenjiro said.

Kenyatta nodded in agreement, not wanting to involve their loyal animal friends. The five warriors dismounted. Kita barely reacted in time to catch the falling ninja.

"How is she supposed to get there?" he asked Kenjiro. "None of us could run straight to the tower alone without meeting battle, much less carrying her.

The samurai thought for a moment and then looked up. "She must ride. Her horse will run so long as Akemi is on her back."

"Will she be able to hold on?" Kenyatta asked. "Her horse will keep her astride," Kenjiro answered.

They helped her back into the saddle and Akemi gripped the horn of the saddle in one hand, and leaned over her horse's neck, wrapping her other hand in the thick mane. She took a deep breath, and blew it out to steady herself.

* * *

IEL WAS SNAPPED out of his thoughts, sensing the five humans had reached the portal site. He channeled a bit of his power on the portal and opened the path for them. Now he could only hope that their arrival could tip the battle in their favor.

* * *

FIVE HUMANS and one horse stepped through the portal. The companions stood in disbelief at the sight before them. Only a few hundred yards away was a wall of impenetrable darkness.

"I guess that's it," Kita said more casually than he felt. "I can hear the fighting, but how are we supposed to see in that?"

"Use our senses," Kenjiro said. "Feel your enemy when you cannot see it. It should be much easier than with a human, since our foes are not from this world and emit such negative energy."

The samurai was right, Kita realized. Even from this distance he could feel the evil. He looked at his best friend, his brother.

Kenyatta was clearly nervous, but an excited light burned in his brown eyes.

Shinobu also stared into the blackness. His right hand over his shoulder, hovering over the hilt of that strange sword.

His face like stone, Kenjiro stood tall, his right hand gripping the hilt of the sword at his side. His loose clothes blew in the wind that slithered through the trees like a serpent through a grassy field.

Kita's gaze again fell on Akemi, and he admired the ninja demon huntress's courage. She was weak, but managed to sit erect in the saddle. Whatever that demon taint was doing to her inside, the woman would hold strong to her last breath. On her lower back, that unusual sword, *Sekimaru,* practically radiated power. He could almost feel a presence within the weapon.

Kita's hand tightened around the shaft of his not yet extended staff. He looked down and realized his knuckles were turning white, and he loosened his grip. Beside him, Akemi let out a barely audible grunt.

"How is she supposed to find her way to the tower in this darkness?" Shinobu asked.

"The same way she led us to where we now stand," the samurai responded.

The five warriors looked at each other, feeling the camaraderie that had developed between them over the time they'd traveled and fought together. Kenjiro moved to stand beside his sister.

"Go to Takashaniel and be healed," he said. "Then join us on the field."

Akemi looked down at him, and it seemed an effort just to smile. "You will have an even greater battle on your hands if I return to see that you have left nothing for me to fight."

Fire raged in the samurai's eyes as he unsheathed his sword and leaned back, roaring at the top of his lungs as he stabbed the sword into the air. The other three warriors thrust their weapons skyward in as well, matching the war cry, and their voices echoed across the land.

Despite her condition, Akemi rolled her eyes. *Men and their war cries,* she thought. Putting her companions out of her mind, she studied what lay before them. It was a great force to be sure, but she had not felt the presence of one Quentranzi, and that worried her. *What is the Drek planning?*

Kenjiro, Akemi, Kita, Shinobu and Kenyatta charged into blackness to face the evil within.

37

The centaurs pounded any fiend that came within reach. The second in command, Warsong, leaped onto the back of a ripclaw, his weight bearing the demon to the ground. Before the demon could react, He stabbed it in the back repeatedly until it had begun to dematerialize. His instincts screamed at him, and he turned to deflect a large pincer aiming for his head.

"You are a strong one, yes?" the Tasarien taunted. It snapped its pincers in and out at the equine warrior.

Warsong growled. "You will learn soon enough when you awake back in our own dark world."

The Tasarien feigned a right hook at the centaur's right foreleg, and when he lifted it, the demon kicked straight out at Warsong's chest.

He stumbled backward but wasn't fazed. The Tasarien hesitated, tipping its head as it studied its adversary.

"I see," the wicked creature said, its voice shrill and thin. "*Coward* magic. I would have expected more, even from a filthy half-breed."

"Amusing that a demon dreg calls me filthy."

The Tasarien screeched.

Warsong charged.

* * *

GRIT BASHED a Kalistyi in the head with his many-spiked club and sent it whirling back to the abyss. He looked over his shoulder and saw yet another one of his warrior's magic fading.

"We ain't gonna be able to hold like this too long!" Strongarm said, magical mist seeping from a wound in his side.

"We gotta get to the open field and away from these blasted trees!" Grit yelled, ducking a swipe at his head. "We're getting outta these woods!"

At that command, the band of sturdy warriors began working their way toward the open field. They managed to fight their way to open ground, and things were just starting to look up when one of Grit's lieutenants went flying by him while his magical body dissipated into nothingness. Grit gnashed his teeth and was about to yell out another order when he felt a burning heat on his back. He turned to see a fiery giant staring down at him.

* * *

THIRD IN COMMAND of the centaurs, Merridius took a deep gash to his hind leg and was slowing as the magic sustaining him gradually diminished. Grimhammer had seen it coming but was unable to act, dealing with two enemies of his own at his side, Warsong was occupied with two ripclaws.

"I fear the climate of this battle will soon change!" the centaur leader yelled over his shoulder.

Warsong had scored a vital blow to one of the ripclaws by then and now focused more of his attention to the other. "What do you mean?" He used his spear to swat aside a claw aimed at his midsection.

"Merridius is not long for this battle," Grimhammer replied.

That news infuriated the second in command. He growled and dodged a swiping tail, then lowered his shoulder and smashed into the demon, sending it tumbling to the ground. Before it could recover, the four-legged warrior was atop it, stomping it into the ground. With a downward swing, his weapon crashed into the demon's head and dark mist seeped from the wound.

The ripclaw made a feeble attempt to rise, but the dark energy that sustained it on this plane was pouring from its body, and seconds later it was gone back to the abyss.

Not wasting any time, Warsong rushed to fight beside Merridius. He reached his overwhelmed friend, and bought him enough time to recover. Despite the relief, Merridius had taken many injuries and Warsong could see tendrils of magical energy seeping from his body.

"We fight together, brother!" Warsong said as he trampled short, silver demon. He stabbed down, then tore the blade up, and a gout of icy mist poured from the wounded demon's chest.

Merridius grabbed another of the silver fiends and hurled it into the ripclaw at its side, but not before it loosed an icy blast of energy at the weakening centaur. The blast knocked him back, but still he managed a weak parry against the ripclaw.

"Brother!" he cried. "My time in this battle is ended, fight on and we will meet again soon." With a roar of defiance, he forced the ripclaw back and slashed it across the chest with his ax. The gash was deep, and dark energy poured out of the fiend's body. It fell to the ground and dissolved back to the abyss.

In that same moment, Merridius also left the battle, his magical avatar having sustained too many wounds. Warsong saw his brother fade away, and though he knew it was not the real Merridius, he still felt as if his brother was truly lost to him. His roar swept the battlefield, and Warsong plowed into another mass of demons, sending one after another back to their world of darkness.

* * *

IEL WATCHED as the battle grew closer to the tower and the second and third wave of his magical forces advanced to meet the advancing evil. Siti had already left with her group and had met battle on the eastern side of the field. The Brunts were the first to strike, and were now somewhere in the middle of that thick blackness. Grimhammer and his clan had followed the Rizanti straight into the middle of the demon mass, but Iel knew the mighty centaur would not lead his forces into the thick of the dark army as the Rizanti had done. They would have branched to one side and cut their way back in to meet the Rizanti, and then force their enemy back from three sides once the Brunts or Siti's forces met with them.

The Rizanti on the other hand, had gone straight into the heart of the evil horde. It may not have been the tactic the Ilanyan would have recommended, but it worked for the magical fighters. Knowing this, Iel had not made any type of strategic plans with any defenders that were spawned purely of battle magic, as they already knew what they must do.

Grimhammer and Grit knew their soldiers and where to best place themselves. Siti was the only one he had made any preparations with, for she spent much time with the gentle guardian. She had never been in a battle before, and was in need of instruction, which the Ilanyan readily gave.

"They are going to break the protective wall surrounding the tower, aren't they?" Mira asked from behind.

Iel glanced over his shoulder. "Within a few hours, yes."

That caught Mira off guard. Usually, the Ilanyan would try to cheer her up or comfort her when things seemed grim. This day, however, he made no such attempt; he did not offer a smile or a comforting tone in his voice.

As if reading her mind, he beckoned for her to stand beside him. "I know you are worried, my student, but now is the time for strength. You are here in the middle of this conflict with no longer the option to retreat. We will stand together." When she didn't respond, he turned to look at her. "What is it?"

Mira was looking in his direction, but her attention was elsewhere. She was feeling something.

"The five warriors are here," she said absently. "One of them is coming straight for us and seems very sick, as if she is fighting for her soul." She focused back on him. "I think it's the ninja."

"Do you think she can make it?" Iel asked.

"Her horse is nearly spent. I don't know for sure if she can make it, but I have to be ready for her when she gets here."

That brought a sigh from the Ilanyan. "Do what you must, but hurry. I will need you soon."

Mira nodded and closed her eyes, drifting deep into concentration.

* * *

AKEMI LEANED FORWARD and wrapped her arms around her horse's strong neck. She smiled to herself in spite of the growing evil that she fought to keep from consuming her from the inside out.

She had run and ridden hard with the others and kept in good spirits, but now she could feel the burn, the inferno that raged inside her body. One thing she had found strange was that she could see clearly in the darkness, no matter how thick. This was a welcomed surprise, as she was more able to guide her horse farther from the battle without losing sight of the tower.

They were speeding along in a straight line now, her horse breathing heavily, but giving her every bit of its strength. She lowered her head to rest on its neck and closed her eyes. Then, she felt a jerk. Her horse had increased its already incredible pace. *What a strong friend you are,* she thought as she gently patted her laboring mount on the neck and closed her eyes, using what little strength she had left to stay astride.

* * *

THE FOUR WARRIORS moved through the darkness, two in front and two in back, facing each direction. The samurai had little trouble, as he had been trained to fight without sight. The other three, however, were at the edge of despair at the overbearing blackness. Guttural sounds and the clashing of weapons and the grunting and yelling of the defending forces polluted the air.

When Kenjiro saw that the darkness had begun to lighten farther ahead, he passed word to the others in attempt to raise their spirits.

"I can see a bit, now," Kita whispered as loud as he dared. The others flinched at the sudden break in silence. "Allow your eyes to go out of focus and you can see more around you."

"He's right," the strider said after a few moments.

"This looks pretty bad," Kenyatta commented after he too was able to see. "There are demons everywhere and coming from every direction."

"And magical fighters to stand before them," the samurai added.

"Get ready!" Kita said, extending his staff to its full length. "I think we've been noticed."

* * *

THEY HOVERED ABOVE THE ACTION, basking in the carnage.

"What a fight this turned out to be!" an elated Szhegaza remarked. "It seems the Quentranzi are not quite as strong as we thought, but at least their numbers give them an advantage."

Zreal cast her a sidelong glance and shook his head.

"What?" the Zitarian demanded.

"After being in the presence of the demon general Kabriza, you still do not know their power?" Zreal shook his head again. "What you see down there is nothing more than fodder."

"Fodder?" she echoed.

Zreal let out a sigh. "There is not one Quentranzi among that army down there."

Szhegaza frowned. They were not the strongest foes, but they were more formidable than any army, human or beast, could have been. Takashaniel was decimating the demon horde, but in the end, it would not be enough. If these were not the fabled super-demons Brit had been summoning, then what was to come?

"I don't think I want to be in the middle of this fight when your master's pets get here," she said.

"I think it's amusing that you speak as if we have a choice," Zreal replied. "If we die, better here than at the hands of our disapproving master."

* * *

BRIT AND KABRIZA watched the conflict through the scrying mirror. Although the darkness was thick, they had no problem seeing the action, as Brit himself had cast the dark cloud. The powerful fiend by his side looked on in amusement.

"Takashaniel has great power," it said in that deep, rumbling voice. "They defend the land well, maybe more than Brit has expected?"

Brit did not even look in the demon's direction. It had been an unrelenting inner struggle not to engage the tiresome demon. He repeatedly had to remind himself that he and this powerful yet immensely annoying creature were allies.

"My plans include you, and since you are included in—" he cast the demon a wry grin "—*my* plans, then you need not worry about *my* concerns."

The demon narrowed its eyes at him, but Brit continued.

"The instrument does not question the wielder, does it, Quentranzi?"

"True," Kabriza responded. "But if the wielder proves incapable, then the instrument might *accidentally* become the bane of the wielder."

Brit had long grown tired of the endless insinuations and mind games. It continued to chip away at his mental armor, and if he showed any loss of control, the demon could exploit it.

"Answer a question for me," he said, turning to face the beast. "How can the army respect the general when the general watches in safety?"

"For two reasons," Kabriza replied with something that looked like a smirk on its wicked face. "The first is, none of my brethren are fighting. Second, if any of them allowed such a thought to enter their minds, their endless torment would be something beyond your earthly imagination." Kabriza's body began to glow.

Brit could feel the evil emanating from the fiend. *After this is finished, I may have to rid myself of this thing before all that I accomplish goes ill.*

Kabriza shot an amused look his way. "The Drek should not think such unkind things about his guest. You might make me nervous." And then the demon vanished in a red mist, leaving Brit to his thoughts. After a few moments, his face twisted into a smile. A final challenge after the tower was taken might not be so bad. He had always wondered how his power would stand against such a foe.

* * *

THEY PAIRED OFF, Kenjiro with Kita, and Shinobu with Kenyatta. Although Kenyatta and Kita knew best how to complement each other's abilities from years of training and fighting together, the samurai thought it better to pair a relatively short weapon with a long-range one. Kenjiro's sword had less reach than Kita's staff, while Kenyatta's two blades were well complemented by the strider's mysterious weapon that seemed to strike even when the blade had not connected.

Kenyatta's swords were a blur that brought defeat to every fiend within his reach. Shinobu was quite impressed with the islander's skill, while Kenyatta as well, was impressed by the strider's mastery of that odd blade, which seemed to slice the air itself, not to mention anything that got too close.

Kenjiro and Kita had worked back to back, turning a circle and cutting down their enemies. A Tasarien rushed Kita who steadied his stance and positioned his weapon in front of him. It struck wildly, but with a bit more precision than the other seemingly mindless fiends. Kita worked hard to avoid and deflect those crab-like pincers snapping at his head and torso. One well-placed snap, and he would stain the ground in two bloody pieces.

* * *

AKEMI CLUNG to the horse's neck as it sprinted across the battle-field. Several times, a monster tried to block their way or lash out at them, but the horse would dart this way and that, never slowing.

Akemi forced her eyes to stay open. Whether a miracle, or the horse's skill, she somehow remained astride despite her depleted strength and overheated body.

With an effort, she lifted her head and managed a weak sigh of relief. They were nearly upon the tower. She couldn't believe how swiftly her horse had traversed the distance of the field.

All concern for herself fell away, and Akemi worried about her loyal companion that was surely running itself to the brink of death.

Within minutes, they reached the tower where Mira stood waiting for them. How she could have known that Akemi coming or where they would arrive, the ninja could only guess. Mira ran up to the horse and laid a gentle hand on its neck and chest area, then caught the limp woman as she fell from its back.

"Please, see that she is cared for," Akemi said in barely a whisper.

Mira responded with a worried smile.

"Let's worry about you for the moment," she answered, and draped the weak ninja's arm around her shoulder. Akemi looked over her shoulder and tears welled in her eyes. Her loyal friend that had borne her full-speed across a great distance huffed and slowly lowered to the ground. She knew that the loving animal had run beyond its limits.

Mira sensed the animal's heart near to bursting, and closed her eyes. She focused on the animal and sent as much healing energy as she dared without depleting herself. The horse's heart slowed, and Mira hoped it would be enough.

Once they were inside the tower an attendant rushed to help Mira get the weakened woman into a healing chamber.

"Help her," Akemi moaned. The woman was near to the end of her life, but thought of her animal companion. "Don't let her die."

Mira closed her eyes and focused on the ninja. An instant later Akemi fell into a deep sleep.

* * *

SHINOBU SLICED a nightmare demon in half, then, as it was diminishing to the dark world, he severed the arm of a ripclaw that slashed at his head. They fought demons at all sides, yet more seemed to just materialize from the darkness. The strider was starting to wonder if there was an end to all this.

Kenjiro's sword worked furiously, severing and thrusting in every direction. Two small silver demons leapt at him, but the samurai had spotted them from a distance despite the darkness. They were flying in pieces before the fight had begun.

* * *

THE LEADER of the Rizanti gave a signal and the magical warriors expanded their diamond formation into the demon horde, slicing through the abysmal creatures. Once they had cleared a large area between them, they held their position, and each of their bodies began to glow with an inner light that flowed from their bodies into the diamond-shaped space between them.

Grimhammer had just taken down a troublesome Ren when he felt the surge of energy.

"Steady yourselves!" he called. "Our Rizanti allies are planning something!"

The centaurs formed a defensive formation and held their ground.

Even from their distance, the Brunts, too, felt the surge of energy.

"What's goin' on over there?" Devjak asked, as he cut down yet another shadow demon.

"Feel like somthin' big." Grit pointed into the retreating darkness. With a crazed smile, the leader of the short but sturdy warriors thrust his club over his head and bellowed for his brethren to charge. There were more demons to slay.

SHINOBU WAS the first human to feel the surge of energy building not far away. "Hey guys!" he yelled as he worked his blade against a Tasarien's snapping pincers. "There's something big building in front of us. It doesn't feel evil, but it's big. We better take cover!"

"How do you know it's something to take cover from?" Kenjiro asked.

"You ever see anything build up this big without there being some sort of release?"

"How do you suppose we take cover in the midst of an endless army of demons that we stupidly marched into the center of?" Kita retorted.

"I guess we should just be ready," Kenyatta answered before the strider could respond with his usual sarcasm.

* * *

THE GROUND RUMBLED under the pressure of the collecting energy that was now on the verge of explosion. As one, the Rizanti dropped to one knee, and the built up energy exploded from the diamond space in a blast of white light that spread outward and vaporized all but the most powerful demons on the field.

Grimhammer and his warriors crouched and held their position, sliding back under the force of the blast. Grit and his remaining soldiers were swept into the air and landed in a pile some distance away. The four human warriors lowered themselves to the ground but were also been swept away. For the span of several heartbeats, it was as if a white cloud had descended over the battlefield.

Iel's concentration was taken away from the weakened horse when the force swept over them. He had felt the energy building, but had not thought it would be so strong. *Well done, Rizanti*, he thought, scanning the area. The darkness was shattered, and now pockets of visibility shown like cracks in a broken glass.

The Rizanti had done their job well. All but the most powerful demons had been burned away. Unfortunately, one of those powerful fiends was not far away. A weakened pit demon climbed to its feet and turned its horned head in the Ilanyan's direction. It turned in and stalked toward him, staring at Iel with red hot hatred.

Iel stood and faced the approaching monster. With a howl to the sky and flames seeping from its eyes, the pit demon charged. The air exploded in a flash of light when the beast crashed into the tower's protective barrier. It shook its head stupidly, then rose again and howled. A lesser demon would have been destroyed, but a pit demon was not much inferior to a Quentranzi.

Another demon slammed into the barrier, and Iel blasted it away, back to the abyss. More attacked, and Iel fought them back, but he alone could not fight them all. More of the remaining demons came at the tower, clawing and racking at the barrier until it finally shattered. The pit demon that had charged Iel raised its clawed hand and a flaming spear appeared in it. It drew back and thrust the spear straight at Iel's chest, but the Ilanyan whipped his hand out and the flaming spear was blasted apart.

Flames danced in the pit demon's mouth as it howled in fury. It lashed out at him, but again, Iel raised his hand and the fiend was immobilized. He then swiped his hand left, then right, slamming it into the ground.

Iel held out his other hand and a white lance appeared in his grasp. He drove it into the midsection of the pit demon, and though it was staggered, it remained on its feet. Its hands glowed with dark energy and a red light emanated from its palms.

"I don't think so," Iel said.

The pit demon threw both hands out at its sides and two waves of dark energy arced toward the Ilanyan. Iel raised his left hand again and blocked the power with the force of his will. Then with his right hand, he launched a wave of pure white energy back at the fiend, enveloping it in a white cloud of pure light.

The cloud receded and formed into a whip, which Iel held with the same hand. White light flashed in his eyes, and the whip pulsated with energy that burned at the demon from the inside out. It howled in agony, but only for a moment. With a twist of his wrist, Iel brought the fiend to its knees before him, and then it burned away, back to the dark realm.

* * *

Mira waved her glowing hands over the ninja's body, sending waves of purple energy to sooth Akemi from the inside. Mira watched the taint recede even as she worked. She said a silent thanks to the Daunyans that Akemi had reached her when she did. Not much longer and she would have perished, or worse.

* * *

WITH A GROAN, Shinobu propped himself up on his elbows. "Anyone want to tell me what just happened?"

"It came from over there," Kenjiro answered, pointing ahead in the direction of the thinned blackness.

"I could have told you that much," Shinobu said. He rubbed his head and looked around. The field was indeed more visible now, and most demon horde had been wiped out by the blast.

Kita squinted as he looked in the direction the samurai had pointed. He could barely see the Rizanti slowly rising to their feet. "They wiped out almost everything, and a good thing, too. After that blast, I couldn't tell which way was up."

The Kenjiro and Kenyatta nodded, still allowing their eyes to adjust. What they saw next had each of them wondering if the blast had shaken their minds, for surely, the figures beating back the demonic forcers were come to life from ancient myth.

A clan of centaurs, a group of short odd-looking men, and various other creatures, all glowing with a pale blue light, cut down every fiend in sight.

Farther away toward the tower, they saw a silver-blue figure gracefully battling a Tasarien. It was as if she danced around every attack the hideous creature threw at her, all the while counterattacking with strength that belied her dainty form.

The Tasarien struck down hard but missed the mark, burying its pincer into the ground. After sidestepping the attack, the silver being—clearly female—touched the fiend's pincer and it froze. When the beast tugged at its embedded limb, it shattered into hundreds of icy shards. The demon's agonized wail was cut short when she blew a mist at the Tasarien that settled over its body and froze it where it stood.

The silver-blue woman casually strode up to the frozen horror and touched a finger to its chest. At the touch of but the tip of her finger, the frozen demon shattered and evaporated, returning to the abyss.

Kita grinned. "Wow."

"Yeah, wow," Kenyatta said, his voice dripping with sarcasm. "And it looks like there's not much left for us. Did they even need us here?"

"Doubtful," Shinobu said, pointing at the tower.

They started toward Takashaniel which stood as a beacon, shining thought the darkness and reaching toward the heavens. The four warriors saw the figure of Iel standing near the entrance and they started toward him. Since the blast of light, the evil cloud had been steadily fading. They sheathed their weapons and Kita retracted his staff. And the ground shook.

38

Quicker than when they'd been secured, the four warriors' weapons were back in their hands. They crouched in the waning darkness, scanning the grounds. The ground shook again, then again, as if in a rhythm.

"By the Gods mighty," Shinobu gasped. "What the hell is that?" The ground shook again, and this time they were thrown to the ground.

"It can't be," Kenjiro said in almost a whisper.

"What is it?" Kenyatta demanded.

"Something is very wrong here," Kita said quietly.

"There!" Shinobu said, pointing high into the air. Through the darkness they saw two giant glowing red orbs.

* * *

"How could it be possible?" Iel stood in shock, staring at the sight before him.

Mira came running up beside him, panting. "I … felt … the … ground shake!" She looked at Iel, then followed her teacher's gaze far into the sky at the two very large red spheres hovering in the darkness. "What are those?" she asked, growing more nervous with each breath.

"I fear to tell you," Iel answered. He raised his hands and began a chant, waving his arms in a rhythmic pattern. Like shears cutting through fabric, white light streaked from his hands and sliced into the darkness.

Grimhammer and his clan had defeated the last of the nightmares and two more pit demons when they felt the ground shake. Visibility was almost completely returned, and they were able to see the origin of the quakes. There was another boom and the earth vibrated again. Following the boom this time, was a high-pitched screech. The centaur leader's eyes widened, and all he wanted at that moment, was to run.

* * *

"You've got to be kidding me," Kenyatta said. They were backing away without realizing it until they had reached the position where the Brunts stood, who also gazed skyward in amazement.

"I'm guessin' yer the ones that's gonna be er helpin' us," One of the short men said distractedly, staring skyward. "So how all of yer gonna help us with that?"

The short man nodded his head in the direction of the enormous figure stalking toward the tower. With every step, the ground shook. Six claws several times longer than a tall man extended from each massive hand. Long, thin black hair waved about its head, and slid away from its face to reveal a huge, gaping maw that housed pointed teeth along with fangs that protruded even when its mouth was closed. The monstrous demon let out another ear-splitting screech, and this time, a host of Bachatttas flew from its mouth.

"What in all hell is that thing?" Kita asked.

"Quentranzi," Kenjiro whispered.

"It must be as tall as a sky building!" Kenyatta said, referring to the few remaining skyscrapers from the Age of Technology.

Shinobu just stared at the thing in wonder while Kita shook his head in disbelief.

"No way," he said. "There is no way we can fight something like that."

"Damn flyin' things er come down this way!" The short man said with excitement.

The humans turned at the sound of his voice with a puzzled look. In the shock of the moment, they hadn't realized they were in the company of these strange men.

"Us be Brunts," the one at the head of the group said when he saw their questioning look. "And I'm Grit. We gonna help you fight those things for er tower Takshiniel!"

The corner of Kenyatta's mouth twitched. Apparently, others found the tower as difficult to pronounce as he had. "Let's do it then!" He exclaimed, finding the brunt leader's enthusiasm infectious.

Kenjiro and Shinobu cast him an incredulous look while Kita shook his head in that all too familiar way.

"You must not understand the situation," Shinobu said, eyeing the advancing monstrosity.

Kenyatta looked at the other two and shrugged. "Nothing to do but that which we came here to do. So let's do it."

Just then, there was another boom and the ground shook again. The Bachatttas were diving toward them. "We gonna die fighting or running?" Kenyatta asked, stepping forward.

The islander had made his decision, and the samurai followed close behind. "I would enjoy death as I have life," he said, sword in hand.

Shinobu glanced over his shoulder at his mysterious blade. "Looks like this will be a good one," he said. "I hope you're up for the challenge, my friend." As if in answer, the blade emitted a glow within its scabbard.

"Well," Kita said, "this is why we're here. I always wondered how I would do with of my greatest challenge." He looked over at Kenyatta. "To the end."

Kenyatta held his swords in a white-knuckled grip and narrowed his eyes at the monstrosity that caused tremors with every step. He smiled deviously in the face of impossibility. The islander was not unlike the samurai, his stoicism manifested by a smile instead of a scowl.

* * *

"BY HEAVEN AND EARTH!" Mira whispered. "Please tell me that this is an illusion or that my eyes lie to me."

"I wish I could," Iel said. "What you see is our true enemy."

"Heaven help us," Mira said.

"Yes," the Ilanyan replied.

Grimhammer and the centaurs steadied themselves. The big centaur ground his magical teeth at the sight of the behemoth quaking its way toward Takashaniel. He turned to his remaining fighters, all calmly awaiting his words. "We came here to fight!" he cried. "Never a greater foe has come to challenge us. Raise your weapons high and proud my brethren, and fight to the end!" The mighty centaurs reared up on their hind legs and thrust their weapons above their heads, and the field echoed with the roar of the mighty warriors, charging toward the monstrous Quentranzi.

* * *

AS WAS THEIR TRADITION, the Brunts had long ago run past the four humans to reach the battle first. The Rizanti also sprinted toward the enormous fiend, but at a much slower pace than before.

Iel noted the slower pace of the magical warriors and sighed. That burst of power had been a boon to their efforts, but was costly. The guardian did not like the prospect of fighting the second half of this battle without the Rizanti.

"How is the ninja?" he asked Mira, who still stood transfixed beside him.

"She will be fine, but I cannot be sure when she'll awaken. If she had come any later, I may not have been able to help her."

"I pray she awakens soon."

Mira said nothing, only watched in amazement as the defenders of Takashaniel charged the behemoth for a fight that seemed impossible to win. Before Siti and her battalion had reached the monster, the Bachatttas had already descended upon them. Not overly powerful creatures individually, Bachatttas' strength lay in numbers. Countless bat-winged fiends darted here and there, snapping and clawing at their intended prey. Siti and her warriors, however, were not easy prey. They fought the winged demons back while still making their way to the huge Quentranzi.

The Rizanti were the first to reach the demon, and struck with all their remaining power at the monster's heels and ankles. Despite the sharpness of their blades, they did little damage. Hardly noticing the tiny flies at its feet, the beast continued to make its way to the tower.

Grimhammer and his clan thundered across the field to meet the new enemy. The centaur leader was formulating a plan in his mind when Warsong practically sat back on his rear legs and moved to the side, just in time to avoid a red oval-shaped light that appeared in front of him.

Grimhammer and one of the nearby warriors to his side almost ran right through two larger ones when they realized the rest of the clan had stopped. Grimhammer looked all about, grinding his teeth again. Those red oval lights were appearing everywhere. "What new evil is this?" he growled.

"Portals!" Warsong yelled, just as a dark blue figure stepped out.

Windglider, a thin, muscular centaur and the fastest of the clan, faced another of the dark figures that stepped through the glowing red hole in the air. The thing stood taller than the centaur, closer to seven feet than six. Its blue skin was so tight that it looked as though it was sown over muscle. It flexed its long skinny fingers, revealing thin claws that looked like needles. Its bat-like wings curled up behind its back like a vulture, the tips nearly touching the ground. One each side of its smooth round head were pointed ears that extended nearly a foot above its head. It narrowed its yellow eyes hatefully at the centaur. Four fangs protruded from its closed mouth, two curving upward and two downward.

Windglider stood frozen from the sheer overbearing force that the creature exhibited. Its lips curled and drew back behind a set of smaller teeth, and it let out a threatening hiss.

"Windglider!" Grimhammer exclaimed. "Get away from it!"

The warning came too late. The beast opened its mouth and spat a foul black mist that wrapped around the paralyzed centaur. In seconds, the mist had engulfed him and eliminated the magic that sustained him.

More portals appeared all around the field, and out of them stepped various twisted and horrific creatures from the lowest level of the abyss.

Warsong roared and charged the Quentranzi that had defeated Windglider. He leaped at the unmoving demon, his body twisted back to drive his spear through the monster's chest. The Quentranzi threw out its hand and a blast of black energy shot forth, stopping the centaur midair. Warsong had just enough time to feel the magic sustaining him being ripped away, and then he was gone.

"The centaurs are in trouble!" Mira said with alarm.

"We cannot worry about them," Iel said. "Our own battle begins." Another portal appeared next to Mira, and she stumbled away at the sight of it. Iel stepped in front of her, and when the creature stepped out of the portal, the guardian launched a wave of cold at it, and engulfed the demon in ice. Once it was frozen, he said a few words in a language Mira had never heard, just as the ice began to crack. An instant later, the trapped fiend broke an arm free, then shattered the ice just as Iel finished the incantation. A shockwave knocked the demon to the ground, but it recovered quickly and was up again and charging toward the Ilanyan.

Iel had to think fast, for the demon would be on him before he could formulate a new attack. The fiend suddenly stopped and was slammed hard into the ground by an unseen force. It rose into the air, slammed into the wall of the tower, then again into the ground and jerked violently left, then right, before finally becoming engulfed in green flames by Iel, who had taken advantage of the help and finished the words of power.

After the beast was fully banished back to the dark realm, the guardian cast a glance at his student. "Improvement," he said with a grin. Mira smiled back, but the smile left her face as another Quentranzi approached.

* * *

"How are we gonna stop that thing?" Kita said as they narrowed the distance between them and the towering Quentranzi.

"This doesn't look good," Shinobu said. "All of those short guys were blown away in one blast by one of those things that materialized ahead of us. They didn't even get to the big one."

"Hey look!" Kita said, pointing some distance ahead. Siti and her group had moved forward and managed to clear a path for them to get through.

"They need our help!" Kenyatta said.

"We cannot," answered the samurai. "They fight to clear a path for us. We cannot let their efforts be in vain."

The four warriors sprinted through the battling fiends and magical warriors and came upon the giant. Kenyatta glanced over his shoulder. "They aren't winning," he said.

"Then run faster," the samurai said.

Kenyatta started to reply, but then the reality of having to fight a host of smaller Quentranzi while attempting to take that big one down stole the words from his mouth.

After covering a few hundred yards, the group came to a stop. The Rizanti had been cutting at the beast to little effect, but now they were falling one by one to the smaller fiends. The magical warriors fought tirelessly, but they had expended too much energy in the blast, and now moved slower and their strikes carried less force.

"We must use their last stand to our advantage!" the samurai said.

The four warriors charged the titanic demon, like ants converging on an elephant. Kenyatta was the first to strike. He cut an 'X' slash across the side of the monster's ankle, and for the first time, the beast acknowledged the tiny fleas at its feet.

"Our weapons affect it!" Kenyatta yelled. "Don't give it a chance to react!"

The others struck hard and fast, slicing and cutting and stabbing at legs and feet. The huge monster stopped and looked down at the insects stinging it. Kenyatta saw a black line streak down its ankle. "These things bleed?" Then, his warrior instincts told him to be anywhere but where he was at that moment. On pure reflex he leapt far to the side as an enormous hand slapped at him, missing and slamming its own leg. The monster then raised its foot and stomped the ground, creating a massive quake.

* * *

"THE CENTAURS HAVE ALL FALLEN," Mira lamented.

"Concentrate on your enemies," Iel replied. "These demons are far more dangerous than the previous horde."

Mira used her mental powers against fiends coming from every direction. She reached into her robe and produced several throwing knives that she hurled at a tall blue fiend that glowed with an inner red flame. The knives missed the mark as the demon disappeared and then reappeared a few feet to the side. It took another step toward her, then started convulsing as the knives had circled around to hit it from behind. The blades tore through its body repeatedly, sending tainted black blood spewing from the wounds.

Just as Iel had defeated two cunning Quentranzi, the earth burst open and out leaped a heavily muscled dark green monster with a waving tongue. Its body was nearly three times the size of the Ilanyan, its thick long tail waving tauntingly in the air. It stood crouched on two legs with one hand on the ground. Its mouth, housing several rows of long, sharp teeth, stretched into what looked like a gaping grin.

Having managed to paralyze her adversary with her mind, Mira picked up a thin branch from a tree and threw it at the monster. The branch transformed midair into a spear that struck the demon through the chest. Such a vital blow would have sent any normal fiend spiraling back to the abyss, but these were Quentranzi. Its black lifeblood poured out, but it resisted the pull of the abyss. Mira blasted the fiend with a telepathic shockwave that weakened it enough for it to succumb to its wounds, phasing from the earth plane back to the abyss.

The sound of hissing and growling drew her attention to where her teacher struggled against a Zzrt, one of the most dangerous Quentranzi to walk the abyss. "Master!" she exclaimed.

"Don't come near!" Iel yelled.

"What?" Even as she spoke, the green monster drove its arms deep into the ground and ripped out a large piece of earth and hurled it at the Ilanyan. Iel rolled to the side and launched a wave of light energy to slam into the hulking fiend to no effect. It still crouched in front of him, tongue waving outside that hungry grin as if tasting the air.

Mira focused on the demon and sent a shockwave to slam into it. If the attack had any effect, the demon ignored it and rounded on her. It stood upright, towering high above the apprentice. Its large white eyes widened and it responded with an openmouthed hiss just as it whipped its tail around and slapped her into the air.

Iel glanced with concern at Mira squirming on the ground, and the brief lapse of attention cost him. The Zzrt leaped the dozen feet between them and slapped him with a backhand, sending him hurtling into a nearby tree.

Despite being dazed from the impact, Iel used the base of the tree to spring forward. He raised his right hand and loosed a powerful blast of light into the demon.

When it staggered, he followed up with another blast of light energy, this one aimed at the creature's face. The monster hit the ground grabbing its eyes and screeching in a mixture of pain and fury. Iel slid to a stop at the sight of the Zzrt slamming the ground with its fist. In a fit of rage, it rolled back to its feet and charged, shredding the ground with its thick black claws.

* * *

KITA TRIED to catch his breath as he backed away. He and the others had done little damage against the titanic demon, and now its attention was fully on them. "We're doing just enough to annoy it!" he said.

"What makes you think that?" Shinobu asked sarcastically, as he dodged a huge fist that crashed into the ground and sent him tumbling under a wave of dirt and rock. The strider recovered quickly and countered with a zigzagging slash across its hand.

The demon yanked its hand back, and with a roar that made the air vibrate, raised its massive foot and stomped the ground once more, sending more dirt raining down. Shinobu dove aside, narrowly avoiding being swallowed by one of the many wide fault lines that trailed from the site of impact.

Kenjiro charged in and stabbed the side of the massive foot, driving his sword in to the hilt. It screeched and lifted its foot high into the air to grab at the wound. Kenjiro held onto his sword until the right moment, then pulled it free and leapt onto the creature's hand, driving the blade into its wrist. The beast reached for the samurai, but then stumbled from the pain of yet another stab from Kita's staff. With his free hand, Kenjiro drew his tanto, reversed the grip, and drove it in next to his sword. He pulled the short sword free and stabbed again. When the monster recoiled and leveled its arm, Kenjiro pulled the blades free and ran up the massive arm.

"I like his strategy!" Kenyatta said as he hopped onto the beast's foot and stabbed repeatedly.

Once he reached the shoulder, Kenjiro stabbed once again, bringing yet another bellow of pain from the creature. Tainted blood oozed from the wound, and the samurai had to fight back his revulsion. The giant fiend twisted and turned, but Kenjiro held on to his embedded sword. He saw a massive hand from the corner of his eye coming directly at him, and withdrew the blade and hopped up the shoulder. The hand missed, but a finger larger than Kenjiro's body slammed into him, blasting the air from his lungs.

While this was happening, Kenyatta backed away, then sprinted at the fiend from the rear. He leaped high into the air, embedding his blades to the hilt into the back of its leg. The monstrous demon shrieked and reached back for the dangling warrior.

Seeing his friend's vulnerability, Kita stabbed the monster in the foot with all his strength, which succeeded in drawing the beast's attention while Shinobu moved to the opposite side of the beast as Kita, and struck rapidly at its feet and ankles.

The demon stomped and swatted at the tiny humans, but they were quick and cunning. In dealing with the annoying specks at its feet, it had forgotten the samurai who lay at the edge of conscious-ness underneath its long black hair beside its neck.

The two warriors worked together to keep the enormous fiend distracted while Kenyatta worked his way toward the still-dazed samurai. Kenyatta made another leap and once again drove his swords into demonic flesh, this time into the monster's lower back. It was a wound that burned from the inside, and the demon ignored the two on the ground and tried to grab at the tiny insect stinging its back.

"What is he trying to do?" Shinobu yelled from the other side of the monster's foot.

"We'll find out soon," Kita answered, dodging another stomp.

Suddenly, the demon went still, and its back began to glow. Dangling from the monstrous demon's lower back, Kenyatta saw the blue skin beginning to glow just before heat started radiating from it. It didn't take long for the islander to realize his danger, and he quickly curled his body and positioned his feet between his embedded swords and pushed. They seemed unnaturally held in place, and now he could feel the heat and mounting energy in front of him. He did not dare release his grip and lose his weapons, however, so he held his position, trying to figure out another way to free himself.

The glow brightened, and explosion of built up energy sent the warrior flying away. Dazed, Kenyatta lifted himself to his elbows and rubbed his head. "Wasn't expectin' dat," he groaned.

* * *

KENJIRO WAS FINALLY able to clear his head and reorient himself. It was not very comforting to awaken and find that he was lying next to the massive creature's head, underneath a forest of slithering hair. He slowly climbed to his feet and gripped his sword in a white-knuckled grip. He lined the tip of the sword with the demon's neck, squared his stance, and drove it forward. Or tried to.

A mass of slithering hair wrapped around his right arm while more of the sentient locks flowed toward him. In one turning motion, Kenjiro let the sword drop from his right hand, caught it with his left, and cut his arm free. No sooner had he freed himself than more of the black tendrils wrapped around his limbs. Though he cut and slashed every stalk of octopus-like hair that entangled him, he couldn't work fast enough, and the bottom half of his body was wrapped tight.

In an act of desperation, he drove his sword into the neck of the beast, behind the jaw. The sword, although tiny in proportion to the massive fiend, struck true, for a thick line of black blood ran down its neck. Still it was not enough, and the hair continued to wrap about him. In seconds, he was cocooned in a mass of writhing black hair.

* * *

KITA PULLED himself back to his feet after nearly being sideswiped by the demon's enormous foot. The blow had sent him spinning through the air to crash to the ground over a dozen yards away. Once he had reoriented himself, he saw that Shinobu was in a bad situation.

Although the strider worked tirelessly, attacking and dodging, slashing and slicing while avoiding a stomp or a grab, he was unable to keep the thing at bay for long before it turned toward the tower once more. He started behind the fiend, but then on instinct, spun and ducked a slashing claw from behind.

Shinobu straightened to face his newest foe. He could feel the sense of wrongness that surrounded the demon. It was not very large, only about five and a half feet tall and of an average size, but the intangible force within it seemed ten times its size. Its dim yellow skin was leathery and hard, and it was difficult to see if the creature was fast but not physically strong, or slow and powerful. It had no defining features that gave any indication of its capabilities. Even its face was negligible, sporting only two red slits for eyes, and no nose or mouth that the strider could see. Its tail was as thick as Shinobu's arm, and whipped from side to side as the fiend studied him.

The strider narrowed his eyes and smiled. "Well at least you can't talk."

The fiend didn't respond, only continued to stare at him. With a shrug, the strider fingered the hilt of his sword while he sized up the foul creature. With a derisive sniff, the strider charged.

* * *

MIRA LIFTED her head to see Iel waiting calmly in the path of the charging fiend. As it drew nearer, the Ilanyan's body began to glow with a soft white aura. He was in the midst of gathering power within himself.

The Zzrt leaped high into the air and descended on the waiting Ilanyan. At the last possible second, Iel released a shockwave from his body that shook the ground and everything nearby.

The Zzrt caught the full force of the shockwave and was knocked from the air to crash back to the ground. Without as much as a flinch, it got up and charged again, and in less than a few heartbeats it was right in front the guardian. It slashed at him with terrifying speed and ferocity, but Iel avoided the assault and rolled to the side.

He was quick to his feet, but the hulking demon was on him. Iel was prepared this time, and slammed it in the chest with the palm of his hand, releasing the remaining built up energy. They flew away and landed a few feet from Mira, who scampered backward.

The beast shook its head and rose, seeming little affected. Mira picked up a rock as she positioned herself so that the Zzrt was between her and Iel. The demon let out a hiss-like growl, spun and charged back toward the guardian.

Iel threw his left hand out and a lance of yellow light went streaking through the air at the raging fiend. The lance struck the demon's chest, and its body pulsated with yellow light.

The Ilanyan's eyes pulsated in tune with the light-filled demon, yellow then blue. As the blue in Iel's eyes darkened, so too, did the light in the body of the disabled Zzrt. The crackling sound of ice creeping over its skin made Mira's skin crawl. In seconds, the demon was frozen.

Mira shook off her revulsion and threw the rock, focusing as it flew at the immobilized demon. The rock elongated into spear, and with a loud *crack* the rock-spear punched into the frozen Zzrt. The apprentice clenched her hand into a fist, then opened it.

The frozen Zzrt shuddered, then pieces of the ice began to chip away. A moment later, the demon burst into thousands of shards of ice that rained down around them. Mira started to smile, but saw that Iel was chanting and drawing energy into himself again.

"What are you doing?" she asked, just as the shards around her feet began to slide toward each other, reconnecting. Several heart-beats later, the shards evaporated into a green mist, then dissipated.

"You fought well," Iel said. "But that was a Zzrt. They are the toughest of the lower Quentranzi, and that was a weaker one." He started toward the field.

"Weak one?" Mira called after him.

Iel had not walked far before he caught sight of three of the four warriors fighting desperately to divert the monstrous titan that stalked unwaveringly toward the tower. A glowing white staff appeared in his right hand, and he whirled it faster and faster till it was a blur in his hands. He began to chant an incantation, and with every word, his voice echoed louder and louder until it filled the air. Finally, he thrust the staff above his head, then pointed it at the abysmal titan. A silver stream of light spiraled from the staff, and gradually formed into an enormous glowing beast of equal size to the giant Quentranzi.

The earth shook under its landing, and it straightened before the massive demon. The giant fiend screeched, and the air hummed with negative energy.

In response, the huge magical creature bellowed and fell upon its enemy. The two monstrous creatures exchanged blows, punching and clawing, and then the magical beast slapped the demon across the head with an open hand and sent it crashing to the earth with a mighty quake.

* * *

KENJIRO TUMBLED TO THE GROUND, finally released from the tightly grasping hair. Ironically, the only thing that saved him from a deathly fall was the very hair in which he'd been entangled.

He opened his eyes and looked at his sword, still tight in his grasp. He rose to one knee and looked over his shoulder at the massive beast lying on its back behind him. The ground shook again, drawing the samurai's attention to another equally large monstrosity stalking toward him. Kenjiro closed his eyes, then took a deep breath and opened them again. This was where he would die.

He climbed to his feet and readied himself, bringing his sword before him in a two-handed grip. The giant monster looked past him at the demon behind, just now climbing back to its feet. Kenjiro kept his eyes on the giant while he trotted aside. To his relief, the beast continued past, and to a titanic struggle with the screeching minion of the abyss.

* * *

THE MAGICAL DEFENDER lifted its foot to stomp its enemy, but the Quentranzi caught the massive foot in its clawed hands, just before it crashed into its chest. It heaved the magical beast backward, and when it stumbled, the Quentranzi was on it.

The defender was the quicker, however. It clasped its hands together and brought them up in a double ax-handle blow underneath the chin of the huge demon, sending it stumbling backward.

The Quentranzi retaliated with a slash across the magical creature's midsection, then a solid punch landing on the side of its head. The punch sent the defender off its feet, and when it hit the ground, it burst into thousands of silver sparks. The monstrous demon threw its head back and screeched in triumph.

Kenjiro had already started toward the monster, but was forced to deal with two smaller fiends. He could feel the power radiating off them, and knew that he would have had an easier time battling four pit demons than these two. They worked as a team, complementing the other's movements, the samurai was hard-pressed to keep them at bay. One stabbed forward, and as soon as Kenjiro attempted to deflect it, the demon withdrew and the other would jump in with an arcing strike.

Though he held them off at the moment, it was only a matter of time before one of them found an opening. Kenjiro redoubled his efforts, trying to gain just an instant to formulate a strategy to turn the tide in his favor. He received that split second that he needed when one of the creatures went to strike and hesitated, stumbling forward. After beheading the creature, Kenjiro focused on the remaining enemy. From the corner of his eye, over the diminishing body, he saw the figure of Kenyatta running toward the titan.

Kenyatta felt an inexplicable building of energy inside his body as he sprinted up behind the giant. He reversed his grip on the sword in his left hand, and held it tightly to his side while holding the blade in his right hand in a forward grip.

With a growl, he leapt, positioning his left blade behind him facing downward, and his right blade in front of him facing up.

Kita fell back on his heels at the sight of his friend, impossibly high into the air and tucked into a tight ball. He spun like a wheel fitted with blades, cutting his way up the back of the beast's leg. He angled diagonally to the right and just as he passed over the hip, he opened and he cut the beast down the leg during his descent. This happened faster than the monster could react, and the deep cuts in the back of its left leg and the front of its right, bled freely.

It was an effective strike, but the sheer mass of the demon

made it possible to sustain the wound without falling. Kenyatta dove aside to avoid the stomping foot, only to roll into the midst of yet another group of twisted monsters.

* * *

SHINOBU DANCED a deadly dance with the fiend before him. He'd never fought an opponent that could match his every move so effectively. Neither had gained an advantage, but the strider was hard-pressed to keep up with the small dark creature's movements. He had received several minor injuries from its whipping tail, and every time he attempted to sever it, the demon would flick it away at the last second. He would not be able to accept many more of these stinging injuries, but he couldn't find an opening in its defense. Blood dripped from his brow into his left eye, and his right leg was beginning to go numb from the four lashes he had received.

* * *

KITA HAD BEEN ATTACKED by two Quentranzi that descended upon him shortly after Kenyatta's amazing maneuver on the big one. He was able to handle them well enough with his staff, keeping them at bay from both sides while he worked them into a favorable position. Finally, he defeated one, banishing it back to the dark world, and batted the other aside to buy him enough time to twist the shaft and release the whip-chain.

* * *

AFTER DEFEATING two more Quentranzi using her telekinetic abilities, Mira leaned against the wall of the tower, trying to catch her breath. All about the field, Quentranzi stepped through red and orange portals. All hope left the young woman as she looked in every direction at the mass of the most powerful race of demons ever to walk the earth appearing everywhere. "How many of the damned things did the Drek summon?" she muttered.

No matter how powerful an assault Iel hurled at the massive fiend, it continued its unerring path toward the tower. He fell into concentration, chanting another incantation that would summon another magical creature, but this one he had reserved as a last effort. Carzan magic was extremely powerful but difficult to control. Mira stood frozen in alarm when she realized what her teacher was doing. She knew that if a beast summoned by way of Carza defeated the Quentranzi too easily, it would turn on its summoner.

Her breath caught in her throat when a bolt of light shot out of the tower and went streaking by. "What in the name of the Daun-yans?" A figure glowing with yellow light energy glided across the fields, past the battling enemies and defenders, and straight toward the gigantic, and seemingly unstoppable Quentranzi. The light shot past Iel, and the Ilanyan stopped in the middle of his casting.

The four embattled warriors also saw the light, as well as the human figure within.

It stopped at the titan demon's feet and shot straight into the air. As it glided ever upward, the light melted away to reveal Akemi, her body glowing from the inside with that yellow light. In one graceful movement, she drew *Sekimaru* from its sheath, and cut a burning path up the demon's leg, up its waist and abdomen and to its chest. With an ease that should have been impossible, she whipped the sword up and through the demon, and as her body turned in the air, she reversed her grip on her sword, and thrust backward at her side, driving the blade to the hilt in the middle its chest.

Suspended in the air by an invisible force, her back to an enemy so large, she looked like a fly, Akemi closed her eyes and the power that filled her body drained away and flooded through the abysmal monster. Like veins carrying lifeblood, the yellow light energy of the Daunyans snaked through the gigantic demon's body until started to glow from the inside out.

As the demon was being infused with the deadly heavenly energy, *Sekimaru* drained it of its dark essence. Helplessly suspended during this struggle, Akemi held on as her anxiety grew. *Sekimaru* was growing more powerful and more hungry with each of her nervous heartbeats. Then, of its own accord, the sword began siphoning the light energy out of the demon.

The sword glowed with Daunyanic light that shone so bright Akemi thought she would be blinded and the sword destroyed. As if with a mind of its own, *Sekimaru* thrust both light and dark energy back into the fiend in one burst. Its mouth agape in a silent cry of agony, the monstrous Quentranzi's body shuddered as the tiny sword ripped its very existence from its body, only to propel it and the deadly god power back in.

Kenjiro stood mesmerized by the sight of his younger sister and that huge titan, engulfed in that searing light.

Kenyatta still fought several of the smaller human sized Quentranzi, but still managed to take in the sight before him. The fight gradually became easier though, for the surrounding fiends seemed to be weakened by the power that radiated from the sword of the ninja demon huntress.

Kita had dispatched his two enemies and was now hesitantly moving toward the spectacle, unsure of whether or not he might be needed when this ended.

Though he had taken several injuries, Shinobu also had dispatched his remaining adversary, and now stood transfixed, hardly believing what he saw. "My kinda woman," he thought aloud trotting—and grimacing with every step—to catch up with Kita.

Kenjiro looked around the field. Other Quentranzi, smaller ones, were appearing everywhere. Smaller they might be, but he could feel power radiating from the creatures, and it made the first horde seem insignificant.

39

Red dimensional holes appeared in the air all over the battlefield, and out of them came the most hideous and powerful fiends that any of the defenders had seen. Every one of the abysmal creatures turned toward the four warriors, and Kenjiro, Kenyatta, Shinobu and Kita put their backs to each other and formed a tight square.

"A challenge is good, but not when the odds are impossible," Kita remarked.

"Then we die in battle with honor," the samurai declared.

Kenyatta frowned over his shoulder. "I made no plans to die today, so save the 'death in battle' talk for another time."

Shinobu sniggered.

Kenjiro surprised the islander with a smirk, then raised his sword.

Demons littered the field, and an overwhelming sense of despair and hopelessness filled the air. The dark monsters circled the four humans, closing the distance.

"Prevail or perish," Kita said. "Though I feel the latter is more likely, I regret."

"I already tell you," Kenyatta snapped, fighting off the effects of the demonic incursion. "I don't plan to check out today! Dem wan war wit us, we bring it to em!"

Kenjiro glanced at Kita, and it seemed to him that for the first time, the samurai actually understood the Jamaican's heavily accented western tongue. With a nod to his companions, Kita snapped his weapon together into its blade-ended staff form. Kenyatta crossed his swords downward, then slowly raised them while sliding them across from each other. When they were eye-level, he flipped his wrists, spinning the blades in his hands, then snapped them downward at his sides.

With one long, slow breath, Kenjiro slid his sword along the side of its scabbard, and when the tip of the sword reached the end of the scabbard, he replaced it in its home, sliding it ceremoniously within the sheath with a *click* when the hilt rested flat against it. With his hand resting on the hilt of his sword, he bowed, not to the malignant creatures before him, but to the ancestors that stood with him now, those who would guide his body in the greatest battle of his life.

Shinobu lowered his stance, fingering the hilt of his weapon his right shoulder. "I'm ready for a vacation," he said.

"And you will have that vacation no matter the outcome," Kita answered. "The length of your vacation, however, will depend on who wins the fight."

"All are one and the same to me," the strider replied. "Perish now or perish later, it makes little difference."

"Then remember the purpose of this fight and perish another day," Kita said.

"So solemn," Shinobu replied.

The four warriors stood in the midst of a small army of Quentranzi demons, many of which were closing in on them, while others made their way toward the tower. To Kenyatta, they looked like an army of demented berserkers, clawing and hacking everything in their paths.

"Primal bloodlust!" Shinobu said dryly. "My favorite kind of foe."

"Then I'll leave more of them for you to deal with," Kita said. "We should try to stay together as long as possible," he added. "We'll know who's at our back."

"Good theory," Shinobu replied. "But I don't think we'll be able to hold this position much longer."

The other three warriors followed Shinobu's gaze above their heads to see one of the fiends descending on them. They held their position, and as soon as the demon's first foot touched the ground, all four of the warriors spun, cut it to pieces, and returned to their original positions. In the middle of their formation, the demon evaporated to a sickly mist that descended back to the abyss.

And then the battle began anew, the four warriors along with the guardian, his pupil, and the few remaining magical defenders, battling the fiercest enemies they ever knew existed. Iel and his student were severely outnumbered, but managed to keep an efficient defensive position.

After what seemed like days, the defenders managed to gain the advantage, cutting through the demon forces and gradually pushing them back. Such progress was not without cost, however. Kenyatta had sustained a nasty rip at his shoulder, which bled freely and slowed the use of his right arm. Kenjiro ignored the pain of a gash he sustained from a narrowly avoided stab at his heart. Kita managed to defeat two of his enemies, only to be attacked by another, while the strider—who fared the best of all at the moment —cut through his enemies with that otherworldly sword of his.

"After this is done, I would really like to know why you're so good at this," Kita remarked between breaths.

No response was forthcoming, however, as Shinobu had been forced away from the group by a bigger threat. Two red dimensional gates appeared in front of the strider, causing him to dive to the side. He was quick to his feet, and spun to face two Zzrt hissing and growling as they slowly crept toward him, tongues waving and red eyes glowing. "You guys look a little tougher than the others," Shinobu said as he backed away from the hulking creatures.

More dimensional doors continued to appear, and Quentranzi demons of all types covered the battleground. "There are too many," Iel said. "We must retreat within the tower, now!"

Mira skittered backward and narrowly avoided a slashing claw that would have cut her in half. She threw a handful of pebbles at the beast, focusing on the harmless missiles until they elongated into spears. They struck home in the demon's chest, and she channeled energy from the Takashaniel that sent the fiend writhing and crashing into the wall of the tower. It shrieked in sudden agony as the pureness of Takashaniel ripped the life force from it, and sent it screaming back to the abyss.

The pupil spun in the direction of a bellow that sounded like a war cry. She looked to eastern hills and saw a large figure, half horse, half humanoid, standing on its hind legs and holding a huge war hammer with a spike on each end, high above its head. It raced down the hill, and behind it came raced a force of howling half-horse, half-men, holding their weapons aloft. A pained smile of relief crept across Mira's face. "Master Iel!" she cried. "The centaurs have come. The *real* centaurs!"

"Not just them," Iel said, still battling the last of a group of demons that had ventured their way. Mira turned to the charging figures once more. After studying them closer, she noticed that they bore passengers. Small passengers.

"The Brunts!" she exclaimed. "They've brought the Brunts with them!"

"Indeed," Iel said, moving beside her after dispatching the lesser demons back to the abyss. "Let's hope it will be enough."

* * *

THE MIGHTY CENTAURS and their unlikely passengers flew down

the hill and across the battlefield, hooting and roaring as they closed the distance between themselves and their prey. On Grimhammer's back rode Grit, the leader of the Brunts.

"Now *this* is a fight, eh horse-man?" Grit shouted.

"Don't call me 'horse-man,'" Grimhammer snapped.

"Err yer never did have a humor about yer did yer, horse-ma ... uh, centaur," Grit teased. "Now, yer get me close enough to one a them err stinkin' quen-thingies and I'll be doin' me stuff!"

The centaurs and their eager riders cut straight through the demonic mass. As they passed, the Brunts launched themselves from the backs of their carriers and hacked into the demon forces with the same bloodlust as their enemies. Now relieved of their riders, the centaurs sped through the battle and out of the other side. Grimhammer led a group to circle to the left, while Warsong led a group to the right. Once on opposite sides of the horde, they began working their way back in, hacking and slashing every fiend in their path.

"This is not going to work," Warsong yelled. "They do not fall to our weapons!"

"Without the right weapons to fight these things, we cannot win!" another centaur yelled. True enough, a strong blow managed to stagger some of the smaller demons, but had little effect on the larger ones. A pained grunt drew Warsong's attention, and he turned to see that one of the smaller centaurs had been lashed by the whip of a green-skinned demon.

The hearty warrior staggered but fought on, growling away the pain through clenched bloody teeth. Warsong could see that the wound was mortal, as the wounded centaur's lifeblood flowed from his body. Still he fought, beating back the relentless creatures. He glanced over at Warsong, and the group leader saw death in those eyes. Warsong cried out, trying to fight his way toward his injured comrade, but the dying warrior bellowed and turned his back to the commander, hacking and slashing, batting demons away in every direction with what strength remained to him. The Quentranzi were too much, however, and soon he fell to many more attacks that descended upon him from every direction.

Warsong felt a coldness settle over him, then rage burned it away. He spotted the green-skinned demon that had struck his friend down, and with a mighty cry, he charged through the demon forces, blasting fiends from his path with strength beyond anything he had known he was capable of. Within seconds, he was upon the green demon. With its double-tipped tail and eagle-like talons extended from four fingers, the fiend thought it would be more than a match for the smaller centaur. It could not have been more wrong.

The enraged Warsong brought forth his spear and impaled the hunch-backed fiend, lifting it into the air and over his head to slam it to the ground.

The enraged commander stomped and trampled the fiend with such ferocity that it startled his own allies. After his rage played out, he backed away from the beast and dodged an attack from yet another fiend. He kicked out with his hind legs and knocked the beast away. The green demon with the whip recovered, and its whip lit afire. It stared murderously at the centaur commander. Warsong was prepared to meet it, but at the sight of his other adversaries, —recovering despite injuries that would have killed any normal enemy—decided against that action. They were doing nothing more than wasting energy.

He searched the battleground, but by now, all of the defenders were engaged and surrounded. A heavy sense of despair settled over his shoulders, but he clenched his teeth and fought it back. At the sight of the green fiend approaching him, the one that had killed his friend, Warsong's rage flared once again. The monster managed to score a few blows, but the enraged warrior seemed immune to any injury.

Warsong ripped and stabbed the fiend so violently that even the other dark creatures kept their distance. With one last thrust with all his strength, Warsong drove his spear so far through the demon that his hands reached its chest. He reared back on his hind legs, and came forward and butted his head into the creature's face. He ripped his spear free and saw that this time, the demon seemed weakened. Black, tainted blood poured from the wound, and it staggered away.

Not wasting the time to figure out his sudden fortune, Warsong beat the demon down until it could no longer sustain itself, and it slowly dissipated back to the abyss.

* * *

MIRA WORKED to protect Iel while he channeled Daunyanic power through himself and into their newly arrived allies. The charges upon their weapons were temporary, but it would enable them to defeat their demonic foes.

Not long after he had fallen into concentration, a Behematranzi materialized before them. The four-legged beast looked as if it weighed tons, and Mira was certain that a swat from one of those tree-sized legs would be the end of her. Two wavy horns protruded from the front of its head, and as it opened its yawning maw, she could see four fangs as long as swords.

The sight of such a beast sent tremors of fear through her body, but she controlled it, grabbed a long stick lying at her feet. She focused on the stick, and it doubled in length and formed into a hissing and spitting Naga serpent. Although she hated to dabble in the dark arts, Iel had insisted that it was necessary for the rare instances when one is faced with a foe that only a similar force could match. She could have changed the stick into a viper with considerably less effort, but a Naga was lethal in a different way. She used it carefully, focusing to ensure that the creature did not turn on her instead.

The Behematranzi reared to strike, but the Naga was quicker, and struck it several times in the belly. Mira lost track of time as

she fought the thing, barely avoiding death, before she and the
Naga were finally able to defeat the tank-like beast. Calling up
what strength she had left, she stood guard with the magical
serpent until Iel awoke from his meditation.

"It is done," the guardian finally said, "but not before the
centaurs have lost a few of their clan, I fear."

Mira fought back the lump forming in her throat. "I heard
Warsong's cry."

Iel laid a hand on her shoulder. "Grief must wait."

Just then, the guardian noticed the angry Naga she held by the
tail, its head waving through the air in search of any would-be
enemies. "Well done." he said.

* * *

HOURS PASSED as the battle raged from midday to night, and now
dawn was approaching. The four humans had fought valiantly, but
time and lack of rest began to wear at them. The enormous titan
had fallen to the bite of the mighty *Sekimaru*, and the struggle had
left Akemi unconscious on the ground when her brother reached
her. He hurried back toward Takashaniel with her over his shoulder, cutting and dodging attack after attack.

"Him not last long like dat," Kenyatta said to Kita.

"Then let's give him a little cover," Kita responded, cutting
down yet another of the twisted monsters. He turned, then grunted
when Kenyatta tackled him to the ground.

He heard Kenyatta groaning over his shoulder, and rolled over
to see his friend's eyes clamped shut in a grimace. He looked over
Kenyatta's shoulder and saw a single needle protruding from his
back. Several feet away, the demon that Kita has defeated
squirmed on the ground, and he saw that it had launched those
poisonous needles before it succumbed to its wounds. Kenyatta
had saved him from taking a fistful of those things in the back, but
one of the cursed needles had found its mark.

Kenyatta scratched at the wound while struggling to his feet. "Dammit," Kita growled, draping his friend's other arm over his shoulder and helping him up. "Now we've got to hurry *you* to the tower." He looked to the strider for help, but Shinobu was having a particularly rough time with two Zzrt, who slashed and leaped at him such savagery, he didn't know how the man was still alive.

Shinobu snarled with dissatisfaction. Despite their savage appearance, they were intelligent and far more lethal than any demon he'd fought so far. It took all of his skill just to keep from being shredded by those sharp claws, or being swatted by one of those thick tails!

"Shinobu!" he heard Kita yell. "We make for the tower. Akemi is down and Kenyatta is injured."

"That sounds like a great idea," the strider yelled back. "But you'll have to pardon me if I'm not fast to join you!"

That left Kita in a bind. The samurai had already made off toward the tower, Kenyatta could probably still fight, but not very well, and Shinobu fought two grinning, hissing piles of muscle that seemed not to be affected by any injury the strider dealt.

GRIT AND DERK fought a green demon Iel had called a corono. They used a simple tactic of spacing themselves in order to position the fiend between them. With Brunts, the strategy was always simple brute force. Per Grit's orders, the clan split, each pairing with another to take a target. They had never fought Quentranzi before and Grit wanted to be sure they were close as a group and could depend on one another to help fight the unpredictable creatures.

The strategy seemed to be working, as they complemented each other's movements. As effective as they were, however, the battle had cost them a number of their clan until their weapons had suddenly become effective against the wretched things.

Mira scanned the once-beautiful fields of Takashaniel, now shrouded in horror. The presence of evil darkened the surroundings, but the worst was the tainted blood of the creatures. One drop of demon blood tainted the land that it fell upon. Everywhere, demons and their adversaries bled, fought and destroyed each other. The apprentice could only look on in despair. Even if they did win this battle, the cost would be heavy. Would the land, torn and darkened, ever recover?

She was pulled from her thoughts by the gurgling sound of a prauna, a human-sized Quentranzi with five tiny spikes protruding from its back. It had a small mouth with no visible teeth, but two horns about half a foot in length extending from each side of its jaw and arcing forward. Its green scaly hide was stretched taught over its hunched body, and it looked to Mira that it could turn easily turn aside the thrust of a sword. Its top set of arms were as long as its legs, while its lower arms were about half that length.

Not taking her eyes off the vile, gurgling creature, she backed away and picked up another rock. The prauna leapt at her and spread its arms. Mira stood her ground as the creature descended upon her, just long enough to charge the rock with explosive energy and hurl it at the demon. She rolled aside just as the rock hit the prauna and exploded. She grabbed a handful of dirt as she rolled back to her feet, and basked in the power of Takashaniel filling her.

The prauna rubbed at its chest with its smaller arms, more out of irritation than pain, its thick scales having effectively protected it from the projectile.

"Let's see how you handle this," she said as the dirt began to glow in her palm. She squeezed her hand tight until the dirt was somewhat solid, then threw it above the creature's head. She held her hand out in front of her with her fingers closed, and when it reached the demon, she spread her fingers, and what was left of the glowing dirt burst into a shower of Daunyanic light. The effect was like acid on the demon's thick hide, and the prauna fell to the ground, twitching and coughing.

Mira thought the beast finished, but it slowly rose back to its feet, its scaly lips drawing back from yellow teeth. "How?" was all the apprentice was able to say before the abysmal creature charged.

40

B rit watched from of his scrying mirror as the battle ensued. Upon hearing Kabriza's guttural voice, he half-turned to regard the demon.

"You chose powerful enemies, Drek," it mocked. "Not long ago you claimed the ability to defeat them and destroy the tower without the assistance of my brethren. It looks as if we may indeed require your mighty intervention if the battle continues as it does."

Brit eyed the creature. One would not think of a demon as well-spoken, even if it is to imply sarcasm. Every other of the sickening creatures he had encountered used more ... crude, forms of communication. "You may be correct," he agreed. "It seems that the prowess of your kind is overrated, rest only a few." He then pointed to the one human fighting a pair of large, bulky specimens. "That one, I must say, must be very skilled to handle two of those ... *Zzrt*, they are called? But what of the other four?"

He turned to face the Quentranzi general. "I do not care how powerful these humans are, they are only five, and still *only* humans. I had expected more from your minions than just tougher versions of the first wave of fodder. They still have yet to reach the tower, and the battle lingers. I am disappointed, Kabriza."

The Quentranzi's face twisted into what looked like a sneer, then straightened to its full height. Brit looked up at the beast, a soft red aura lining his body.

Kabriza tilted its head to regard the Drek, then let out a shrill, grinding sound that might have been a laugh. "Do I frighten you, Drek?" it taunted.

Brit knew better. By the demon's change in posture, he knew that his point was well-received. Although he was sure he could send the creature back to the abyss if it came to that, it would be no easy task. Still, he needed to be sure that the Quentranzi understood that he was up for the challenge.

"Mighty Brit," the fiend chuckled. "The weak come in larger numbers. Surely you know that."

"Your point?"

"Why not have fun diminishing their forces," Kabriza continued, "while waiting to strike the fatal blow? What you have seen is not more than a sample of what I command."

Brit could feel his temperature rising. Why did the hellish beast not just send his more powerful minions to the battle and wipe out the defenders after the first wave of lesser demons was defeated? Why the games?

The demon general stood for a moment as if allowing Brit more time to ponder the matter. "I do admit that I had not expected those half-breeds and runt warriors to show themselves, especially with humans fighting." Another horrible laughing sound. "As always we have found your world to hold many surprises."

Kabriza stepped back a few paces, and the floor trembled. Brit followed the demon general's gaze to the far end of the room. It was empty save the scrying mirror and themselves. Brit waited to see what it was the unpredictable creature could be looking at. After speaking in the guttural tongue of the abyss, the fiend smugly eyed Brit, who now could see the outlines of two creatures not much taller than himself. The winged demons stepped forward, and with each step, the invisibility that surrounded them seemed to trail off in wisps.

Kabriza snickered at Brit's incredulity, but the Drek hardly cared. How could those things have been in his fortress without his knowledge, and how long had they been there?

* * *

HOVERING NEXT TO ZREAL, high above the battlefield, Szhegaza looked on in amusement. "The guardian chooses his allies well," she said. "Five humans, a clan of half-breeds led by the biggest centaur I have ever seen, and a group of short, smelly-looking things that are much stronger than they look." She smiled.

"Let's not forget the magical creatures he's summoned," Zreal added.

Szhegaza didn't respond, her focus trained on the samurai carrying a woman toward the tower. "It looks like things are turning more in our favor. I'm sure Master Brit will be pleased if we were to destroy them and lead the destruction of the tower ourselves." If a serpent could smile, it would look like the devious expression on the Zitarian's face. "Let's help them die."

Zreal eyed her carefully. "I will handle the samurai and the woman. You can deal with those two." He pointed at the human holding the large silver spear and supporting another over his shoulder.

Szhegaza looked the scene over and favored him with a grin, then dropped from their altitude, descending to the earth below. Zreal never felt anything other than mistrust for the Zitarian, but he could not dismiss the possibilities of aligning himself with one as capable as Szhegaza. And the potential rewards she spoke of were not untrue. Perhaps he could use her to accomplish his goals, and if she were foolish enough to betray him, he would deal with her then. For the first time since his master's plan came into reality,

Zreal felt he had some control over his part in it. He smiled to himself as he descended toward the samurai.

* * *

SHINOBU FOUND himself gradually giving ground against the Zzrt, who seemed to have no limit to their endurance and felt no pain. *One of these things would have been more than enough,* he thought, *but two are outside my comfort zone.* The strider smiled despite his desperate situation. Beads of sweat trickled down his forehead, and the muscles in his arms burned from constant use and his movements were beginning to slow.

The larger of the two leaped at him, and he threw himself into a roll under the monster. Instinct nudging the back of his mind, and the strider planted his feet and darted into another roll to the right of the second Zzrt that ripped up four large strips of ground where the strider had been only an instant before. Shinobu jumped out of the roll into a spin and slashed the creature's arm with three swift cuts while in midair. The beast seemed not to be affected by the injury, regardless of the black blood streaming from its wound.

Shinobu would have sighed if he didn't need every ounce of energy. He'd driven the blade down with enough force to sever the thing's arm. Instead, he'd only dealt it a deep cut, which it ignored and charged him again! He could feel the triple thud in the ground as the hulking beasts loped toward him.

One leaped at him and he stood his ground, crouching low and striking at the underbelly. The other Zzrt lunged at him as if to tackle, but the strider, ever agile, came out of the crouch and back-stepped. In that same instant, as the beast flew by, he ducked and rolled forward, avoiding a swipe from the creature he'd just cut across the midsection. He spun out of the roll to face the two monsters who stalked toward him, slower this time. *Maybe I did hurt them a little,* he thought as he stared into those permanently grinning maws filled with rows of sharp teeth.

He noticed Kita holding Kenyatta up by the shoulder, undecided whether to help him or get his friend to the tower. He sprinted toward his waiting companions, but was cut off by the smaller of the two Zzrt. He tried to dodge to the left, then right, then left again, but the demon matched his movements so precisely that the strider had to wonder if the thing was reading his mind.

* * *

NOT FAR AWAY, the clan of centaurs had been slowly but steadily gaining ground since their weapons had suddenly become effective. Grimhammer suspected it was the tower guardian's work, which meant it was most likely temporary. They drove as hard as they dared, trying to destroy as many of their enemies as they could before the effects wore off.

He noticed one human fighting two of those ferocious Zzrt. Unshakable though he was, Grimhammer didn't want to think of what would become of the human if those things got a hold of him, which from his perspective, seemed like only a matter of time. He also saw two other humans not far off, one of them injured. Clearly the human holding the other wanted to help, but was hesitant to leave his injured friend unguarded.

The third thing Grimhammer saw was what prompted him to order two of his fastest warriors to follow him toward the humans. A strange-looking creature was gradually descending upon the two humans, as if it were savoring the moment before the kill. As he and the two centaurs at his side raced toward them, Grimhammer remembered Iel mentioning that five humans would be pivotal in the outcome of the battle. The shape that these three were in didn't offer much hope. And where were the other two?

* * *

HE SAW NO IMMEDIATE DANGER, but Kita's instincts screamed at him. Without thinking, he jumped and turned, positioning his feet under his friend's arm and at the side of his body, saying, "You're gonna hate me for this." As gently but with as much power as he could, Kita pushed off his friend. Kenyatta was thrown in one direction, rolling and cursing on the ground, and Kita in the opposite direction. If he'd acted a hairsbreadth later, both of them would have been skewered by the winged creature that came crashing to the ground.

"I'll admit that I am impressed by your instincts," it purred, straightening. "I wasn't expecting to enjoy this."

Kita had already recovered and was on the winged reptilian-looking thing. He struck swiftly and with deadly precision, but to his surprise, the thing dodged every attack without much effort. He backed off and held his staff in front of him at a defensive angle.

"Come now," the thing said. "Do human males not treat females with better manners?"

Kita frowned at her. *Females?*

"Should we not at least be introduced?" she continued.

"What are you and why did you attack us?"

"Attack?" The thing leaned backward and placed her clawed hand over her chest as though shocked. "I simply wanted to introduce myself and see if I might assist you in your plight." Her smiled could have dripped venom.

"No, thank you," he replied.

"Perhaps your friend would be of a different mind," she said. Kita glanced at Kenyatta, who looked in worse shape. He circled around until he was between his friend and this apparently female creature.

"We'll manage."

She smiled even wider and took a step forward with her arms spread open. "I hold no weapon to harm you with. I make no move to attack, even though you stand ready to strike me down with your very nice silver stick."

Kita almost laughed. Who did she think she was fooling? She

held no weapon aside from the ones naturally attached to her fingertips. Those claws could slice him to pieces.

Suddenly his thoughts began to haze. He shook his head, keeping his eyes on the approaching creature. With each step that she took, Kita found her less threatening. He could not strike her down, but in fact he yearned to welcome her help. She closed the distance between them, her movements graceful and seductive. She seemed to glide rather than walk, and with each step, she no longer looked like a winged reptilian creature, but a woman of flawless beauty.

"It hurts me that you have forgotten me already," she cooed. "Has it been so long, traveling warrior?"

And then he remembered. She was the beautiful woman from Toyotomi Village.

"I can make all of your problems disappear," she said. Her voice echoed in his mind, pushing aside the sounds of battle. He was oblivious to all but this alluring woman moving ever closer. The warnings screaming at his mind were pushed further and further back until they were no more than muffled cries in the back of his consciousness.

He closed his eyes as she reached out to touch him, then a sudden burst of pain snapped his eyes open and he back-stepped, following with a horizontal spinning cut at the woman's waist. She reacted much quicker than expected, and Kita once again saw her for what she was. He glanced at his bruised shoulder, then at Kenyatta, who was on his knees with a devious, 'that's two you owe me,' expression on his face. Kita knew that he and everyone else would hear about his apparent demise before Kenyatta had saved him.

The once again reptilian-looking thing cast a venomous glance at Kenyatta that made his blood freeze. "Hate to be her boyfriend," he said.

"Your friend cost you an easier death," she said.

"What happened to all the sweet talk?" Kita replied.

With a tip of her head, and then that poisonous smile again, her wings rose above her head and divided.

What is she supposed to be now, a dragonfly?

He'd barely finished the thought when the winged creature flew at him.

* * *

THE SAMURAI WAS BEGINNING to tire. He had fought an endless battle and now carried his sister on his shoulders to Takashaniel. They desperately needed her in the fight and there was no time to waste. He felt her body tense over his shoulder.

"Kenjiro, stop." Akemi raised her head and looked over her shoulder at him as he slowed and let her down. She stood, a bit shaky at first, but then strength seemed to flow into her.

Kenjiro looked her over. "Can you fight? Danger is everywhere and I don't think I could defend you from more than one or two of those things at a time. They are much stronger and more cunning than those other demons we fought."

The ninja cast him an insulted look. "When have I ever needed you to protect me?"

"When you were lying on the ground unconscious not long ago."

"As the guardian aided you when you were tangled in the hair of a towering demon," came the retort.

The samurai was disarmed. How did she know about that?

The sight of a winged creature speeding toward them from above cut short the argument. Having recovered most of her strength, she stood as casual as if they were having a cup of tea when she pointed to the sky.

The samurai looked up. "What do you suppose that is?"

"Looks like a giant reptilian dragonfly or something."

"It doesn't look like a demon to my eyes," Kenjiro said.

"It isn't," Akemi replied. "It exudes no demonic presence that I can tell."

Kenjiro was unsure whether or not that was good news. He moved to stand side-by-side with his sister.

Zreal found it amusing that the two humans stood as if his appearance was no concern. *I will have to change their perception of me,* he thought as he pulled up at the last minute, his wings beating rapidly to hold him aloft.

Kenjiro and Akemi shielded their eyes from the dirt and rocks that those beating wings stirred.

"A bit of a rude entrance, don't you think?" Akemi remarked, one hand gripping the hilt of *Sekimaru.*

"Must feel the need to make a grand entrance," Kenjiro replied.

"Are all humans as confident as you?" the thing asked.

Akemi's eyebrows twitched at the raspy sound of the creature's voice. "You sound as if you need a throat-soothing tablet," she said. "If you will wait a moment, I can see if I have one with me." Her older brother arched an eyebrow.

Zreal studied the humans. Both had great power emanating from them, like nothing he had ever seen from their species. They stood casually, but he had no doubt that they could spring into action in an instant. He decided to gauge their skill. In the blink of an eye, he launched himself straight at them.

Akemi snapped *Sekimaru* out of its sheath and sidestepped to the right while she cut diagonally down and then vertically up.

Kenjiro, in one motion, unsheathed his sword and sliced straight up and then diagonally down to his right while stepping into the motion.

To their surprise, the reptilian-looking creature dodged both of their attacks and landed safely behind them. From the corner of his eye, Kenjiro saw a long, thin cut that had almost removed the sleeve of his *haori*. He glanced at Akemi, her hair hanging freely at her shoulders. The band that held her hair back fell to the ground.

It didn't take much to realize that the creature had dodged their attacks, sliced his arm and cut the band from her hair.

"I wished to see your hair unbound," the creature said.

Akemi stepped forward, her foot on top of the band, further burying it in the dirt. "Show me your weapon, creature, so that I may remove it from your corpse."

It chuckled at her statement. "All of my weapons are natural, *human*," it spat the last word. "Try as you wish, but you've little hope to survive this."

Zreal had their attention, and there was no doubt in his mind that they believed him. They attacked, one cutting low while the other cut high, one left, one upward. Their tactics were systematic and precise, indicating years of fighting together that surprised Zreal. His surprise was nothing more than amusement, however. They were fast and they were skilled, but they were humans.

Kenjiro feinted a stab, then changed the motion and cut a circular strike that surely would have removed the creature's head if not for its tremendous speed and reflexes. The creature dodged his attack, then dropped to the ground to avoid the ninja's low strike that would have removed his legs. It hopped from the ground between them while turning its body diagonally. It straightened midair, delivering a powerful kick to the samurai's chest, and a head to the ninja's stomach.

Launched in opposite directions, Akemi tumbled head over heels backward while Kenjiro's body skipped over the ground like a pebble across a body of water until he slammed into a tree.

Zreal looked a mixture of amused and disappointed. "This cannot be the extent of your abilities?" he said. "Two of you against me and this is all you can do? The tower should be rubble by now if all depends upon you."

Kenjiro struggled to his feet. That had hurt more than he wanted to admit to himself. Whatever this thing was, it was definitely strong enough to have killed him with that kick to the chest.

It was toying with them. He noticed that Akemi was slow to her feet as well.

Akemi was also hurt more than she wished to admit. The demon huntress was no stranger to being struck down in a fight, but she always managed to recover with the grace of a cat. This reptilian thing had sent her tumbling out of control for several dozen feet before she finally slid to a stop. She stood, partially bent at the waist and trying not to grab at her stomach. Kenjiro would need to buy her some time to recover. As if reading her mind, the samurai raised his sword once again and stalked toward their enemy.

Zreal looked at him in mock surprise. "Up again? You wear a brave face, but don't move so fast. You really don't want to play with me anymore, do you? If you admit it now, I can end all of this quickly."

Kenjiro continued toward his enemy. *It knows nothing of the samurai.*

* * *

THE HUMAN'S quick reaction surprised Szhegaza. She'd thought to rip out his intestine and be done with it. Her underestimation had earned her a slap at her wrist from the human's staff. He followed the blow with a reversed horizontal swipe at her head, which she slipped underneath. The fact that she had to expend this much energy on a human irritated her.

The Zitarian was nothing if not vain, and such vanity was the source of her irritation at having to get dirty. Her vanity also could have cost her more than a stinging wrist. If there had been a blade in place of that staff, she might be cradling a nub instead of her hand.

Now he was on her, feigning a left swipe, then reversing the motion and nearly slapping the Zitarian on the side of the head. Szhegaza was getting angry. This human was a much better fighter than she'd anticipated, and it had damaged her pride. She dodged his every attack, even parrying a few with her hands, then ducked another horizontal strike and darted in low. He sidestepped and barely avoided her right-handed slash at his midsection.

Kita did well to hide his surprise at this creature's prowess. He hadn't expected her to parry his staff with her bare hands. He was obviously not fighting a demon. This thing kept him on his toes, and it was difficult to establish a solid footing long enough to formulate some sort of strategy. She was faster than he was, but how much faster, he was unsure. Kita knew that he had caught her off guard only because of her arrogance at the start of the fight.

"Time to finish our little dance," the thing hissed. "I don't know why you are still alive, but that doesn't matter much to me now." Its spread its dragonfly-like wings and half-flew, half-jumped toward him in a confusing zigzag motion that was so fast, Kita had trouble following the movements. He barely avoided being cut across the face by a clawed left hand that he didn't see coming till the last minute.

Quick to improvise, Szhegaza followed the attack through and slammed her shoulder into his chest and blasted the wind from his lungs. The human flew a dozen feet and hit the ground in a backward roll.

Wheezing for air, he looked up and saw a clawed hand stabbing for his chest. He turned aside just in time to avoid those razor sharp claws, and rolled backward again to put some distance between them.

"This is it, my human friend. I hope you don't mind." That same venomous smile crept across her striped green face. And then the smile was gone, along with the reptilian-looking female. Kita flinched away as a blur of movement whipped by him and knocked her into the air to crash into a group trees.

"Not at all," a deep voice replied.

Kita's eyes widened at the sight of a half-horse, half-man peering into the distance with a grin of satisfaction on his face.

Kita was still in shock as this new ally helped him up. "Thanks," he said. "I hate to admit it, but I think that might have been my end."

"Do not say that," the centaur said. "Even the greatest of fighters need help at one time or another. Besides, I think your friend was determined to help you despite his injury." The centaur nodded over his shoulder at his Kenyatta, holding one of his swords in the hand of his strong arm.

"He might be mad that you beat him here," Kita chuckled. "He'd like nothing more than to have another save to hold over my head." He straightened and extended his hand. "I am Kita."

"I am Warsong," the centaur replied, taking the human's hand in a powerful grip.

Kita waved a hand. "My struggling friend over there is Kenyatta."

Warsong smiled and tipped his head.

Kita's smile disappeared when he remembered the others. In his fight with that green winged thing, he'd forgotten them.

Seeing the concern on the warrior's face, Warsong placed a reassuring hand on Kita's shoulder. "Fear not for your friends. My clan battles with you." They walked over to help Kenyatta get to his feet, and after careful inspection of his wound, Warsong lifted the protesting islander in his arms and started toward the tower.

Kita insisted on remaining behind so that he could help Shinobu, despite Warsong's assurance that his leader was more than able to deal with the creatures. Kita soon found that it was no exaggeration. The—much larger—centaur leader had come to the strider's aid, and now battled those two frightening Zzrt. The big centaur inflicted grievous damage on the two demons, but they seemed more tolerant of the enchanted weapons. The one named Grimhammer pounded one of the hulking fiends to the ground, and struck a gaping hole in the chest of the other, only for it to mend almost immediately.

Kita joined the fight, and with Shinobu and the giant centaur, together they managed to defeat the two demons, beating at them until they finally succumbed to their numerous wounds and faded back to the dark realm. After the centaur leader inspected a nasty wound Kita had received from one of the Zzrt, Grimhammer declared that they must make haste, and grudgingly offered to carry them both on his back to the tower.

On the way, Grimhammer explained the strategy that had begun before the five of them had arrived, and what was happening now on the fields of Takashaniel. The Brunts were fighting their way back to the tower and may have reached it by now. The remaining magical warriors fought with the last bit of power that sustained them, but would not be able to hold their physical forms much longer. Aside from the five humans, the guardian and his apprentice, the Brunts and the centaurs were the only other mortal warriors on the battlefield.

Once they reached the tower, they found a battered Kenjiro and an exhausted Akemi. Kita was surprised to see the siblings so worse for wear. Kita whistled through his teeth after listening to a recap of the fight with a reptilian-looking creature similar to the one he'd fought, and that the centaur Lightlance had tipped the scale in their favor. None wished a rematch with those two any time soon.

Across the field, the battle was turning for the better. The Brunts had fought their way back, and most of the remaining demons were not as powerful as the first wave that had attacked before. Though the centaurs had suffered the loss of three of their clan, the Brunts had not fared so well. Grit reported that he had lost his fifth in command. (Traditionally, a clan of Brunts would have as many as ten in command). It was that loss that had brought them closer to winning the day. When Leader Ghrass fell, the Brunts had gone into a frenzy. Although they lost a few more numbers, they'd sent many demons screaming back to the dark realm.

41

B rit prepared himself for a tough battle that he had known was inevitable from the start. Kabriza had summoned two subordinates and housed them in his fortress without his knowledge. Surely a face-off would follow, as Brit could sense power emanating from the twin winged demons standing to the side like statues.

To his surprise, however, Kabriza made no threatening gesture. Instead, it spoke a word in its guttural tongue, and they ran past Brit toward the balcony, leapt over it and glided into the distance. Brit never took his eyes off of the Quentranzi general.

"A plan of your own?" the Drek inquired.

"A precaution for an ambitious plan that might have proven beyond the Drek's means," Kabriza rumbled. Brit let the insult pass. He was more concerned with the demon before him, the two that just left, and how strong they might be if their efforts were joined. If Kabriza was able to summon those two without his knowledge, how many more could it bring? How was that even possible since Brit himself was the demon general's *tether* to this world. The prospect of battling two Quentranzi interested Brit more than it worried him. What did concern him, was the prospect of battling those two along with the demon general. That might prove to be a challenge unlike any Brit had experienced.

42

The defenders regrouped for a final stand against the closing demons. The centaurs formed a simple formation and awaited Warsong's order. The Brunts formed a two-group, arrow-shaped formation, ready to charge at Grit's command. Despite their determination, Iel was concerned for his human allies. They had fought beyond anything he thought a human capable of, and were looking the worse for wear.

The sound of hooves pounding the ground drew the guardian's attention, and Iel looked out to the battlefield to see Grimhammer racing toward them with Shinobu and Kita riding his back.

The defenders readied themselves, but at the sight of the resistance that the two remaining warriors met in the field, half the centaurs and half the Brunts, per Warsong and Grit's orders, charged the field to aid their friends. Iel moved to the humans and offered what he hoped was a confident smile. "You need not—"

"Do not even bother, guardian," the samurai interrupted. "We have no intention of leaving without finishing this."

Iel could only nod at that declaration. He had expected such from them, but still he had to try.

"I have a bad feeling," said a voice from behind. Iel turned to his worried apprentice. "Only a handful of demons are left, and there is no sign of any new threat, but I can't help this feeling I have."

"I feel it also," Iel responded. "There is no sign of the Drek or his ally."

"Not only that," Kenjiro added, "but those two reptilian things are still alive." That brought a worried expression to the Ilanyan's face, for he received a full account of the two winged creatures that were even more formidable than any of the demons they'd fought, save the titan.

* * *

THE TASTE of dirt in his mouth, and the sound of the remnants of battle awakened Zreal from his unintended slumber. He lifted his head and immediately regretted it when the pounding started. That huge centaur had crashed into him with so much force, he'd been launched far away from those humans. The last thing he remembered seeing was the fast approach of a tree.

"I think we would do well to leave while we may," said a familiar and unwelcome voice. "The tide is turned against us."

Zreal lifted his head—slowly this time—to see the haggard-looking Zitarian on her hands and knees. There was no sarcasm or deviousness in her tone. She must really be hurt.

"The master would disagree with you, Szhegaza," Zreal responded through gritted teeth. His head felt like it might split.

"Oh?" Szhegaza said. "He would prefer his two most loyal and competent servants to perish in an already lost battle?"

Zreal almost laughed at that last question. Surely they were indeed the most competent of Brit's forces, but loyal? Surely Zreal's loyalty was not in question, but amongst the Zitarian race perfidy was a way of life.

Szhegaza had finally regained her feet, and upon seeing Zreal's dubious expression, she grabbed his arm and hoisted him upright.

"You have no choice, Zreal." She draped an arm around his shoulder. "You must trust me." She grinned at her groaning companion. "If it makes you feel any better, I would never take advantage of a helpless ally or adversary. There is simply no honor in it." She shot him a sly grin. "Or fun."

With some effort, and no small amount of pain, the unlikely allies took flight, and put as much distance between themselves and Takashaniel as possible.

43

The surviving defenders gathered about the base of the tower and tended their many wounds. The last of the demon threat had been put down, but not without further loss. The centaurs stood gathered together, silently mourning their fallen comrades. The Brunts had begun singing songs of the times of old, as well as those songs that would help to usher their fallen brethren into the next world.

The human warriors sat with their backs against a wall, exhausted and glad that the battle had finally ended. Iel and Mira joined them.

"Not bad, my friends," the Ilanyan said. "I have never seen humans fight as you do. I am honored and thankful to you. Takashaniel is a place of great power, but also a place of sanctuary. I can have all of your wounds mended and your energy returned to you within but a few days if you will be my guests."

Akemi was more than happy to remain, but she looked to her brother. To her relief, he nodded in agreement. The stubborn samurai must be as hurt and tired as she was to accept the invitation.

Kita and Kenyatta needed no coaxing. They had been amazed

with the tower when first they'd visited during their non-physical excursion that seemed a lifetime ago.

"How long is the invitation for?" Kenyatta asked with a smile that quickly disappeared after he was elbowed in the ribs by his friend.

"As long as you wish," Iel answered.

Mira noticed Shinobu sitting away from the group, seeming submerged in private thoughts. She sat next to him and the two said nothing for a time.

"Thinking about the road," Shinobu finally said, gazing into faraway places she could not see.

"Do you not intend to at least stay with us for a short while?" she asked. "You have many wounds that could be mended with little time."

The strider never shifted his gaze. "I have quite a bit to do, Miss Mira. My road has much ahead, and I cannot let time escape me."

"Maybe so," the young woman persisted. She removed a strand of hair from in front of her face and slid it behind her ear. "But if you take the road too soon, you won't have a chance to recuperate. I need you to grant me two days before you leave."

When the strider turned a curious look on her, she explained, "I can sense the contamination in your body. It has affected you deeper than you realize. If you take to the road in your already-fatigued condition, your body would not hold longer than a few days before you fall. I will need time to properly expel the taint."

"Darker things than demonic poisons haunt my path Miss Mira," Shinobu whispered. After another stretch of silence, he finally looked at her, and saw the concern on the woman's soft and youthful face. He sighed and grudgingly promised to remain long enough for her to do her work.

Two days after the battle, the animals and inhabitants of the surrounding fields made their gradual return. The guardian had put forth a great deal of effort in cleansing the land of the vile residue that resulted from the tainted blood and presence of the demonic horde. In some places, the ground was as black as tar where the Quentranzi had bled.

It would take time to cleanse the area of the taint, and Iel and his student had begun immediately. Now, after two days, he lay at rest in his private chamber. Around the tower, the simple presence of the animals, large and small, helped to heal the battered and beaten rolling hills of Takashaniel.

A week had passed before Shinobu finally packed his few supplies, along with some fresh provisions given to him by Mira. He had stayed a few days longer than planned, to help with cleaning up. The Brunts, the centaurs, Mira and Iel, and Shinobu's four companions bade him farewells that ranged from warm to gruff. Once he left the tower, the other four companions escorted him to the borders of the lands. It was during this leisurely walk that they realized how strong their friendships had become. After spending nearly half the day remembering their adventure together —and promising to share another in the future—Shinobu departed to the northwest on an errand he was less than willing to discuss.

"The man seems to have some unfinished business waiting for him in the northwest," Kenjiro remarked as they watched the strider on horseback, disappearing over the distant hills toward the soon-to-be setting sun.

"He won't be able to stay away from us for long," Kenyatta remarked. The others glanced at him curiously. "We're too much fun," he added with a grin.

A few more days passed and Taliah arrived to aid Iel. She had spent most of the time watching the battle with Grandmaster Akutagawa. She had felt guilty in not helping, despite her instructions by the Daunyans not to interfere. Watching her brother and the others struggle through such a time, not knowing if they would survive or perish, had proven to be a challenge in itself. Sensei Akutagawa had been her crutch during that time.

As soon as the battle was over, Taliah had begun preparing for

her and the Grandmaster to travel using a network of portals that
would take them there. Normally, the process took no time at all,
but with the presence of so many portals that transported so many
demons from the dark world, she did not want to take the chance of
unintentionally passing through a portal that would have dropped
them in the throne room of the Quentranzi lord Grala himself!

At the end of the second week, the four remaining warriors
informed that they would take their leave. The night before their
departure, Iel called them to the same observation chamber they'd
gathered in during their out-of-body visit.

"I felt no need to speak to the strider about this because I feel
he already knows," Iel began. "It is with you four that I wish to
share this information." They faced the largest wall of the room, Iel
facing them and Mira and Taliah standing to the side. "I told you
once before that the world is changing at a rapid pace. I know that
you have already discovered that humans are not the only beings
inhabiting this world. I know of your encounter with the Stonecliff
Clan."

Iel looked each of them over. "They and the centaurs and
Brunts are not the only beings you share this world with."

"Without your technology to help you control the world and
change its physical makeup to suit your desires, the world has
begun to reshape itself, and those who have remained hidden may
one day resurface. The return of magic brings with it beings and
forces unlike anything your species has experienced in countless
years. Landmasses will change, becoming larger or smaller, and in
a relatively short period of time. People, animals, even the names
of your towns, cities, countries and provinces will change. Some
traditions will remain, others will change, and others will evolve. I
tell you this because you and the strider will continue to play a part
in the changes to come."

Iel smiled and continued. "One last thing, and this message
actually comes from Taliah here. The extraordinary abilities that
have aided you in defending Takashaniel will not come to your call

at will. You were each born with the gene gifted to you by the Daunyans. This gene gives you enhanced abilities beyond any normal human, but it was implanted in your parents to pass to you for the sole purpose of battling evil not born of this world, such as the Quentranzi incursion. In their wisdom, the Daunyans understand that for a human, having the benefit of such a powerful gene at any time would hinder your evolution and in effect, slow your growth, both personally and as a species. You as humans learn little without struggle involved. I tell you this for your own safety so that you will not expect the same of your bodies as you do now. Such a miscalculation could have devastating results.

"This gene will not automatically activate in any circumstance other than when you are battling a being that is not from this plane of existence. In human conflict, if your life is at stake, the gene will not activate. This may seem cruel or unfair, but your growth and evolution as a species depends on you living your lives the way they are supposed to be lived, without the constant interference of the Gods or their gifts to you. If it is your time to pass from this life, so it will be."

It was with that that the four companions, the four friends, remained at the tower for one night and one day longer before departing the following morning before sunrise. Iel and Mira, along with the Brunts and the centaurs, bade them farewell with promises of future meetings.

The humans thanked them once more for the extra supplies and took their leave, traveling with the aid of Taliah's portal to expedite their return home. It was a difficult departure, but the road-weary friends were happy to return home.

44

B rit watched his two servants not so quickly making their way from the Tower of Balance. He'd never been one to accept excuses, and surely both were careless in allowing the centaurs to blindside them. Still, he knew that the mighty beasts along with those annoying little runts would have proven too much for the two.

Fortunately for them, he was in more of an understanding mood than usual. Actually, things had gone a bit better than he had planned, surprises notwithstanding. Brit hadn't been foolish enough to expect his first attempt on the tower to bear much fruit, but he had achieved his first goal. He had a gauge of the tower's defenses and the capabilities of the guardian. The five humans that aided him were strong, but not much of a threat to hold his attention.

He'd anticipated treachery from the Quentranzi general—could one expect anything else from a demon?—and though he hadn't expected the appearance of those two winged fiends in his fortress, he was not unprepared. With all of the other demons back in the dark world, and Kabriza on the loose, things were moving more or less according to plan. The addition of the other two fiends made little difference. Indeed, their presence might be a boon in dealing with Iel's humans.

The Drek's face twisted into a smile. Things had not turned out quite that bad at all, and now he had a firsthand report of the landscape and abilities of those who would defend the tower again. From his balcony, Brit gazed out at the sick and twisted surroundings, home to countless wretched forms of life that infested the lands.

This place had once been colorful and filled with life until the Drek had made his home here, and drained the land of its life to strengthen his own. Such was the result of the presence of his leeching species.

Although it sickened Brit to see himself lowered to such a classic aspiration as world domination, the truth was that this world was much larger and more bountiful than his own, and much easier to manage, given the less harsh atmospheric conditions. Besides, the humans didn't seem to be doing much with it beyond wasting and destroying it, so why not take it for himself? While it was true that his kind, by nature, siphoned the life out of the land they lived on, humans just wasted it.

Brit leaned against the back wall of his balcony with his arms crossed. He had nothing but time. Patience came with little effort, and with Kabriza's pets roaming the lands, time was all that was required. He withdrew back into his chamber to retire with the amusing thought of how those insects would react when he did decide to show himself. They would try to prepare, but they couldn't. There was nothing they could do. And they would perish.

ABOUT THE AUTHOR

Ramón Terrell is an author and actor who instantly fell in love with fantasy the day he opened R. A. Salvatore's: The Crystal Shard. Years (and many devoured books) later he decided to put pen to paper for his first novel. After a bout with aching carpals, he decided to try the keyboard instead, and the words began to flow.

As an actor, he has appeared in the hit television shows Supernatural, izombie, Arrow, and Minority Report, as well as the hit comedy web series Single and Dating in Vancouver. He also appears as one of Robin Hood's Merry Men in Once Upon a Time, as well as an Ark Guard on the hit TV show The 100. When not writing, or acting, he enjoys reading, video games, hiking, and long walks with his wife around Stanley Park in Vancouver BC.

Connect with him at:

ALSO BY RAMÓN TERRELL

Legend of Takashaniel

Legends of a Shattered Age

Heroes of a Broken Age (coming soon)

Hunter's Moon Series

Running from the Night

Hunter's Moon

Darkness of Day

Revenire (coming soon)

The Fairies

Out of Ordure